"Take whatever you want and get out."

"I have what I want. Drive." The gun and his hold on the weapon remained level. He took up more than his own seat, his arms and torso solid muscle. His face was hard and angled—cut in a way that almost looked unreal.

His words chilled through her. How was she going to get free of him? She pressed the gas pedal again and drove along fresh graves, spotting the exit farther ahead. Her heartbeat increased its force, and her ribs ached. "What do you want from me?" She held her breath.

"Just your brain," he said, the sound raw.

She jerked, her head turning to him again. "To eat?" she gasped.

He blinked. Once and then again. "No, not to eat." His wince drew his cheeks up and his darker brows down. "Geez. To eat? Why would I eat your brain? Ick."

Her kidnapper had just said "Ick" and looked at her like she was insane. She eyed him with her peripheral vision so she could better describe him in a police report—if she survived this. At least six foot six, long dark blond hair with even darker streaks strewn throughout, handsome face. Somewhat rugged but also sharp, and with healed burn marks down his neck.

His eyes were world-weary and wounded, and he'd obviously survived hell. Now she had to survive him.

Also by Rebecca Zanetti

The Dark Protector series
Fated
Claimed
Tempted
Hunted
Consumed
Provoked
Twisted
Shadowed
Tamed
Marked
Talen
Vampire's Faith
Demon's Mercy

The Realm Enforcers series
Wicked Ride
Wicked Edge
Wicked Burn
Wicked Kiss
Wicked Bite

The Scorpius Syndrome series
Mercury Striking
Shadow Falling
Justice Ascending

The Deep Ops series
Hidden
Taken novella
Fallen

ALPHA'S PROMISE

Rebecca Zanetti

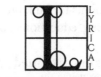

LYRICAL PRESS
Kensington Publishing Corp.
www.kensingtonbooks.com

LYRICAL PRESS BOOKS are published by

Kensington Publishing Corp.
119 West 40th Street
New York, NY 10018

All Kensington titles, imprints, and distributed lines are available at special quantity discounts for bulk purchases for sales promotion, premiums, fund-raising, educational, or institutional use.

Special book excerpts or customized printings can also be created to fit specific needs. For details, write or phone the office of the Kensington Sales Manager: Kensington Publishing Corp., 119 West 40th Street, New York, NY 10018. Attn. Sales Department. Phone: 1-800-221-2647.

Lyrical Press and Lyrical Press logo Reg. U.S. Pat. & TM Off.

First Electronic Edition: June 2019
eISBN-13: 978-1-5161-0747-6
eISBN-10: 1-5161-0716-0

First Print Edition: June 2019
ISBN-13: 978-1-5161-0751-3
ISBN-10: 1-5161-0751-9

Printed in the United States of America

This one's for every girl who's seen a hot guy with a hint of the extraordinary on the street and thought, 'Yeah. He could be a vampire.' Come on. You know who you are.

Acknowledgments

Thank you to the readers who have jumped into this new era of the Realm vampires. I have many wonderful people to thank for getting this book to readers, and I sincerely apologize to anyone I've forgotten.

Thank you to Big Tone, Gabe, and Karlina: for their love, support, for making my life better every day.

Thank you to my eximious editor, Alicia Condon, as well as the innovative group at Kensington publishing: Alexandra Nicolajsen, Steven Zacharius, Adam Zacharius, Vida Engstrand, Jane Nutter, Lauren Jernigan, Elizabeth Trout, Samantha McVeigh, Lynn Cully, Kimberly Richardson, Arthur Maisel, Renee Rocco, Rebecca Cremonese, April LeHoullier.

Thank you to my wonderful agent, Caitlin Blasdell, and to Liza Dawson and the entire Liza Dawson Agency.

Thank you to Jillian Stein for the absolutely fantastic work and for being such a great friend.

Thanks to my fantastic street team, Rebecca's Rebels, and to their creative and hard-working leader, Minga Portillo.

Thanks also to my constant support system: Gail and Jim English, Debbie and Travis Smith, Stephanie and Don West, Jessica and Jonah Namson, Kathy and Herb Zanetti, and Liz and Steve Berry.

Finally, thank you to the readers who have kept the Dark Protectors alive all of these years. It's because of you that we decided to return to the world of the Realm.

Chapter One

Across the windy cemetery, beyond the rows of gravestones, a man leaned against a pine tree and watched her. Even at the distance, the deep blue of his eyes cut through the day. He stood to at least two meters, his chest broad, his legs long. His gaze was almost physical and alight with something that caught her by surprise. A rare tingling, one she'd never been able to explain to herself, much less to anybody else, morphed into an instant headache at the base of her neck.

Dr. Promise Williams shivered and broke eye contact to focus in front of her.

Meager September sunlight glinted off the coffin as it was lowered into the wet earth. The clouds had finally parted and stopped dropping rain on the mourners. She closed her umbrella and tucked it into her overlarge bag, wet grass marring her smart boots.

"It was a nice service. Earlier, I mean," Dr. Mark Brookes said at her side, wiping his thick glasses on a handkerchief. He wore a tailored black suit with a muted tie, his eyes earnest and his thinning hair wet from the earlier rain.

Promise nodded, her stomach aching. The group standing around remained silent with a couple of soft sniffs piercing the quiet. She knew all of the mourners. Six professors, a dean, and two grad students. The earlier service had been packed with students, more faculty, and even the local press. This part of the day was reserved for family.

Dr. Victory Rashad hadn't had any family. Other than the faculty, of course.

The wind picked up, brushing across Promise's face. She shivered. Who did she have? If she died tomorrow, who would attend the burial part of her service? Unwittingly, she looked toward the pine tree.

The man was gone.

Not a surprise. While he'd visited the dead, no doubt he'd just looked over at the assembled group in passing. His focus hadn't been solely on her. She shook her head and tried to dispel the dread she'd been experiencing since the police had found Victory. The woman had been missing for nearly three days before being found. Torn apart.

Who would do such a ghastly thing?

The gears of the lowering device stopped, effectively concluding the burial for the bystanders. "Well." Mark held out an arm, and she naturally slipped her glove into the crook of his elbow. "Would you like to get something to eat?" He turned and assisted her over the uneven ground to their vehicles, parked on the silent road.

"Thanks, but I'd rather go home." She'd attended an Irish wake once where the family members drank into the next day, toasting the dead with stories. A wealth of stories, and all told with love and shouts of laughter. What was it about her world that lent itself to quiet services and no humorous anecdotes? "Thank you, though."

Mark paused at her new compact car and waited for her to unlock the door. "I hadn't realized you and Victory were close."

"We weren't," Promise said quietly, opening the door. The other professor had joined the physics department at the university during summer semester, and so far, even though the school was a month into fall semester, they'd merely politely greeted each other at department meetings. That was it. Maybe a lunch or two in the cafeteria, but she didn't remember the details. "Are we, any of us, close with anybody?"

Mark scratched his chin. "I am. Two brothers, both married with kids. In fact, Mike is having a barbecue this Sunday, probably the last one before winter. I've been meaning to ask you."

"I should probably work." The idea of witnessing a happy family was too much to think about right now. What was wrong with her?

"Okay." He waited until she'd sat before leaning over the open door. "Two dates, and now I'm not sure what's going on." His intelligent brown eyes studied her, while the too-musky scent of his cologne wafted in her face. "I'm thirty-five and don't have time for games, Promise. Are we going out again or not?"

She forced a smile. "No." He was a nice man, but she'd rather work with supersymmetry or cosmological inflation than spend time with him. Of course, who wouldn't? "I think we're better situated as friends."

"Well. I do appreciate your honesty." As he straightened, his tone indicated that he did not, in fact, appreciate the truth. "I'll see you Monday." He shut her door with extra force.

Cripes. Maybe the truth had been a mistake and she should've worked harder to soften her words. Like usual.

She started the engine and pulled away from the curb, winding through the cemetery and wondering about Dr. Rashad. The police hadn't indicated any movement on the case, but Promise felt she should do something. Perhaps she'd call on Monday and request a status update.

She sped up slightly, and her doors locked. Her shoulders relaxed. It had to be a coincidence that Dr. Gary Fissure, a colleague from Great Britain, was also missing. She'd collaborated with him on a paper several years previous.

The wind picked up, and rain splattered against the windshield again. Several roads spread out in different directions. She hadn't been paying close attention when she'd driven in. How stupid of her. So she took the first left, allowing her mind to wander as she drove among the peaceful dead. She flicked on the wipers and turned down another road in the sprawling cemetery.

Suddenly, her passenger door was wrenched open and the damaged lock protested, emitting a screech-popping sound.

A man forced his way inside, rocking the car, and slammed the door. Droplets of rain wettened her leather seats.

She reacted in slow motion. How was this happening? How had he broken the door lock of her new car? Her eyes widened, and she turned her head to fully face him. That quickly, she recognized him. "You were watching me."

"I was." His voice was low and mangled, gritty and surpassing hoarse. Those blue eyes were even darker inside the vehicle.

Adrenaline flooded her, and she finally reacted, slamming on the brakes and reaching for her door. Her seat belt constricted her, but she fought it, silent in her desperate bid to escape him.

He manacled one incredibly strong hand around her arm and yanked her back into place. "Drive."

Her shoulders collided with her seat back, and she opened her mouth to scream. Her headache blasted into a migraine instantly.

He pressed a gun into her rib cage.

Her scream sputtered into a whisper. She looked frantically around, but the road ahead and behind her was empty.

"I said drive," he repeated, no infliction in his tired tone.

She swallowed, and fear finally engulfed her. The sound she made was so much of a whimper that she winced. "My purse is on the floor. Take whatever you want and get out." Her voice shook almost harder than her hands on the steering wheel.

"I have what I want. Drive." The gun and his hold on the weapon remained level. He took up more than his own seat, his arms and torso solid muscle. His face was hard and angled—cut in a way that almost looked unreal.

His words chilled through her. How was she going to free herself from him? She pressed the gas pedal again and drove along fresh graves, spotting the exit farther ahead. Her heartbeat increased its force, and her ribs ached. "What do you want from me?" She held her breath.

"Just your brain," he said, the sound raw.

She jerked, her head turning to him again. "To eat?" she gasped.

He blinked. Once and then again. "No, not to eat." His wince drew his cheeks up and his darker brows down. "Geez. To eat? Why would I eat your brain? Ick."

Her kidnapper had just said "Ick" and looked at her like she was insane. She eyed him with her peripheral vision so she could better describe him in a police report—if she survived this. At least six foot six, long dark blond hair with even darker streaks strewn throughout, handsome face. Somewhat rugged but also sharp, and with healed burn marks down his neck. His eyes were world-weary and wounded, and he'd obviously survived hell. Now she had to survive him.

Wait a minute. His words registered even deeper. Her brain? Heat spiraled through her chest. "Did you want Victory Rashad's brain too?"

"Yes."

Oh, God. He was going to kill her—just like Victory Rashad. Panic took Promise again, and she slammed her foot on the gas pedal.

"Wait," he said, grasping her arm. "I won't hurt you. I'm here to help you."

Affirmative. Yes. The guy with the gun was interested in providing assistance. Right. She ducked her head and floored the gas pedal, bumping out of the cemetery and speeding down the quiet road.

"Slow down," he hissed, his hold tightening enough to bruise.

She zipped around a corner and into traffic, driving as fast as she could.

He swore and grabbed for the key, which wasn't in the dash. She'd used the starter button. She swerved around a minivan and finally spotted a police cruiser up ahead. Slapping at him, knowing if he got her out of the car, she was dead, she took the chance of being shot in order to gain freedom.

Yelling, finally, she slammed into the rear of the police cruiser.

Everything stopped for a second and then sped up. The crash was thunderous. Her passenger bellowed and flew through the window. The airbag deployed right into her face and propelled her back into the seat.

She blinked, her ears ringing as the bag deflated with a soft hiss and a smattering of dust.

A police officer ran up and opened her door. "What in the hell?" he muttered, blood on his chin.

She coughed and shoved the airbag down. "Where is he?" she gasped, her eyesight blurry. Her assailant lay sprawled on the pavement, blood coating his face as the rain pelted down to make the red flow to the ground. The other officer leaned over him, talking into a radio at his shoulder.

Then the kidnapper jerked awake and leaped to his feet. Blood covered his face and his neck, while his left arm hung at an unnatural angle. He stood several inches above the officer. "What did you do?" he bellowed. His eyes were so dark they appeared black, and his gaze was piercing.

She screamed.

The cop tried to grab him, but he shoved the officer into the side of the car. Before the officer next to Promise could draw his gun, the kidnapper turned and ran into an alley.

The police officers quickly pursued him.

She panted, her mind buzzing, her body aching.

The police officers soon returned, both shaking their heads.

Oh, God. He was gone.

Chapter Two

Ivar Kjeidsen limped up the stairwell inside the high-rise building, blood trickling from cuts in his neck and down one arm from flying through a damn windshield. He hadn't expected the harmless-looking physics professor to defend herself so well. The healing cells he'd focused on his injuries were doing their job slowly—too slowly. The scar tissue down his neck semi-blocked the cells. Shit. He might even need a bandage, just like a human.

His boots echoed dully on the cement steps, and even though he was the only one in the entire high-rise crazy enough to climb thirty stories, the walls still pressed in too closely. But it wasn't nearly as bad as an elevator, which he'd avoid at all cost.

He'd had to walk all the way from the accident, having lost his fledgling ability to teleport the second he'd been injured. Being temporarily fragile sucked. He shoved open the door to the top floor and eyed the sheen from the white and gray tiles forming a sophisticated design down the long hallway. Beige-gray slabs of tile, thick and luxurious, made up the walls until the office opened into a center reception area surrounded by glass—one whole wall of it windows to the outside.

All glass and chrome and soothing materials.

He fucking hated this penthouse office space. It even smelled like recycled air and environmentally friendly cleanser.

Keeping his head down, he maneuvered through the hallway and past the deserted reception area to one of the many conference rooms down yet another hallway. The lights were too bright, the air too relaxed, and the height from sea level too damn far.

Banishing any hint of the pain still attacking him, he strode into the room and waited for the explosion to come.

None arrived. Instead, Ronan Kayrs looked up from a stack of maps that had been spread across the inviting and perfectly smooth light tan conference table, where he was apparently working alone at the moment. "Hello, Viking. The local news has already reported the attempted kidnapping. You had to go after her."

A familiar slash of guilt cut into Ivar. He barely kept his hand from trembling as he drew out an environmentally friendly chair to sit. "I didn't intend to take her." Sometimes his instincts still overruled his brain.

Ronan's eyes flashed a deeper aqua than usual. The vampire-demon had odd eyes, even for a hybrid. "You were on a reconnaissance mission. To watch and learn. She might be the exact wrong physicist based on the opinions expressed in some of her articles."

Ivar nodded. "I'm aware." The burn scars marring his neck went much deeper into his tissue than merely marring the skin outside, and his voice would always remain hoarse. Not as mangled as a purebred demon's, but close. Considering he was half demon, he really didn't give a shit. But right now, he couldn't let that hoarseness be gauged as weakness. "I saw an opening, and I took it."

"You failed," Ronan said simply, his eco-friendly chair squeaking as he leaned his impressive bulk back. The hybrid crossed muscled arms, looking just as deadly as the entire Kayrs vampire family was known to be, even with the recent cut to his black hair, which made him look more like a businessperson for this mission.

Ivar flushed, and his damaged skin ached. It was rare for a vampire-demon hybrid to scar, and when it happened, it hurt. Most of his burns had healed, but his neck and larynx still retained their rough texture. The inside of his throat was ribbed and uneven and annoying. Maybe hell wanted to stay with him as long as it could. "I made a mistake." One of many. When would he return to a thinking being instead of one propelled by survival instinct? He'd been trying so hard.

Ronan nodded, his mouth in a pinched line, which only accented the ones by his eyes. "She's going to be more difficult to get to now."

Ivar nodded. Taking him by surprise, a lightness caught in his chest. Nowhere near what humor had felt like years ago, but something different from pain and guilt. "She is smarter than I'd thought. Better thinking on her feet, anyway." He'd studied Dr. Promise Williams for months while he regained his sanity—somewhat—and she was obviously intelligent. But he hadn't expected her to ram her vehicle into a police cruiser. "She is in danger and needs to be locked down."

Ronan pinched the bridge of his nose. "We have got to quit kidnapping people," he muttered.

Ivar shrugged. "I don't know. It worked out well for you." Ronan had kidnapped a neurologist he'd ended up mating and adoring like a puppy that had found its place. "Where is your mate?" She was a doctor—maybe she could stem the blood Ivar still felt dripping beneath his dark T-shirt.

"Back computer room with her sister, researching that list of human physicists most likely to be targeted next," Ronan said.

"Promise Williams is next," Ivar said flatly. A couple of her academic papers had held cautions about messing with the universe, which might cause him problems. But there had been something about her. A tingling that had attacked him right before she'd tried to kill him. "And she's Enhanced." It had been the first time any of them had been close enough to her to sense her gifts, whatever they might be.

"Ah, fuck." Ronan shook his head. "I'd say the Kurjans wouldn't kill her if she's Enhanced, but now we know better." Their enemy, another immortal species, needed Enhanced human females as mates just like the vampires did.

"The Kurjans have lost their minds," Ivar muttered. The woman who'd been buried earlier that day had been Enhanced, and the Kurjans had torn her apart. Or rather, their Cyst faction, their religious soldiers, had done so. Ivar's duty began to yank him in opposite directions once again. "We have to get to her before they do."

"She might not have been on their radar until now," Ronan said.

Ivar's chest heated. "Bullshit. She's one of the best in her field, maybe *the* best, and she's next. We will get to her first." When he'd seen the crime pictures after the Kurjans had finished with Dr. Victory Rashad, even he had felt sickened. And he'd suffered through more hell worlds than he could count. They often blurred together in his nightmares. "This is as important to you as it is to me. This is our only way to save Quade. He's your blood brother."

Ronan sighed, the sound tortured. "So are you. Blood and bone, brother."

Ivar slowly nodded. Seven of them, all vampire-demon hybrids, had been bonded together in a ceremony of blood and bone that went beyond mere genetics or ancestry. "We have to free Quade, and I'm done waiting. I have a feeling this woman will get us what we need." The obsession to free Quade from a bubble world dimensions away pricked beneath his skin like live wires. His leg trembled, and he slapped a hand on his thigh to stop it. *Calm. Stay calm, damn it.* Desperation was the only emotion, the only feeling, he could truly identify these days. So he held on to it with both hands.

An elevator door in the distance dinged, and power immediately swam through the oxygen.

Ivar started to rise, and Ronan shook his head. "Logan and Garrett are finally back. Stay for their debriefing."

It was about time the two youngest members of the Seven returned from their missions. Ivar had actually missed them during the last month; they were his brothers now too. Logan had probably saved his life, and Ivar would do anything for that demon. He regained his seat. Five of his brothers, those created by the painful ritual of the Seven, had hidden him, protected him, and helped him for the three months he'd been back from hell. "You want me in a meeting? With other people?"

"I'd hardly call them people," Ronan drawled, looking up as two males entered the room. "Family doesn't count."

Ivar partially turned. "Welcome back."

Logan Kyllwood flashed a smart-ass grin. "You still batshit crazy, Viking?" He drew out a chair and lowered his muscled body into it.

"Yes," Ivar said shortly, missing his days as an actual Viking before the world had changed. Out of habit, he shared Logan's grin, even though he didn't feel what a smile was supposed to feel like. Not anymore. He'd do anything for the young warrior. He owed him. "Unlike your mate. Now that's a sane female." There was no doubt Mercy O'Malley was crazier than the rest of them put together. Most fairies were. As was Logan's mum. Maybe that was his type.

Logan snorted. "She's not crazy. Just high energy."

Fair enough.

Garrett sank into a seat with a sigh of relief. He'd been dealing with the Realm, the coalition of immortal species run by his family. His genetic family. The youngest Kayrs soldier glanced at Ronan. "Hello, Great-Uncle."

"I thought we'd finished with that nonsense." Ronan rolled his eyes. "You didn't realize I existed until three months ago, so shut up."

Garrett chuckled. "I know, but it makes you feel old and me delighted. I must be an imp."

Ivar zeroed in on the seriousness lurking in Garrett's eyes. The kid was supposed to smooth things over with the vampire king and the Realm in general. The Seven had kept their existence a secret for a thousand years, until they'd lost members and had to recruit, which had ended up outing them. Well, to nation leaders, anyway. "I take it your mission to smooth things over with the Realm wasn't roses and hugs?"

Garrett lost the grin. "Nope. The King of the Realm is a little pissed that he's still dealing with the, ah—"

"Cluster fuck," Logan said helpfully.

Garrett cleared his throat, his metallic gray eyes sizzling with intelligence. "Yes. In his words, with the mess we all have created by, ah—"

"Just existing," Logan added. "Or rather, perverting the laws of nature and the witch nation, binding our torsos into impenetrable shields, and creating a force called the Seven."

Garrett cut his best friend a look. "You are not helping."

"Not trying to help," Logan drawled.

Garrett grimaced. "I just spent the better part of a month being yelled at by several uncles, several aunts, and my mother. It was a shitstorm, and not all of us have a new mate who's happy to see us, like you do, Logan. Some of us are mateless, you know."

Logan rolled his eyes. "I know for a fact that you spent last weekend with a couple of feline shifters. Not one, but two. Female shifters are very bendy. So don't tell me you're pent up."

Garrett's lips twitched into a smile.

Logan cleared his throat. "I've been dealing with the Fae nation and trying to glean as much information about teleporting as they have learned. Unfortunately, they haven't actually studied the ability any more than we have." He leaned forward. "I've been talking to Kane Kayrs a lot, and he's getting caught up on the science behind teleporting."

Ivar glanced at Garrett. "Your uncle is willing to help us?"

Garrett nodded. "Yeah. Kane is intrigued by the whole notion, and since he's the smartest being on the entire planet, I say we tell him everything. We need to find the best human physicists and get them working with him. It's a good plan, Ivar."

Ivar nodded. "Agreed." He had to get back to that one hell world and save Quade Kayrs. His eyes met Ronan's, which all but glowed with guilt and pain. Ronan had escaped the bubble world where he'd been trapped, but Quade was still stuck in his. "We'll get him out, Ronan." It was a vow, and Ivar meant every word.

Garrett scrubbed both hands down his face. "I don't think I'm a good diplomat. It's so much easier to just hit people."

"The kid reminds me of his father." Ivar glanced at Ronan. "Though I agree. I liked it so much better when we were a secret."

Ronan nodded. "Yeah. It was easier to maneuver, but now at least we have more people working on the problems."

Garrett held up a hand. "Only the leaders of the nations know about the Seven. They're not making our existence public, by any means. At least not yet."

Ivar cocked his head. "What else did Kane say?" If the brilliant Kayrs brother was on the problem of finding Quade, then maybe they wouldn't even need to use humans.

Garrett tapped his fingers on the table. "He's been studying the cosmology of extra dimensions, cosmological inflation, baryogenesis, and dark matter. Everything every species has learned, including the humans, who actually have put a hell of a lot more time into these subjects than we immortals."

Ivar's breath caught. "Has he figured out how to get to Quade?"

"No," Garrett said shortly. "Even the Fae don't know how to find his world. The Viking here is the only one who has actually been there. When we messed with the universe to create those bubble worlds, we apparently created new rules that not even those who can teleport can follow."

Ronan leaned forward. "We did what we thought was necessary at the time."

Garrett slowly nodded. "I get that. Fourteen hundred years ago, you didn't know what we do now, and even though Logan and I are new members of the Seven, we take responsibility as if we were there and took part in the initial rituals. That might be what's pissing my uncle the king off."

Ivar could understand the king's irritation. The original Seven had created three worlds—far away from this one—with the ultimate evil, a Kurjan Cyst named Ulric, in the middle, while

Ronan and Quade had manned the outside worlds as guards to keep him contained. Recently, Ronan's bubble had burst, and he was home now. It was time to bring Quade home as well. Ivar cleared his throat. "We all know that Quade's bubble will burst, or Ulric's will. So let's make it happen on our time."

Garrett lifted his chin. "Kane said that there's a chance we'll destroy *this* world if we blast open the ones created for Ulric and Quade. It's not like we understand dimensions or parallel universes or whatever the hell we created."

Ivar flattened his hands on the table, and the pace of his heart picked up. There was a piece of him, one he'd never admit to, that thought the risk of ending the world was worth it if it gave Quade a chance at survival. Yeah, that probably made him a sociopathic bastard. "Then let's get the experts in here and find out. We need to bring in Dr. Promise Williams immediately."

Ronan sighed. "You're right." He glanced at his watch and then looked back at Ivar. "She'll be here tomorrow at 9:00 A.M."

Chapter Three

The darkness of night carried additional rain. Mature trees scented the air with pine as drops drizzled from rolling clouds and splattered up from the leaf-covered ground. Thick branches protected Ivar as he leaned against a tree trunk, munching on peanuts, watching the quiet bungalow at the end of a private street. He ducked to the other side as a police cruiser drove by and turned around in the cul-de-sac, apparently conducting an hourly check of Promise's home. Either the local police force lacked manpower, which was likely, or they thought his stupid kidnapping attempt earlier that day had been random.

Promise slid open filmy curtains at the front of her house and waved at the officer. He waved back and drove away.

Leaving her alone.

It was near midnight, and she had changed into soft-looking gray yoga pants with a matching top. Her thick hair was pulled up on her head, and her hand trembled slightly on the curtain. She had long, very curly black hair, high cheekbones, and caramel-colored skin. Her ancestry wasn't obvious, but her beauty certainly was.

Relief had soothed some of his guilt earlier as he'd watched her walk from a different police car to her front door without a hitch in her stride. So he hadn't hurt her. Good. The curtain fell, and she disappeared from sight.

A loneliness drifted through him that caught him up short.

Her home was perched on cliffs overlooking the Pacific Ocean, and the water crashed loudly against rocks below. Trees and branches blocked his view of the water, which was fine, because his interest lay in the woman. If he had found her, his enemies soon would as well. He slid down onto his butt and extended his legs, resting his head on the rough bark. Protecting her from afar should've been his default position.

Yet there had been something about her at the funeral. Something sad and solitary that had called to him. So he'd tried to kidnap her. He banged his head against the tree, enduring the pain as bark dug into his skull. Being half-crazed didn't give him the excuse to be a moron.

He closed his eyes and let the sound of rain, wind, and waves ground him in this moment and in this world. He was home, and for the time being, he was safe. His mind drifted, and he returned to hell.

He'd been forced into world after world through a portal, and somehow in this loop, he could escape by imagining other portals that soon appeared. Most led to worse places, so he'd try to jump again. Time moved differently—one minute felt like a hundred years of torture and pain. His spirit hung in tatters by the time he reached his brother's world. Quade was one of the Seven bonded in blood and bone, which made them family.

Quade had pulled him out of the fire and secured them both in a dirty cave littered with crumbled leaves and discarded bones. Fire and glass-filled wind roared in a maelstrom outside. The other male had scar upon scar upon scar on his body, but his nose was Ronan's. Exactly the same.

Even though pain had engulfed Ivar, he finally knew why he'd been through so many hells. "Ronan's world exploded, and he's home now. It's time for you to go home too. I'll take your place," he said.

Quade's dark aqua eyes barely showed the existence of his pupils in the dingy cave. "It's almost over, brother."

Ivar eyed the sharp rock. "Just tell me what to do." His memories were already dim, but hadn't Ronan said he'd needed to move rocks and balance the magnetic poles in his world to keep Ulric trapped? If so, what was Quade doing every day besides being tortured by an environment too horrible to believe?

Quade's torn lips twisted in a parody of a smile. "I feed the dragon, Viking. Not you."

"Dragon?" Ivar asked. They existed other places as well as back home?

"No," Quade said, his voice raw. "It's getting harder, and soon it'll end. Everything will. Me." He grunted the last, sounding more hopeful than resigned.

Ivar tried to reason with him. Was he mad? How could anybody have stayed sane here? "You'll be free, Quade. Ronan survived the end of his world, and so will you. You can heal and find a new life."

Quade's lids dropped to half-mast. "Already dead...Viking." He stood and dragged Ivar to his feet. "You go now. Portals will open, keep following. Maybe you'll get home." Even with his body damaged so badly, his strength was beyond that of a normal hybrid. "Tell Ronan. Tell all my brothers..."

Ivar clutched Quade's arms, fighting the unholy wind that pierced through his skin to his soul. "Come with me," he begged.

"Tell them goodbye." Quade pushed Ivar hard, sending him through a portal that swallowed him with a gleeful shriek. He screamed, but the void allowed for no sound. He hit ice in a new world, rolled, and came up fighting.

Through portal after portal, through hell dimension after hell dimension, he hung on to Quade's last words. Soon they were all he had. After a while, he vaguely remembered who he'd been. But Quade, he never forgot. Saving Quade, rescuing his brother, was the only thought that kept Ivar alive.

Until he finally arrived back home, on a peaceful lakefront, with his brothers surrounding him.

Ivar jerked back to the present as the police car patrolled again, this time slowing down in the cul-de-sac. The cop was talking on a phone, but his gaze was alert. Good.

Ivar reached for more peanuts, needing the salt. When he went back in time to that period of being just an animal, a metallic taste always filled his mouth. Blood or adrenaline or just fucking fear. He wasn't sure. But the peanuts helped.

The car moved on, and he angled his head to see one light go out at the far end of the house. Dr. Promise Williams had gone to bed. What did a beautiful scientist like her wear to sleep? Something silky she hid from the outside world? Or something practical and comfortable? Either way, her full curves would be perfect.

He shifted his weight in his suddenly tighter jeans. It had been too long since he'd touched a woman, and considering he'd just tried to kidnap that one, she sure as shit wasn't going to give him a chance. Not that he could blame her. He sucked down more salt, trying to banish the bad taste that went all the way to his soul.

A sound alerted him, and he stretched to his feet, remaining in the tree line as he made his way to the cliffs. He stopped short at seeing Promise on her back deck beneath a sloping roof, her arms hugging her body, her gaze out at the far sea.

His heart cracked. Her melancholy stirred a part of him he'd long forgotten. His chest aching, he lifted his head to scent the wind.

No fear. The woman wasn't afraid. Just lonely. And her scent, wild purple heather, engulfed him. He inhaled sharply, taking in as much of her as he could. Light spilled out from the house, glimmering on her long curls and smooth skin. The almond shape of her eyes gave her a mysterious appearance, and the night masked the pretty bourbon color he remembered from the other day.

He twisted to the side to get a better view, and a leaf rustled beneath his foot.

She jumped and swiveled toward him.

He held his breath, not moving. The trees covered him, but he was a predator, and most prey could sense danger. For his kind, humans were definitely prey.

She searched the tree line and then turned, hustling back inside to shut her sliding glass door. The lock echoed loudly, and then curtains blanketed the remaining light from within.

He let out his breath. Crap. He hadn't meant to scare her. Damn it. He stuffed his mouth with peanut shells. It'd serve him right if he choked. Instead, his fangs worked on the shells, and he discarded them, eating more of the peanuts. Then he sank to the ground, scanning the rear of the home. The cops could watch the front.

Would she have liked him before he'd gone to hell and tried to kidnap her? He'd been the organized member of the Seven. The guy who kept everyone else in line and secured headquarters and homes for them all. Heck. He'd even made sure Benny had his favorite red Swedish fish candy on demand.

Then he'd ceased to be him. He closed his eyes, wondering how he'd survived. There had to be a bigger plan in play. He should most certainly be dead, even with his torso fused into a solid shield by the Seven ritual, forever protecting his internal organs. For the rest of his life, no matter how long he lived, he'd never forget the joy on his brothers' faces after he'd fallen from hell. They'd lifted him off the ground, engulfing him in hugs. Benny and Adare had held on the longest, for they'd known each other most of their lives.

He'd endured their touch on his destroyed body as long as he could, finally breaking free and backing away. His head down, feeling nothing but pain, he'd tried to escape. To go into the lake and just disappear.

They wouldn't let him.

From that day on, they didn't touch him. But they were always around. Benny telling jokes and Adare trying to engage in small talk. That alone was torture. Logan and Garrett, the two young members, had been thoughtful and kind. Welcoming with no pressure.

But Ronan. Ronan had seen the torture in Ivar because he'd felt it himself. They had to get Quade free.

It had taken Ivar a month to relearn how to speak, first in Swedish and then English. To make his vocal chords create sound that made sense. His body had healed, except for the burn scars down his neck and the ones inside his throat. His mind was another matter.

Mostly he was lucid unless he was sleeping. But he made mistakes. Stupid ones like trying to kidnap Promise Williams.

The acceptance and support of his brothers had helped him to regain his sanity, and his brain was probably as good as it could get. He could mimic humor and other emotions, but he wasn't sure he fooled anybody.

His soul was something else altogether. He had never given much thought to the soul—not until his had been ripped apart by forces not found in this world. Even now, pieces of it had to be still struggling with those shards of ice and boiling flames so far from this peaceful rainy night. He didn't know much, but one thing was absolute.

He'd never be whole again.

Chapter Four

Promise finished her coffee, facing Detective Jones across the desk in her office at the university. It was Saturday, and the faculty hallway was silent, just the way she liked it. "That's all I remember," she reiterated. "I told the other detectives all of this last night." Then she'd barely slept, even though the police had patrolled her private road all night.

Her one dream had consisted of running through a forest, away from the kidnapper with the cunning blue eyes. Even in her dreams, there was something about him that intrigued her. How in the world did that make any sense?

The detective, a sixty-something black man with reassuring brown eyes, sat in one of several leather chairs in the room. The only one not stacked high with books and papers. He flipped another sheet of paper over in his slim notebook. "The only connection we can find between you and Victory Rashad is that you work at the same university. You have nothing else in common." He looked her over, his gaze intent. "Not the same age, race, religion, or anything else." He leaned forward. "What I'm trying to say is that our profiler doesn't think your kidnapping and her murder are related."

She swallowed. "But the kidnapper said—"

"The guy was obviously high on something and nuts—while hanging out in a cemetery." Jones had a kind voice, and he was apparently trying to be gentle. "None of what he said to you in that car made sense, and the fact that he ran away after hitting the ground so hard proves he was on a strong hallucinogenic drug. He should've been in too much pain to breathe, must less flee."

Promise tossed her latte cup in the garbage, which was already overflowing with discarded papers. Light filtered through the wall of windows, dancing through dust motes in the air. "You're saying you don't believe I'm in danger?"

He flipped his notebook closed. "I'm saying we don't know. The guy saw you and tried to kidnap you, but he didn't say anything specific about you, did he?"

She slowly shook her head. The would-be kidnapper hadn't said anything that would lead her to believe that he actually knew her personally. Sure, he'd said he wanted her brain. But had he just been under the influence of drugs? She had been the person to mention Dr. Rashad, and all he'd done was agree. "There was just something about him." She couldn't explain it to herself, much less this man.

The detective stood and slid his business card through stacks of papers and a couple of books on the teakwood desk. "We do think this was random, a crime of circumstance."

Promise's pulse sped up. "What about Dr. Fissure?" He was still missing, although he'd disappeared in a different country. The coincidence was interesting but probably not connected to her.

The detective shook his head. "We talked with Scotland Yard, and so far, it looks like Fissure took off for Scotland with a grad student. Doesn't seem to be related to this incident."

That did sound a little like Gary. The guy was a known flirt, but even so. Promise rubbed a bruise on her arm from the airbag. Her entire body had been sore all morning from the crash. Her kidnapper had to be in worse pain, and he deserved it.

The detective smelled like citrus cologne. He gave her a reassuring smile. "We're a small police force, and we can't provide protection for you based on these facts. Perhaps the university can arrange something?"

"I'm not sure," Promise said. The university security force was composed of three retired police officers—all in their mideighties. Student organizations volunteered as designated drivers and campus escorts after dark. "I'll look into the matter." How? She didn't have any idea.

Jones nodded. "All right. Please call if you remember anything else, or if you see him again." He pushed his chair back and stepped lightly over the different stacks of books and research covering her office floor, wincing as he had to hop to avoid two open notebooks illustrating diagrams she'd created to show students that supersymmetry could be consistent with unification as well as warped extra-dimensions theory. "You, ah, study dark matter and planets, right? My niece plays video games with stuff like that."

She needed to finish those diagrams before class next week. "Yes. I'm interested in elementary parcels and fundamental forces, as well as extra dimensions of space."

"Um, okay." He safely neared the door. "I'll call you if there are any developments on your case or on that of Dr. Rashad. Which, again, we think is probably unconnected."

That statement did not sound promising. She watched him leave after he successfully avoided two more piles of books.

Was the kidnap attempt random? It hadn't felt like it. She turned and looked out the window at the vibrant fall colors. Red and gold spread as far as she could see from tree to tree and even covered the ground. As a leaf fell, she automatically calculated the air motion necessary for it to land among the other crumbling leaves.

"You ready?" Mark poked his head in. "We're running late."

Right. The grants. How could she have forgotten? "Yes." She claimed her briefcase and maneuvered around the piles of books, grabbing her raincoat by the door and heading through the quiet hallway to the breezy fall day outside. The staff parking lot was right around the corner, and she kept silent until Mark opened his car doors. "We have a good chance at getting at least one of these grants," she said, attempting conversation as she sat and shut her door. These were the biggest grants ever created for the study of the cosmology of extra dimensions, multiverse theory, math, and quantum mechanics.

"Maybe." Mark slammed his door, started the engine, and pulled sedately out of the quiet parking lot. "The money involved is impressive."

She let Mark drive, her pitch forming in her head. "If we get either of these grants, we'll have better resources than MIT, Caltech, Montana Tech, and Harvard put together." She'd studied at all the schools but had decided to teach at her alma mater, West Coast Technical University on the Oregon coast. It was a coincidence that both of her parents had taught there. Although, sometimes when she was working late at night, she remembered them doing the same thing at the same place. As silly as it was, she somehow felt closer to them in those moments. When was the last time she'd placed flowers on their graves?

It was the proper thing to do, and the flowers looked pretty. But why was that a tradition? Her parents were long gone, and only dust and bones remained in that place. Her parents weren't there.

Mark drove through the campus arches and headed toward town. "You ready?"

"I think so," she said, patting the briefcase at her feet. "They have our applications; now they just want to talk. I imagine it'll be like defending a dissertation, and that's not very difficult."

"For some," Mark muttered.

She kept her gaze out the window, running through arguments as to why her university should win at least one of the grants. Pressure pounded through her and elevated her heart rate. For some reason, she flashed back to seventh grade, when she'd brought home an A− in advanced calculus and ended up grounded for three months.

Her knees shaking in her uniform, she forced herself to walk into her father's study. Unlike her mother's office, which was light and stacked with books, her father's study was pristine and organized, surrounded by heavy mahogany shelves. His dark hair was cut short, and his black beard neat. He looked up from behind his desk, his dark brown eyes covered by perfectly cleaned glasses. "What is it, Promise?"

She took one step inside and threw up all over the antique Persian rug.

"Right?" Mark's voice yanked her right back into the present.

She coughed. "Right." She shook her head. "Sorry. I was thinking about my childhood." Her father had been a brilliant mathematician. "I'm sorry if I hurt your feelings yesterday. I'm not good with people." She never had been. Science and discovery were so much easier.

Mark sighed. "Was it something I said or did?"

She chewed on her bottom lip. "No." Supersymmetry made her breath catch and her mind expand. Mark was just a body to see a movie with. Would she ever feel about another human being the way she did about dark matter? "I have the characteristics of a sociopath," she murmured.

Mark snorted out a laugh. "You are not a sociopath. I've seen you sad and I've seen you more than empathetic with students. Sympathetic, even."

That was true. And she'd cried when her fish had died in high school, so there was that. "Thank you for not being angry with me any longer."

"No problem." Mark drove into an underground garage, slowing down to reach a parking spot near a clearly marked elevator. He cleared his throat. "I think you should stay with me until they catch the guy who tried to kidnap you. No pressure. Just some protection."

She tilted her head. "The police think the attack was random." Though his offer was sweet.

"What if they're wrong?" Mark put the car in park and shut off the engine.

That was a good question. She'd dreamed about the kidnapper the previous night, but in the dream, he was holding her hand and showing her wild purple flowers by an ocean. Maybe she had hit her head in the car accident. She smiled at Mark. "I'll think about your offer. For now, thank you for the ride." She stepped out of the vehicle and took note of the several brand-new, shiny black SUVs also parked in the private garage.

"Anytime. Good luck today." He locked the doors and walked her way.

"You too." It was a good thing they had applied for different grants. How awkward would it be to compete against each other? She shrugged and led the way over the new cement to the elevator, which opened instantly. Then she pushed the button for the top floor. "I've researched this company. They have a good reputation for supporting the sciences, but I can't quite figure out what they manufacture." They seemed to create products for rockets and other vehicles, but even that limited information had been difficult to ascertain.

The elevator doors closed, and it smoothly lifted. Mark straightened the beige tie that melded into his light shirt. The blue suit jacket and khaki pants made him look like the studious professor he was known to be. "So long as they give us millions, I don't care what they do."

Excitement flushed through her, and she calmed it. "I'm sure we're competing with every university out there that has physics and math departments."

"Yeah, but we're due. And we're the best." He finally smiled, reminding her why she'd found him appealing in the first place. Well, besides the fact that he understood supersymmetry and could argue general relativity with the best of them.

The elevator opened, and they walked out into a bright reception area with muted tones and new furnishings. The place smelled like unwrapped furniture and new paint. Even a small hint of drywall and construction cleaner wafted around.

"Hi." The receptionist, a twenty-something redhead with one green eye and one blue eye, smiled from behind a wide bamboo counter. Petite with pale features, she looked like a sprite in a bright green suit with topaz jewelry. "I'm Mercy O'Malley. You must be Drs. Williams and Brookes."

An ice pick of pain slashed into Promise's nape, and she gasped, her vision blurring from the outside in. She stopped cold and then swayed.

"Whoa." The woman rushed around the desk and reached for her arm.

The pain increased, exploding into red bursts behind Promise's eyes. Blackness followed the red, and she dropped to the ground, with one final thought that gravity wasn't as weak as astrophysicists believed it to be.

Unconsciousness took all the pain away.

Chapter Five

Promise regained consciousness with a slow opening of her eyes. The pain had ebbed. She lay flat on her back on something hard, and above her, a bamboo platform holding lights hung suspended from a tall ceiling. Where in the world was she? She swallowed and partially sat up.

Oh, cripes. She sat on the middle of a smooth conference table made of what appeared to be reclaimed wood. Mark stood adjacent to the table next to another man—a colossal man with intriguing bluish green eyes. Almost a true aqua.

"Dr. Williams." Mark reached for her hand to help her swing her legs around. "Are you all right?"

Heat burst into her face, and she straightened her skirt to keep from flashing her plain white panties at them. "I do apologize." She pushed an escaped spiral of her dark hair away from her face. "That has never happened before." At least the losing consciousness part hadn't. She'd felt the pain before. Her sensible heels caught the edge of a chair, and she pressed her knees together.

"My, ah, wife will be here in a few minutes," the other man said, no expression on his face but definite concern in his eyes. Concern and curiosity. "She's a doctor."

"I don't require medical assistance." Promise scooted off the table to stand. "But thank you, anyway." What in the sphere of all reality had happened? Did she have a tumor or perhaps a blood

clot from the accident? High blood pressure could account for
such an attack as well. It was time for a physical, clearly. "I was
in a car accident yesterday. Maybe I'm having a residual reaction."
She rolled her neck. No pain. Not any. "I feel centered now." She
studied the man. He stood to about six foot six and filled out the
black designer suit as if his body were metal and the fabric just
a finish.

He held out a hand mammoth enough to palm a basketball.
Maybe two. "Ronan Kayrs."

She shook. "Dr. Promise Williams." Her body still trembled
from the pain, even though it had evaporated. "I must apologize
for my attack. I am so sorry."

He smiled, turning his face from rugged into sheer male beauty,
although he dropped her hand rather quickly. His palm had felt
rough and raised. Scarred? "No apology necessary. I'm quite used
to women fainting in my presence."

"Oh, for Pete's sake." Another man entered the room, this one
just as big as Ronan Kayrs with hair as dark and a blue suit just
as expensive. But his tie was an intriguing bright pink, while
Ronan's was a deep blue. "You need new material." He held out
a hand. "Dr. Kane Kayrs. It's nice to meet you."

Another Kayrs. She shook hands, and Kane released her as
quickly as Ronan had. These businessmen didn't believe in the
long shake, now did they? And his skin had felt odd as well. Like
it had been branded. But she couldn't very well ask to see his
palm; that'd be odd. "Brothers?" They certainly had similar bone
structure and physiques. But Kane wore light-refracting glasses,
so she couldn't see if the uncommon aqua eyes were a family trait.

Kane snorted. "No. Distant relations."

"Very distant," Ronan said, his grin flashing again.

Kane smiled. "Good one. My presence was requested around
midnight, and here I am. See? Family."

She looked from one handsome man to the other, her curiosity
piqued. They obviously shared an inside joke. She'd never had
one of those. What would it be like to have family again? Not

that she'd ever experienced much family time, anyway. "I hope my losing consciousness doesn't influence your decision for the grants." How could this have happened?

"Not a chance." Kane gently led her to a chair and waited for her to sit, making her feel all feminine. "Are you feeling better?"

"Yes. I'm fine." She frowned, rubbing the base of her neck beneath her braid. "Just fine now. I don't understand."

A rustle sounded by the door, and the receptionist stepped partially inside. "Dr. Brookes? Since Dr. Williams is feeling better, how about you follow me for your interview for the grant for research into ordinary differential equations?"

An ice pick ripped into Promise's neck, and she bit her lip, trying not to cry out. If it was a tumor, would the thing just explode and get it over with? She just had to complete this interview, and then she would make an appointment with a neurologist immediately. The room swam.

"Sure." Obviously not noticing her distress, Mark patted her shoulder and followed the petite woman, disappearing from view.

The pain receded and then sputtered out. What were these attacks? Promise exhaled slowly and let her shoulders relax. Okay. Time to concentrate. She'd figure out her health problems right after the interview.

Ronan cocked his head. "You okay?"

She nodded, bewilderment filling her. What would account for the pain coming and going so suddenly? "Yes. I experienced another sudden headache, but the pain has receded."

Kane looked toward the door. "Completely gone now?"

"Yes." She breathed in, filling her chest, and then exhaled again, slower this time. If she'd just destroyed her chance at the grant money, then her brain could up and explode. The good the university could do with such funds was inspiring. She had to turn this around. "I'm fine, gentlemen. Shall we get started?"

The two men exchanged a glance and then took chairs across from her at the table.

Ronan cleared his throat. "We don't have a lot of time to mess around, so here it is. Based on your application and a background check, you're one of several finalists for this grant. We're interested in studying different dimensions. I mean, the possibility of travel between and to different dimensions."

She blinked. That hadn't been mentioned on the application. Was he serious? "As a practicality instead of theoretically?"

"Yes," Kane said, leaning forward, his elbows on the table.

Oh, for goodness' sake. So much male beauty and no darn brains. She sighed. "All right. So, first we probably need to get the terminology straight. Dimensions refer to distance, so you don't travel to another dimension. At least we don't. We're third-dimensional beings, so we're in the third dimension. If there are other dimensions, and I believe that there are, we don't go there. Or rather, they could be all around us right now, and we wouldn't even know it, because we can't see them—just like a two-dimensional being wouldn't be able to see, well, off the page." It was as elementary as she could make the explanation.

Kane blew out air. "We should've never shared that word with the humans. Ever."

Ronan nodded. "They have perverted it. Dimensions don't even mean dimensions anymore. Damn Einstein. I blame him for taking the word and screwing it all up."

She looked from one to the other, her heart rate increasing. "Um, excuse me?"

Kane flattened large hands on the table. "Just kidding. Quote from an old sci-fi book I read as a kid. All right. So say we somehow travel through space, time, whatever...and end up in another third-dimensional world. One not here."

Who were these men? Some billionaires who'd been watching too many television shows? "Are you talking about the multiverse?" she asked.

Kane shook his head. "Not in that there are identical universes with different paths. Not at all. I'm talking maybe different universes. Or even other places in this universe, though I'm thinking that's not it. Universes with places you can get to only by, well, jumping through dimensions. Or black holes. Or wormholes."

Her eyebrows rose. "All right. Then bubble theory? That our universe is one of an infinite number?"

"Yes," Kane said. "Bubble theory accounts for black matter, so it's possible."

She nodded. "That is one of many theories for black matter."

"Exactly," Ronan added. "We're interested in that kind of a study. More specifically, how we could jump to another place in this universe, or a different universe, or world, or bubble—not a parallel universe but one different from this one. Whatever."

There had to be a way to earn the grant and somehow not insult these men. As a child, she'd dreamed often and vividly about such possibilities until her parents forced her to face reality and study accordingly. "I understand the appeal of such a theory. I truly do." She cleared her throat. "If you subscribe to superstring theories, then you'd have to believe that the D-brane expends over three spatial dimensions. But those can't move at right angles, so there's no exploring the universe outside of the brane." Did they even comprehend that much of string theory?

"Perhaps we're looking at an alternate theory about the D-brane," Kane said. "Something outside of the box, if you'll pardon the expression."

Alternate theory? "Physics does have some laws we follow," she murmured.

"Really?" Ronan's gaze darkened to more green than blue. "The most prevalent theory right now is that the universe is made of strings—that we've never seen. The laws of physics are constrained by our understanding of the universe, and we're probably dead wrong."

Well, gravity probably did warp time. She smiled. "You're sounding like one of those conspiracy groups who were sure the Large Hadron Collider would make black holes and destroy our entire planet." Which, of course, hadn't happened. Initially, she'd been concerned too, but the science behind the machine had reassured her.

Kane smiled. "Maybe we were just lucky that space and gravity reacted as we'd hoped. As we'd theorized."

There was some truth to his statement. She nodded her head, relaxing finally. "So you at least do understand what you're asking with this grant."

"Yes." Ronan Kayrs tapped long fingers on the table. "I'd also like to discuss a couple of your academic papers."

That made sense, considering their focus. "You're concerned about my declaration in the paper about fracking that the possibility of a positive outcome doesn't always justify the risk involved."

"That's one of the papers," Kane said. "And I'm not saying I disagree with your analysis. But we do need to discuss your general belief system."

"Do we?" she asked.

Ronan leaned forward. "Risk versus reward. If there is a way to bend time and alter gravity to travel through dimensions, there could be risk factors."

She coughed out a laugh, allowing herself a moment to descend into their fantasy. "Yes. Say that we figure out a way to do what you want, and say it doesn't take two hundred years, then we definitely would need to look at the risks involved. You're talking about math and science, about possibilities that aren't even imagined fully right now. We don't even know if we have the other dimensions correctly identified."

"You are a theoretical physicist," Ronan said quietly. "Theorizing is wonderful, especially when you use the absence of something to prove the existence of something else. But we're looking for somebody willing to experiment along with theory. To take the chance—take the risks."

Risks were for the foolish. As a scientist, she had a duty to protect life.

However, even the risks were theoretical at this point. She kept her smile in place. These guys were bored Star Trek fans with millions to donate to a good cause, like her school. Yet intelligence showed in their eyes, and their knowledge base had been impressive so far. But they were dreaming. She cleared her throat. "Any theory would have to take into consideration risks of altering the known laws of physics. It'd be irresponsible otherwise."

Ronan smiled. "Well, you're one of the brightest minds of this century, so have a little faith. Come up with a theory, some sort of plan to find a theory to get us what we want, and we'll grant you five hundred million dollars to use as you please at your university in order to prove it. You have one week."

Chapter Six

Ivar kicked back in the control room, watching the interview in the conference room through one of the several monitors set up on the long table. His area was windowless and quiet, which suited him just fine. Promise Williams was even prettier today with her gray suit and pale pink blouse. Her curly dark hair was secured in a no-nonsense braid that highlighted her strong features, her cheekbones high beneath her very smooth, warm beige skin.

The suit was form fitting in a classy way. Though the shoes had to go. Sensible, square heeled, boring. She had slender ankles made for sparkly sandals. Something told him there hadn't been much sparkle in Promise's life.

Not that he'd had much either.

It was an odd name. Promise. No doubt a hope for her large intelligence and expected contributions to science. He'd researched her family. Both of her parents had been professors who'd appeared to be more involved in work than with each other. The pictures of the skinny and awkward little girl had interested him. She'd attended math camp, space camp, even chess camp. No ponies, no lakes, no campgrounds. Only books and huge brown eyes and a sense of loneliness that he could feel in his own bones. A sense he lived with daily. Her parents had died when she'd been a sophomore at Harvard, but she'd looked alone even before that. Long before that.

The need to join her in that conference room pricked beneath his skin and up his neck. Even his blood felt more aware with her in the building. He glanced at the other monitor of Mark Brookes giving his spiel in another room. Boring. He picked up his phone and called Mercy at the front desk.

"What?" The sound of her typing furiously came over the line while she no doubt moved currency through markets as she pretended to be their receptionist for this week of grant interviews. The female did love investing.

"Would you do me a favor? Poke your head in the conference room and ask if they want any water," he said, his adrenaline flowing way too freely.

Mercy sighed. "They can get their own water."

He grabbed onto his temper with both hands. The last thing he needed was a pissed-off fairy in his day, and Mercy could be mean when she wanted. With her mate, Logan, and Garrett having left early that morning to secure a secondary safe location, the sprite was already cranky. So he chose his words with care, even though they burned through his already burned throat. "I know, but I'm asking for a favor. Don't go all the way in. Just stop at the door, ask, and then leave when they say yes or no."

"Fine." She slapped the phone down.

Ivar winced as his ears rang. Then he leaned toward the monitor, his instincts humming. His muscles vibrated with the effort it took to keep himself in that chair, in that room, and away from that woman. *Promise.* Even her name jolted something inside him. Mercy came into view through the monitor, her feminine green suit flouncing. She reached the doorway to the conference room and asked if anybody wanted a drink, her tone polite.

The color fled Promise's face, and she visibly tensed. Her pupils widened, and her chest rose rapidly. She shook her head, as did Ronan.

Mercy shrugged and strode back down the hallway, looking up at one of the cameras to stick her tongue out at him.

He turned his gaze back to Promise. The color filled her face again, and her breathing smoothed out. She rubbed the base of her neck as if something had stung her. Why would being in Mercy's proximity give Promise a raging headache? That was three for three times—so it wasn't a coincidence, and it had nothing to do with the car accident the day before. At least he didn't need to carry that guilt. For now.

Was it because Mercy was a Fae? Did Promise, as an Enhanced human female, have some sort of allergy to the Fae? Was that even possible? Damn it. Where could Ivar find another fairy to test his hypothesis? They weren't just hanging around, and most of them didn't like the Seven. Mercy was definitely an exception, and frankly, he wasn't sure she liked him very much.

The back door clanged, and Ivar turned toward another monitor. Benny was back. Good. Benny was usually on Ivar's side, and he'd understand why Ivar had tried to kidnap the physicist the other day. Oh, he'd have plenty to say about the mission being a failure, but at least he'd still be supportive. Besides Ivar, he was probably the member of the Seven most removed from sanity, which wasn't a terrible place to be. Reality often sucked.

Benny high-fived Mercy and then kept walking, finally reaching the first conference room.

Ivar cocked his head and turned up the volume on the speakers. It'd be riveting to see how the cerebral woman interacted with Benjamin Reese. Benny was around six foot eight with size sixteen boots and an even bigger ego. His hair was dark, his eyes a metallic mesh of colors, and his laugh booming. At the moment, his T-shirt was torn, his mouth bleeding, and his left hand full of candy corn.

Ronan's face hardened to that granite look he got when his plans weren't going as he wanted. He partially stood and introduced Promise and Benny, his gaze all but shooting blades at the newcomer. "Why are you bleeding?" he asked, way too calmly.

"Was sparring with my bastard demon cousin," Benny said, munching on the corn. "The guy who helped Ivar with the shrink?"

Ivar groaned. They had to get Benny out of there before he said something he shouldn't. Something else, that was. Hopefully Promise would think "demon" was an expression and not meant literally. Of course, she might just think Benny was nuts, and she'd probably be correct.

Ronan nodded. "All right. Why don't you go find Ivar and report on the shrink?"

Benny leaned against the doorjamb. "I don't know. I'm part of this organization, and I like conference meetings." He looked up at the camera and winked.

Ivar reached for his phone again to call Benny if he didn't comply. Then he noticed Promise's face. Pinched with wide eyes. She clutched the armrest of her chair so hard, her knuckles had turned white. She swayed.

"Time to go, Benny," Ronan growled.

Benny rolled his eyes and strolled away, heading down the hallway toward the computer room.

Promise slowly released her hold on the chair. Her breathing smoothed out. She smiled at Ronan, but her lips trembled a little. "I'm sorry. I think my headache is returning." Her voice was soft but clear.

Huh. This was getting weirder.

Benny stomped through the doorway of the computer room, dropping candy corn on the way. "Hey, buddy. Heard you screwed up on a simple kidnapping mission yesterday."

"Affirmative." Ivar narrowed his gaze to watch Promise's every reaction. Something heated in his chest. Something strong and protective and totally fucking weird. He didn't like how she kept ending up in pain, and it wasn't making a lick of sense. "What do you and Mercy O'Malley have in common?"

Benny dropped into the only other available chair—another eco-friendly piece of crap that was too small. It lurched and groaned in protest. "We're both here in a high-rise when we should be at a better holding somewhere underground?"

"Agreed," Ivar muttered. For decades, he'd provided mountainous headquarters, one after the other, to keep them safe. Two had been blown up, and he'd disappeared into hell places for too long, and now they were here? In a human building way too far off the ground. Hiding in plain sight was stupid, as far as he was concerned. For now, he had to play along and find the right human physicist to help them. His gut told him Promise Williams was the person he needed. "What else, Benny? You and Mercy must have more in common than we know," he murmured.

"Mercy hit me in the nose yesterday because I called her a fairy instead of a Fae. She had to jump up to do it, but it still hurt. Both names are wimpy sounding, if you ask me, and they mean the same damn thing." Benny shook his head. "That fairy is crazy."

Well, so was Benny. Maybe Promise had some sort of "insane" detector? Could that be a human enhancement like being an empath? Ivar bit back a grin. "What else?"

"Nothin'." Benny chewed thoughtfully. "She's Fae, and she loves numbers and shit. I like to fight." He held out his hand to offer candy, and when Ivar shook his head, he went back to chewing. "We both don't like strawberries, but she lied yesterday about being allergic to broccoli. Just doesn't like that salad that Faith makes and didn't want to hurt her feelings. I hate broccoli and had no problem telling Faith her salad sucked. Then she punched me." He shook his head sadly. "I don't know why the females around here like to hit me."

Faith. She was a neurosurgeon as well as being Ronan's mate. "Where is Faith?" Maybe the doctor could explain some of this.

Benny shrugged. "How should I know? I just got here." He popped the rest of the candy into his mouth. "When did Kane Kayrs show up in town?"

"Last night."

"Figures." Benny wiped blood off the side of his mouth. "The Realm just can't butt out and let us do our jobs, can they?"

Ivar watched Promise as she obviously regained her strength and kept talking to Ronan. "He's smart." Though Benny was right. Dage Kayrs, King of the Realm and Kane's brother, was in everybody's business. Period. "I think we should tell her the truth about everything. So she can really do the calculations we need."

Benny shook his head. "Nope. We agreed we wouldn't tell any humans until we've chosen the grant recipients. She's one of many applicants." He tilted his head. "Though she is pretty. What color are her eyes?" He squinted and leaned closer to the monitor.

"Brown. Light brown with golden flecks." Ivar shifted in his seat. "And she smells like a springtime breeze off the ocean through purple heather." The flowers of his youth. He couldn't take waiting anymore. "Enough of this." Shoving away from his chair, he headed for the door.

Benny partially swiveled in his crappy chair, and one of the wheels rolled off, tipping him to the side. He swore and regained his balance. "What are you doing?"

"Making a mistake," Ivar said grimly, heading into the hallway.

"Well, make it a good one," Benny said cheerfully, turning back to the monitors, no doubt for a perfect view of the mess Ivar was about to create.

Ivar rolled his still aching wrist. Even though he'd healed the bone within an hour of crashing through the windshield, residual pain still thrummed toward his elbow. His healing powers were getting stronger but still hadn't reached a hundred percent, even in the three months he'd been back home.

It really was as if hell, several of them, still had a grasp on him.

His boots made absolutely no sound as he maneuvered the hallway. Traveling through terrible places had taught him stealth beyond a mere immortal's, and someday maybe he could use that fact for fun instead of survival. For now, he went on instinct.

He reached the conference room doorway and entered the room before Ronan or Kane could react.

Promise partially stood, her hand going to her throat. She gasped.

He forced a smile, and no doubt made a grimace. He'd pretty much forgotten how to smile, or rather, how to feel a smile. "Hello."

Then she screamed.

Chapter Seven

Promise leaped to her feet and pressed back against the table. What was going on? She looked frantically toward Ronan Kayrs, who glared at Ivar with what looked like prickly irritation. "Who are you people?" She hadn't even brought her purse in with her. There was nothing she could use as a weapon. Even her pen was the cheap rubbery kind.

Ronan stood. "You're safe, Dr. Williams. I promise."

Safe? Right. Safe with the man who'd tried to kidnap her. He stood between her and the door. The other two men didn't move any more, as if not wanting to spook her. "What is happening?" Her voice shook.

Her would-be kidnapper leaned against the frame in a lame effort to appear harmless. "It's not what you think. I'm sorry about yesterday." His voice was even more hoarse than it had been in the car.

"Sorry?" She gulped. "You put a gun in my side." She partially turned to see Kane Kayrs watching, his gaze alert, his body relaxed. He'd seemed like the most rational person she'd met in the office, so the sight of him remaining calm was somewhat reassuring.

"Yeah. Sorry about that." The guy at the door winced. "I'm Ivar. Ivar Kjeidsen." He cleared his throat but didn't move toward her. "People call me 'Viking' or 'Vike.' You can call me anything you want."

This was not happening. Her phone was in the car. If she screamed again, would anybody come? Maybe she hadn't screamed loud enough. Mark Brookes was somewhere in the office, wasn't he? She drew in air.

"Please don't scream," Ivar said, holding both hands up. "I made a mistake yesterday, and I'm sorry."

His eyes were so blue it almost hurt to look at them. Today he wore ripped jeans and a black button-down shirt that didn't look right with the jeans. The mismatch should've made him appear endearing. It didn't. He looked lethal.

His boots were black and large, and he'd tied his dark blond—streaked with black—hair at the neck, revealing those scars down the right side. Those burn scars. Was that why his voice was so low and hoarse? He stood at least a foot taller than she, and he had a hundred plus pounds on her—all muscle. If he wanted to block the door, she'd need the help of the other two men to get out.

Neither had moved again.

She drew on her professor voice. "Somebody explain. Right now."

"I'm, ah, your security detail," Ivar said. "The gun wasn't to threaten you, but I thought you were in danger at the cemetery, and I was trying to convince you to drive out of there quickly." He shook his head. "I was wrong."

Security detail? Where was logic?

Ivar nodded toward Ronan, whose jaw tightened like one long muscle currently being strained.

"Right," Ronan muttered. Then he cut Kane a look. "All right. We have the grant award narrowed down to six of you already, and one has been murdered, while the other is missing."

"Excuse me?" Promise's stomach jumped, and not in a good way. Nerves pinged along her scalp in a flood she identified as adrenaline. Her body received the fight-or-flight message, and she wanted to flee. But the massive man remained at his post at the door. "You're telling me that you assigned me a security detail, based on a grant I have not as yet received, and that detail was this lunatic with a gun?"

Laughter boomed down the hallway, and she jumped. It sounded like that Benjamin Reese man she'd just met. What was going on with these overgrown males? They were all so big and hard cut.

Ivar's eyes twinkled, for the first time losing that overly intense expression. "Yes. The grant is for a hundred million dollars, and it has put you in danger. We're taking your safety to heart."

The man appeared serious, but this was insane. "What about Mark? Nobody tried to kidnap him."

Kane cleared his throat. "The math grant he's working on is for far less money, and he's not in danger, unlike you. The Viking wasn't supposed to approach you."

The Viking. Truth be told, the man did look like one. She could imagine him leading a raiding ship years ago. An odd tingle spread through her abdomen, and she frowned. What in the laws of physics was that? Her body was really on the blink. She'd need to make a doctor's appointment as soon as she escaped from this place. "I do not need security, and I think it's time I went on my way."

Ivar straightened. "You have security until the grant is awarded and is safely transferred. Whether you like it or not."

Ronan snapped his lips shut, and Kane groaned softly. More laughter bellowed down the hallway from that Benny.

Promise put her hands on her hips. This was not making any logical sense. Not that there was illogical sense. She shook her head. "This isn't right."

Ivar slipped his thumbs into his front jeans pockets in the worst "aw shucks" attempt imaginable. "Everyone is mad at me now."

Her heart didn't soften in the slightest. Not a bit. "You said I was in danger. How so?"

His chin dropped as he no doubt went for a harmless and apologetic appearance. Instead, he looked like a predator who'd just found dinner and was trying to blend into the flora. Unsuccessfully. "It was a false alarm," he said, his voice rough sandpaper over wood. "Again. Sorry."

Ronan's fingers curled over the back of the chair he'd vacated. "We can put somebody else on you, Dr. Williams."

"No," Ivar said shortly. "I'm her protection detail. Period."

The hair on the back of her neck stood up. And her abdomen did the odd flop-roll it had endured earlier. Her skin flushed and sensitized. What in the world? She recognized the feelings of physical attraction, but there was no way she was feeling something for this old-world Viking. Of course, biologically, there was some logic there. From an anthropological perspective, he appeared to be capable of protecting an entire village, and she was being told she was in danger. Naturally, that made him attractive to her body, if not her brain. All right. Her brain, too. "I can hire my own protection," she said.

Ivar snorted. "Not as good as me."

That was probably true. The man could stop a truck if he wanted, probably. "Even so, I can take care of myself."

"No." He tilted his head to the side. Studying her. There was intelligence in those hues of blue—a lot of it.

She forced a smile. "If you follow me, if you harass me, I shall call the police."

"Is that a fact?" he drawled.

"Ivar—" Ronan warned.

She nodded. "Yes. I know your name and where you work. I could have you arrested for attempted kidnapping, and I believe you assaulted a police officer in your bid to run away yesterday." Her mind calculated the best way to respond to him, and this seemed to be it. So she kept her voice level and matter of fact, even though her heart rate had sped up. "I suggest you leave me alone, or your entire business here could be in jeopardy." She glanced over her shoulder at Ronan. "I have no problem suing you civilly as well."

"Man, I like her!" Benny's loud voice boomed from down the hallway. "She's a keeper."

She jolted. Who were these people? "What kind of business is this, anyway?"

Ivar pushed away from the door frame. "We manufacture certain parts for crafts. Rockets, planes, and so on."

Yes. She'd managed to dig that up herself. The secrecy probably had something to do with government contracts. These guys looked like soldiers. Maybe ex-marines turned CEOs? She cleared her throat. "What else?"

Ronan sighed. "We're ex-soldiers, and we provide security services to many governments and private individuals around the world. All legal and all confidential. We're the best in the business if you need protection."

She believed every word of that because finally something made sense. "I need to meet my colleague and return to the university," she murmured.

Ivar smiled now, and it wasn't a completely unpleasant sight. His features were straight and strong, his jaw firm. The darker streaks through his hair intrigued her. "Dr. Brookes left fifteen minutes ago to visit one of our facilities. We assured him we'd secure you a ride back to the campus."

If the mathematical modeling grant was in the millions as well, it wasn't surprising Mark had done as they suggested. Of course, he didn't know that her would-be kidnapper was among them. "I see."

Ronan gestured toward the door. "I'll have my driver return you to campus. I strongly recommend you hire a security force until the grant money is awarded."

One week. She had one week to introduce a theory they liked enough to pursue. An impossible task, really. But if everyone was under the same constraints, a mere theoretical approach was all she required. Then she could have decades to prove or disprove it. "All right."

Ivar stood straighter. "I'm for hire." He held up his hand before she could protest. "I'm trained in firearms, knives, swords, and strategic defense, as well as in hand-to-hand and several martial arts disciplines. I'm a former soldier, and I've worked security detail on people marked for assassination. Not one of them died under my watch."

It was hard to imagine she was actually in danger just because of a grant. "You held a gun on me."

His eyes widened. "I am extraordinarily sorry about that and will not let it happen again."

There was something about him that just threw her off. She couldn't put her finger on it. Sure, he was handsome and sexy and had that dangerous thing going on that so many women liked. She did not like that. Her biological clock must be going haywire all of a sudden. "I appreciate the offer."

Three phones dinged through the room in unison.

Ronan glanced at his first. "Ah, shit."

Kane slammed his fist on the table. "Damn it."

Keeping her gaze, Ivar drew his phone from his back pocket and read the face. His body didn't move, and his expression didn't change. He looked up, and his eyes had somehow darkened to a deeper blue. "Dr. Fissure was found an hour ago in eastern London, torn apart piece by piece. He's been dead at least a week."

Her mind jittered, and she swayed. *Not Gary. Oh, God.*

He grasped her arm. "The crime scene looks nearly identical to that of your friend Dr. Rashad."

"We weren't really friends," Promise said. How did this make sense? She pushed her hair away from her face. "You're telling me that somebody is butchering grant applicants? How? Why? To earn a grant?" That was insane.

Ivar glanced at Ronan and then back. "There was another killing in Sweden this morning. A Dr. Polantski was taken early and has already been found dead. The deaths were just connected this morning. The police think it's a serial killer, and it looks like the only thing the victims have in common is that they're the leading experts in the area of physics."

That was an odd thing to have in common. She coughed, even as her mind quickly reviewed possibilities. Serial killers played by their own rules. She'd studied a couple while taking abnormal psych as an undergraduate. "Physics."

"Yeah," Ivar said softly. "And you're one of the best, right?"

"So it isn't because of the grant," she said, tearing her gaze away from that impossible blue and looking at Ronan.

He shook his head. "Doubtful. Although the publicity surrounding the grant might've put you all on a killer's radar, and we take responsibility for that."

A serial killer didn't need a reason. "This doesn't add up for me," she murmured.

Ivar rubbed his damaged neck. "I understand that, but at the very least, you know you're in danger, right?"

Three colleagues, all working in similar fields to hers? Yes. She understood the danger. And the men with her right now, they couldn't have gone to Sweden and back in time to meet with her this morning. So at the very least, none of them was the killer. Of Dr. Polantski, anyway. "I—I understand I'm in danger," she acknowledged. "But I am not your responsibility."

Ivar frowned, his eyebrows slashing in the middle.

She breathed deep, her mind banishing any emotion. She'd done her research—these men had decades of ownership in the company. They were authentic, and now she understood why she hadn't been able to find all the details. "However, I'm willing to hire you until they catch this killer." While she might be confused at the moment, she was not stupid. Ivar Kjeidsen had more training than anybody else she'd find in this small college town, and she'd be a moron to refuse his help while a serial killer was targeting people like her. "Though I expect to see your personnel file before we reach an agreement."

His shoulders relaxed, and his smile was slow. Sexy. "I bet we can drum one of those up for you."

Chapter Eight

Ivar scouted the area outside the gray cottage, tuning in his senses for any threat. He chewed on a couple of cashews and swallowed the salt. The private road of established single-family homes was silent except for the crackle of falling red and gold leaves from thriving trees, while the ocean rolled on the other side. He followed Promise to the whitewashed front door and took the key from her. "I enter first. Every building, every time," he said. "Understand?"

"Yes." The woman had been shaky since discovering that two more of her colleagues had been brutally murdered, and trusting him to protect her had to feel odd after the way they'd met. But he appreciated her ability to follow logic and not emotion in the situation.

He couldn't relate to emotion any longer.

He released the lock and walked inside, closing his eyes to listen. Nothing. And no energy signatures he couldn't identify. But he searched the living room, one bedroom, and bathroom before taking in the clean kitchen and nook. Nothing except the slight scent of purple heather—her scent.

She followed him inside and shut the door to lock it.

He whistled and moved toward the sliding glass door beyond the breakfast nook. A small but private yard led to cliffs overlooking the Pacific Ocean. In late September, the sea rolled gray and white, promising a chilly winter to come. It reminded him of his early days, on the sea, with his family. There had been a Realm headquarters somewhere in the cliffs of Oregon, and he made a mental note to find out where it had been, just in case. Of course, it had been blown up. Why did their headquarters continually get blown up? Maybe leasing the high-rise office wasn't a bad idea. "It's beautiful."

"Yes." She tossed her jacket over a chair and yanked several notebooks out of her briefcase. "I need to get to work."

"Um, how about dinner?" he asked, studying her. The flimsy silk blouse followed her contours as she tossed the notebooks onto the coffee table, and his mouth started to water for anything but food. He paused and turned to survey her place. Muted colors, artfully arranged, clean and uncluttered. Even the bedroom had been so.

"There are delivery menus in the right-hand drawer on the other side of the island." She pointed toward the kitchen and settled herself on the sofa.

Delivery? He walked around the island and past the stove. "How about I cook something?"

She looked up and blinked a couple of times until her eyes focused on him. "You cook?"

"Yeah." Taking up the hobby had been part of his recovery the last three months, and he found he liked the exactness of it. And he enjoyed eating, so it was a practical hobby too.

"I don't have much food," she said, not seeming concerned about it.

He moved to a quaintly old-fashioned refrigerator to find several batches of vegetables already cleaned. The woman probably took them raw to eat as snacks at work. "I'll make it happen." He found a pot and filled it with water to start boiling before searching for a knife. Then he started chopping.

She glanced away from her notebooks. "You are remarkably fast."

He slowed his knife to a more human range. "I just make a lot of noise." He smiled and scanned her home. Besides a few framed photographs of her with her parents and her as a student with other kids, there wasn't much of her in the place.

"What?" she asked, finally concentrating fully on him.

He shrugged. "Dunno. Figured your house would include rich colors and wild paintings."

She smiled, twirling a highlighter in one hand. "Direct opposite of what I show the world?"

"Yeah." He'd also imagined her in a scarlet-red panty set but figured she wouldn't appreciate that revelation. He couldn't tell what she wore beneath the pink silk, but it obviously wasn't bright red. Or black.

"No. What you see is what there is." She looked into the quiet living room. "Hired a decorator right when I moved in, and she bought the pieces. Said they were tranquil and went well with the ocean outside."

Books were lined neatly on the shelves, and no television was visible anywhere. She drew him in a way he didn't understand, especially since they seemed too much alike to arouse any "opposites attract" flow of hormones. Although her choice of vocation might negate that theory. There was more to her than he could see—he just knew it. "What do you do for fun?" he asked, dumping the vegetables into the water.

"I work." She kicked off her shoes. "My few friends are colleagues, really. We've come up with new experiments together." She mulled it over. "I play some VR multiplayer games online sometimes."

"Dealing with science?" He grinned.

"Of course." She shrugged and rolled her feet around.

He swallowed. There was just something about her ankles. He searched through the cupboards and found a set of herbs that remained protected by their plastic coatings. Had probably been a gift. "I see."

She shrugged, her face turning a lovely pink. "Must seem boring to you. Cold and logical."

"No," he said, relaxing for the first time that day as he sprinkled in different herbs. His brain finally made the connection. "You're a romantic, Promise Williams. You just don't show it."

Her chuckle was low and feminine, and he felt it right in his balls. "A romantic? Not in a million years."

Her lack of self-awareness was intriguing. He nodded. "Not true. Anybody who studies the cosmology of extra dimensions, supersymmetry, and dark matter is truly a romantic. All of you deep thinkers are big dreamers."

She rubbed her nose, her gaze meeting his. "Nobody has ever called me either a romantic or a dreamer."

"Then they don't see you clearly," he returned, moving to the freezer and finding a decent pack of meat he could use for the stew. He tossed it into the microwave to defrost, his gaze trailing back to the woman. What was it about her?

She glanced down at a page in her notebook. "I don't wish to take advantage of your business group, but I really want that money for the university."

Ah, the sweetheart. "You think we're crazy?"

She winced. "Not crazy, just misinformed. Dreaming, rather. There's no way we're going to find another dimension or travel to another universe in this lifetime. In several, actually."

Not with the laws of physics she knew. Man, he'd like to tell her everything about the world that humans didn't see. Didn't know. "We can take care of ourselves. You just come up with your best theory, and I hope you'll get the grant." He waited until her gaze met his. "In fact, I'll make sure you do." He had enough of his own funds to give her five hundred million or so without missing any.

She sighed. "Can you imagine? The breathtaking danger and risk we'd create if we tried to bend time? It'd be a horrible mistake."

So not what he wanted to hear. Not even close.

Her gaze moved to his damaged neck.

"You can ask me," he murmured, shoving aside her remarks about risk and danger. "I don't mind."

She shrugged slim shoulders. "None of my business."

Yet he wanted to tell her. When he'd first returned from his hellish trip through other places, he had to relearn how to speak, even though he didn't want to. Then he'd forced himself to talk to a shrink and get it all out. But he'd hated every second of it. Now, for the first time, he really did want to tell the truth, and he couldn't. "I was on a mission, things went bad, and I was burned."

She nodded. "I surmised it was something like that. I'm glad you survived."

Had he? Sometimes, in the minute before dark turned to dawn, when he hadn't slept all night, he wondered. Maybe he was actually still back in hell. Just dreaming that he'd escaped. "I'm still figuring things out, and I make dumb mistakes." His IQ was unmeasurable, but he hadn't acted like it in too long. "Yesterday, I'm really sorry if I scared you."

Her head jerked. "You terrified me."

The words were like a knife to the gut. "I'm sorry." Maybe he wasn't ready to be around humans yet.

She exhaled. "You're forgiven. Just don't do it again. To anybody. Ever."

"I promise," he said, meaning every syllable. Kidnapping wasn't his style. Not that he had a style. Her easy forgiveness was a balm to some of his guilt. Much of his hurt. He liked her brain, and now he was seeing her heart.

"Should I help you make dinner?" she asked, sounding as if she were offering to attend a twelve-hour lecture on dentistry.

"No. I've got it." His movements were quick and economical. "I enjoy cooking. The preciseness of it."

She smiled. "I can see that, although I don't understand. Cooking has never been my passion."

Passion. The word hung in the air for a moment. He nodded. "I like it. Maybe someday I'll teach you." Why the hell had he said that?

She cleared her throat, obviously skipping right over the offer. Smart girl. "We've agreed no more kidnappings. How about no more guns?"

"Not a chance," he said. If she had any idea of who was after her, she'd want to carry a gun herself. "Sorry."

"Do you have a gun right now?" She tapped her bare foot, meeting his gaze directly.

In answer, he withdrew the pistol from the back of his waist and set it on the top of the island. "Yes."

She frowned. "I don't know anything about guns. It's green. Well, a light metallic green. What kind is it?"

He looked at the weapon. It fired green lasers that turned into hard projectiles when hitting an immortal body. "It's a prototype. You've never heard of it."

She shook out her dark hair. "You and your colleagues seem to have good connections. I couldn't find out much about you, however."

He nodded. The woman had no clue. He tucked the gun back in place, which relaxed him even more. How screwed up was that? "How's your head? Any more pain?"

"No." She chewed on the end of the pen, looking adorable. "But I'll make an appointment for an MRI next week at the hospital. Just in case." She rubbed her eye. "The losing consciousness concerns me."

Yeah, but it was because of Mercy and then Benny. Ivar stirred the stew. "Has that ever happened before?"

She ducked her head. "No." Lying. She was definitely lying.

"All right. We both obviously have things we don't like to talk about. Let's make it even." He flattened both hands on the cool granite as the stew began to thicken and bubble. "I sometimes go a couple of nights without sleeping because the nightmares get too bad." When she looked up again, he nodded. "Your turn."

"This conversation is peculiar," she murmured, tilting her head to study him. When he didn't respond, she sighed. "All right. Yes, there have been a few times in my life that I've gotten an odd tingle in the back of my neck that led to pain. It's usually fleeting." Her eyes widened. "In fact, I felt it a little when you first tried to kidnap me, but it went away."

He stiffened. "Do you feel it now?"

"No," she said. "Haven't since that first moment, so I concluded it was just adrenaline or panic. You know. From the gun you pressed into my ribs."

He winced. "I've apologized." Repeatedly. What the hell did she want? "I'm the one who flew through glass and hit the asphalt."

She lifted her head slightly. "Speaking of which. Shouldn't you have more injuries than you do?"

"Nope." One good thing about logical people was that they believed what they saw. Although she might take the news of his real genetics more easily than most humans; after all, she worked with outlandish theories all day long. "I tucked and rolled. Sure, I have some cuts, but nothing is broken." He smiled. "Though you're welcome to check me out." Oh, he did not just say that. What was wrong with his damn mouth?

Her dark eyebrows rose. "The police theorized that you were under the influence of strong drugs."

"I'm sure." He stirred the pot, which was finally smelling like dinner. "I don't do drugs, and I have the training necessary to protect myself during an event such as flying through your windshield."

She studied him. "I'm not going to apologize."

"You shouldn't," he said. "You reacted quickly and intelligently to what you considered a threat." In fact, he was still impressed by her—especially since she'd just gotten him off track. "When were the other times you experienced the tingling and then the pain in your head?"

She frowned. "I don't know. Once on a train, once in a crowd in New York City at a conference, and once in a restaurant at Harvard. I didn't lose consciousness any of those times. It's odd." She glanced at the clock. "I'm planning to make an appointment tomorrow to get my head examined." She chuckled, her pretty eyes lighting up. "You can make a joke about that now."

"I don't joke." He stirred some more.

She sat back. "Never?"

He shook his head. "No. Even before I went through the mission that went bad, I was the serious one—the one who planned everything and kept our operation running smoothly. It was my place, and there wasn't time for jokes." Even when he'd been a kid and then a Viking on the open seas, life was rarely calm enough to go for the one-liner. He wouldn't know how, anyway. "There isn't much I find funny." That was the truth, so he gave it to her.

"Me either." She crossed her legs in the slim skirt. "A lot of times, when other people catch a joke, I completely miss it. I think I interpret words too literally. Subtext, sarcasm, and even humor escape me sometimes." She sounded more thoughtful than regretful.

Man, she was cute. Nerdy and sexy and brilliant. An alluring combination for a scarred former Viking who figured he'd die in the battle coming up and was just fine with that fact. For now, his blood pumped through his veins. He wanted to choose his words carefully, but after more than a millennium of not doing so, it was probably too late to try now. "You intrigue me, Promise Williams."

Her eyebrows rose now. "You intrigue me as well. Not the kidnapping part. But the cooking dinner and being so deadly combination." Her gaze raked down his chest. "And you're certainly good looking."

Good looking? With his scars? "What are you saying?" he asked.

She sat back, for the first time looking uncertain. "What are you saying?"

Cute. So damn cute. They were under pressure, and there was a fantastic way to release that, so long as no expectations were created. He couldn't be there for a mate, or even a girlfriend. "I was trying to find a smooth way of seeing if you wanted, to, ah—"

"Have sexual intercourse with you?" she asked.

Surprise zinged through him, and he coughed out a laugh. A real laugh. "Yes." Then he held his breath as the stew started to bubble over.

Finally, she spoke. "Yes. I think I would like to do so."

Chapter Nine

Promise finished doing the dishes after eating a remarkable stew while the Viking scouted outside the home for any threats. Who'd have thought the muscled badass would be such a good cook? Dinner had been delicious and comfortable as they discussed current politics, movies, and the possibility of religion. The meal had been enjoyable and relaxed. Every once in a while, he'd study her with that brilliant blue gaze, and her hormones would wake right up.

It was good they'd determined they'd have a sexual relationship while he served as her bodyguard. Oh, it might be improper, but she didn't care. She hadn't had a good orgasm in way too long, and these things were physical—not emotional.

He appeared at the sliding glass door and opened it, letting in a rapidly escalating wind. "We're clear."

She wiped her hands on the dish towel and hung it on the proper hook. "I imagined we would be." She waited until he closed the door and locked it. "Do you really believe I'm in danger?" Based on the financial report of his corporation, he didn't need the extra money for protecting her, so there didn't appear to be an ulterior motive for the claim.

"Yes." His size overwhelmed the breakfast nook, and a stray red leaf clung to the right shoulder of his black shirt, which was still shoved haphazardly into ripped jeans. "What do you think?"

She ran through the facts in her head again. "I'm uncertain. There does seem to be a killer targeting physics experts, as bizarre as that sounds. Of course, killing in general is bizarre, so that tracks." She thought it through as he watched her with that incredible blue gaze. "My instincts, which I rarely heed, are telling me that something is going on and that I am in danger." Hopefully the authorities would catch the killer soon.

Ivar nodded. "Good. If you realize you're in danger, you'll take precautions."

"Like hiring you," she murmured. "Speaking of which, we should negotiate a contract." They should get all the business out of the way before retiring to the bedroom.

Amusement tilted his upper lip. At least, it looked like amusement. "Ah, Missy. Let's just consider my protection services as part of the grant process. I don't need your money."

No, it did not appear that he did. She stilled. "Missy?"

He blinked. "Sorry. Nickname for Promise? It just came out."

She warmed anyway. "I tried to use it as a nickname in high school but my parents wouldn't allow it." They thought it made her sound too, well, something. "I guess since we're talking about becoming intimate, it's something you could try."

His eyes lightened, and humor filled them. For some reason, it made her feel good. As if she'd made him happy for a moment. She cleared her throat. "I think our business and personal interactions should be kept separate," she said.

He nodded. "Okay."

The man was so agreeable. She nodded and crossed the kitchen, her breathing accelerating enough to be noticeable. They'd already agreed to have relations, and she'd shaved her legs earlier that day, so there wasn't anything to be nervous about. This was a normal bodily function. "So, are you tired?" she asked, moving toward the bedroom.

"No," he said, following her close enough she could feel the heat off his body. The man was definitely hot blooded.

Warmth trickled into her face. "For some reason, I'm experiencing nervousness about this."

He paused at the foot of her bed and looked around. "I could find some candles and play music." His hand looked big and broad when he ran it through his thick hair. "I don't have much experience with seduction."

Seduction? She didn't need to be seduced, and with a body like his, he probably had women jumping all over themselves to bed him. Even with the scars down his neck, or maybe because of them, his features combined into a combination that was as deadly looking as beautiful. Add in the spectacular blue eyes, and no doubt he rarely lacked for female companionship. So that probably meant he'd never had to work for it. She sighed and moved to the bedside table. "Don't worry about it."

"I'm not," he said, rather dryly.

She opened the drawer and withdrew two condoms, their wrappers only a little dusty. It had been quite a while. Then she placed lube and her pocket rocket on the table, shutting the drawer and turning to face him.

His head cocked to the side in almost slow motion, his gaze on the narrow pink cylinder. "What is that?"

Tingles swept up her skin, and her cheeks burned. Why, she didn't know. "It's a personal massager. To provide clitoral stimulation." It wasn't worth the time and mess if he was the only one who reached orgasm. With all the stress in the past week, she could use relief.

For several heartbeats, he just stared at her. "Ah, baby. You're not gonna need that."

She swallowed. How did he know that fact?

An unidentifiable light glittered in his eyes, and then he prowled toward her, all muscled grace. When he came close enough that she could smell his masculine scent, he reached around her for the light pink device and flipped it on with one hand, drawing it between them. It instantly sprang into a familiar buzz, and she swallowed, trying without success to read his expression. Had she somehow insulted him? Being practical and adultlike about sex was necessary to reach satisfaction. "You're not supposed to turn it on yet," she murmured, her skin suddenly feeling too tight.

He glanced down at the device between them, his heat washing over her. "Ah. When do I turn it on?" Without waiting for an answer, he lifted his hand and ran the pulsing tube down her neck.

Vibrations tickled through her skin. She shivered. "When it's closer to time."

"Closer to time?" His voice deepened even more, the hoarseness almost a physical burn. "You mean when I'm balls deep inside you—fucking you hard enough to rattle the walls?"

His words sank even deeper than the vibration. "I'm amenable to dirty talk, but I don't require it." It was necessary to be up front in situations like this.

"Amenable?" He continued exploring, sliding the massager across her clavicle. "What else are you amenable to?"

She blinked several times as the pulses dug beneath her skin, somehow zinging down her chest to her breasts, even though he'd kept the massager just at her collarbone. What had he asked? Oh, yes. "Well. What pleases you?" She blinked, trying to concentrate on those glittering eyes studying her so intently. "I'm open to different positions. I, ah, believe most men are drawn to what's commonly called 'doggie style.'"

The sound he made was a strangled groan. "Baby, if I fuck you from behind, you'll be more than amenable."

Oh, lord, she had insulted him. "I should've waited until we were in bed before taking out the provisions. I'm sorry, Ivar." She met his gaze directly as she made the apology.

His smile came out of nowhere, making him look both boyish and lethal. "God, you're sweet. And cute."

She amused him? Well, that was better than hurting his feelings. And she truly was curious about his hard body, so perhaps she hadn't ruined the chance of physical intimacy for the night. "Okay. Shall we get in bed?"

His entire body tensed, and he turned his head, his gaze going down and his ear lifting. Both of his nostrils flared like a hunter catching a scent. He flipped off the massager and tossed it on the bed, grasping her arm. "They're here. We have to run."

* * * *

A wave of power rolled over Ivar, and he settled into battle mode even as he grabbed Promise's arm and all but dragged her from the bedroom. He'd been so thrown by her vibrator and lube, not to mention her willingness to sleep with him, that he had allowed himself to become distracted. Energy signatures cascaded from outside, from the street, drawing closer and making his muscles vibrate with the need to fight.

The enemy was there.

His blood heated and then flowed faster, providing him with oxygen he needed to battle. He recognized the signatures as Kurjans, coming from north and east. Kurjans were white-faced monsters with fangs who drank blood and enjoyed killing. It was rumored they were cousins to vampires, and that made sense, except vampires could venture into the sun. The sun killed Kurjans, which was why they'd waited until night to attack.

And he'd been busy playing with Promise and her personal massager.

He kept his grip firm and led her through the living room to the sliding back door. Thunder bellowed high and strong, and the clouds opened up with a roar. The grass looked already soaked. When had it started raining hard?

She fought his hold. "What are you doing?" Her small feet tried to dig into the sensible tiles, and she pulled back, fighting as she slid where he wanted her to go.

He yanked the door open, and rain splattered inside, thrown by the chilly wind. There wasn't time to grab her shoes or a coat, but at least it wasn't too cold outside. "They're coming down the street. We'll have to go this way."

She bent at the waist, pulling back, trying to free her arm. "What are you talking about? I didn't hear anything."

Neither had he. Panic tried to grab him, and he pushed it away. Promise's safety was all that mattered. "I sense them," he muttered.

The doorbell rang, and they both froze. Her eyes widened. "The killer is ringing my doorbell?" she whispered, incredulity tilting her mouth.

So they didn't know he was there. They'd sense him any second. He needed to find safety for her and now. "Guess so." Without waiting for an answer, he tugged her into the storm, all but forcing her across the fenced backyard toward the cliff, where the ocean crashed far below. Rain poured down, sliding into his eyes. Wet grass covered his boots. The wind battered them as if trying to force them back inside. He shook his head, reaching the edge and pressing his lips toward her ear to whisper, "Is there a way down?"

She elbowed him in the ribs and yanked wet hair out of her eyes. "No, you crazy bastard." The rain soaked her pink blouse, molding the material perfectly to high breasts. Full breasts in perfect proportion to her curvy hips.

He tore his gaze away from her and searched wildly around. They couldn't go out the front door, and no doubt the Kurjans had the street covered. He leaned closer to the edge and peered down into the darkness. Way down. The tide was high, and waves pummeled over rocks to the shore. "There has to be a way to the beach."

She pointed her wet hand to the west. "About a mile that way, there's a trail. You go that way, and I'll answer my door."

They couldn't go that way. The Kurjans were too close. The storm blanketed their signatures, but even so, he'd spent lifetimes hunting and fleeing predators too unimaginable for this world. Even when he had nothing else, he was a survivor. But the female next to him, the one fighting his hold again, was all human. Fragile and breakable.

Giving her a jerk toward him, he freed his phone from his front pocket and pressed speed dial.

"Ronan," his brother answered easily, munching on something.

"I'm at Promise's home, and the Kurjans are out front," he said quickly. "Get to the beach below her house as soon as you can." He clicked off.

She slapped at his hand. "You really are crazy. I should've trusted my instincts, but no. I had to believe the guys in suits just because they had money to grant the university."

He dragged her to the nearest side fence and looked over to see a Kurjan jumping the fence at the other side of a wide yard. "Shit."

She bent over and bit his hand, trying to dislodge his grip.

Without pausing, he pulled her back toward the edge of the cliff again, ignoring the pain.

She stopped fighting him, gasping, her chest rising rapidly. "What in the world are you doing?" she hissed, her voice clear through the pounding rain.

Oh, she wasn't going to like this. Not at all. "Do you trust me, Missy?" he asked, seeing her easily in the dark.

"No." She kicked him in the shin with her bare foot and then winced, setting it back down in the wet grass. "Let me go, you lunatic."

It hurt a little that she didn't trust him. It shouldn't, and usually nothing hurt him, but they'd almost had sex. "You probably shouldn't sleep with people you don't trust," he said, angling his head to see better. Even with his preternatural eyesight, the bottom of the cliff was dark. Way too dark.

"I didn't sleep with you." She kicked him again, this time in the knee. "Let me go. I won't call the cops. Just go away."

A flash of white caught his eye from the corner of the house. "Sorry about this." He picked her up, holding her against his chest.

She froze for a second and then sucked in air to scream. "No!" Her nails scraped down his damaged neck.

He jumped, rolling in the air and wrapping himself around her as much as possible. Then he let gravity win.

Chapter Ten

Cold air rushed her, even while raw male heat surrounded her. The storm stole her screams. She shut her eyes, frantically fighting Ivar, until a spray of ocean caught her. They hit the beach hard, his back taking the brunt as he remained wrapped around her. The wind flew out of her lungs, constricting her entire torso. Wet sand sprayed in every direction. They bounced once and then smashed down again, burrowing into the sand.

Promise panted out air, gasping to breathe.

Water crashed over them, nearly reaching her face. She struggled to her hands and knees on his limp body. "Ivar," she croaked, shaking violently.

He lay prone on the ground. No way had he survived. She rolled to the side and partially stood, grabbing his T-shirt at the shoulders. When the water rolled in again, she used its momentum to pull him farther up the beach and out of the spray. Then she dropped to her knees next to him, listening for breathing.

The rain pounded down, while the surf sprayed all over. Even the wind blew sand wildly around. She spit out sandy hair and tried to see. Was he breathing? She'd have to perform CPR. She flattened her hand on his chest, and it rose against her. How was he breathing? A rattle caught her attention.

She shoved his shirt up and gingerly felt along his very ripped abdomen to his rib cage. His skin was smooth over wildly powerful muscles—harder than steel. Actual, real steel. How was that possible? He had to have a broken rib or several, but she couldn't feel any damage. Not one. She looked frantically around. If a rib was broken, it would puncture his lung, if it hadn't already done so. Where could she get help? Leaving him defenseless against the elements on the beach was a horrible idea, but running for the trail a mile away was her only chance to help him.

Her hands shook, and she sucked in several deep breaths to stay calm. His life depended on it.

He coughed and jerked conscious, immediately leaping to his feet, already crouching into a fighting stance.

She dropped to her butt, her eyes widening to see better in the storm. How was he moving? Who was this guy? He should be dead. She trembled and tried to crab-walk away from him.

He looked around, shook his head, and then spotted her.

She stilled, her gaze trapped.

His blue eyes lasered through the darkness of the storm, his long body one hard outline against the cliffs. Blood flowed down his face from a deep gash near his eye, and his left arm hung at an odd angle. The same arm he'd injured the other day. She'd forgotten his forearm had appeared broken when he'd run away after the car accident.

"How are you even standing?" she asked, trying to make sense of the situation. He should be in unbearable pain or even shock. She glanced up the cliffside, which disappeared into the storm. The calculations didn't make sense. Their weight, their rate of speed, the angle of impact, and the solidness of the sand. They should both be dead—he especially. There was a slight chance she could be alive, but she should have several broken bones and most likely internal injuries. Right now, she just had a headache.

He spun around, obviously seeking a threat that wasn't there. The only dangerous thing in sight was him. The man was a lunatic. One who was somehow standing while spectacularly injured.

"What are you on?" she yelled through the twisting wind and sand. While she was unfamiliar with pharmacology, there had to be some drug that was keeping him on his feet. "You're probably bleeding out internally." She stood up, fighting the wind. Sand stuck to her lips, and she wiped it away.

He reached for her hand. "We have to run."

From what? The disastrous storm? She thought about fighting him, but his grip remained strong, and remaining on the beach with the increasing storm was insane. The man had mental problems, and right now, she couldn't be any more vulnerable. So following his lead to the trail and up to safety was the only smart thing to do.

Then she'd run away from him.

She kept her head down to protect her eyes from the slashing sand and followed him, oddly grateful he kept her hand. How he found his way in the darkness and through the storm, she had no idea. His training as a soldier must've been impressive.

Her bare feet sank into wet sand, and she struggled to stay upright. Darkness and sand and water surrounded them, but adrenaline kept her moving, even though her heart rate accelerated until her lungs fought her.

She shivered and tried to walk faster, needing to keep her body temperature as high as possible against the chill.

A light cut through the darkness over the ocean.

Ivar paused, and she tumbled against his broad back, fighting to stay on her feet. He turned and grasped both her arms. "Can you run?"

Gulping, shoving wet hair off her face, she nodded. "Can you?"

He turned and watched the light grow near. "They might be friendly."

She swallowed and stared up at his still bleeding face. Friendly? Was he having some sort of war flashback or something? "It's okay, Ivar. Let's get to the trail." The storm was so thunderous, she had to lean up to yell close to his ear.

Lightning ripped across the sky, deadly and beautiful. It lit up a helicopter rapidly moving their way.

She gaped. "Who in the world is flying through this storm?"

Ivar's shoulders relaxed, and his body stilled. "They're ours. Saw the side of the copter."

She shook her head, turning to see the craft pitch crazily in the air. "There's nowhere to land," she whispered, her words stolen completely by the wind. A gust of wind attacked her, throwing her into Ivar. She hit him midcenter, already trying to backtrack. Had she hurt him?

He planted an arm around her shoulders and hauled her into his side, protecting her from the wind, rain, and sand.

Oh, no. She could inadvertently damage his possible internal injuries more. She gently tried to extricate herself, but he held firm. She stood stiffly, trying not to touch him.

The light shone down from the helicopter, and a rope became visible.

Panic attacked her, and she shook her head, trying to move away from him.

"You're okay." With one hand, he grabbed her arm and swung her around to land on his back.

She cried out, instinctively wrapping her arms around his neck, her knees clapping to his rib cage. The movement itself should've dropped him to his knees. Instead, he secured her wrists together at his collarbone with one hand and reached for the rope with the other.

There was no way in the scientific universe the man would be able to climb the rope in spite of his injuries, especially with her perched on his back.

With one hand and both legs, with her on his back trying not to scream, he started to climb.

They were going to die.

* * * *

Every muscle ached, and Ivar's broken arm bones clattered against each other and repeatedly sliced through his skin while he climbed the rope. The wind fought him with a powerful wail, while rain somehow slashed sideways to turn him around. On the beach, he had tried several times to teleport Promise to safety, but only a sputter echoed through him. Sputter and broken bones and fucking agony.

He'd lost his ability to teleport before it had strengthened enough to be used again.

Promise tucked her nose into the back of his neck, her mouth moving, probably in some sort of prayer. She held herself as stiff as concrete, no doubt theorizing how quickly they'd fall if he lost his grip on the rope.

Rain attacked his eyes, and he blinked water away, gauging the distance to safety.

The copter pitched and rolled, throwing him wide.

Promise screamed and dug her nails into his clavicle, her foot scraping along what felt like a break in his femur. He growled low but kept climbing, having to reach with his one free hand and then use his knees for leverage. His right knee was going numb, and he sent emergency healing cells to it. He just had to get the woman inside the helicopter, and then he could pass out.

The cut in his forehead kept bleeding, the liquid burning his eye. The gash went beyond his skull to his brain, and the healing cells were stitching the skull back together too slowly to make a difference. He hadn't regained his strength after his ordeals in hell, and crashing through a windshield the other day had taken its toll, especially on his slowly regenerating ability to teleport.

The helicopter pitched again, and his hand slipped, burning along the rope. He growled and fought to stay in the air.

They dropped several feet before his grip caught purchase. Promise burrowed closer to him, now making soft mewling noises.

"It's okay," he said, turning his head so his mouth brushed her forehead, his muscles straining so much he could feel them unravel.

She shuddered.

He drew deep for strength, fighting his body once again for survival. "This is nothing," he grunted, climbing once again. After a guy had been to a few different hell worlds, getting caught on a rope in a middle of a fall storm really was a mild nuisance. The human on his back probably didn't understand that, however.

Of course, she could die easily. He needed to be decapitated to be finished and had healing cells to fix everything from his brain to the tendons surrounding his knee. At least he'd been able to protect her from injury when they'd hit the ground. "I'm not gonna let anything happen to you, Promise. Just hold on." He'd swallowed enough sand that his normally hoarse voice sounded raw, even to his damaged eardrums. Healing cells started to fix them, and he let them go to work.

Although she didn't have any choice except to hold on, he kept a firm grip on her wrists.

Finally, a large hand reached out of the helicopter and grabbed his, pulling hard. He looked up to see Adare hanging out of the twisting aircraft, his face one hard line of concentration. When had the Highlander gotten back to town? Ivar used his knees to help and was soon on his belly, half inside the craft. "Get her," he ordered, his face down.

Adare lifted Promise free and sat her on the side bench before hauling Ivar all the way inside and plunking him next to her. Then he closed the door and turned around. "How bad?" His brogue was unusually thick with stress.

Ivar opened his eyes to see Ronan nod from the pilot's seat. He banked a hard left and turned away from the ocean. "I'm fine," Ivar said, mentally checking the healing cells. They were slower than they'd been before he'd run through endless dimensions and fought hell beasts, but they were still working. He turned toward Promise, whose eyes were wide and frightened in her sand-battered face. Was she all right? "What hurts, sweetheart?"

Sand covered her wet hair and clothing. Her mouth gaped open and then shut. Her full lips began to turn blue, and she trembled so violently her shoulders shook against the helicopter's metal side. But he couldn't see blood or any broken bones.

She gulped and then looked toward Ronan, at Adare, and then at Ivar. "What in all reality?" she croaked.

He leaned his head back to relieve some of the pressure in his skull but kept his gaze on the woman. She seemed in shock but not physically injured. "Promise? This is Adare. He's another ex-soldier at the business."

She looked toward the Highlander, taking him in from head to toe. For the mission, Adare had dressed in black cargo pants, complete with a myriad of weapons visible in every pocket. He wore a sidearm strapped to both thighs as well as a knife in the holder at his waist. His dark T-shirt covered his hard chest, and he'd tied his unruly black hair at the nape.

"Hi," he said, holding out a hand.

Hers trembled as she reached for it. The second they touched, she winced, yanking back to press her palm against her temple.

Ivar straightened. "You okay?"

She winced and partially turned away. "It's that headache again," she slurred.

Adare was studying her with those black eyes of his. Slowly, he reached out and poked her in the arm.

She coughed and drew away, pain leaching away the color beneath her skin.

Ivar's chest hitched. "Adare? Go up by Ronan, would you?"

Adare nodded. "Aye. Just give me a sec." He tugged his thick T-shirt over his head, handing it to Promise. "It's dry." Then he turned and crouched down to walk to the copilot seat. The farther away he got, the better Promise looked.

Interesting.

Ivar noted that her breathing had leveled out. "Better, Missy?" Yeah, he liked having a nickname for her.

"Yes." She fumbled with her hand at her neck, looking toward the cockpit. "That's quite the tattoo on your friend's back."

It wasn't a tattoo. The fusing of the ribs and entire torso that occurred during the Seven ritual created a type of dark shield that made the ribs visible. "Promise," Ivar said, waiting until she focused back on him. "I need to know if you're injured, honey."

She drew Adare's shirt over her head and then hugged her body with her arms, her movements jerky. "I'm okay." She rocked back and forth, holding herself tighter, her lips still trembling. "But I really don't understand." She was quiet for a minute and then swept her hands out. "Any of this. I mean, how in the world are you still breathing? There's no way you should be. This defies all logic."

Ivar opened his mouth to say something, and he wasn't sure what. Then the helicopter banked a hard right and spun, battered by the storm.

Promise banged her head back. "We are so going to die."

Chapter Eleven

Like any puzzle of the universe, Promise was going to figure out this one. She walked from the en suite bath to the vacant bedroom and finished toweling water from her hair after a hot shower in an apartment in the high-rise downtown, just a couple floors below the office she'd visited earlier. They'd landed the helicopter, midstorm, right on the gravel covered roof.

Ronan had explained the building would serve as a safe house for the time being.

How was her life in such a state that she required a safe house? She had already dressed in a nice pair of yoga pants and a T-shirt sporting Snoopy meditating on what appeared to be a human brain filled with shoes. Who in the world would wear such a shirt?

She glanced down at the yellow material. At least it was soft and clean.

As was she. She eyed the scrapes down her right arm from fighting the sand. She'd been in fight-or-flight mode on the beach and hadn't felt the pain. Unlike now. Now her arm stung.

The room held high-end furniture with an overlarge king-sized bed covered in a dark blue comforter. A dresser and two nightstands were the only other fixtures, and they were lacking in knickknacks or anything personal. But the bed. She eyed it. The item was huge.

She quickly secured her wet hair in a ponytail holder from the cosmetics bag left for her in the bathroom. All new makeup, lotions, hair clips, and so on that had been provided.

The low rumble of male voices came from the living room just beyond her door, and she recognized Ivar's from his hoarse rasp. Were they arguing about something? She had just moved to press her ear to the door when somebody knocked on it. She yelped and jumped back. "Um, come in?"

The door opened, and a woman walked inside carrying a black doctor's bag. "Hi. I'm Faith." She was tallish with sharp features and brown eyes that shone with intelligence. Her brown hair was swept atop her head, and she wore a lovely red silk shirt, pressed jeans, and stylish brown boots. "Rumor has it you might need a doctor." She shut the door and looked Promise up and down.

Promise backed away. "What kind of a doctor?" Who were these people?

Faith smiled, showing a dimple in her right cheek. "Neurologist. Dr. Faith Cooper, at your service."

Wait a minute. Faith Cooper? Promise narrowed her gaze and tried to picture the vivacious woman the way she'd last seen her in a black-and-white magazine photograph. "I read your article last year regarding quantum neuroscience and the limits of consciousness. It was fascinating."

Faith's eyes sparkled. "Thank you. We had tons of fun researching that and just played around with existing theories to question whether there could be temporal patterns of electromagnetic fields that could somehow affect levels of brain space."

Okay. So this definitely was Faith Cooper. "What are you doing here?" Promise asked, her body aching everywhere from the fall.

"Well, it's a long story," Faith said. "Short version is that I'm engaged to Ronan Kayrs and am taking a sabbatical from the hospital to help my sister heal from being in a coma for a few years."

Every brain cell in Promise's head bellowed that there was a lot more to the story than that, but Faith had tried to give her a short version. Promise's left ankle protested against standing any longer, so she backed away and sat on the edge of the bed. "I have you to thank for the clothes?"

Faith's smile widened. "Yes. They're for yoga, and I didn't know how bruised you might be, so I figured loose would be better."

"It is. Thank you," Promise said, her mind reeling. "Where is Ivar?"

"Outside the room. I thought I could check you over before we grab something to eat." Faith glanced at her watch. "It's well after midnight, and I'm starving. How about you?"

Food? The other woman could think of food right now? "How did Ivar and I survive a leap off a cliff that high?" she asked, her skin pricking. Enough with the secrets that didn't make sense.

Faith eyed the scratches on Promise's arm and opened the bag to draw out ointment. "He's trained to jump and roll."

"Malarkey," Promise burst out. "Nobody is trained to survive gravity at that height." She accepted the tube and began to rub the clear lotion into her skin, relieving the pain almost instantly. She tried to make rational connections. "This is a supersoldier type of business with unlimited funds. What all do you research? Have you somehow genetically altered the human physique?" The mere idea was folly for suspense novels and streaming television. But what else made sense?

"No. No genetic manipulation here. Not a bit," Faith said cheerfully. "Are you hurt anywhere else?"

"No. Just neck to ankle contusions." A couple of bruises wouldn't kill Promise. "If Ivar hasn't been altered in any manner, why isn't he in the hospital right now having his ribs and lungs operated on? As well as that gash in his head. He needs stitches, at the very least."

Faith closed her bag. "Ivar does have the ability to heal quickly and from surprisingly damaging wounds. I'm sorry, but I can't tell you more than that. Proprietary information and all of that bullshit."

Promise straightened from her perch. "I take it you don't agree with keeping secrets?"

"Not usually, and definitely not when somebody is in danger." Faith lost the smile. "You're pretty much in this now, whether you want to be or not, so we might as well tell you everything. But that's Ivar's decision, and I'm trying really hard not to step on his toes. It's nice to have him being rational again. Well, mostly."

Curiosity cut thorough the irritation in Promise. "He wasn't rational? After the mission where he got burned?"

Faith snorted. "He called that a mission?" At Promise's nod, she continued. "No. He didn't speak at all for a month when he returned. It was like he had to relearn how to live without fighting for his life every second," she said, her voice thoughtful.

A pang hit Promise's chest, and it took her a moment to recognize the feelings. Empathy and concern. Was she getting attached to the Viking? How was that possible? He wasn't even being honest with her. "Ivar seems much better now." In fact, the memory of how easily he'd put her on his back, despite a myriad of broken bones, turned her abdomen all mushy. She paused to interpret the feeling.

Faith watched her closely. "Ivar told me about your headaches."

Promise perked up. This woman was one of the premier neurologists in the world. "Yes. I feel fine now, but I had another attack in the helicopter."

"When Adare was close to you. Then when he returned to the cockpit, your pain receded," Faith said, ducking her head to examine Promise's eyes. "Follow my fingers." She put up two fingers and moved them slowly left to right.

Promise complied. "What could Adare have to do with my headache?" She pursed her lips and followed Faith's fingers up and then down. "It doesn't make sense, but that receptionist yesterday. My head hurt when I entered the office, and I passed out. Then I was pain-free in the conference room, and when she came inside and asked me if I wanted water, my head hurt again." Same with that Benjamin man. "I don't understand." What was the connection between those people and her brain? It had to be coincidence, but she didn't believe in those. Everything had a rational explanation.

Faith dropped her hand. "I don't know. Honest."

Promise's breath caught. "How about an experiment?"

Faith lifted her chin. "I'd enjoy one." She glanced toward the door. "Are you sure?"

"Definitely." Promise clasped her hands together on the yoga pants. "Let's do this."

Faith clapped her hands together. "Excellent." She sat on the bed and turned toward Promise, tucking one leg beneath the other. "Face me."

Promise mirrored her pose, excitement flushing down her arms. She loved a good experiment. "What now?"

Faith put her fingers on the pulse point on Promise's wrist. "Keep your eyes on mine so I can record any pupil reaction." She waited until Promise had done so and then lifted her head very slightly. "Adare? Come in here for a second, would you?" she called out clearly.

The door opened. Promise kept her gaze on Faith and didn't look over her shoulder. Nothing happened to her brain or neck. No sensation whatsoever. She sighed. It had been a silly experiment.

"What's going on?" Ivar asked from behind her.

Hope filtered through Promise again, and she kept her eyes opened and wide on Faith's pretty brown ones. "Nothing. Would you please ask Adare to come here?" she asked.

Ivar sighed. "Adare? Come here."

Pain slashed into Promise's neck before she heard Adare's footsteps.

"What?" he snapped. Man, the big guy with the brogue was cranky. Promise's eyes watered, and she finally winced, shutting her eyelids. Her brain felt like it swelled.

"Go away," Faith said urgently.

The pain receded again. Promise opened her eyes.

Concern filled Faith's. "That was pretty conclusive."

"*Res ipsa loquitur*," Promise agreed.

"The thing speaks for itself?" Ivar asked from the doorway.

Promise jumped and swiveled toward him. "You speak Latin?"

His eyebrows rose. "I'm not your ordinary boy toy, sweetheart."

Fire lit her face, because she had been thinking of him as such. He was brave and strong and impossibly muscled. She hadn't looked for intelligence. Her body had wanted him before, and now her mind slid right into being intrigued. This might be detrimental to her well-being. "Does Adare wear a cologne?"

"This is way beyond scent," Faith said. "Are you willing to try again?"

Promise swallowed. Anything to solve this puzzle. "Yes." Her hands trembled.

"Somebody find Mercy," Faith yelled.

Promise winced. Enough with the loud noises. "What did you observe?"

Faith peered closer into Promise's eyes. "When Adare approached, you experienced an elevated heart rate, and your pupils expanded and then severely contracted, more noticeably in your left eye," she said. "Is the pain worse on the left?"

"Slightly." Promise rubbed the back of her neck, where it still ached a little.

Ivar cocked his head. "So, the sympathetic pupillary deficit is greater on the stronger affected side."

Okay. Now the man sounded like he'd studied medicine. Promise stared at him, and then her breath stopped. He'd showered, and his wet hair appeared darker than normal. An intriguing scruff covered his jaw, and his blue eyes were clear and direct. Those masculine features were all Viking. Then she blinked. What the heck? "Your head. The wound has healed." Not even a scar was visible. She jerked away from Faith. "I don't understand this. I'm missing elements here. Facts." What was going on? It didn't make sense. None of this, not one bit, made a darn lick of sense. Even the badass Ivar talking like he had a two hundred IQ was throwing her.

"Did you guys call me?" Mercy tossed open the door and all but bounced inside, reaching the bed in a couple of strides.

An ice pick of sharp pain slashed into Promise's head so quickly she gasped, her heart all but stopping. She coughed, and her body seized.

"Lie down." Faith pushed her to a prone position as the convulsions grew stronger. "Mercy? Get out. Run away. Now."

Promise shut her eyes as mini-explosions ripped through her entire head. Her brain pounded against her skull, and blood dripped from her nose and ears. She whimpered, no longer seeing anything but a red haze. Tremors shook her eyes, and they rolled back into her head.

When unconsciousness took her this time, she welcomed the darkness.

Chapter Twelve

The rain pattered outside in the wee hours before dawn, and Ivar held Promise close, running his hand up and down her arm. He lay on top of the covers, while she was safely ensconced beneath them. Her heart rate had returned to normal, and the waves of pain had stopped rolling from her. His touch seemed to calm her, so he caressed her good arm, letting her know she was safe.

What the fuck had he been thinking? He'd noticed what caused her pain, and he'd allowed Faith to experiment with her brain. Promise had asked him to protect her, and he was doing a craptastic job of it. So far he'd held a gun to her side, thrown her off a cliff, made her climb through a storm into a pitching helicopter, and now had almost let her brain explode. When he'd seen the blood dripping from her ear, he'd nearly lost his own mind. She had probably been perfectly safe before he'd entered her life. He should've protected her from the Kurjans from afar.

"You're thinking so hard I can feel it," she mumbled, opening her eyes.

"Sorry." He stopped rubbing her arm and gently smoothed the curly hair back from her face. "For everything. I really am sorry."

"You have to stop apologizing." She yawned and stretched, blinking sleepily. "What happened?"

He should probably leave her alone in the bed, but his body didn't want to move. "Mercy came inside, and you seized and passed out." Again. "You've been sleeping for about three hours, no doubt so your brain could heal itself."

"Brains can't heal themselves," she whispered, her pink lips curving in a small smile.

Hers probably could. If the pain was related to an enhancement, which it no doubt was, then she had gifts she didn't understand.

"So." She lifted her free arm and ran her fingers along his healed forehead. "Want to explain this?"

Her touch was soft and her skin smooth. The gentle glide slid right beneath his skin, offering comfort. "I heal easily?" he rumbled.

"Nope. There's more. And while you're at it, you can explain what Adare, Mercy, and that loud Benjamin gentleman have in common. What is it about them that attacks my mind?" Her eyes remained sleepy. "It's time you told me everything."

There was no doubt the woman had a high IQ, so lying to her would just be silly. From the very moment she'd challenged him so bravely and knocked his ass out of her car, he'd wanted to know her. Wanted her to know him. The real him. "All right. Here it is. There are seven of us in this business, and we make decisions together. I am going to tell you everything, no matter what, but I'd like to wait until everyone agrees. Ronan, Benny, and Adare are fine with it, so I've reached out to the two on mission, and I'd like to give them the respect of waiting for their agreement." It was the least he could do after they'd pulled him out of himself the last three months. Without his brothers, he'd be dead, and he wouldn't have cared. They'd made him care again. "If that's okay with you."

She explored the side of his face, watching her finger as it dipped over his cheekbone. "Since you jumped off a cliff with me, I think it's time you told me everything. I didn't see anybody coming for us, so you're asking for a lot of trust here. Besides, counting you, that's only six people. You said there were seven business owners."

"One is unreachable at the moment." Ivar's body tightened at her soft exploration. "That's, ah, part of what I'd like to discuss with you. Tomorrow." If he didn't hear from Garrett or Logan by noon, he was telling Promise everything.

She drew back her hand, and her eyes cleared completely. "You know, certain high frequencies can cause piercing headaches. A raging headache can affect the body to the point of convulsions. And when the central nervous system overloads, so to speak, unconsciousness follows."

Fuck, she was adorable. Look at her trying to find a rational explanation for everything. He levered himself up on his elbow to see her better in the darkness. "What about the cut above my eye?"

"And your broken arm." She pressed her fingers against his already healed skin.

Pain ticked into him, and he winced.

"Hmm." She pulled away. "Not broken any longer, but apparently bruised. That's impossible."

"Apparently not." He sent healing cells through his body to take care of the bruises in case she did it again. "What causes that kind of fast healing?" He really wanted to know where her mind would go with the problem. Smart women had always done it for him, and this gorgeous, curvy creature in his bed was beyond brilliant. "What's your hypothesis, Professor?"

She shook her head, her dark hair catching on the pillow. "I don't know. My guess is that your brain trust, the one giving millions for grants, has been doing so for a while. I do know that scientists have been working on the MG53 protein, which the human body naturally creates to help repair injuries." She pursed her lips, obviously thinking. "The study I read about involved using a cytokine protein that also heals wounds but does so too quickly. Combining those into a way that inhibits the cytokine while promoting the MG53 protein could lead to compelling results."

"Like healing a broken bone in a manner of hours?" He wanted her hands back on him. Now.

"Yes," she said. "If the science has developed to the point of human trials, which apparently it has, then you owe the world the data. You can't keep this kind of discovery to yourselves."

His chest filled with warmth. She'd figured out rational reasons for almost everything by using science and logic. Maybe when she knew all the facts and all the possibilities in the universe, she'd be able to get him back to Quade. He had to save his brother. "Interesting."

"Even so, none of that makes you the good guys." Her dark brows drew down, making her look like a grumpy math professor. "All I know is that somebody rang my doorbell last night and then you threw us off a cliff, claiming the enemy had arrived." She blinked several times and then pinned him with that soft brown gaze. "Am I free to leave this apartment, or are you keeping me a prisoner?"

* * * *

Promise asked the question and waited for an answer, wondering if Ivar would tell the truth. The bed was comfortable and the man very nice to look at. Her fingers still tingled from her exploration of his hard face. Logic proved that if he wished to harm her, he wouldn't have wrapped himself around her and taken the brunt of the fall from the cliff. He also wouldn't have somehow used one damaged arm to carry her safely into a helicopter.

But what was going on? Why did they need her specifically? "Ivar? I'd appreciate an answer."

"I'm trying to think of an answer you'd like, Missy," he said, his breath minty with a hint of Scotch.

Oh, he didn't get to use her nickname, one she'd always wanted, to charm her. He still smelled lightly of the ocean, salty and woodsy mixed together. She inhaled his scent. "Do you know why my head hurts when those people are in close proximity to me?" she asked.

"Yes. We think we've figured it out." He brushed her hair back from her face again, watching his fingers play with a spiral. The rain pattered against the window, lending a sense of safe intimacy to the room. "Of all the disciplines you could've studied, why did you focus on dark matter, the cosmology of extra dimensions, and cosmological inflation?"

"Those subjects were of interest to me," she said calmly. If he wasn't going to share, neither was she. Her crazy childhood dreams of traveling to other worlds were better left back with the Easter bunny. Not that she'd been allowed to believe in any mythology. "Now answer my question. Am I free to leave or not?"

He exhaled and dropped his hand away from her hair. "No."

That's what she'd concluded. "Your attempt at kidnapping is finally successful."

He grinned. "Took me several tries and a helicopter, but hey."

She was not amused. Yet, she did like the sense of safety, and the conflicting feelings were bewildering. She tried to drum up some anger, but her energy levels were depleted. "I have to teach tomorrow." It had to be Sunday morning by now. Nobody would know she was missing all of Sunday until she didn't show for her freshman seminar particle physics class Monday morning. "So the kidnapping must end by nine tomorrow morning." Logic would have to rule since she couldn't find anger.

"Can anybody cover your class for you?" he asked.

"No. It's my last lecture before their first test, which causes a great deal of angst. I need to teach that class." She gave him her sternest expression. So far, he'd at least listened to her.

He nodded. "All right. We'll figure something out."

"Good." A sense rose in her, a surprising one, that she wanted to out-maneuver him, and it had nothing to do with safety. How odd.

He glanced around the bedroom, tension rolling from him. The rather heated kind. "For now, we're in bed. Didn't we have plans?"

"I don't have my pocket rocket," she snapped, feeling the walls close in.

"You won't need it," he returned, his jaw tightening just enough to show he also had a temper.

Her breath caught in the same way it had earlier. She was having a physical reaction to his show of—what was that? Blatant masculinity? She'd read about that phenomenon in a magazine at the dentist's office. There was a connection between bravado and female sexual response, based on years of biology and the necessity of survival as a species. Even so, butterflies swarmed throughout her abdomen. However, she refused to engage in sex with him until she solved the mysteries suddenly surrounding her. "We no longer have a plan," she said, gritting her teeth together.

"I assumed as much, but it never hurts to ask." He rolled off the bed, leaving a chill around her. "Faith and Ronan are in an apartment down the way, but the rest of the building is vacant. We bought the entire thing, and Mercy hasn't had time to squeeze money out of it yet."

So she only had to get by him. "Where did everyone else go?"

"Different safe houses," he returned. "This one is temporary. I don't like being in the middle of town like this, and we'll move after dawn, when the sun is high and bright. Or at least up there shining down enough to illuminate the earth somewhat."

What an odd thing to say. She enjoyed being confused even less than being shielded from the truth. Though she didn't believe she was in danger from Ivar and his friends, the secrets they kept appeared substantial. They'd said the physics grant was to study the ability to move through dimensions to other points of existence. Was that just a ruse? If so, why did they need her? If not, then... why keep her here? "I don't like unsolved puzzles," she muttered.

"Yeah, I get that." Ivar loped toward the door. "I have hearing like a bat, so don't think about leaving. Plus, this door locks." He added the last almost cheerfully, shutting the door and loudly engaging said lock.

She breathed deeply for several moments, listening to the rain against the windows. Her hand fumbled when she reached over to twist on the table lamp. Then she stood, making sure her legs held her. No residual weakness remained. Good. First she checked the window, which didn't open. Then she moved to the door and examined the lock.

A deadbolt secured the door above the doorknob. Well, she didn't have three PhDs for nothing. Tiptoeing as quietly as she could, she went into the bathroom and rummaged through the cosmetic bag for two bobby pins, pulling one wide open to make a feeler pick.

Most people didn't know how to pick a lock. It was just a matter of mechanics, really.

She slightly widened the middle of the other pin to create a tension wrench and then bent down by the lock. She inserted it, twisting slightly before adding the end of the first pick, scrubbing over the pins from outside to inside. She did this for several moments.

Nothing happened. Cripes.

She removed both picks and then started over, putting her ear to the door. It took nearly an hour and a multitude of tries, but finally, the pins set. Using a barely there tension, she twisted to the right, slowly forcing the bolt to retreat.

Triumph filled her as if she'd solved a truly problematic formula.

Yes, there was also something exciting about putting one over on Ivar. The man was just so male and strong, and it turned out he apparently had a decent intelligence quota too. She opened the door, very slowly, peering out to the darkened living area.

"You know, that took you about fifteen minutes longer than I expected," Ivar said, his big body sprawled across the lone sofa in the room.

Chapter Thirteen

Ivar kept his gaze on the woman straightening to her full and not very impressive height. Not many women knew how to pick a deadbolt, but she wasn't just an ordinary woman, now was she? What would she do now? He'd lay odds she'd confront him instead of slamming the door and going back to bed.

Her shoulders went back, and she stepped toward him.

Yep. She was complex, but he was slowly getting to know her. Each new facet of her personality, of her intelligence, of her cluelessness with males—just intrigued him more.

"You know," he murmured, "most people are afraid of me. At least a little." Of course, they'd seen him at his batshit craziest. Even so, many humans instinctively avoided him, even on his best day.

"Well." She moved closer, bringing that enticing heather scent with her. She perched on the far end of the sofa by his feet, looking unbelievably young and fragile and human in the Snoopy shirt. "I can understand that. In a physical altercation with you, my only recourse would be to render you unconscious swiftly before you could retaliate." She bit her bottom lip. "I am uncertain how to accomplish that."

With her mind, she'd figure it out quickly. He'd have to protect his temples if she ever got her hands on a golf club. Of course, if she swung one, that'd give him an excuse to put his hands on her again. Something he desperately wanted to do. Yet, he had to be fair. "You don't want to try it, sweetheart. You wouldn't like the result."

She rolled her eyes in such a feminine move he could only watch, fascinated by her. Passion and humor lurked beneath her uberlogical facade, and he wasn't sure even she realized how much. Could he unleash that passion? Just for him? Or would she be repulsed by his natural violence and brutality when it came to his enemies? He lived in a world she couldn't comprehend.

She smoothed her hands down her yoga pants. "You don't sleep, do you?"

"Not much. Nightmares," he said, giving her the full truth.

She patted his ankle. "I understand. There was a time in my youth when I had terrible night terrors—I thought I was traveling to other worlds. Some scary ones and some nice. Even convinced myself that part of my body had gone during the night. But I saw a professional, learned the difference between imagination and reality, and soon healed."

Imagination and reality. His shoulders perked up. "Tell me about your imagination."

"I—" She paused and looked toward the wall of windows where a light cut down. "What is that?"

He jumped up, rushing to the window. A helicopter flew above, shining its lights down. "Fuckers."

She stood. "What's happening?"

He lowered his head, thinking rapidly. "If I were the Kurjans, I'd conduct a grid search for the helicopter that picked us up on the beach. Looking for places on the outskirts of town to hide a helicopter." Which they'd probably been doing for hours. He'd figured they'd regroup before searching. "When that didn't work, I'd do a cursory check downtown for a helicopter." He was talking to himself at this point.

"You mean the one on top of this building?" she asked.

He'd thought they were safe. That his people were so well known for living in mountains and underground that the Kurjans would never really search a populated area. A high-rise was so out of character for the Seven, for the entire Realm really, that it seemed like a safe place for one night. "Shit."

"Ivar?" she asked.

He ducked away from the window and reached her in a second. "The sun should be up soon. Maybe thirty minutes?"

"So?" Her voice emerged breathy, and her arm tensed beneath his hand.

The light cut out, and the helicopter high above banked and angled away. Had they seen the sun coming up? Ivar grabbed his gun off the coffee table and tucked it into the back of his jeans.

She gulped. "Are you sure we're being chased? That could've just been a medical helicopter or something."

Not with the searchlight flashing down through the buildings. But the approach of daylight might've scared the Kurjans off. Without a doubt, they'd return as soon as darkness fell. "I'm sure." He needed to tell her the entire truth so she'd understand the danger. They had to be ready to run as soon as the sun appeared. "I think we're okay now."

He'd no sooner gotten the words out than lights slashed down from the north and east walls of windows. Soldiers on ropes swung in, crashing glass in every direction.

Promise partially ducked, covering her head, and screamed high and loud.

* * * *

Promise struggled through the panic, opening her eyes to gauge the level of threat. The two men who'd jumped through the windows quickly released their ropes, which flew back out into the storm. She blinked. Once and twice. The men had frighteningly pale skin and horribly bloodshot eyes. In fact, their eyes appeared red through the dim light. Both men were bald, save for one strip of stark white hair down the middle of their heads that ended in long braids.

She took a step back. Her stomach clenched, and the hair pricked up along her arms.

Ivar pivoted, putting his body between her and the ghoulish men. "Only two of you?" he asked, his back one long line of vibrating threat.

"More breaching the hallway," the first guy said, his substantial jaw barely moving as his bloodred lips curved. "Though we won't need backup."

Who were these people? Rain splashed inside, covering black outfits that looked like they included bulletproof vests, only partially hidden beneath their dark jackets. Promise shivered, looking toward the door to the hallway. Were more of these weird-looking soldiers coming?

The second guy settled his stance, his boots crunching glass. "We don't want you right now, Viking. Give us the professor, and we'll let you live."

What was this? A bad B movie? She moved to the side, partially out of Ivar's shadow. "Why do you want me?"

The guy didn't even look her way, keeping his focus on Ivar as he patted the hilt of a knife at his waist. "Well?"

Ivar rolled his neck, and it lightly cracked. "Come and get her," he rasped. But he didn't wait, instead leaping over the coffee table, his gun already out and firing rapid green lasers toward the first intruder. Blood spurted from the guy's neck, but he somehow still jumped forward, colliding with Ivar in a clash louder than metal impacting metal.

Heat rushed up Promise's throat. She screamed and scrambled around for some sort of weapon, her hands grasping a candlestick off the sofa table. She swung as hard as she could as the second attacker reached her. He swiped the unsatisfactory weapon out of her hand, and the metal clanged off the wood floor, rolling beneath the sofa. His prodigious gloved hand clamped over her entire shoulder, and he hauled her toward him. Pain rippled up her neck from his fingers.

The sound of fighting came from Ivar at the window and from an altercation in the hallway outside, but she kept her focus on the guy bruising her clavicle with just his hold.

Her breath panted out, and her lungs seized. The room narrowed in focus, and all sound dissipated while adrenaline flooded her entire system. She grabbed the nearest sofa cushion and pivoted, hitting him in the face with the decorating tassels, aiming for his eyes.

He growled and twisted his head, his hold tightening so painfully her stomach cramped.

Then he was jerked away from her as Ivar threw him toward the broken window.

She stumbled back, dropping the pillow, hyperventilating.

Ivar punched the guy in the neck, and he turned, already swinging. His fist impacted with Ivar's cheek, and the bone crunched loudly.

Promise gasped and looked for the other soldier, who was down on his stomach near the window, surrounded by broken glass, not moving. His head was under the drape, and blood flowed from his neck area.

Tears filled her eyes, and she blinked them away, struggling to breathe. She spotted the edge of Ivar's green gun over by the door to the kitchen. While the two men traded nauseating-sounding blows, she ran for the gun and picked it up, stumbling back over the rain-soaked floors to point it at the men. Then she paused, her mind scrambling to catch up.

They hit and kicked so rapidly, their movements were mere blurs of movement and sound. How was that possible? Shock took her, and even the sounds tunneled into a faint buzz. She wavered, her legs shaking so hard her left knee hurt.

The other soldier punched Ivar in the stomach and then howled, pain etching his face as he drew back his hand, which showed several broken fingers.

Promise hesitated, her mind reeling. Was Ivar wearing some sort of protective gear? She couldn't see it beneath his tight T-shirt.

She pointed the gun again, moving around the sofa, her hands shaking so much her finger slipped off the trigger. She lifted her other hand, steadying her aim, but her shoulders trembled, and the barrel of the gun jumped from point to point.

The soldier kicked Ivar beneath the chin, and his head went back. With a furious growl, he ducked and punched the other man in the jaw, following up with a series of hits so quick they had landed and bounced off before the sound was even audible. Then he kicked the soldier in the knee, knocking him to the ground.

Promise edged to the side, trying to aim the gun at the white-faced attacker.

Ivar grabbed the guy's long braid and jerked his hair back, quickly striking his mouth at the guy's neck and pulling. Blood, tissue, and cartilage flew around as Ivar lifted his head, having torn out the soldier's neck.

With. His. Teeth.

Ivar turned toward her as he let the corpse drop to the glass on the ground. Fangs hung out of his mouth, their sharp points glistening with blood. His eyes had turned a shade of intense green beyond normal emerald. Nearly translucent, heavily metallic, they glowed with a deep blue border around the iris.

Her mouth opened and closed. The smell of rain, blood, and death filled her nostrils, and she hitched away from him, swinging the gun barrel toward his head.

This was not happening. It was a nightmare. She could not be awake.

He straightened to his full height, and his fangs retracted. Blood still bracketed his full mouth and discolored his already multicolored hair. He studied her, no human recognition in his feral eyes. "Gun, down." His voice was a brutal rasp.

Her hands convulsed around the butt of the gun. She slid her finger closer to the trigger. "You're not human," she whispered, her throat feeling like it was on fire.

"Not even close." He reached down and secured a firearm and two knives from the corpse, sliding them into the back of his jeans.

The door burst open behind Promise, and she yelped, accidentally pulling the trigger. A dark green laser shot out of the gun, hitting Ivar square in the chest and turning instantly into round, bullet-shaped pieces of metal. They dropped harmlessly to the floor, bouncing around the dead soldier's head.

She gaped and partially turned to keep both Ivar and the door in sight. Her body went numb with what had to be shock.

Ronan ran inside, bare to the waist, blood pouring from a wound in his right shoulder. Faith was behind him. She wore pajamas decorated with bright pink stethoscopes, her eyes wide and a gun in her hands.

Ivar stepped over the corpse, his face a hard mask of anger. "Status?"

"Two down in the hallway, more breaching the roof, I think." Ronan partially turned. "We take the stairs down. It's the only way."

Ivar grabbed the gun right out of Promise's hold and took her hand with his free one. "We have to run. Now."

Chapter Fourteen

Ivar finished covering the black SUV beneath a thatch of branches. He'd parked the vehicle in between two massive pine trees with canopies of branches and needles, so there was no way anybody could see it from the sky. A river rushed by beyond the weeds, and he'd already jumped in and washed off the blood before changing into clothing he'd borrowed from Benny, who had been staying in a secure cabin since the night before.

Ivar turned to survey the smattering of other cabins along the full banks. He had hoped to find somewhere more comfortable for Promise. The summer camp had been deserted for winter, and the starkness of the dead foliage and rapidly browning trees cut through him more intensely than the chilly wind off the water.

They'd driven an hour away from the city, and now the sun illuminated the area from behind clouds. It was light enough that the Kurjans and their white-haired, creepy Cyst soldiers wouldn't be able to survive outside.

Even so, he couldn't relax the taut muscles down his back. The ride to safety had been tense and silent, out of necessity. He shook out his arms and strode inside Adare's cabin, kicking pine needles off his boots first.

"Hey." Adare finished putting more wood on the roaring fire in the fireplace before standing up and dusting off his hands. There was a small kitchenette in the corner, a big bed in the other corner, and no other furniture. "You okay?"

"Yes." Ivar glanced toward the silent brunette who was putting the finishing touches on the bed. "I'm glad you're here, Grace."

Grace Cooper turned around, her pretty face set in hard lines. "That's nice, Ivar, but I'm not staying."

Adare didn't look at her. "You are staying, and that's the end of that." The Highlander's brogue deepened in a way that conveyed both warning and annoyance.

Grace and her sister Faith shared similar bone structure and stubbornness. "Ivar? Now that your physicist is safe for the time being, you promised to fly me to Realm headquarters so I can get the virus that will negate our stupid mating and get rid of this asshole." Grace's smile was both smart-ass and kind of cute. "No offense, Adare. I do appreciate your saving my life."

Adare still didn't look at his small mate. "You're welcome. Now stop being ridiculous. There is no way you're going to be infected with a virus after being mated only four months, especially since you're recently out of a coma. I will not discuss it any further."

"Whatever. I didn't ask for your opinion." Grace crossed to the door and brushed by Ivar. "We'll talk later."

"Where are you going?" Adare growled.

Ivar looked longingly at the door. Why had he dropped by there?

"To see my sister, although it's none of your business," Grace returned, all but stomping outside and slamming the worn wooden door.

Adare glared at the closed door.

Ivar shuffled his feet. His friend had mated the young human to save her life. Usually mating took love, sex, and a good bite, but Grace was special and the bite alone had done it. "No peace on the domestic front, huh?" That seemed a bit of an understatement.

Adare snorted. "No. She doesn't seem to understand that mating is forever. You'd think she'd at least be appreciative of immortality. But no. Not that woman."

Interesting. Usually nothing upset Adare. "Why don't you court her?" Ivar asked.

Adare swung around, and his eyes widened. "Are you kidding me? I want nothing to do with humans, even one who has become my mate. We'll go our separate ways once the Seven completes its destiny."

Destiny? Was there truly such a thing? "It could take decades, even centuries, for us to kill Ulric. His world, dimension, whatever it is…might not fail for a long time." It would make a hell of a lot more sense for Adare to get to know his mate. Perhaps Fate had had a hand in their meeting. Maybe not. Who knew? "Perhaps you should try and make it a genuine mating. A relationship, or whatever."

Adare's black eyes narrowed. "Why are you a romantic all of a sudden?"

Ivar frowned. "I'm not."

"Are too."

"Am not." Centuries ago, he'd lost a sister who'd only been in her teens, and he had a soft spot for females who needed help. Since he had identified his trigger, it was okay. At least, that's what his shrink had said. "I just want to keep Promise safe until we take out the Kurjans. And the Cyst. Everyone who wants to use or hurt her needs to die." There. That made perfect sense.

Adare whistled, both of his eyebrows rising. "I hate to lower myself to the vernacular of the day, but what the hell. Dude, you have it bad for her."

Hearing the Highlander say the word "dude" lightened Ivar's spirits just enough that he no longer needed to kill somebody right this second. He'd been pissed off since the Cyst had attacked the apartment. The image of Promise trying to ward off a deadly soldier with a fucking sofa pillow kept running through his mind like a bad film. Now he had her ensconced in a crappy cabin with barely working electricity. "I just want to keep her safe. Don't make things up in your crazy head," Ivar returned. He wasn't sane enough for a relationship, and since he was planning to go back to hell to take Quade's place, he didn't have anything to offer a female.

Except protection for now.

Adare finally smiled. "Well, I'm going to go fight with my mate some more. You've put off your interaction with the pretty Dr. Promise long enough. Stop being a wimp."

Ivar wanted to get ticked and argue, but the guy was right. "Fine." He turned and exited again, walking past two cabins and reaching the one he hoped to share with Promise. Sitting outside all day and night would suck. He opened the door and walked inside, his senses instantly tuning in to her.

She sat on a torn sofa, bundled in a homemade quilt provided by Benny, her gaze on the crackling fire in the old stone fireplace. The light danced across her smooth features, highlighting her glossy dark hair. She sat with her legs extended on a rickety coffee table, her lips pursed. Different expressions filtered through her beautiful eyes. She didn't look his way. "What are you?" she asked quietly.

* * * *

Promise banished all feeling, ignoring the tingling around her lungs. The body dealt with stress in some odd ways.

Ivar shut the door, and the room instantly warmed. "I'm a hybrid."

She turned then, surprised to see him in clean clothing with his hair wet. He'd jumped in the river? A plain dark T-shirt stretched across his strong chest, while faded jeans covered his long legs. "Part human and part what?" She'd seen fangs. Both he and the white-faced scary soldier had shown fangs. So vampires truly existed.

"Not human. I'm a vampire-demon hybrid." His eyes had returned to the wild blue-green mix of the night before.

Vampires and demons. "Oh my," she muttered, unable to help herself. She swallowed several times. "You're from hell?" So much for being agnostic.

"No." He strode forward, all grace and purpose. "I'm from here. Vampires and demons are just different species from humans." He sat on the sofa, rocking her toward him. "Humans have twenty-three chromosomal pairs, right?"

She nodded.

He extended his legs, his boots making her stocking-covered feet look ridiculously small. "Demons have thirty-two, vampires thirty, Kurjans thirty, witches twenty-nine, shifters twenty-eight, and mates of any of us twenty-seven."

She withdrew her legs and turned to face him on the sofa, tucking one foot beneath her. "What?"

He grinned. "There are many different species. We've only recently learned the chromosomal differences. Score one for human geneticists."

She shook her head. "Wait a minute. Witches? Shifters?" Reality was splitting in two in the worst application of fissure imaginable.

"Yes." He turned his head, his gaze direct. "Witches use the elements to create fire. They do not turn people into frogs." His voice was low and soothing. Well, as soothing as his rasp could be. "Shifters can change shape into canine, feline, or ursine. Oh, and dragons, but that's a secret."

That was the secret? Even her feet felt stunned. How was that possible? "Wait. Mates?"

"Yeah." He rolled his neck, looking back toward the fire. "Enhanced humans, mostly female, can mate an immortal. When that happens, the female's chromosomal pairs increase until she reaches a state of immortality." He held up a hand before she could ask the question. "No, they can't be turned into any other species. There's no turning into vampires, demons, or any of the rest."

Her mind scrambled for the first time in a decade to deal with a solution to a problem. A bizarre and almost incomprehensible solution. But she'd seen the fangs, and she'd seen him fight. "Urban legends have some truth to them," she murmured.

"They usually do, although vampires are fine in the sun and would rather eat steak than drink blood. We only take blood in extreme situations like battle or sex." He exhaled, moving his broad chest. "You're Enhanced, sweetheart. Customary enhancements are psychic ability, empathic ability, telekinesis."

She didn't believe in any of those false sciences. "You have got to be jesting."

"No."

"I'm not psychic." Not even close.

He shook his head. "Nope. That's not your enhancement."

She straightened. "Well?" If he continued to be coy, she was going to punch him. Oh, she'd never attacked another person in her entire life, but he wasn't a person, now was he? The guy was immortal. "Tell me."

He turned and snagged her hand, imprisoning it between his much larger palms. "We think you're some sort of identifier for immortals who can teleport." His hold was firm and warm. Very warm.

Teleport? In truth? "What?" She let him heat her hands. Just for a minute.

He nodded. "Adare, Benny, and Mercy can all teleport. Adare and Benny, like many demons, can go through space and time to end up somewhere here on earth. I used to be able to do it too, until I was injured. I thought the ability was coming back, but now it's gone again."

Teleport. Actually move through dimensions, or possibly something else, and land where one wanted on earth? How was it possible? Could it be that her dreams as a child had actually been real, and somehow she'd learned to block them? Her mind started compiling scenarios. But it was all too much.

"And Mercy," he added. "She's a fairy, and they have the ability to teleport to other worlds. They're the only ones who can do so, as far as we know. That makes her more powerful than the others, which is why I think the pain in your head is worse with her."

She blinked. "How many chromosomal pairs do fairies have?"

He shrugged. "I'm not sure we've ever tested them. Until recently, most of them lived off-world. And by the way, when you talk to Mercy, call them Fae. For some reason, they think that sounds tougher than fairy."

Thoughts zinged through her mind so quickly that her head jerked. The explanations, although she hadn't had time to process them yet, at least added up to some semblance of logic. That is, if she discarded everything she believed about reality. "Why do you need me, Ivar? If people can already teleport, as you say, what do you want with a human physicist?"

He winced, wrinkling the skin at the corners of his eyes and making him look more approachable. Maybe more human, even though that appeared to be impossible. "Because we don't exactly know *how* we teleport." He crossed his ankles, and his boot clunked heavily on the table. "Science is actually a human study. We've always accepted our abilities as normal and not questioned them much, maybe because we've been at war so often."

"You're immortal and you go to war?" she asked, her brain reeling.

He grimaced. "A lot. We go to war a lot."

Maybe immorality came with a strong dose of moronism. "That's stupid."

"Yeah, it probably is. But evil is evil, and it's here." He caressed the side of her hand with his thumb. "We've always treated teleportation like, I don't know, breathing, making fire out of air, or using elements to our advantage. Or even just being able to shift into a bear. For shifters, I mean."

"All of those are out of the ordinary," she protested.

"For humans. Not for us." He cocked his head and looked toward her again. "Why you? Because you can help us figure out the *how* of what we do. More importantly, you can give me the one thing I need."

His words softened something inside her she hadn't realized even existed. "What do you need?" she whispered.

He released her hand and ran his palm along her face, gently cupping her jaw. "I need you to send me back to hell. As soon as possible."

Chapter Fifteen

After a day of securing the campground, Ivar finished scouting the area beyond the river and made his way back toward a firepit near the cabins. His brothers, all of them except for Quade, sat around it. He took an empty seat, easily catching the beer Garrett tossed to him out of a dented cooler covered in bumper stickers. He popped the top and drank down several swallows. "Area is secure," he said, when he'd cooled his throat.

Adare kicked out his feet toward the fire, letting them get close enough that the rubber on the bottom of his boots started melting. He pulled them back slightly. "The Kurjans won't look for us here."

Ivar took another drink, appreciating the full moon shining down. It was nice to have a cloudless night for a change, and it certainly helped when keeping an eye out for the enemy. "I didn't think they'd search the middle of town."

Ronan crumpled his beer can and tossed it in a garbage bag set up yards away. "Logan? I should give you a warning before your mate finds out. Just received word that the Kurjans blew up our entire building. Well, to be more accurate, they set fire to every floor and shattered the windows."

"Ah, damn it." Logan's head went back, and he shut his eyes. "Mercy is gonna be so pissed. She believed we'd make a fortune from rent."

Chuckles erupted around Ivar, and he tried to find amusement in Logan's comment, but it just wasn't in him. Had joy been in him before? He vaguely remembered it. And he had thought Promise was amusing on a few occasions. Perhaps humor was coming back to him. Or maybe it was just Dr. Promise Williams. He felt more in her presence than he had for centuries, even before going through so many hells. It was too bad he couldn't explore that attraction. "Where is your mate, Logan?"

"Talking with Faith and Grace," Logan said, his overlarge body sprawled in his chair. "She'll be out here when they go to check on Promise. You know, you're gonna need to teach her to shield her mind because she'll want to get close and interview beings who can teleport."

"Or I could teach her," Garrett offered, a slight smile playing on his lips.

Spots danced across Ivar's vision. "No. I'll teach her." He clenched his teeth until his jaw hurt and then forced himself to relax.

"So it's like that, is it?" Ronan asked, turning away and barely masking a laugh with a lame cough.

"No." Ivar crossed his arms. His ears started to burn, and he growled.

Garrett tossed his beer can in the garbage and reached into the cooler for a purple drink. "Sorry, Ivar. Just messing with you."

Ivar glanced at the drink. "Grape?"

Garrett shrugged. "Yeah. Damn things are addictive. I stole a couple from my uncle Dage last month, and before I knew it, I wanted a grape energy drink every morning."

"I hope you get fat," Ivar returned, losing his tension. He'd forgotten how friends liked to banter; it was a skill he needed to work on. Maybe at some point, he'd actually feel amusement. It was possible. "I'll teach Missy what she needs to know."

"Missy?" Adare asked, turning his head.

Ivar's back straightened. "Yeah. It's a nickname. But I'm the only one who gets to call her that," he hastened to say. It was special and just for him. He didn't want to analyze why that mattered.

Garrett snorted and took a deep drink. "In all seriousness. My aunt Amber, who's mated to Kane, can shield from a demon mind attack and could do so even when she was human. We've studied her ability but can't really explain it. She might be able to help you with…Promise."

Ivar stretched out in the chair but kept away from the fire. He'd been burned enough in this life. "I haven't told her that demons can attack minds." He hadn't wanted to scare her any more than he already had. Oh, she'd kept calm and collected, asking tons of questions. But behind each query was fear. He couldn't blame her. "I figured since her mind was already being attacked, I'd skip that part of her introduction to our world."

"Seems fair," Benny agreed, which meant the plan was probably crazy. He rubbed his flat belly, his gaze on the dancing flames of the fire. "We don't do this enough. Just us hanging out and not talking about the world ending." He rubbed his whiskered chin, his eyes morphing from their normal metallic color to his secondary color of blackish green. Most immortals switched eye colors during extreme situations. Not Benny. Contentment brought the change out in him. "I like spending time with you guys when we're not ripping necks out of people."

"Yeah," Ronan said, looking around the fire. "This is nice. I mean, all six of us in one place." A roughness deepened his voice. "Someday we'll have my brother, I mean *our* brother, here with us. Quade will survive, and we'll help him start a new life. Right, Viking?"

Ivar nodded. "Yeah." It did feel good being with his brothers again. Almost complete. Their ages ranged from fourteen hundred years old to Garrett and Logan's mere twenty-five years, but each had survived an unsurvivable ritual to create their own brotherhood. Age didn't matter, and neither did family lines, because now they shared blood, which made them brothers. For the first time since he'd returned so broken, he felt a sliver of hope. They were strong enough to save Quade and kill Ulric. They had no choice. "I, ah, wanted to say thank you. For the last three months."

Adare reached over and clapped him on the back hard enough to rattle his teeth. "Of course. We're family."

They were. It was true. Ivar stared at the fire, no longer needing to run away from flames. Who did Promise have? She didn't have this type of support system. A part of him, one he would not examine, wanted to draw her into the fold. Give her a secure place.

But that wasn't his to give. Not if he was going to live out the rest of his days in Quade's hell dimension.

He glanced at Adare, who was the last remaining O'Cearbhaill remaining on earth. The clan had been one of the deadliest of the Highlanders, and surely he had plans to continue his line. "Your mate asked me to take her to Realm headquarters so she could be infected with that new virus." Would Adare allow such an act?

"No," Adare said shortly, reaching for another beer. "The virus has only negated mating bonds in mates that have been widowed for centuries. A new mating bond would be too strong, and she'd end up getting killed. The woman needs to be protected from herself."

Ivar cut a glance at Ronan, who shrugged. For centuries, Ivar had tried to pull Adare out of self-destructive and dangerous situations after Adare's shifter love had mated another shifter. Was he still in love with that twit? "Is it your decision?"

"She's my mate. Everything about her is my decision," Adare said.

Huh. Ivar wasn't certain Grace Cooper would agree with that. She was a modern woman from this century, even though she was now caught in a war between immortals. Was Adare staying distant because the final ritual might kill them all? Even the human women they called the Keys; the ones who'd be involved in the blood ritual that could kill Ulric? Ivar didn't understand females, and he sure as shit didn't understand relationships. But something told him Adare was fucking this one up but good. "Why don't you try for a real matehood?"

"With a human?" Adare mumbled. "Not a chance. They're too fragile."

Ronan shook his head. "She's immortal now, numbnuts. And she's a Key, which is well known by the Kurjans. Without her and the other Keys, Ulric can't be destroyed."

"So she's in constant danger and has no choice but to let me protect her," Adare snapped. "Discussion is closed. Now."

Ivar shrugged. "Fine. How about a status report? Any news on the Cyst?" The white-faced monsters were supposedly a monk-like sect within the Kurjan organization, but they were also a fierce fighting force, determined to rescue Ulric from his prison world. "The two last night fought well."

"They're still kidnapping Enhanced women across the globe—probably to force matings and increase their numbers," Garrett said somberly. "The Realm is tracking each disappearance down, but no luck stopping the kidnappings so far."

Ivar shook his head, his chest aching. They had to take out the Kurjans and their Cyst fighting force for good.

Mercy emerged from her cabin and made her way toward Logan, who pulled her down onto his lap and snuggled her close. She leaned back into him with a sigh of contentment, her long hair brushing down his arm.

Ivar studied them. Was that what happy looked like? It seemed like it. Logan handed her his beer, and she took a drink, her gaze caught by the fire. She kicked out small feet, her legs only extending to Logan's calves. She turned her head and smiled at Ivar. "Faith and Grace are going to talk to your lady. Make sure she's okay." Mercy's bottom lip pouted out. "I wish I could go."

"I'll teach her how to shield her brain," Ivar was quick to reassure her. "Then you can become friends." He'd like to secure some friends for Promise before he left. "I think she needs that."

Mercy's eyes sparkled. "That's sweet, Ivar."

Sweet? He'd never been sweet. Not even before—not even the old him. When he was organized and made sure they had what they needed for headquarters. The old him never would've never put Promise in a high-rise building in the middle of town. "Thanks?" he murmured.

Logan chuckled and dug his face into Mercy's neck. "I'm sure Ivar will teach her, and then you can take her through dimensions, baby."

"No," Ivar said instantly. "Missy, I mean *Promise*, can study the issue all she wants, but nobody is transporting her anywhere. That's final." He hunched his shoulders and stared into the fire, pointedly ignoring all the chuckles masked by coughs around him. What did they know?

Chapter Sixteen

Surrounded by scraps of yellow legal paper, Promise finished drafting the string solution for an open string, leaving the ends open and what was commonly referred to as floppy. Oh, she had so much work to do. The wind blew gently outside, while the bright moonlight streamed in through the windows. During the day, Ivar had installed a powerful generator, so she had plenty of electricity and was using the internet on her phone. Even so, she missed her office at the university.

Somebody knocked on the door, and she called out for them to come in. It was probably Ivar. She had so many more questions for him and turned to start asking.

"Whoa." Grace Cooper stepped gingerly over several loose pieces of paper. The brunette wore a thick green sweater and jeans with hiking boots, her hair piled high on her head, giving her that classic look some women just seemed to have naturally. "Obsessed scientist at work." Lifting her camera, she sidled three steps to the right and leaned forward to take several candid shots.

Promise blinked. She'd met Grace earlier in the day before the young woman had disappeared down the river to photograph wildlife. "Hello."

"Hi." Grace smiled, her hazel eyes sparkling.

Her sister walked in behind her, holding a bottle of red wine and three red plastic cups. "Promise." Faith wore a light gray sweater over darker gray jeans with spectacular cream-colored boots. Just how many pairs of stunning boots did she have, anyway? Her dark hair was long and loose around her slim shoulders. She looked around at the disheveled papers strewn about the room. "Working hard, I see?"

Promise looked at the mess she'd made, for the first time seeing the jumbled confusion. Even the bed was covered with solutions, equations, and theories scribbled over yellow legal paper. "I need my chalkboards."

Grace snorted and gingerly gathered papers off the old sofa to stack on the coffee table. Then she moved closer to the fire, turned, and snapped several more shots. "I'd love to get a few photographs of you in your work area, surrounded by chalkboards, your hair full of chalk."

Promise calculated the available light, dimensions of the room, and space. "You've studied fractal light?"

Grace lowered the camera. "Huh?"

"Your positioning for both series of shots. They made the best use of light and space," Promise said, her interest piqued.

Grace shrugged. "I'm a photographer. That's my job."

One she apparently did instinctively. Fascinating.

Faith set the wine bottle on the rickety coffee table, twisted it open, and started pouring three cups. "This is a decent Shiraz. Nothing to set your hair on fire, but it'll do." She motioned for Promise to get off the floor.

"Oh." Promise let the papers slide off her knees and stood, stretching her back. She'd changed into dark jeans and a red silk shirt that Ivar had procured from her home earlier. She had twice the curves of either woman, a fact that had always been fine with her. She was healthy, and her brain worked well, so life was good. But her neck ached. Just how long had she been sitting on the floor? What time was it?

Faith motioned her forward. "Let's chat a little."

Promise stiffened and then stretched over different stacks of papers to reach the sofa and sit. Girl talk. Wonderful. She never knew how to do this, unless one was discussing entropic gravity or something similar. But Faith was a world-renowned neurologist. She could go with that. "I've been thinking about the possibility of moving through time and space and wondering why motor functionality doesn't seem to be diminished in the subject afterward."

"Probably because that study about going to Mars only involved humans." Faith handed her a cup and sat on the sofa. "I thought we'd start a bit more generally with getting to know each other. Like, what do you do for fun besides study baryogenesis?"

"I can see I'm going to be mostly lost in this conversation once it gets started." Grace chuckled, took her cup, and moved to sit on the floor by the side of the fire. She extended her legs. "Any hobbies, Promise?"

Promise looked down at the thick red liquid. "I work for fun." Her mind scrambled for some sort of connection. The women were attempting to make her feel welcome, and the pressure to please them rolled her stomach over. "Though I did spend some time working on supersymmetry just for a break." She smiled, looking up.

"Well," Faith breathed into her cup. "That would make for a relaxing hobby."

Oh, good. They'd connected. Promise took a drink of the wine, finding it full bodied and delicious. "I thought about studying yoga or Pilates for a bit, but then scientists at JGU reported finding a new spectral line with an energy of 3.5 keV in x-ray light from distant galaxy clusters. So, it was back to studying dark matter."

Grace lifted her glass. "That's exactly why I stopped going to the gym too."

Promise started and then laughed. She took another drink, her shoulders slowly relaxing. These were nice women, and they wanted to spend time with her. "What do you do for fun?"

Grace played with her camera. "I used to travel and take pictures, but then I ended up in a coma for a few years, got mated to a vampire-demon to come out of it, and now am regaining my sea legs, so to speak."

An unusual warmth filtered through Promise's blood. That was a subject she hadn't had the courage to broach with Ivar. "What exactly does mating entail?" Such a barbaric word.

Faith blushed prettily. "Well, usually it entails a whole lot of crazy vampire-monkey sex, which is a phrase coined by the vampire queen that truly nails the experience. There's also a bite that slashes right to bone, and a branding. A marking appears on the male's palm, at least on a demon's, and it ends up on the female mate's body." She turned and tugged down her shoulder to show what looked like a deep tattoo of an intricate *K* surrounded by sharp and somehow beautiful lines. "The letter comes from the demon's family surname."

Promise nearly dropped her wine. "It's a brand?"

Faith shrugged. "They call it a marking."

Promise looked toward Grace. "Adare had sex with you when—"

"No." The woman held up a hand. "Not at all. He bit and branded, but no sex. I'm unique. One of the three unfortunate Keys."

Okay. Information overload. Promise sat back and mused over the problem for a minute. "I understand that mating made you immortal."

"Mostly," Faith said. "We can be beheaded." She cleared her throat. "Also, mated beings can't touch a member of the opposite sex for more than a minute or so without suffering an extreme physical reaction that's like a horrible allergy."

Promise sat back. What type of mathematical solution would explain that? So much happened on the chromosomal level that nobody knew about. Maybe that could be her next hobby. Explaining the genetic changes from a mating that seemed impossible based on current science.

Grace sighed. "She has that look on her face again."

Faith nodded, smiling. "I know that look. I get it when I'm close to a discovery. Or when I find a new path to take that scientists haven't gone down yet."

Promise focused on Faith. "I'm confused. I understand that the Seven are all demon-vampire hybrids. But they call Logan a demon while calling Ronan a vampire."

Faith swirled the liquid in her cup. "Right. Apparently, immortal hybrids take on the traits of mainly one species. So Logan is a lot more demon than vampire, and vice versa for Ronan. Even if their genetics say otherwise, they're usually one or the other. Which makes Adare kind of different."

Grace snorted. "Adare is different because he's an uptight jackass."

"Who saved your life," her sister reminded her.

Grace tilted her head. "True." She crossed her legs at the ankles over a few of Promise's papers. "Adare has the black eyes and hoarse voice of a purebred demon, but they usually have white-blond hair, and his hair is black. He has gifts known to both. He's probably the truest hybrid of them all."

So the woman had given this some thought. Was there more to Grace's feelings for Adare than mere annoyance? Promise didn't know how to gauge the other woman's emotions better than that. So she concentrated on what she did know—scientific inquiry. "You said you're special because you're one of three Keys. What does that mean?"

Grace winced and pulled down her shirt to show a perfect outline of a key above her breast. "That's what this is all about. Short version? We're planning for a ritual to destroy Ulric once and for all. It'll take three Keys, which means three Enhanced women, and the blood of a lock to actually kill him. I'm one of the Keys."

Okay. That sounded like crazy science fiction, but so did the rest of the information she'd gleaned lately. "You must be studying the genetic composition of the Keys," Promise said.

"The Queen of the Realm and I both are," Faith agreed. "She was a geneticist before becoming the Queen of the Realm, and she's pretty obsessed with the genetics of the entire situation. But so far, we haven't found anything."

Then it probably came down to the lock. "What or who is the lock?" Promise whispered. If the Keys were human, it stood to reason that the lock would be as well.

Faith sighed. "The lock is a seven-year-old hybrid, Hope Kayrs-Kyllwood." She shook her head. "With both vampires and demons involved, most of them her relatives, I don't think anything is ever going to go as planned."

Promise straightened. "It all comes down to a young girl?"

Faith nodded, taking another sip of her wine.

Just who was this Hope Kayrs-Kyllwood?

Chapter Seventeen

Hope Kayrs-Kyllwood twirled in front of the mirror, checking out her party dress. Green and purple and pink colors sparkled through the material that fell beneath the bandage on her knee covering the big bruise she'd gotten falling out of a tree the day before. Her flat green shoes sparkled along with the ribbons tied in her brown hair.

"I like that dress better than the yellow one," Libby said from the bed. She'd had her eighth birthday party the previous week and wore her birthday dress again today. It was a wild orange color, which was the feline shifter's favorite out of the whole rainbow. Probably because she hoped she'd be an orange cougar when she finally learned to shift in her teens. Her hair was blond, however, so her fur probably would be too. "I made you a scrapbook for your birthday."

Delight filled Hope, and she turned around. "That's so nice. I love your scrapbooks." She hadn't expected Libby to hold off on giving her gift until it was time to open presents. Libby was terrible with secrets. Usually.

Somebody knocked on the door, and Paxton walked in. His dark hair was slicked back, and he tugged at his button-down shirt. He held a present wrapped in newspapers in his hand, and he awkwardly handed it over. "Happy birthday." His jeans were ripped and only a little dirty.

She took the gift, smiling widely. "Thank you, Paxton."

Then she looked at her very best friends in the entire world. Well, Libby and Paxton and Drake, who was her dream friend. "We're gonna throw you a party next week when you turn nine years old, Paxton. Whether you want a party or not." He hadn't let them throw one when he turned eight, and his daddy didn't seem interested in parties, so he didn't get one.

Paxton flushed red and shrugged, moving to sit next to Libby on the purple bedspread covered in butterflies. "My dad said parties are for wimps." He winced and held up a hand. "I mean for guys. Not girls. Girls aren't wimps and should love parties."

His dad was kinda a jerk, but Hope didn't say that. Ever since Pax's mom had died, his dad had been not so great. Pax's mom had been a really cool demoness, and his dad was a vampire soldier. "Okay, Pax," she said quietly.

He brightened. "Open your present."

She ripped open the paper to see a box, which took a second to open. "Oh, Pax," she breathed, taking out a shiny silver ring with sparkly butterflies. "It's so pretty." She slid the ring onto first her right ring finger and then her middle finger.

"You'll grow into it," he said, his eyes silvery.

She swallowed. "How did you get this?" He must've spent all his money from working with the Realm soldiers.

He shrugged. "Wanted you to have a good birthday." His cheeks turned red.

"I am." She smiled at him. What a good friend. Her stomach went all fluttery. "Okay, but I wanna ask for something else from you both also." She held her breath, waiting for her friends to nod. "We have hours before the party, and I want to go and meet Drake in real life. But I need you guys to help me get there."

Libby bounced on the bed, her twin ponytails bobbing. Her soft brown eyes widened. "Are you for real? You can see him?"

Pax frowned and shook his head. "Are you kidding? He's a Kurjan. There's no way your parents are going to let you go meet him. What's he doing nearby, anyway? The Kurjans don't live here in Idaho. Last I heard, they lived somewhere really cold up in Canada."

Hope clasped her hands together, trying to be cool like the kids on television before they went off on an adventure. "I know, but I talked to him in a dream last night."

Pax's eyebrows slashed down even farther, making him look like his dad. "You said you weren't meeting in dreamworlds anymore."

"I never really said that." Hope clutched the box closer to her chest. "I need your help to do this."

"Okay," Libby said, bouncing again.

Paxton shook his head. "No. Definitely no." He picked at a scab on his elbow, his silver-blue eyes looking more silver than blue as his face got redder. "The Kurjans aren't even supposed to know where we live. Our headquarters and demon headquarters are secrets. How could you tell him?"

Her stomach hurt. "I didn't, Pax. I promise." She waited until he looked up before trying to explain better. "He guessed when we were talking. Said they knew we lived by this lake and had for a long time. They don't wanna be enemies anymore, and I think it's up to us to find the peace." She'd always known that would be her path. She rubbed the deep blue marking down her neck and side that proved she was one of the three prophets chosen by Fate.

Pax looked at Libby and then back at Hope. "We're just kids, you guys. We're not supposed to do anything but train right now."

Training was boring, and Hope wasn't as good at it as Libby. Neither was Pax, since his big feet tripped him all the time. Hope was a hybrid and the only living female vampire in the history of the entire world. All vampires, even hybrids, had just made boys until she was born. She might suck at training, but she must be special in a different way. It had to be her ability to meet Drake in the dreamworld. He was a Kurjan, and he was her friend. "You know my mama and daddy met in dreamworlds, and they saved the entire world when they got together." Why did she hafta always remind Pax about that?

Pax's lips got a white line when he pressed them together. "This is not a good idea."

She had him. Right then, she knew she'd get what she wanted for her birthday. "Okay. I have a plan. The hardest part will be to keep our dresses from getting dirty, Libby."

* * * *

Ivar knocked and stepped into Promise's cabin, stopping short when he caught sight of the torn-off yellow papers everywhere. The woman sat on the floor, furiously scribbling a mathematical equation on another pad, an empty cup of wine next to her. It was one of the sexiest sights he'd ever seen. She looked up, and her pretty brown eyes focused. "I need more information."

He lived with obsession daily and recognized the signs. This side of her was way too enticing. "Sure." Shutting the door, he stepped over various pages and reached her, dropping to his knees to face her. "When did Faith and Grace leave?"

"Don't know." She looked down and shuffled papers. Her scent of heather filled his senses. "I need to experience teleporting."

He took the papers from her and set them aside. "Yes."

She blinked, surprise lifting her eyebrows. "You agree?"

"I didn't earlier, but when everyone laughed at me, I figured I wasn't thinking clearly," he mused. "I'll work harder to regain the ability, and then I'll take you." That had to be a good plan. He hadn't found much enjoyment in life since returning, and yet, that sounded almost fun. So long as they managed to keep from hurting her in the process.

She frowned. "I could go right now with Mercy, if I could control the headaches."

"No. Just me." He cocked his head, searching for the right words. This close, with the fire crackling softly and the moon gliding across the sky, an intimacy wove around them that fired up his blood. It had been way too long since he'd bedded a female. That probably wasn't even the correct terminology any longer.

He tried to concentrate. "But you're right that we need to teach you to shield your mind against whatever brain waves harm you."

She leaned back. "Why just you?"

"Because then I can control the outcome," he said easily. That seemed obvious, didn't it?

Her face cleared. "Listen, Viking. I appreciate a control freak as much as the next absentminded professor, but you're overstepping."

Was he? He thought it through. "I believe you're wrong. It's my fault you're in this situation." He held up a hand before she could argue. "Yes, the Kurjans would've probably targeted you at some point, but we don't know that for sure."

"I'm one of the most visible physicists in the world right now. Of course they would've targeted me."

Had he just insulted her? That truly hadn't been his intention. "I think I could've protected you from afar. Let you go for the grant, work on the problem, without your view of the world having to change so drastically."

Her chin jerked down. "That's the most condescending thing I've heard all day. And that's saying something."

He paused. Condescending? Damn it.

"Besides, it's stupid." She said the words casually, as if she hadn't just insulted him.

Irritation clawed down his back, melding with arousal in an uncomfortable mixture that made the blood pound between his ears in a roaring sound. "How so?" he asked, keeping his hoarse voice somewhat mild.

She rolled her eyes. Actually rolled those intelligent eyes like a teenager. "There is no way to solve this equation without a full knowledge of the facts. Of the ability to teleport—or rather, the different abilities and possibilities. The solution might be found by researching the differences between the Fae and the demons. Why they can both teleport but the Fae can actually travel to different worlds."

Man, when she started talking in science jargon, his jeans became too tight. "Be that as it may, we've broken many laws by telling you the truth."

"Since when do you care about laws?" she challenged.

He straightened his back. "Are you trying to pick a fight?"

She considered the question, her gaze directly on his. "No. I am challenging your supposition that you have any control over what I do or do not...do."

Cute. "You sound like Shakespeare. Whom I've met, by the way."

Her head did an adorable little spiral in the air. "You've met Shakespeare?"

"Yep. Guy drank like a fish." Ivar leaned in to whisper. "And I've met Einstein."

Her gasp was pure joy to his ears.

"What was he like?" she asked, her tone reverent.

"Kind. Thoughtful, smart, and very nice." Ivar had liked the guy from the start. "He and Kane Kayrs were actually pretty decent friends. We'll get you back in touch with Kane to collaborate. He had to return to headquarters, but we'll make it happen."

Delight absolutely lit up her entire face.

He grinned. "Now, it's pretty late. Why don't you get some sleep so you can teach tomorrow?"

Surprise joined the delight. "You're not going to try and stop me?"

He ignored the hint that he wouldn't be able to prevent her from leaving. "No. We've diagrammed a good plan so you can teach tomorrow and gather all of the resources you need from your office. But you'll have to put in for leave. Maybe claim that after Dr. Rashad's death or your car accident you need a sabbatical." If she fought him on this, she wasn't going to like the result. "We can't keep your students safe, Missy. If the Kurjans come for you, they won't care about collateral damage."

She swallowed. "Well. Since you put it like that."

Yes. He had thought his argument through thoroughly. "I hope you understand."

"I do, and I can get my doctoral students to cover my classes for the remainder of the semester." She looked at the notes strewn around. "I'm captivated by this problem, anyway. I need to follow the math."

He stood and assisted her up. "Then we're in agreement." The woman barely came to his chin, and he wondered once again how he was going to keep such a fragile human safe in his violent world. "I'll let you get some sleep."

She looked up at him, her gaze direct and a pretty pink suffusing her dusky skin. "Why don't you stay with me?"

The blood drained out of his head and rushed south so quickly his ears rang. He glanced at the sofa and back up to her face.

She pressed her lips together in an obvious attempt to stifle a smile. "I mean in the bed. With me." She placed her hands on his chest, spreading out her fingers with a soft hum. "I like how hard you are."

The woman had no fucking clue. He swallowed.

"I understand that mating is a part of sex. Or vice versa," she murmured.

"You don't have to worry about that," he said quietly. "We can control the mating process." He struggled to regain his composure, but her soft touch was wreaking havoc on his system. "Unless you want to mate." He attempted the joke.

Thus his shock when she didn't reply. Instead, her lips now pursed, and rapid thoughts altered her expression.

He almost stepped away. "I was joking. Mating is forever."

"I might need forever to solve the theories you've presented to me," she said thoughtfully. She blinked. "You don't believe in romantic love or any of that, do you?"

"No," he croaked.

She smiled. "Logic and biology explain everything. We're on the same page here." She tugged his shirt free of his jeans and slid her hands over his bare abs. "And you've given me my first nickname. That matters. We should see if we're compatible. Then we can discuss the matter."

His cock hit his zipper so hard he winced. "You need to understand." His words came out garbled, sounding like Russian. "Logic and mating don't belong in the same universe." Oh, she didn't get it. Not at all.

"Logic belongs everywhere." She leaned up and kissed the side of his neck. "Are you staying or not?"

Chapter Eighteen

Promise made the offer with her eyes wide open. The male had intrigued her even before she'd discovered he was a vampire-demon mix. They were working well together and were possibly becoming friends, and she loved having a feminine-sounding nickname that only he used. Missy. It didn't fit her at all, and yet, she enjoyed it. And they could both use a healthy outlet for the stress pounding against them. When he'd mentioned mating, she hadn't been put off in the slightest. They might make a good pairing.

First, he had to agree to stay. Then if they were compatible physically, she'd broach the subject. Immortality appealed to her on many levels, and she liked Ivar, especially since she'd discovered he had a vast intelligence.

His hands folded over her shoulders, and he set her lightly away from him, his gaze darkening. "I'm a demon-vampire hybrid." His words came out clipped.

She nodded. "I know." Was there something about that fact that would matter to her? "I can't be infected with some demon or vampire illness, can I?" She'd left her condoms back at her house, and it appeared that Ivar hadn't grabbed them when he'd secured her clothing.

"No." His voice sounded strangled again. "I'm trying to explain. We don't approach mating or even sex as a logical matter."

Ah, passion. Now she understood. Did immortals have the same brain chemistry as humans? If so, elevated levels of dopamine, norepinephrine, and serotonin led to the physical connection between love and body. "I understand," she said.

His eyes flashed to that odd iridescent green. How marvelous that immortals had secondary eye colors. "I don't think you do. Let's change that." The intriguing color of his eyes and the intensity of his gaze trapped her in place. Or perhaps that was her own curiosity. She caught her breath as he reached out and cradled her chin.

Tension rolled from him and surrounded her. She tilted her head. How was that possible? She opened her mouth to ask him, and he lowered his head. His lips touched hers, and an electrical shock zinged through her blood. She gasped, and his lips firmed, his tongue sweeping inside her mouth.

His other hand slid to the small of her back and pulled her closer, into unimaginable hardness. Desire flooded her, much faster than ever before.

He released her mouth, his own hovering just above her lips. "You still thinking?"

She blinked, trying to hypothesize. "There's chemistry at play here." She needed a notebook.

"Guess you're still thinking." He pressed her up against him, his mouth taking hers again. This time hard and full, he kissed her, bending her entire body to fit him. Hunger rode his low growl, and he kissed her deeper, forcing her to take what he was giving.

Her head fell back, and she shut her eyes, captured by the storm he created. She might've whimpered. He growled again, and the sound reverberated through her, awakening nerves she'd thought long dormant. Never in her life had she been kissed like this. Whatever this was. Heat flowed beneath her skin, making her nipples pebble and her breasts heavy. Her thighs trembled, and her panties dampened.

He lifted his head again, and the dark blue rim around his eyes seemed to glow. "Still in your head?"

She stared at him, bemused. What had he asked?

His smile held both challenge and an intriguing arrogance. "Now we're getting somewhere." A dark flush spread across his harsh cheekbones, giving him the look of a Viking marauder.

Her legs trembled.

"Better." In one smooth movement, he swept her up and carried her to the bed.

She gasped and planted one hand against his chest to balance herself. This was out of her experience. Normally she'd be drawn to the newness. Instead, a feminine thread of caution wound through her brain. It was as if her body had a life of its own. Were the chemicals in her brain being affected by him?

"You're thinking again." He laid her down while yanking her shirt over her head in one easy motion. His nostrils flared, and he reached out one finger to trace along the top of her plain cotton bra. "Beautiful."

She swallowed, recognizing her trepidation for what it was. She'd always been in control in the bedroom, and now, her body was following his lead and not her brain. A part of her, one she hadn't known existed, wanted to wrest control from him in the most intimate of ways. So she grasped his shirt and yanked.

He ducked his head to let her remove it.

Finally, his physics-defying chest was revealed. Hard planes, smooth muscle, taut skin. Male perfection she'd never even imagined, much less thought to touch. Her hands trembled as she explored his pecs and moved down to the ripples of his abdomen. "How are you real?" she whispered. How was any of this happening?

He flicked her bra open and dragged it down her arms. "You ever been tied up?" he rumbled.

Her lungs constricted right before her sex did the same thing. "No."

"Maybe next time." He tossed the bra over his shoulder. His big hands flattened across her breasts with his thumbs caressing beneath them. "You're beautiful, Promise. Thought you should know." His touch electrified her skin, and she moved against him, needing something she couldn't quantify. Then his mouth followed his hands, his tongue swirling around and so hot it nearly burned.

She slid her hands into his thick hair, holding on, her eyes wide on the ceiling. What was happening?

He kissed down her abdomen and quickly dispatched her jeans. "Now I'm gonna show you how I'm better than a pocket rocket." His breath brushed sensitive skin, and he kissed her clitoris.

She jerked as spasms took her. Light ones, not nearly strong enough to orgasm. But something new. She gaped down at him.

He nipped her. "Spread your legs, baby."

Her knees tensed, and her body rioted in a way that probably wasn't healthy. She tried to make sense of his words. To think. To just be herself.

"Now." He licked her again, his tone beyond firm.

Her body reacted before her brain could catch up—probably for the first time in her life. She widened her legs. He made a hum of appreciation and then licked her again, once and then twice. On the third time, he slipped a finger inside her, and she blew apart, crying out before she could bite her tongue. He carried her through a truly excellent orgasm and then moved back up her, shedding his jeans.

She blinked and slowly smiled. "That was great." Definitely better than a pocket rocket.

His eyebrow lifted. "That was nothing."

Huh. The male was crazy. She reached for him, surprised by his size. His penis was thick and long and heated. Her belly warmed again as she stroked him from base to tip.

He rolled more on top of her.

"Wait." She released him. "Condom." Oh, hopefully he hadn't forgotten those.

"Not necessary." He kissed her deep, his body surrounding hers with unreal warmth. "We don't have diseases, and I can't impregnate you if we're not mated. This is as safe as sex gets."

Nothing about this felt safe, and her liquid reaction to the realization shocked her. She wanted more of him. Her nails scraped down his chest of their own accord. "All right." Sprawled on the bed with him over her, she suddenly understood all those romantic movies she sometimes watched alone. It'd take her a year to analyze these feelings, and right now, she just wanted more of them.

He held himself on his elbows, not crushing her but somehow surrounding her. She lifted her knees and pressed against his warm hips. Sensations coursed through her, new and deep.

"Having fun?" he asked, his lips wandering over her forehead, down her cheek, to bite her earlobe.

"Yes," she whispered, caressing along his flanks to his lower back, which felt like stone that had baked in the hot sun all day. "You?"

"Yes." He poised himself at her core and then slowly began to push inside her.

She gasped, widening her knees, her eyes widening too. Physically, her body was meant to take him in, but he was rock hard and monolithic.

"God, you're tight," he muttered, a vein protruding in his neck as he held himself back.

"It has been a while." In fact, she couldn't remember the last time she'd engaged in sex. At the moment, every man in existence except for the one inside her disappeared. He kept his pace slow but steady, stretching her with delicious tingles along the way. "I've never felt like this."

He paused, his dark gaze cutting to her eyes. "You are so sweet sometimes." Then he pushed harder, blending pain with pleasure. His big hand banded around her wrists and drew them up above her head, pinning them to the bed. Her back arched, and her breasts scraped against his chest.

She tugged at his grip, finding herself helpless in his hold. A shiver took her. "I, um, I don't like this."

"You sure about that?" He finally slid all the way inside her. "Your body just quivered, you got wetter, and you all but pulled me the rest of the way in." His hold remained gentle but unrelenting.

The way he kept her in place shot excitement through her nerves. "Let me go." She didn't sound remotely convincing.

"No." At the denial, her body bucked, heat flowing down her torso. Triumph filled his gaze. "Oh, we have some exploring to do, Professor." The erotic threat had the desired effect of trapping the air in her lungs and flinging protons throughout her abdomen. His smile was devastating. "One thing at a time."

Then he pulled out of her, paused, waited three heartbeats, and shoved back inside so hard the bed hit the wall. Pleasure rippled through her.

"More," she murmured, locking her ankles around his firm butt. She might not be able to move her hands, but her legs were free. So she used her leverage to push him farther inside her.

He tangled the fingers of his free hand in her hair, finding purchase and taking control. Then he moved his lips over her jaw, finally taking her mouth again and kissing her deep. Still kissing her, possessing her mouth as fully as he did her body, he started to move.

Sensations rippled through her. The heat at her mouth, the hard length inside her. She lifted her hips to take more of him, meeting him thrust for thrust. Sensations tore through her, way too fast for her to catalog each one. Hunger overcame her, and she returned his kiss, taking everything she hadn't realized existed.

He pounded harder, his breath harsh, his body everywhere. She closed her eyes to experience every sensation.

"Eyes on me, beautiful." He paused inside her.

"No."

He didn't move.

She opened her eyes, caught by the raw possession on his face. The intimacy of the moment, of watching him take her, sent a charged jolt through her to where they remained joined. Followed by a hint of vulnerability she hadn't expected.

"That's better." He pulled out and then pounded back in, setting up an impossible rhythm that reached a sensitive area inside her she'd only read about. His hammering matched the wildness suddenly pouring through her entire body.

Live wires began uncoiling inside her, sparking to the far reaches of her atoms. Breathing became difficult and then unnecessary. The only thing that mattered in the entire universe was where those wires led. Inside her, he was hard, pulsing, demanding.

Her body quieted for the briefest of seconds. Then ecstasy caught her. She reared up, into him, as she broke with a brutal cry. Her internal muscles spasmed with increased velocity, rippling stirring sensations into violent pleasure throughout her entire body.

He continued to thrust, and his fangs dropped low and sharp.

She gasped, instinctively turning her neck, no longer calculating anything. His fangs pierced her flesh. Pain slashed into her skin and went deeper, somehow intensifying her orgasm until she had to close her eyes or have them blast completely out of her head. The waves took her away until she finally sighed in defeat, her body sated, her mind peacefully blank.

He ground against her and growled low as his body shook with his own release.

His fangs retracted, and he licked her neck like a lazy puppy, releasing her hands.

She drew her arms down and ran her palms along his quivering muscles. Her mind tried to awaken, but only a nice buzz filled her ears. "Ivar." She'd truly underestimated what sex with him would feel like.

"Mmm?" He kissed along her cheek and down her nose.

"I had no idea what my body was capable of," she whispered.

He paused and partially lifted his head so his now blue gaze met hers. His burst of laughter was as unexpected as it was endearing. His grin remained, making him look more boyish than she would've thought possible. He licked her bottom lip. "Let's see what else this body of yours can do, Missy, my girl."

Chapter Nineteen

Ivar stretched awake right around dawn with a snuggly woman in his arms. He lay on his back, and she'd curled into his side, her nose in his neck. His woman didn't move much during the night. He blinked. His woman? What the hell? He didn't have the right to claim anyone right now. Yet having the brilliant physicist tucked into his side felt right. More right than he'd experienced in hundreds of years.

She stretched against him like a satisfied cat. "I wish I could diagram last night in a mathematical equation."

He grinned into the darkness. "I bet you could figure it out."

"Most certainly, but I won't have time with the new theories I have to prove about dimensional jumping." Her warm breath brushed his neck, and he fought to keep arousal at bay. "And today I need to start practicing mind shields."

"You will." He caressed her hair, loving the feel of it between his fingers, wanting to know more about her. Everything about her. Would she share with him? He hadn't felt this complete in much too long, and he wanted to hold on to the feeling as long as possible. Just who was this woman? What had made her? "What were your parents like?"

She stiffened slightly. "They were good parents. Taught me to love math and physics, and I believe they liked each other well enough."

"Sounds cold." He pulled her closer.

"It was sufficient." She sighed. "When I was eight, I wanted a puppy for my birthday. My dad bought me my first book on black holes and the mystery of the universe instead. I can't complain. Look how my life turned out."

He could see her. A little girl with those big brown eyes. She should've been given the book and the dog.

She rolled closer and blinked up at him. "What year were you born?"

"The year 1107," he said quietly.

She lifted her head more. "That's mind-boggling. You've seen everything. The moon landing. The invention of the internet. Not to mention running water and electricity." She moved up his body, her gaze on his. "You said you met Einstein. Who else?"

He started naming scientists he thought she'd be interested in hearing about, and soon, the sun started peeking through the window shades. "And van Gogh wasn't crazy like everyone says. He just saw the world differently."

Delight crossed her features. "I have so many more questions."

"Go ahead." He hadn't relaxed like this in eons.

"What about your family? Do you have anybody left?" Her voice softened.

"No," he said, for once not feeling uncomfortable about discussing his past. "My parents were killed in a war a century ago, while my brother was killed by the Kurjans and I took his place on the Seven." Their deaths still felt raw. "I had a sister, one my folks had adopted. She was killed by a man who courted her, and I killed him afterward." The idea of anybody hurting a woman still pissed him off, and he had no problem killing abusers. Never had and probably never would. "Does that frighten you?"

"No," she said, kissing the area right above his heart. "Should it?"

He shook his head.

She tilted hers. "I thought I heard Logan talking about teleporting during the ritual to become a member of the Seven, but being near him doesn't hurt me. Can you explain?"

"Not very well." Ivar rolled toward her. "Logan can't teleport. But during the ritual, we all saw dimensions, or other worlds. Our bodies stayed in the circle here, but our consciousness moved on somehow. He saved me, even though he was still here."

She bit her lip, thoughts flashing across her face. "So how did you end up traveling through hellish places?"

"An evil Fae named Niall teleported me to a hell world in a murder attempt, and then I was dragged through the different worlds." He shook his head. "The bastard is still alive too."

Her expression cleared. "Okay. That all adds up nicely. I can't deal with the Seven ritual right now when there's a more critical theory to explore: the demons teleporting and the fairies jumping to other worlds."

"Is that what's happening?" he asked, his pulse quickening.

"Heck if I know," she retorted, her smile warming him. "But I intend to find out, especially since I think when I was a young child I could maybe teleport to a dreamworld? Or more likely, since I'm human, I just dreamed of immortals doing so."

Man, he wanted to keep her. How, he wasn't sure. Not if he was to take Quade's place. But now that she was fully awake, perhaps they could get a quick lesson in. "How about we start trying to protect your brain?"

She looked over at the dying fire. "I guess we could go see Mercy."

Ivar snorted. "You won't be starting with the fairy. She's too powerful."

"Adare, then." A small pout made Promise's lip bitable, so he took a nip. She chuckled. "Should we get ready?"

"I'm a demon, Professor." He caressed down her spine to her delicious ass and pinched. "We can attack minds. The pain we cause is imaginary, but it feels like hell." Could he hurt her? Probably not. They'd start with something easy. "Okay. Feel this." He slid into her mind way too easily, planting scenes of puppies and butterflies.

Her eyes widened. "Incredible."

He added a slow glide of pain.

She closed her eyes and slapped his arm. "Stop."

"No. Imagine shields coming down and stopping me. You're the only one who can do it." He kept up the pressure, careful not to add any more pain. "Take control of your mind."

Shields slammed down so quickly, he could hear their echoing clang in his head. "Nicely done."

Her eyes opened, and her pupils constricted. "That was astounding." Her smile lit up the entire room. "Did you feel that? Truly?"

"Yes." He kept his hand planted across her butt since she hadn't protested the intimacy. "That block was remarkable. Are you sure you haven't done this before?"

"I haven't." She wiggled closer to him. "I was unaware that it was even possible. Now that I know, I can do it. I think. At least here in bed with you where I feel safe." She traced circles across his chest. "I hadn't realized that I didn't feel safe before."

Sweet words from a sweet woman. "I won't let anybody harm you, Promise Williams." He kissed her nose and tugged her back down to rest on him. "You can trust me."

"I do," she murmured, kissing him beneath the jaw. "Are you waiting for love to mate?"

"No." He leaned back until he could see her face. She was back to thinking logically, and that was fine with him. "If we can't break Quade's world and let him out, I'm going to take his place."

Her spine straightened. "You're going to sacrifice yourself?"

He couldn't lie to her. There was also no reason to be coy. He knew exactly why she'd asked about mating. "Yes. If you mate me out of a desire for immortality and the chance to solve all of the world's equations, you might be doing so alone for eternities." Yeah, there was a virus that negated the bond, but nobody had figured how exactly how it worked. If he still lived, even worlds away, would the virus kill his mate instead of breaking the bonds? "Also, I think there should be more to a mating than a logical plan. Or math." He shifted his weight.

"What could that be?" she asked.

He couldn't answer the question, because whatever it was, it was starting to beat in his heart for her.

* * * *

Never in her life had Promise been tempted to lounge in bed when there was an equation to solve. But cuddling with the Viking, her body pleasantly sore, she couldn't find a pressing need to hurry and dress. The previous night had been unquantifiable. She'd discovered elements to herself that she hadn't identified before, and she was uncertain how to process the information.

Her question about mating him the day before now seemed naive. An abstract thought with no understanding of the real-world consequences. In speaking with Ivar, she'd learned he was educated and knowledgeable about pretty much every subject.

She'd underestimated him.

Even now, after the night they'd shared, much of him remained concealed. Maybe not purposefully, but she sensed in him aspects that she couldn't understand, much less define. The need to solve the mystery of him drew her more strongly than any equation ever had.

He rolled from the bed to pull the shades over the one window more firmly shut, his nude body a study of muscle and sinew.

She partially sat up, holding the sheet to her chest, her gaze on his back. "Oh my."

He looked over his shoulder at the dark shield of his rib cage. "Our torsos are fused front and back, protecting every organ. It happened during the ritual, and that part was more painful than any other hell world."

She shook her head. "How?" There wasn't a scientific theory that came close to explaining such a phenomenon.

He smiled and slid back into bed, grasping her hip. "How about you figure that out after the other problems? Dimensional jumping comes first." He gave a gentle tug and landed her on top of his solid body. "How is your mind now?"

"The temple pain is still gone," she said, a juvenile delight flickering through her. "Did I really expel you?"

"Yes." His smile brightened his eyes to a light cerulean. A color nowhere near human. "We'll practice throughout the day, before and after you teach, and then you can try with Adare later."

She caressed his jaw, letting his whiskers tickle her palm. They were more auburn than his hair. She reached up and tugged on a strand above his ear that reached his shoulders. "These darker streaks in your hair. Were they always there?"

"No. Got those recently," he said lightly.

Oh. Another change he'd endured. "They suit you," she said, hoping that was permissible to say.

He grinned and wrapped one of her long curls around his finger, pulling hard enough that her scalp protested. "Okay."

She smiled, looking at their hair together. The contrast of her black strands and his deep blond were intriguing. They looked right together. Was that a romantic thought? She liked him. She really enjoyed having sex with him. Maybe this was romance. They were lovers now. Did that mean they were dating?

If so, it would be temporary since he planned to sacrifice himself for his brother. "I like you," she said quietly.

His eyes softened. "I like you too." He blinked. "Huh. I really mean that." His expression turned thoughtful. "Haven't actually felt anything in a little while."

Her entire being lit up from within, just like one of those silly girls back in high school. Was this really what a first crush felt like? She'd liked past boyfriends, and she'd enjoyed spending time with them. But she'd never experienced this rush of heat and wildness. The feeling that she could do anything—that the laws of the universe wouldn't hold her back. For now, she'd just try to be honest with him. "I appreciate your taking me back to school today." She couldn't get an Uber so far out of town.

He caressed down her spine to her butt, his hand warm and firm. "No problem. The sun is out, so we won't have any problems from the Kurjans. But it's your last day of teaching for a while."

His tone ignited an awareness within her. She blinked. "Agreed. I already said I wanted to start working on the equations for teleporting." In fact, she wouldn't be able to stop herself. "But that's my decision. You understand that, correct?"

He studied her, losing the lazy contentment he'd exhibited all morning. "It's a good decision."

Tension ticked along her arms. "I think we should be sure we understand each other."

"I think we do," he said lightly.

"I'm uncertain," she said, her knees falling on either side of his hard hips. They were still naked, and desire began to pulse between her legs, right where he was hardening. Her mind fuzzed, and she quickly marshaled her thoughts. "The reason I'm taking leave is because it's the right thing to do."

"I totally agree." His flattened hand pressed her down onto him.

Her eyes nearly rolled back in her head. "Wait." She scrolled through correct phrases, even though electricity was arcing through her body. "I enjoyed last night. The male dominance you exhibited during foreplay and sex."

His grin was quick.

Heat infused her face. "But that was during sex. A sense of role-playing, if you will."

"I wasn't exhibiting anything." He rolled them over, his hard body bracketing hers. Heat flashed along her nerves as he settled against her. "I showed you exactly who I am." He slowly began to penetrate her.

She lifted her knees to give him better access and slid her hands around his ribs to that hard shield protecting his back. The subject was important, but she was experiencing difficulty retaining her line of thought. "I'm not following your reasoning," she said, her body on fire.

"Let me help you." He kissed her, forcing arousal through her blood like a heavy drug. "If you don't like being dominated, then you're going to want to revisit your thoughts on mating me." With that, he grasped her hips for leverage and pulled out to push back in, his speed and depth increasing.

She grabbed his biceps, her head going back on the pillow. Pleasure swamped her. Mini-explosions rocked through her, and she moaned. She'd solve the problem later.

Chapter Twenty

Ivar ignored the itch between his shoulder blades that urged him to grab Promise and drag her back to the campground. She stood in front of her classroom, gathering her papers and reading over her notes. Students filed in carrying laptops and backpacks. The room was stacked with desks stepped down on different levels to her big table in front of a few chalkboards. She greeted students as they sat, her smile easy and light. In her black jeans, pink shirt, and blazer, she looked approachable and knowledgeable.

He knew what lurked beneath that clothing. A sexy and energetic woman with smooth skin and soft moans. His arms still bore a couple of scratch marks from her, and he purposely hadn't let them heal yet. He liked wearing her mark.

"South entrance is clear," Adare said through their earbuds.

"Affirmative," he said quietly, scouting the quiet hallway. Most of the students had taken seats. "Benny?"

"Man, some of these professors are hot," Benny said through the comm lines. "The east entrance is clear, and I'm liking the food in the teacher's lounge. There's a volleyball coach here from Brazil with legs up to her ears. Think she'd like a big bastard from Chicago?"

Ivar tried to hold on to his temper. "You're not from Chicago."

"She doesn't know that," Benny said reasonably. "For her? I could be from Chicago."

Ivar's attention returned to the pretty professor. She had started lecturing, and even her equations on the chalkboard looked elegant and sexy. Man, he had it bad. She turned when a student asked a question and then answered, striding gracefully to the next chalkboard to draw out another solution before turning back to the student.

She looked up, and her gaze caught Ivar's. She stumbled, looked around, and then moved for her notes. His chest filled. Damn if that didn't feel good. He got her out of her head—even if it was for just a second.

A bunch of students exited a classroom down the hallway, talking boisterously about films they'd produced.

A student in Promise's class stood and shut the door. Ivar straightened, his gaze on the closed door. If he went inside, he'd disrupt class. There was no question he wasn't a student. He looked down at his cargo pants and black shirt, which nicely hid his knives and even a gun. Yeah, it was illegal to have weapons on a college campus, but it wasn't like security was prepared for the Kurjans.

Not that the Kurjans could go outside on such a sunny day. He began to patrol the hallway again, checking out the exits and any shady areas—just to make sure. But he stayed within earshot in case Promise set up an alarm.

Benny came through the earbuds next. "I'm on the lawn outside—lots of trees but I don't see a path from the parking lot that would be in shade." He whistled. "By the way, you looked awfully relaxed today, Viking. You and the professor play naughty schoolgirl last night?"

Ivar's retort strangled in his throat. How in the hell should he answer that? "Shut up," he muttered.

Benny chuckled. "I thought so. Her gait was loose today too. Haven't seen the professor so relaxed before."

Ivar's fingers closed into a fist. If Benny were near, he'd break his nose.

Benny cleared his throat. "Don't get your panties in a twist. It's just nice to see you happy. Or at least, not bone-crushing angry and defeated. You deserve some good times, Viking. You really do."

Geez. Just as Ivar was planning to bring Benny's cabin down on him during the night, the guy had to go and say something nice. "Thanks." It was more difficult being calm than planning death, but he owed his brothers, and he could try. "I do like her."

"Would you two stop acting like little girls in high school?" Adare growled through the comms. "I swear. If you start talking about flowers and kisses and shit, I'm going to puke."

Benny chuckled, the low tone echoing loudly through the earbuds. "You have a mate, Highlander. It's your own damn fault you don't make her yours."

Ivar pinched the bridge of his nose. Sometimes he missed the solitude of hell.

The door to Promise's classroom burst open, and she ran outside. He drew his gun and ran toward her. His heart thumped and then nearly stopped as he grabbed her arm and pulled her behind him. "What? Do we have a breach?" He snapped. "What's happened?" She was safe. He looked rapidly around and edged toward the door to find students staring at him, their mouths open.

Promise grasped his arms and pulled him around. "Your head. The other day. You said that you were relearning to teleport and after you went through the car, you can't." She panted out air, her hair escaping its braid.

Benny ran full bore from the east, while a second later, Adare came barreling from the opposite direction. Both had guns out, and Benny held a knife in his free hand. Their boots made loud bangs on the tile floor, and their gazes took in everything. Watching each other's backs and his at the same time.

Ivar clutched Promise's arms and gave her a little shake. "Are you in danger?" Where was the enemy? He wasn't sensing anything.

She shook her head, her mouth forming a small O. "No." She coughed. "Not at all. No danger."

His brothers reached him. "No danger," he said. "False alarm."

Adare immediately tucked his weapon out of sight, his gaze still scouting the area for threats. Benny dropped his hands, still holding weapons. "Really? There's nobody to fight?" He kicked at a small pebble on the tile. "Are you sure?" He craned his neck to look into the classroom.

"Benny," Ivar growled, heat trickling up his neck.

Benny sighed and hid his weapons on his body. "Geez." He looked down, way down, at Promise. "What's going on?"

She held a hand to her chest. "All right. Two theories hit me at once, and I had to tell you." Her eyes lit up like it was Christmas and she was ten years old. Her words came out in a rush. "Demons can teleport anywhere on earth."

Ivar winced. "Lower your voice, Professor."

She nodded. "Oh. Yes. I forgot," she whispered. "Like I said, demons anywhere on earth. But fairies, or rather, the Fae, can go other places outside of here." She frowned and stepped back, her head turning slightly. "Wait a minute, the Seven have an unusual out-of-body experience during the ritual." She tapped her finger against her lips. "That would fit too," she mused, going silent and staring at the wall.

Adare sent Ivar a look. "What's wrong with her?" he mouthed.

Ivar shrugged. "Missy? Sweetheart?"

The nickname brought her back to the present. "Oh yeah. Okay." Her face flushed, and she seized his thumbs, lightly shaking. "We've been assuming everyone has the same ability, just used differently." She shook her head, and more dark hair escaped her braid. "What if it isn't? I mean, what if the ability is different in the two species?" She leaned up, drawing him closer. "What if it's controlled in the brain? I mean, everything is controlled in the brain. You want to move your arm, your brain tells the muscles to move your arm."

Benny looked through the open door of the classroom. "Doc? Are all of those students in their twenties? Or do you have a mom or two going back to college?" He angled his neck to see better. "Any forty-year-olds?"

Ivar shoved him in the arm. "Go back and patrol the east side."

Benny huffed but turned and jogged back the way he came.

Adare drew closer. "What are you saying?"

She exhaled. "I'm saying that we need MRIs. Need to see what part of the brain lights up when a being teleports." She flattened her hand over Ivar's heart. "What if you injured that part of your brain? Maybe you don't even know it's hurt." Her eyes prominently glowed. "Faith Cooper is a renowned neurologist. She will have better theories than I do."

Ivar's chest filled with something warm and soothing. Was it pride? Or just affection? Maybe both. "You're saying I had a brain injury that was healing on its own, and when I flew through your windshield, I reinjured myself?"

She rolled her eyes. "I am sorry I slammed on the brakes and you crashed through glass. All right? Are you happy now?"

He grinned. "Yeah." Was she correct? "Though I may have a brain injury."

She shook her head. "Don't you see? If you discover the injury, you can heal it the same way you did the cut over your eye or the broken arm." She straightened. "How did you do that, by the way?"

"Healing cells," Adare said, his gaze thoughtful on Promise. "We all have them, and we can direct them mentally to where they need to go." He turned and leaned in, right over Promise, to look into Ivar's eyes. "Does your brain feel damaged?"

Ivar swallowed. "I don't know." Sometimes he barely remembered what it felt like to be healthy. To be complete and whole. "It might be." He tried to concentrate on his brain and any empty spots, but his temples began to ache.

"The MRI is probably the way to go. If I can see where your brain lights up when you teleport, maybe I'll know where to concentrate the cells." Promise gave a slight hop. "Isn't this exciting?"

Ivar nodded, more than a little entranced. He had to find more puzzles for her to solve so he could see that look on her face again. He sobered. Solving the next puzzle would send him back to hell, but he'd made peace with that a long time ago. It was just as well.

He was playing at being a nice guy, at being a soldier. The real him, the animal he kept inside, would just scare her. Their time was limited, but he wanted to enjoy her while he could.

Her eyes widened, and she slowly turned to look through the doorway of her classroom. "Cripes. I forgot I was in class." Red slid beneath her smooth skin, and she moved back toward the doorway. "I'll be out in an hour." She shut the door after reentering the class.

Adare exhaled. "Man, she's smart. Absentminded professor smart."

"I noticed," Ivar said dryly.

Adare looked him over. "You're calmer with her. More natural."

"I'm faking it," Ivar said. "I'm being who she needs me to be right now as she works on the problems. And I want her to like me." There was no shame in being honest with his brother.

"You don't think she'd like the real you?"

Ivar snorted. "The pissed-off, damaged, brutal soldier who not only lived through hells but became the most dangerous thing in them? No. I don't think the sweet and brilliant Dr. Promise Williams would like that beast."

Adare scratched his whiskered jaw. "You're probably right." He shrugged and moved to return to his post. "Although, who the hell knows. Women are hard to read sometimes."

Amen to that.

Chapter Twenty-One

It was odd having a bodyguard. Especially one so sexy that several of her students followed her to her office after class, trying to engage Ivar in conversation. Promise couldn't blame them. His size alone made him intriguing. Add in the badass masculinity, unreal blue eyes, and hard-cut features, and he was the epitome of the alpha male. For the first time in her life, she understood the appeal.

Heck. She'd orgasmed four times the night before. Four times! That was more than appeal.

They reached her office, and she pulled him inside, shutting the door and accidentally pushing back a stack of notebooks with the edge of her pump. "Stop flirting with coeds."

His eyebrows rose. "Flirting? I was trying to keep from stepping on a couple of them."

Amusement tickled her, and she smiled. "That's fair." She moved aside a couple of articles she'd written on protecting the ozone layer.

"Hey, Promise?" Mark Brookes opened her door and poked his head inside, his eyes widening at the sight of Ivar. He pushed the door all the way open. "Hello." His shoulders went back, and he adopted his "lecturing" voice. "Dr. Mark Brookes." He held out a hand.

Now only one of Ivar's eyebrows lifted, and it was more of a twitch. "Hello," he said smoothly, shaking hands. He towered over the professor by at least six inches, and Mark was tall. Well, for a human. "Do you always barge in?"

Mark pulled his hand free, and Ivar let him. "Promise and I go way back."

Pinpricks danced along Promise's spine. What was happening? Tension filtered through the room, and she pondered the puzzle, finally reaching a conclusion. They were posturing? Over her? She leaned back against the crammed bookshelf to watch. This was new.

Ivar smiled, and the sight was a threat. "Well, Missy and I are enjoying the present."

Red flushed through Mark's face. "Missy?"

Ivar lifted a shoulder. "Nickname. Just mine. You can't use it."

All right. This was quickly descending into something that would destroy the organized chaos in her office and probably result in Mark enduring broken bones. Promise pushed off the bookshelf. "Mark? Don't you have a class to teach?"

The math professor looked at his watch and then straightened. "Yes. I was just popping by to tell you I could cover your supersymmetry class for the rest of the semester, since we don't have grad students advanced enough to do so." He smiled at Ivar. "I read her sabbatical request in the office."

"I helped her compose it," Ivar returned.

Oh, for Pete's sake. Promise fought a laugh and made herself nod. "That's wonderful. Thank you, Mark."

He hesitated. "I understand that you need to take some time off." He eyed Ivar. "For personal reasons."

Ivar growled, and Promise jumped, looking toward him. He looked back with a guileless expression on his hard-cut face. "What?" he asked.

Had she imagined the noise? Maybe. "I'm healing from the car crash and working on a theory for that grant," she said. "It's got me, and I want to work the problem all the time. I'm sure you understand."

Mark looked Ivar up and down. "I understand the math problem."

Ivar took a step toward him. "Perhaps I can help you understand the personal issue."

Promise held up a hand. "Mark? I appreciate your help with the class, and I'll make sure to keep you appraised of my work on the theory." She used her crispest voice, and it was a clear dismissal.

Mark paused and then nodded, disappearing back out into the hallway.

Promise crossed her arms and stared at Ivar.

"What?" he asked, his rugged face the perfect picture of innocence.

Why did she feel so good? Almost delighted at the moment? She'd have to explore that later. "It's going to take me an hour or so to get organized, and you're way too distracting. Any chance you can patrol the hallway without causing gaggles of girls to follow you?" Most were in class right now, anyway.

His smile was more than mildly arrogant. "Distracting, huh?" He pulled her close for a hard and what felt like possessive kiss. "Okay." Then he was gone, smoothly shutting the door behind him.

Her lips tingled along with the rest of her body. From one kiss. A proprietal one. At least, that's how she'd qualify it. The only way to know would be to ask what he was feeling when he had kissed her, and she'd learned early on that most people didn't like to be questioned about their feelings. Ivar might be different, but she didn't want to make him uncomfortable right when they'd become lovers.

She'd really like to engage in sex with him again. He was superb at it, and she'd never felt like that before. Ever.

She shook her head to regain control of herself and then moved to one of the file cabinets, where she thought she'd left a partially used notebook on a theory seeking evidence of a higher dimension. She had set it aside months ago to follow new math on Standard

Model observables. Ah. There it was. She took it out and then considered what else she'd need for the next month or so. Or longer.

Her office was a mess. Well, she knew where everything had been placed, but the piles of books, papers, and notebooks might amount to a fire hazard. She should probably organize it a mite more before leaving on sabbatical.

The cast-iron vent in the ceiling opened, and a tall male body dropped down in one smooth motion. Papers and a couple of notebooks scattered across the floor.

She blinked. Shock kept her immobile for about a second, and then she opened her mouth to scream for Ivar.

"Don't scream." The man pulled a gun from the back of his waist. A green gun.

Her breath stopped. She swallowed.

The man had long black hair tipped with red, deep green eyes, and pale skin. No way was he human. He stood to at least six seven, and he held the gun casually, slightly pointed away from her. "I just want to talk."

She held the notebook to her chest. The desk was between them, but that wouldn't stop a bullet. "Then you shouldn't have a gun pointed at me," she said, her voice shaking.

"It's not pointed at you." He smiled, revealing smooth white teeth.

She'd expected fangs. Not sure why. She tilted her head. "Who are you?" If Ivar came crashing in the door, he'd get shot. And that green gun was one of those laser-spurting immortal guns.

His smile smoothed out. "My name is Dayne, and I'm the leader of the Kurjan nation." When she didn't panic or scream her head off, he continued. "Honestly, I just want to talk to you. I'll leave as soon as you've heard me out. I waited to come near your office because I didn't want the hybrid to sense me. It was uncomfortable in that vent system."

She looked toward the sunny fall day outside, her stomach cramping painfully. Sweat broke out on her hands. "I thought the sun killed you."

"It does. Hence the trip through your ancient and rather dusty ventilation system." He wiped off his dusty gray button-down shirt, which was tucked into black jeans over large boots. Very large. "Wouldn't you like to understand the composition of our skin, of our muscles, even our bones, that makes them susceptible to the sun?"

"I would very much," she admitted. "But last time I checked, you people were tearing apart physicists." Her heart beat so fast it hurt to breathe.

He rolled his eyes. "That wasn't us. Why do the damn vampires blame us for everything?" He shook his head. "They have a wolf in the sheep pen, and they're blaming us." He lowered the gun even more. "I swear, it's hard being everyone's villain. Day in and day out. I should grow a mustache."

Promise lifted one eyebrow. "I should tell you that not once in my life have I found anybody charming."

He straightened and drew back a bit, his face classically angled. "Really?"

"Yes."

"Huh." He looked around the messy office, his voice low and light. "That's unfortunate. Charm is my strong suit."

She tilted her head, her body on alert in case she needed to flee. "It still isn't working."

His gaze sharpened, and he looked at her fully. "You are smart. I like that."

"What do you want, Dayne?" she asked, edging toward the open window to stand full in the sunlight. It heated her, providing a slight sense of protection.

He watched her move, waiting until she had found a spot before continuing. "I'm asking you to use logic and not emotion. Ulric is the leader of our Cyst sect, which is our religious arm. They're monks who look creepy." He spread out his hands. "A thousand years ago, the Seven decided Ulric was becoming too powerful, and they imprisoned him in a hell dimension far away."

She huffed. "Nobody is in a dimension. A dimension is not a place. Ulric is at a point somewhere in this universe or another universe. I assume in this time, but who knows if time was warped. But he is not in a dimension."

Dayne shook his head. "Why did we ever give humans that word? We used it long before you did. I've heard rumor it's Einstein's fault."

She swallowed. The conversation was getting odd. "You should leave."

He sobered. "We want your help to get him out so he can be safe again. Sooner rather than later."

"I've seen your Cyst at work," she returned softly. "They're soldiers, not monks."

Dayne lifted his chin. "If you've studied religion at all through the centuries, often soldiers and monks are one and the same. He didn't do anything wrong, but the Seven passed judgment all on their own. No trial, no defense, just imprisonment in hell. His bubble is going to break anyway, and we'd like to make sure he survives the event. Please help us."

She steeled her shoulders. "Did you kill Dr. Rashad?"

"No." Dayne kept the weapon pointed at the floor. "I'm telling you, it's a different faction. Not Kurjans. Somebody within the vampire world, within the Realm, who doesn't want the bubbles to burst. They don't want Quade Kayrs back on earth any more than they do Ulric. Having the Seven in one place represents too much power. This world, the one you're still trying to figure out, will implode from it. Gone. All of us." He shrugged. "Except fairies. They can go elsewhere. At the end, the crazy fairies will survive."

"Fae," Promise said automatically.

Dayne smiled again. "I'm just a single dad trying to save the world. Please help me."

The guy really did have the charm down. "You're a dad."

He tugged a worn wallet from his back pocket and flipped it open, holding up a picture of a cute kid with really green eyes.

The kid looked more human than his dad. "His name is Drake. Named after a relative. He's visiting family close by right now."

"Where's his mother?" Promise asked.

Dayne shook his head. "She didn't survive the last war." He swallowed, his throat moving as he put the wallet back in place. "Please just tell me you'll consider what I've said."

"I already have." She backed up until she all but sat on the sunny windowsill. "Ivar!" she screamed. "Help!"

Chapter Twenty-Two

Ivar tore into Promise's office, smashing the door into the back of something solid. He kicked it open, and a bookcase fell over with a loud crash. The second his gaze landed on his woman, his heart stopped trying to burst out of his ribs. Fury caught him, and he tried to banish emotion for the first time in months. His blood felt like it was about to boil. "You okay?"

She sat on the windowsill, clutching a notebook to her chest. "He shoved the bookcase in front of the door with one hand," she said, her eyes wide. "Just one hand. Like it weighed nothing, and his movement was too fast for me to see. The guy was just a blur. Then he jumped."

Ivar looked frantically around, his gaze catching on an open grate in the ceiling. "Who?"

"Dayne. Kurjan leader. He's—"

Before she could finish, Ivar was already in motion, leaping up and yanking himself into the opening. His shoulders were too wide, and he crashed through the adjacent ceiling tiles, sending them spiraling down. The metal cut into his hands as he held himself aloft. "All alert. We've got a Kurjan in the ducts," he said into his comms, looking one way and then the other down the empty tubes. What the fuck? He couldn't leave Promise unguarded, and the ducts probably wouldn't take his weight. He'd end up falling into a classroom and probably killing whoever he landed on. Even though Kurjans were tall, they weren't as large as hybrids. The need to chase the bastard was a physical burn through his blood.

He dropped back down, his boots cracking more tiles on the ground. "The ducts are different than on the blueprints," he said, taking in Promise from head to toe. She appeared unharmed. The need to touch her, to pull her close, shocked him.

"Renovations in the fifties, I think," she said. Her eyes widened. "There are tunnels from even before that time—from the first incarnation of the school. As undergrads, we'd go down there and diagram equations on the walls. There are some famous ones there." She pushed off the windowsill and dropped her notebook. "I'll show you."

He grabbed her hand and ran into the hallway, grateful it was empty during the class hour. Her touch calmed him so he could plan. The rest of the team had to move and now. "We have a rabbit," he said into the comms. "Head north and down."

She struggled to keep up as they ran through the halls to the north entrance, her breath panting. "Slow down. Keep going to the end of this hallway, and there's a boiler room down a couple of flights. It's a way into the tunnels that the students don't know about. Only faculty. As students, we went to the edge of the campus to enter in order to follow the tunnels. They go in many directions."

"Where?" he growled, slowing down enough that she didn't trip. "Where did you enter them?"

"Beyond the parking area by the east side of campus. It's by what's now the water reclamation facility," she gasped, partially bending over as they reached a locked door that was just opposite the double doors leading out to a courtyard.

"Tunnel entry at east end—forget the north," he barked into the comms. "Get there, now." He put his boot to the door, springing the old metal open to slam into the wall. Narrow cement steps, dirty and marred by oil, led down into darkness. He had to get her to safety before he followed the enemy. She was all that mattered. "Go outside into the sun and stay there. Right in the middle of the lawn and away from any trees."

"I can lead you down," she said, angling her head to look beyond him.

Energy signatures wafted up, and his gut settled. His hackles rose, and his muscles elongated. "There are too many soldiers down there." He could feel them. Dayne hadn't come alone, which made sense, because he was the fucking leader of all the Kurjans. And he'd been in Promise's office, alone with her. He could've done anything to her. Rage filled Ivar, but he shoved it away as fast as he could. "Missy?" He used the nickname on purpose. "Get your ass into the sunlight."

She huffed. "You might need help finding your way."

"I can sense them. At least four of them, maybe more." His thigh muscles bunched with the need to run down there. To fight and attack. "Get outside."

"Four of them? You can't take four of them by yourself." She pulled on his arm. "The tunnels go in a lot of directions, and you might be walking into a trap. Get backup first. Even I know that."

He shook his head. "Four is nothing. Now do as I say."

She turned toward the outside, hesitating. "Dayne showed me a picture of his child. A cute boy."

"He talked to you? For how long?" Ivar hadn't been doing his job if the enemy had time to freaking have a discussion with her.

She shrugged, the color finally returning to her pretty face. "I don't know. Ten minutes? He said there's a rogue vampire killing physicists. Asked for my help."

And yet she'd yelled for *him*. Good. She trusted him. "Go." Ivar pushed her not so gently toward the outside door.

"He's a single dad. Maybe you shouldn't kill him," she muttered, finally following his command and walking toward the door. The second sunlight filtered over her, he finally breathed easier. A little. Not much.

Oh, if he got his hands on Dayne, he'd rip the Kurjan's head right off. "I have no doubt his kid is just as dangerous as he is— if not more." With that, Ivar turned and leaped down the stairs, taking five at a time. He hoped to God there were soldiers to fight at the bottom.

He really needed to punch somebody.

* * * *

He hadn't gotten to hit anybody. Hours later, after having extensively searched the tunnels, Ivar reined in his temper, absently noting that it was alive and wanted to blow. One night with the sexy professor, and he was feeling again. He wasn't sure that was a good thing. "You okay?" he asked.

"Yes. Ronan can't teleport, so he doesn't make my head hurt. And Benny did at first, but not as badly as last time. I think I have it under control now." She smiled. "My head doesn't ache at all." She leaned against him in the backseat of the SUV while Ronan drove with Benny in the passenger seat. Adare drove a Harley up ahead, scouting the way back to the campground before circling around and making sure they weren't followed.

Nighttime was starting to fall, and the sun had disappeared, leaving a definite chill. A promise that winter was soon coming.

Ivar set his head back and closed his eyes, breathing deeply. The Kurjans had been familiar with the tunnels beneath the college and had escaped easily. How long had they been studying the facility? The idea that they'd been close to Promise for a while sent bile up his throat. He needed his peanuts. His fangs dropped, and he forced them back into place before she could notice. "Tell me everything Dayne said to you." His voice was a low growl.

She sighed, grabbed his arm, and shifted her weight to straddle him.

His eyelids opened fast, and he jerked. "What in the hell are you doing?" Benny and Ronan were in the front seat, for Pete's sake. Nobody caught him off guard—except this intellectual professor.

"Trying to get you to calm down and focus on something other than the fight you just missed." With dusk falling outside, her eyes were a light bourbon color inside the vehicle.

Ivar angled to the side to find both of his brothers staring straight ahead. Benny's mouth twitched almost in a smile, but irritated lines cut along the sides of Ronan's mouth. He hated missing a good fight as well. The road remained clear ahead, and Adare zoomed by once again, scouting in every direction. Well. If she didn't mind their audience, neither would he. Ivar planted his hands on her hips and pulled her even closer. "I'm not thinking about my missed fight any longer." His cock pulsed in his cargo pants.

"Well." She tried to lean back. "There's no call to get fresh."

Had she said *fresh*? Cute. Very cute. He tightened his hold, keeping her exactly where she'd put herself. "All right. Now you can tell me again. Go over every word, every movement, everything you thought or felt."

She rolled her eyes, along with her hips. "Fine."

Was she flirting with him? He narrowed his gaze. An impish smile played on her mouth. For the first time since discovering a Kurjan had talked with her, his muscles loosened from rock hard to just tense. "Missy," he murmured.

Pretty color flowed into her face. "All right." She went over the entire encounter again, stressing Dayne's insistence that he wouldn't hurt her and just wanted peace. And that she thought his child appeared precocious.

Ivar listened intently, trying to figure out Dayne's plan. There was something missing, but he couldn't put his finger on it. Even so, he ran through the entire episode in his head. The Kurjan wouldn't have been able to get her out of the building, not if he'd tried to drag her up into the ducts. So what? He'd tried to sow discontent? Set it up so she felt safe speaking to him again if there was an opportunity? Wait a minute. "If he didn't hurt you, and you weren't scared, why did you call for help? For me?" Ivar asked.

She slid her hands over his shoulders. "Well, you said he's a bad guy, and I decided to trust you. Not him." Her eyes were clear and her expression earnest.

His mouth opened and then shut. Warmth infused him, all through his bonded torso, sliding around what should be his heart.

She'd trusted him. Even when not in danger, talking to a guy who'd tried to charm her with a picture of his child, she'd yelled for Ivar.

Loudly.

"I like her," Benny whispered to Ronan. "A whole shitload of a lot."

Ivar grinned. Yeah. He liked her too.

They reached the campground, relatively sure they hadn't been followed. He helped her out of the vehicle so Ronan could camouflage it beneath the trees and then took her hand and led her to a cabin closer to the river than theirs.

"Where are we going?" she asked, stepping gingerly over upturned roots and still damp weeds.

He'd thought to get her flowers or something after their night together, but then he'd had another idea. One he'd had Grace and Faith work out for him. He led her to the cabin and opened the door, flicking on the light. "Benny will bring in all of your file boxes and notebooks from your office."

She walked inside, her gasp one of pure delight. Five whiteboards were stacked against the side wall, in front of a wide table. New markers and thick erasers were lined up neatly on the table next to pens, yellow legal pads, and a stapler. "Oh, Ivar," she murmured.

Most women made that sound at being given diamonds. Or property. Not her. No. Markers and whiteboards made joy roll off her like heat.

She turned and jumped for him, her lips smashing against his. "Thank you, thank you, thank you." She held him tight. "I love it. This is the best." She dropped back to the floor and turned to grab a marker, running to the nearest board and quickly drafting a problem that held a hint of Einstein in it. "I've been thinking." She kept scribbling. "We need to get Adare and then Mercy in here as soon as possible. I want to teleport—and I need to interview them. As much as I can."

He wanted to start slow, to keep her from experiencing any pain. "All right, but first, let's eat something and get some sleep. We can work tomorrow." And maybe he wanted to protect himself.

To let himself live for a short period with her, enjoying everything about her. But that wouldn't do.

There wasn't time.

He cleared his throat. "Promise? Did Dayne say where his kid was?" He wasn't sure why he asked the question.

"No." She kept her gaze on the board. "Just said he was visiting family. Does that mean something?"

Ivar rubbed a bruise across his wrist. "I'm not sure." Probably not. So why was his neck tight?

Chapter Twenty-Three

Hope Kayrs-Kyllwood finished tucking her dress in the backpack along with Libby's. They'd changed into jeans and sweaters after telling their parents they were going to walk around the subdivision in their party dresses like princesses. Nobody would suspect a princess of riding her bike to town.

Paxton shook his head, leaning back against the pine tree. "We can't do this. Your parents will kill us. Or at least, my dad will kill me." He didn't sound like he was kidding. Not even a little.

They were beside the shoreline of the lake, and Hope tugged her bike away from the stairs. "All we hafta do is walk the bikes to the boat launch, and we can ride to town from there." The small town was only a couple of miles away, and she knew the patrol schedules, so it should be easy to avoid the guards.

Pax grabbed his bigger bike, already following her with Libby next to him. "We have missiles, land mines, and a bunch of other stuff that protect headquarters. You're gonna get us blown up."

She snorted. "We're gonna stay right off the road on the trail, Pax. Geez." Yeah, there were probably land mines there too, but they weren't armed. It was too dangerous. Somebody had to flip a switch in the main control room, and nobody was gonna flip a switch without lots of warning or an attack. Why did Pax worry so much?

Vampire and demon headquarters were located about a mile apart on a very cool lake in Idaho, and she went in the opposite direction from both. If any patrolling soldiers saw them, they'd be stopped.

Good thing no one expected them to ride to town by themselves. She was almost eight years old, and everyone still thought she was a baby. For today, that was a good thing.

So long as they didn't get caught.

They kept their heads down and slid between trees until they hit the trail alongside the road. She felt tough as she jumped on her bike and started riding, letting the fall breeze behind her push her along. Libby scouted up ahead, as usual, unable to ride slowly. Pax stayed right behind Hope, his worry smelling like lemons in the fall.

Why didn't he understand?

Hope's mama and daddy had met in a dreamworld, and one day they'd saved everybody. Then they got mated and had Hope. While she never wanted to mate anybody—like, gross—she wanted to be Drake's friend, and they met often in a dreamworld. The dreamworld was there for a reason, and not just to hold a special green book that she knew was hers, somehow. It was her job and Drake's job to find peace for the Realm and the Kurjans. That mattered. It was why she was a prophet. Well, probably. Maybe it was just one of the reasons.

The trail slanted down, and she could ride faster. The wind burst through her hair, and she laughed, having fun. It felt good to sneak to town. That was probably bad.

They entered town along the lakeside, away from traffic, and rode to the park in the middle. It had swing sets, teeter-totters, and a whole wooden jungle gym. She ditched her bike and climbed the stairs, using the rope. This was where she had told Drake to meet her.

She got to the top, which was covered by a thatched roof and should be safe for her friend. A building with an overhang for bathrooms and picnic stuff bridged the space to the parking lot, so she knew he'd be safe from the sun if he came that way. She gulped in air and looked around. Tunnels, yellow and big, spread out in both directions, going to slides and other climbing areas. Had he gotten confused?

Libby leaped on top of the nearest one and perched there just like a cat. How did she do that? Paxton, his bluish silver eyes dark, leaned against a railing and glared. When he got cranky, there was no talking him out of it. "We should go," he muttered, the wind lifting his black hair.

"Hi." Drake pushed himself out of the nearest yellow tube and stood. He dusted off his jeans. His black hair was long and straight, and his eyes were even greener than in the dreamworld. His face was paler too. He stayed safely out of the sun.

Hope couldn't speak for a minute. She was standing there, in real life, with Drake the Kurjan. The future leader of the Kurjans and the boy Pax wanted to punch. She looked wildly around, but there were no grown-ups close. And she didn't sense any other power in the wind, which she usually could. They were alone. At least for now. Her hand shook, but she held it out. "Hi."

He took her hand, shaking gently with his much larger one. His skin was cool but not cold like she'd expected. "Are you going to get in trouble for being here?" he asked, his eyes almost a human green except for the thick gold band around the green part.

"Only if we get caught." She tried to sound brave. In the dreamworlds, she hadn't noticed the gold band or the light strands of red through his black hair. Barely there, but they were super neat. "What about you?"

He nodded, his eyes widening. "Yeah. I was with family on a farm, an actual farm, and I borrowed a truck."

She gasped. "You drove?"

He shrugged. "I just moved the seat closer to the steering wheel. I'm eight now, you know. And I'm tall."

Way tall. Even taller than Libby. Hope looked at Pax. "That's Pax—he's gonna be nine—and that's Libby. She just turned eight." She pointed to the feline shifter.

Libby waved, her eyes wide, her face so pale her freckles stood out. Pax just lifted his head and didn't change his face. He sure didn't smile. Instead, he kind of looked like every mad vampire Hope had ever seen. "They're not sure about this," Hope said.

"Me either," Drake said. "We could get in so much trouble."

Pax edged closer. "This much sun doesn't bother you?"

Drake stayed beneath the awning. "No. In fact, I can step in the sun for a few seconds without getting hurt. Some other kids my age can also. It's called velution."

"Evolution," Libby whispered from her perch.

Drake shrugged. "That does sound better."

Hope smiled. He was just as nice in real life as she'd hoped he would be. "It's awesome we could meet." What else should she say? "I want us all to find a way for the grown-ups to stop fighting."

Pax moved closer until his elbow touched hers.

Drake watched him, and a small smile curved his red lips. A look passed between the boys, a weird one that didn't make any sense. Hope wasn't even sure they knew what they were fighting about. Or why they didn't like each other. If they got to know each other, they'd probably be friends. In fact, they all had to be friends for her peace plan to work.

Pax jerked his head toward a black watch on Drake's wrist. "Is that a fitness tracker?"

"No. Just a watch." Drake leaned to look at Pax's wrist. "Do you have one of those?"

"Yeah," Pax said. "I took it off before we left the compound so nobody would follow us. How did you know where we were, Drake?"

Hope gave him a look. He sounded grouchy.

Drake laughed, and the sound was nice. "The world isn't that big, demon. Or vampire. Whichever you want to be called."

"Hybrid works for me," Pax muttered.

Drake nodded. "Okay. Everyone knows where Realm vampire and demon headquarters are now. Just like the witches are in

Ireland and Seattle, and the feline shifters in Montana. We all have defenses."

"Wow. You know a lot, Drake," Libby said.

"We have to study geography," he groaned. "It's so boring. I like art class better."

Drake could draw? Hope smiled. Maybe he'd give her a picture someday. "I like art too."

Pax snorted. Okay. She couldn't draw good at all. But it was still fun.

Drake's chest puffed out. "Lately I've studied your Seven. The guys who want to blow up the world?"

Pax gave Hope a look. The Seven were a secret, and she only knew about them 'cause Fate told her in dreams. She'd told Pax and Libby. "Nuh-uh," Hope said, her face getting hot. Two of her uncles were on the Seven, Garrett and Logan. "They're good. They want to keep a bad guy away."

"Ulric is not bad," Drake said, his fingers curling into a fist. "He was good, and they were wrong years ago. Don't you see that?"

"My uncles are good," she snapped. Pax slid kinda in front of her, and she shoved him to the side. Nobody ever needed to step in front of her.

Drake took a deep breath. "They might be good. But what they're doing is wrong."

Hope wanted to convince him, but what were the right words? She started to tell him, and then the whole world exploded.

Helicopters rushed above them, and black SUVs screeched to a halt outside the park.

"Shit," Pax said.

Hope gaped. Pax never said naughty words. Ever.

Drake's eyes widened, and he looked panicked, running to the yellow slide.

Soldiers dressed in full black gear dropped from the copters, their big boots slamming into the wood of the jungle gym. Hope's daddy was the first to reach her, and he scooped her up, climbing back into the helicopter so fast that she had to shut her eyes to keep from puking.

Seconds later, Libby and Pax were right next to her, and Drake was across from her. Vampire and demon soldiers crowded in, and they zoomed off.

Drake had gone stark pale, and he looked around.

"It's okay, Drake," Hope said, her voice shaking. Her entire body shivered.

Her daddy's green eyes had turned nearly black, and he looked super dangerous with his gun strapped to his thigh and his black hair tied back. He looked at the Kurjan boy. "Who are you?"

Drake's voice came out all funny. "Drake, son of Dayne, leaders of the Kurjans." His chin went up, and even though he seemed scared, he looked her daddy right in the eye.

"Ah, shit," Uncle Max said from the other side of Hope. He was her main bodyguard and the bestest Gold Fish player in the universe. He looked kinda mean, but he was always nice to Hope. "Just holy fuck."

Her daddy cut him a look and then stared back at Drake. "We won't hurt you. I want you to know that." Then he looked at Hope, Pax, and Libby. "We had no clue you could get to town like that. Not one clue. You three might've just started a new war. Welcome to your first international incident."

Chapter Twenty-Four

Ivar kept the scratch marks from a wild night with Promise on his shoulders all the next day, not wanting to use healing cells on them. He'd bitten her again, his fangs going deep. Her blood tasted like the finest of wines, and he found himself wanting to bite her throughout the day.

He'd never felt like that before. Sex with her was unique, and he was starting to crave more.

After suppertime, he leaned back at the fire, sitting next to Adare, who stared broodily at the flames. Mercy sat on his other side, all but bouncing next to him.

Promise had spent all day with her equations, and by dinnertime, every board was covered with them. Watching her work was the most fun Ivar had had in years. She'd asked them more questions than he could count about the Seven ritual and the other ritual that had bound Ulric, Ronan, and Quade in different worlds.

He'd interrupted her every hour so he and Benny could take turns messing with her brain, and she'd quickly learned how to block out the pain. Benny could teleport, but he sucked at it, so it had been easy for her to learn to block him. She needed to try with Adare and then finally with Mercy.

Ivar finished warning both of them not to hurt her. "You're up, Adare."

Adare remained sprawled in his chair. "If she can block Benny, she can block me. It's time to hit the ground running with Mercy."

What the hell? Ivar partially turned to look at his old friend. He'd gotten the Scottish bastard out of more scrapes than he could count. Now Adare was refusing to help? "What is going on with you?" Ivar asked.

Adare yanked his black hair back into a ponytail at the neck. "You don't need me." The bottom of his boots started smoking again. Instead of pulling them back, he watched the melting rubber with a dispassionate glare, his eyes somehow blacker than usual.

Ivar studied him. "What's going on?"

Adare hunched his shoulders. "Don't want to talk about it."

"That's unfortunate," Ivar said. "Explain now, or I'm tossing your ass in the fire."

Adare sighed. His chin went down. He turned toward Ivar, his expression tortured. "I'm drawn to her."

Ivar lifted his head. *Now* Adare wanted to take about his mate? Talk about crappy timing. "Well, all right. You're mated to the woman, so is it so bad to be drawn to her?" The guy was nuts.

Adare dropped his gaze. "Not Grace. I mean, I am drawn to Grace, but not like this."

Not his mate? Ivar took a second to comprehend. Wait a minute. "What? You're fucking kidding."

Mercy tensed next to him, looking past Ivar to Adare. "You're drawn to Promise?"

Adare nodded, looking more miserable than Ivar had ever seen him. "Yes. I'm sorry."

Mercy hopped in her chair. "I'm drawn to her too. Big-time."

Adare straightened. "What?"

Ivar pivoted toward her. "What?"

Mercy shrugged, her one blue eye bluer than usual. "Can't explain it. Whenever she's close by, I want to be there. At first, I figured I just wanted another friend or felt left out that I couldn't be in the room with her like Faith and Grace can. But it's more. I need to be close to her." She rubbed her nose. "Not in a stalkerish way or anything. It's like, I don't know. When you're thirsty and there's water nearby. Promise is the water."

Adare's face cleared. "Yeah. That's it. Exactly."

Ivar looked from one to the other. Then he spotted Benny loping their way after having gone for a run. Sweat ran down the huge vampire's face, pooling on his bare chest. "Hey. Do you feel drawn to Promise?"

Benny wiped his forehead off with one arm. "Shit, yeah. She's hot. Why? Does she want me?"

Jesus. Ivar barely kept his seat. "No, she doesn't want you. But do you feel a compunction to be near her? Like she's, I don't know, drawing you in some way?"

Benny exhaled and bent over, stretching his back. His gaze sobered. "Yes. Figured I was just being an asshole. Has it been obvious?"

"No." Ivar looked toward Ronan and Faith's cabin. He most likely knew the answer, but might as well confirm. "Hey, Ronan," he yelled, waiting until Ronan had walked outside, munching on what looked like a ham sandwich. "Are you drawn to Promise in any way?"

Ronan finished chewing and swallowed. "Huh?"

Yeah. That's what Ivar had figured. "So anybody who can teleport is drawn to her." He was drawn to her too, but he couldn't teleport. So he won. His attraction to Promise was not based on her enhancement. "All right." He chewed on the facts, reconsidering thoughts he'd earlier discarded. "If you're all drawn to her, maybe others have been too. Maybe those other headaches happened to her because demons or fairies were drawn temporarily to her in public?"

Adare exhaled, his entire body relaxing into the chair. "Thank God. I felt like such a dick." He grinned. "It's not attraction. It's something else." He lifted a hand. "Not that she's not attractive, because she is. Very pretty."

Ivar rolled his eyes. "Thanks."

Mercy tapped him on the arm. "Hey. So. Since she's a draw to us and can identify people able to teleport, and since you've lost your ability, do you think mating her would help you get it back faster?"

He wanted to pretend that the thought hadn't dawned on him. "I don't know. Mates usually acquire each other's abilities, so I'd gain hers, and yeah, that might strengthen mine." How could he consider mating a woman and leaving her as soon as possible? He'd already made a vow to Quade. He couldn't make an opposing one now. Except Promise had brought up the subject before he had.

Adare pulled his burning boots back finally. "If you mate her, she'll be able to shield her mind better."

How practical. Ivar ground his palm into his right eye to combat the tension headache attacking him. If he brought the subject up with Promise, she'd probably agree as a logical matter. She wanted immortality, and right now, she didn't care if she was alone for eternity.

But she was selling herself short. She was a woman who needed warmth, love, and protection. She just didn't know it.

* * * *

After a second morning of working on equations, Promise stood back and studied her latest model. This wasn't good. Not at all. Building from Einstein's theory of relativity, she'd been theorizing about dark matter and the effect time and gravity had on each other.

To give her brain a break, she looked over at the computer running searches of hell worlds and then snorted. A couple of posters for B movies scrolled across the screen followed by a series of books, including Clive Barker's. She let the screen computer continue its search. Just in case.

"Shield yourself, lady," Mercy chirped from outside.

Promise mentally tugged shields into place. "Come on in."

Mercy slipped inside, and pain boomeranged into Promise's head. She gasped, her eyes tearing, and imagined the shield growing. The pain lessened. Slightly.

"Um, all right. You're pale. Good try. We'll try again later." Mercy began to back out and paused, her gaze stopping on the computer conducting the searches. "What is that?"

Promise blinked water from her eyes and focused. "I'm searching human popular culture for anything on hell dimensions. That's a book." She squinted. "No. Painting. Wow. Several of them. Those are beautiful."

Mercy leaned to the side. "Modern art by Haven Daly."

Promise stepped closer to the screen to watch the stunning landscapes go by. There wasn't one she recognized. A couple looked alien. The woman must have a fantastic imagination. An image came into focus; this one much different than the others. She tilted her head, studying it.

"What is that?" Mercy whispered.

Promise bit her lip and squinted, barely able to discern the outline of a human brain camouflaged by trees and bushes that were unfamiliar to her. Waves cascaded out from the middle, darkening each level of forest until the final trees lay dead on the ground. "If I had to guess, that's some sort of brain attack." Oddly beautiful and ominous.

Mercy took a step back. "Um, yeah. That's what I see, too." Her lips looked bright pink against her pale skin.

"Everything okay?" The pressure against Promise's temples increased, and she winced. Shielding her brain wasn't easy.

"No." Mercy retreated for the doorway and took her phone from her back pocket. Her eyes were round and her mind obviously spinning.

Promise wanted to follow the woman, but her head was about to explode. "Are you all right?"

"Yep. Just have work to do." Mercy shut the door and disappeared from sight.

The pain stopped completely. Promise let out breath she hadn't realized she'd trapped inside her lungs. With one last look at the stunning oil paintings still sliding across her computer monitor, she returned to her equations.

After about an hour, heavy footsteps sounded on the stairs outside. The door slowly opened.

"It's about lunchtime, and I think Mercy is cooking. She was on the phone for an hour with her people and now seems like she's in a snit about something. So we might die by tomorrow anyway if we eat her cooking. How's it going?" Ivar stepped into the room, stress lines fanning out from his eyes. Even though the last two nights had been sensational, he appeared to be getting more and more cranky.

How could she tell him? She didn't even have a conclusion yet, and considering he'd been in a mood ever since she'd talked to Dayne, this probably wasn't the time. But the truth was the truth. "This will take years. For now, as far as we can tell, although Ronan's world burst, the other two have remained intact."

"Yes," Ivar said. "For now."

"Newton's first law of motion," she murmured, glancing down at the different marker colors all over her hand. She hadn't even noticed.

Ivar came up behind her, bringing warmth and an electricity that heated her skin. "Meaning what?"

"It's too early for me to say anything definitive," she said. "But since there hasn't been another event, we can assume the two remaining worlds have found a balance. Maybe with other worlds, perhaps in a void. There's no way to know."

He was quiet for a moment, but tension spiraled from him. "We will find out."

She bit her lip. "I want to tell you what you want to hear, but the math is going in a different direction." In other words, it'd be a mistake to try to affect Quade's world ever again. "I think when the Seven bound those three worlds together, they used gravity in a way that messed with time. Or vice versa. Or they used a

dimensional tool I can't even imagine yet and haven't discovered."
Her stomach cramped just like that time she'd brought home an
A-. "The composition of these created worlds now might end this
one." And many others.

He looked at the covered boards. "But you're postulating. I
mean, you don't know for sure, do you?"

"Newton on a cracker, not even close," she admitted easily.
"Like I said, problems like this take centuries and many different
minds to solve." She turned toward him so suddenly, his body
tensed. "I want centuries." She winced. That wasn't smooth at all.

His chin lifted, and his eyelids dropped to half-mast. "Now
isn't the time."

But the idea was in her head, so she had to push it. "It is the
time. Exactly the time."

His gaze hardened. "You want to mate."

She swallowed, deliberately ignoring the warning in his tone.
"Marriages of convenience are statistically stronger than those
founded on chemicals in the body. On love. I can't imagine that
matings would be any different." The memory of him biting her
the night before threatened her reasonable line of thought. Her
nipples hardened, and she glanced down to make sure her bra
was doing its job. It was.

"You don't understand." He stood his ground, but his gaze darted
to the doorway and back. His biceps bunched, and he shoved his
hands in the front pockets of his soldier cargo pants, as if to keep
them occupied.

"I do understand." She turned more fully toward him. When
the equation was solved, she wanted to be there. To protect the
world, if nothing else. The science at play was deadly. "You need
to be rational about this."

He changed in front of her eyes. Something barely held together
snapped. Nothing obvious, and nothing she could identify, but
she *felt* his control shred. He grasped her arms and hauled her
body against his, shocking the oxygen from her lungs. His face
set in brutal lines, tension ripping from him, he leaned down and

trapped her gaze. His dark eyes glittered with a need even she could identify. Primal fury darkened his face, proving he was nowhere near human. "You think hybrids have survived this world by using logic?" he rasped.

She shivered and slapped at his chest, trying to push him away. It was too late for that, and deep down, she knew it. Sparks arced through her body, firing nerves, arousal shocking her even more than his unrelenting hold. "Ivar."

"A name. Just a name I gave up in hell. I'm a demon, I'm a vampire, I'm a fucking Viking." His breath burned her mouth, while his anger overwhelmed the atmosphere around them. "We don't sign a nice contract for life ever after, Professor. We fuck hard, bite deep, and take." His hold tightened, and he pulled her up on her toes. "You want to be mine? Make sure you damn well understand what that means."

She stared up at him, a buzzing sounding between her ears. What had she said to bring this on? What was this? "I...I don't—"

"No. You don't."

"I—"

He cut off her next word by slamming his mouth down on hers, stepping into her and lifting her onto the table in one smooth motion. She fell back to her elbows, and pain tingled through her skin. He kept her there, barely stable, kissing her so hard she couldn't breathe.

His tongue slipped inside her mouth, warm and demanding. Her eyelids closed, and she opened her mouth wider, taking more of him. Wanting all of him.

A groan rippled up his throat, and he dug his hand into the back of her hair, twisting and taking control. His other hand banded at her hip, drawing her closer to him and forcing her legs to widen and make room for his hips. He caressed her butt, partially lifted her against his hard groin, his hand spread across both buttocks, his mouth furiously working hers.

Then he stopped, releasing her lips. Holding her against him with one hand, he twisted the other and pulled her head back. She was helpless in his grip, a shocking hunger burning through her lower body. He lowered his chin, and his eyes blazed a furious metallic green with that raw blue border. "This is me. This is what you get if you want to mate." He kissed her hard, his eyes remaining open. "No logical agreement. No rational partnership. You get the real me, the one still bound to hell. I'll take, and then I'll take some more. And if you agree, you'll fucking give me everything."

She shuddered, and it wasn't from fright. Well, not completely. The craving for him shooting through her obfuscated every other feeling. Every other thought.

"I'll mate you. Without question, if that's what you decide." His nostrils flared, giving him the look of a hunter finding prey. "You want it, and you want me right now. Make sure you can live with the decision in the cold dawn of morning when you're not hot and so ready to be taken."

With that, he released her.

Her butt smacked the table, and she shoved off her elbows to regain her balance and sit up. She blinked, trying to regain control of herself.

He turned on his heel and strode out the door, his steps deliberate and sure.

She touched her bruised mouth, desire still raging through her. For the last few days, Ivar had worn a facade. Of a humanesque, handsome, and almost easygoing soldier who wanted to sacrifice himself for his brother. He wasn't human. He'd tried to tell her, and she hadn't comprehended the difference. Additional chromosomal pairs didn't result in an evolved species. He was more animal than human.

She'd just met the real Ivar the Viking.

Worse yet, she wanted him. Immensely.

Chapter Twenty-Five

Ivar stormed out of the research cabin, already at a jog. By the time he hit the dirt road, he was running full out. His breath panted. It took him several heartbeats to realize a pint-sized fairy was running right behind him. He looked over his shoulder. "I thought you were making lunch."

"I started the kitchen on fire. Again." She increased her pace to his.

"What are you doing?" he asked.

Mercy's dark red hair bobbed behind her in a ponytail, and her small white tennis shoes easily found purchase as she matched his pace to run up alongside him. "You looked like you were bent on destruction. Thought you might need backup."

He didn't want to smile. He didn't want to feel any amusement, but a slight amount slid through him anyway. The idea that the small stockbroker could back him up was cute; it warmed something inside him. "You're the younger sister I never, ever ever ever, wanted."

She grinned, her one blue eye and one green eye lighting up. "I get that a lot."

He took in her stride to make sure he wasn't overtaxing her; if anything, she looked fine. Fairies must be good runners. Figured. They probably had to run away from blown-up buildings often. "You okay?" he asked.

"No, but I don't want to discuss it yet. Not until Logan has a spare moment to talk," she murmured. "What's up with you?"

"I think I just scared Promise," he admitted, jumping over a pothole.

Mercy nodded. "Did ya get all *grrrr*?"

Ivar's eyebrows lifted. "Huh?"

Mercy ran around a downed batch of pine tree branches and returned to his side. "You know. *I'm all immortal and fanged and dominant.* Grrrr. *I will take you back to my cave and have my way with you.* Grrrr. *This is how I kiss when I really want to.*"

"Grrrr?" Ivar asked.

"Yep." Mercy spit out a piece of a leaf.

His shoulders hunched, slowing his pace. So he straightened them. "Yes. I believe that's an accurate description."

"Oh, don't go back to being a tightass," she muttered, plucking a pine needle out of her hair. "You're a vampire-demon hybrid who has survived torture most of us can't even imagine. To survive, you sucked deep for that animal that lives in all of you, and he isn't going anywhere now. Either she gets it or she doesn't. You can't think of mating her unless she can accept and deal with all of you." Mercy rubbed her nose. "And you shouldn't have to hold yourself back and be somebody you're not. Even if the real you isn't exactly politically correct. Or at all."

Ivar increased his pace, not surprised when the fairy easily did the same. Her legs had to move twice as fast as his to keep up, but pleasure bloomed across her pixie-like face. "Where's your mate, anyway?" he asked.

"He and Garrett are teleconferencing with the Realm," she said, her arms pumping. "Bo—ring."

Ivar smiled. "No kidding." He used to enjoy that kind of work, but now he'd rather run or hit something.

She gracefully jumped over a mudpuddle. "Has your lady figured anything out yet? About dimensions?"

"Yes." Well, maybe. Ivar told Mercy about Promise's theory concerning the brain and teleporting abilities. Since he'd noticed

Faith slipping into the research room right after he'd left, no doubt they were coming up with a plan for MRIs at the moment. "It's an exciting theory."

Mercy was quiet for about a mile, her mind obviously working through the issue. "If Promise is correct, and demons and the Fae actually draw on different talents to do something similar, you know what we could really use?"

"A demon-fairy hybrid," Ivar joked. The fairies only numbered about sixty, and twenty of those had been created in test tubes a quarter of a century ago, with Mercy being one of them. "Can you imagine?"

She stumbled and quickly righted herself, splashing mud on his boots.

Everything inside him stilled, even as he kept pace. "Mercy?"

She lowered her head and started to run faster.

He quickened his strides, his mind rioting. Wait a minute. No way in hell. "Mercy?"

She slowed to a stop, her chest panting, her head down. "All right. So this just happened, and I'm a little torn. Your lady found paintings on the internet by somebody who has seen what I've seen somehow—while moving through dimensions. Except this artist also drew, or rather painted, what looks like a demon mind attack. Well, it's an attack from the brain, and that wouldn't have freaked me out so much, except this terrain around the brain is a place I've actually teleported to a few times. A place nowhere near the earth."

Ivar ran through the entire monologue. "Then it's probably just a painting from a fairy who's been to that place." The entire immortal world knew about demon mind attacks, so maybe the artist was just playing around.

"Yeah, that'd make sense, except I've never heard of the artist. And I know every fairy alive right now."

Okay. Good point. "So there's a fairy you might not know? Maybe one from eons ago who's still on earth." Ivar started jogging again.

"Maybe. I got to thinking and called the president," Mercy said, running around the puddle.

"Of the US?" he asked.

She snorted. "No. Of the Fae. Our president. Turns out she wasn't shocked by my revelation. Well, not completely, anyway."

He stopped cold, his boots sending muddy water in every direction. Sweat rolled down his back. "So you're saying that some fairy has been painting different dimensions. So what."

She shook her head and halted, her breathing even. "No. All of the Fae are accounted for. I mean, I know them all, and nobody has been painting anything like that."

"Obviously that isn't true if the paintings you saw were of actual places." What was he missing?

She was quiet for a minute. "All of the full-bred Fae have been with me on other worlds until recently. None of them painted what I saw earlier on that screen."

Full-bred Fae. The words hung heavily in the air. "What are you talking about?" She could not be saying what he thought she was.

She turned and started running back the way they'd come.

He easily caught up to her. "Talk to me. Now."

"It's probably treason," she muttered.

Who the hell cared? "Mercy," he warned.

She sighed, running faster, her small legs just a blur. "Fine." Her breath remained easy. "The president confirmed my suspicions. When the elders created my generation with leftover genetic samples, they might have experimented a little bit. Most of the experiments didn't make it."

"But?" His ears burned.

She winced, running smoothly again. "They combined Fae and demon DNA—and apparently found success."

They reached the campground, and he stopped, grasping her arm to halt her motions. Shock dropped a series of hard rocks into his gut. "Say that again."

She shuffled her now dirty tennis shoes. "The Fae elders apparently created a demon-Fae hybrid." She winced and tried to kick off the mud, spraying his calves. "Female too. You know how rare female demons are."

They were rare but existed. Energy ricocheted through him. "Where is she?" They had to get her on board. Now.

Mercy grimaced. "Well, that's the thing. They couldn't take her to the other world with us. A hybrid like that would be too volatile. Probably. They left her here on earth."

"Where?" He released her before he bruised her arm.

She paled. "The president wouldn't confirm, and truth be told, I don't believe she knows. I think they left her with humans."

His head jerked. "Humans? A hybrid like that?"

Mercy kicked a rock, and it rolled toward a tree. "Yes. I mean, teleporting is a learned skill, so if she was raised human, she might have no idea what she's able to do. If she survived childhood. Who knows. The images she creates—could be from dreams. Or... maybe she has traveled dimensions and knows how to commit a demon mind attack. It guess it's possible. Somehow."

The Fae were fucking nuts. He'd love to get his hands on those elders right now and squeeze until their heads popped off.

The doors to the cabins burst open, and his friends poured out. Logan reached them first, his jaw set in battle mode. "We have to get to demon headquarters. There has been a breach. A huge one."

Ronan brought Faith and Promise out of the research room, a gun already in his hand.

"Stop." Ivar held up a hand toward Promise. "Stay there for a minute." He didn't want her brain shutting down if she stood too close to Mercy. She'd had enough training for the day.

Ronan and Faith kept coming, while Promise hesitated on the cabin steps.

Garrett jogged out right behind Logan. "They want Promise there since she just talked to Dayne the other day. Thinks that might calm the guy down since the meeting was cordial."

"Dayne?" Ivar asked, his body going hot and then ice cold. "What the hell does he have to do with a breach?"

Garrett reached him at the same time as Logan. "Long story, but his kid is at demon headquarters. Might've run away to meet up with our niece, but who knows? Could be a setup."

Ivar growled, and his fangs itched to lower. "Promise is not getting involved in this shit."

"She already is," Logan said, wrapping an arm around Mercy's waist and drawing her near. "There are kids involved here, Ivar. We have to avoid a full-out war."

Faith clutched her mate's hand. "Let's all go. There's a medical facility between Realm and demon headquarters with top-of-the-line machinery. That's where I wanted to go, anyway."

"There's no time for helicopters," Ronan said, tucking his gun at the back of his waist.

Ivar evaluated the group and who had the ability to teleport. "Okay. Mercy, you take Grace, and Logan, you get Garrett." The fairy was strongest, but Logan had gained some of her teleporting powers after mating her. "Adare? You get Promise and me." He could help her shield herself from Adare but probably not Mercy at this point after having her mind attacked all day via training. "And Benny? You can take Ronan and Faith." He figured Ronan wouldn't let anyone take Faith without him.

"Ah, shit," Ronan muttered.

Benny rubbed his hands together. "I can do this. No problem."

Adare shook his head. "Grace is coming with me. I can take all three of you."

Ivar wouldn't let Promise teleport for the first time without him, and Adare had a right to protect his mate. Teleporting three people would tax the Highlander, but it was his decision.

Mercy pouted. "I want to take somebody. It's not fair, otherwise."

Ronan pushed his mate toward Mercy. "She's safer with you, Mercy. If Benny dumps me in an ocean, you'd better come looking for me."

Mercy grinned and slapped an arm over Faith's shoulders. "Hey, Doc. Want to stop off in Paris for a quick shopping spree for some new boots?"

Glee filled Faith's face.

"No—" Ronan started just as Benny jumped forward and hit him in a tackle, tumbling them toward the ground and then disappearing.

Promise let out a gasp from across the campground and then dropped to her butt on the stairs, her eyes wide and her chin lowering.

Ivar moved toward her across the uneven ground. There wasn't time for shock.

She lifted her head and watched him. He'd expected fear after the way he'd treated her earlier. Color infused her face. No fear. Not even warning or uneasiness. Instead, she watched him walk, her gaze intense. She licked her bottom lip. Holy shit. She was scrutinizing him like he was a chalkboard covered with equations. Trying to figure him out and solve him.

The woman should be scared shitless.

Instead, she stood as he got nearer, her blood pumping faster than usual. He could hear it. "We're going to have a crash course in mind shielding and teleporting." He paused in front of her. "Adare will take us, and since he's teleporting three of us, it's going to be bumpy. It'll take longer than usual, but don't be frightened."

Excitement lit her brown eyes.

"Are you up to shielding some more today?" he asked. They'd already asked a lot of her brain for one day.

She nodded, her gaze moving past him to where Adare had fetched Grace from her cabin. The young woman was drawing on a jacket, her hazel eyes serious. "Why can't I bring my camera?" she asked as they approached.

"Metal doesn't teleport," Adare said. "Unless you're with a Fae. Somehow they can do it." He'd obviously removed his gun and knives. Then he paused about three feet away. "Promise? You good?"

She rubbed her temple. "Slight ache but not bad. I've been practicing shielding all day while working on equations."

Adare grasped Grace's bicep and smoothly swung her onto his back. "I need you to hold on, sprite," he said, manacling her wrists at his clavicle with one wrist. "Secure your ankles together at my waist."

The woman did so, setting her head on his shoulder and turning her face into his neck.

His eyes darkened, and he exhaled sharply. "You're safe, Grace. I won't let you be harmed."

They made a nice couple. Why the heck didn't they see that? Ivar pulled Promise in front of him and wrapped both arms around her waist, plastering her body to his. They both faced Adare. "You can hold on to my thighs, sweetheart." Ivar had her arms trapped.

She dug her nails into his cargo pants, her body trembling with what was probably anticipation. Maybe a little fear. "What should I do?" she whispered.

"Nothing," Ivar said. "There's nothing you can do once we go. Just hold on and trust me." He nodded to Adare. "You ready?"

The Highlander cocked his head. "As ready as I'll ever be. Brace yourself." Then he charged.

Chapter Twenty-Six

Adare hit Ivar in the shoulders right above Promise's head, not touching her in the slightest. Then no sensation. Darkness pressed in, and then a heaviness, followed by an unbelievable weightlessness, and finally pure light.

Her vision focused first. She stood on a thick lawn next to a firepit facing a lake surrounded by mountains. Adare stepped away and shook his head. His mouth moved as if he was talking. He bent over at the waist and sucked in air, letting his mate easily slide off his back.

Then sound roared in. Heavy boots running, a couple of shouts, Ivar's breathing above her.

She blinked. Soldiers dressed in full combat gear, armed with sleek rifles, ran in directed chaos along the lake, obviously securing the perimeter.

Ivar hugged her close and turned her toward the building, which was a rustic example of a beautiful Frank Lloyd Wright–style lodge. "Welcome to demon headquarters," he said.

The doors opened, and a large male dressed in all black stalked out with a gun strapped to one thigh and a knife to the other. He tossed guns toward Adare and Ivar, and they caught them easily. His black hair was tied at the nape, and his green eyes sizzled. The jaw was familiar—he looked a lot like Logan. He reached her. "Hi. Zane Kyllwood. I need your help."

Pain lashed into her temples.

Ivar pulled her back into his body. "Shield, Professor. You can do it. Grab my hands and draw strength."

She did so, mentally imagining those shields slamming into place.

Zane frowned. "I didn't attack her mind."

She blinked, her heart rate slowing back to normal. Well, slightly above normal. "You can teleport."

He nodded.

Garrett and Logan popped up on their right, and a second later, Mercy and Faith appeared on their left.

Promise barely jumped.

Mercy grinned. "You okay? Covering your brain?"

"Yes," Promise said. The shielding was actually becoming easier to accomplish.

"Good," Mercy said. "What did you think of teleporting? Of there being nothing?"

Promise frowned. "I'd like to do it again. But there wasn't nothing." How could any of them think that? "We were there, so there was something. And there was a path, so again, something." It appeared that the immortals hadn't spent the time in their long lives studying physics. It was a pity, really. "Even at a reduced energy level, fluctuations occur in the quantum vacuum of any space," she said.

Zane lifted his eyebrows and looked at Ivar.

Ivar leaned down. "One thing at a time, Missy."

Oh, yes. That was right. She looked up at the demon leader. "You said you required my assistance." Too bad it couldn't be to discuss and study physics at the moment.

Faith looked around. "Hey. Where's Ronan?"

As if on cue, Ronan and Benny slammed down, cracking the asphalt around the firepit. They had icicles in their hair and covering their boots.

Faith gasped. "Where did you go?"

Ronan shoved away from Benny and started picking the ice out of his black hair. "Greenland? Arctic Circle? Russia?" He shook his head. "Next time somebody else goes with Benny."

Zane's gaze sharpened, making him look frightening. "Long story short. We have the leader of the Kurjan nation's kid in our possession. We'd like to give him back, but there's a great chance we're about to be bombed instead. Promise, I thought you could talk to the guy since you've had the most recent contact with him. According to my brother, it was a friendly meeting."

Promise drew in air, trying to fill her lungs. "I'm the only one who's met him?"

Faith shook her head. "Nope. I met him, and he handed me over to a psycho Cyst who wanted to cut me apart and study me."

Promise gaped. "Were you, I mean, are you—"

"Oh, I punched him in the eye and then Ronan ripped off his head." The neurologist grinned. "Good times."

Promise's legs weakened. "All right. So he truly is a bad guy."

Faith frowned. "Didn't you know that? I heard you screamed for Ivar when Dayne was in your office."

Promise swallowed, her head still aching a little. "I decided to trust Ivar, and he said the Kurjans were dangerous and were the enemy, so I yelled for him when the time came."

Zane's chin lifted. "I like you."

"She gets that a lot," Benny said, shaking ice out of his shirt.

Ivar growled.

The sound brought everybody back to the present. Promise nodded. "I'm happy to speak with him. It'd probably be beneficial if I could see for myself that his child is here and is safe." She looked up at the clear blue sky. How would bombs be delivered? Did the Kurjans have missiles, or would a plane provide warning?

Benny chucked Garrett on the arm. "While they deal with this, why don't you and I run over to Realm headquarters? My nephew Chalton is there, and your mama is there, so let's go visit."

Zane tightened his gun strap. "We've activated the land mines around both headquarters. You'll be blown up before you get ten feet."

Benny sighed. "We'll teleport, then."

Garrett grabbed his shoulder, his odd gray eyes sizzling into a deep metal color. "How about I lead?"

Faith took Ronan's hand. "We want to come. The queen and I have been working on some genetics, and I'd like to see her."

"Damn it," Ronan said, shaking his head. "All right. I'm with Benny."

"Wait," Ivar said. "Real quick. The Realm has the best computer system in the world. We need to find a female demon-Fae hybrid born around twenty-five years ago and probably raised by humans. Have the computer guys go through all databases they can find to search for her. Somehow."

Benny's chin dropped. "There's a fairy-demon hybrid? A *female* one?"

Mercy kicked at the firepit. "Yes. When I was created, the leaders experimented a little bit. That's all I know."

Benny rubbed his chin. "Where do you suppose they got demon sperm?"

Zane turned toward the doorway. "We don't have a lot of time here. Please come this way."

Ivar's warm palm slid down her arm to take her hand, and Promise held on tightly. The world was changing in front of her. Or rather, it was revealing itself to her, and her senses were experiencing an overload that tilted her vision.

Her head held high, her gaze seeking new discoveries with each step, she walked into the headquarters building of the demon nation.

* * * *

Ivar kept a good grip on Promise's hand as they followed Zane through the maze of headquarters, taking a second to admire the architecture. Logan had designed it, using sharp lines and elements of stone, wood, and stained glass. Zane barked orders into his comm unit the entire time, even sending up the Blackhawks. This was serious.

They'd just gotten out of a full-out war and were currently succeeding in keeping the Mission of the Seven to a strategic battle.

Maybe seeing the way the immortals lived would change Promise's mind about mating him. Or perhaps she'd find another immortal among the demons.

The idea flashed like a knife through him, and he growled again, his fangs pricking his lip.

She jumped and turned her head.

He forced his fangs into place and gave her a smile. Her eyes widened. Man, it had been too long since he'd gotten in a fight. If they survived the current crisis, he'd ask Benny to spar with him. Benny never held back.

Zane paused outside of a closed door at the end of a hallway. "The Kurjan kid seems okay, but I'm sure he's taking notes."

Ivar exhaled. "You don't think this was deliberate, do you?"

Zane shrugged. "Dunno. The Kurjans have never hesitated to take advantage of any situation. Apparently my daughter and Drake have been meeting in a dreamworld, and I sure didn't know about it. If the Kurjans did…"

Ivar shook his head. "I can't imagine a father would send his eight-year-old into danger like this." But the Kurjans were evil, so who the hell knew? "Did you check the kid for recording devices?"

"No," Zane said, sighing. "We brought the kids from the park to headquarters in the back of a van. If he's recording, let him. I'm not searching a child."

"Dreamworld?" Promise asked.

Zane pushed open the door. "Could be another universe, one she gets to without her body leaving here." He shook his head. "Sounds like the Seven ritual, and I did the same thing as a kid. But we thought we blew up what we considered the dreamworld." He looked down at Promise. "Guess it's one more theory for you to solve."

It didn't surprise Ivar that Zane was well versed about Promise. The demon nation had excellent resources.

Zane led them into a colorfully painted room containing game consoles, a small golf putting course, air hockey tables, and dartboards with plastic-tipped darts. Plush beanbags were strewn about along with bookshelves overflowing with books. A costume area stood in the far corner with princess dresses, sparkly shoes, and tiaras.

A massive vampire with sizzling pink eyes stood guard at the other end of the room, while two kids sat in the beanbags, not playing, both pale.

Zane pointed. "This is my daughter, Hope, and her friend Drake. The other two pint-sized escapees went home with their parents." Hope was a cutie with blue eyes and brown hair, and Drake a pale kid who looked almost human. In fact, he could probably pass for human if necessary. Very rare genes for a Kurjan.

Drake jumped to his feet. "Have you contacted my father?"

"Not yet." Zane motioned toward Promise. "This is Dr. Promise Williams, and she met your dad yesterday. We want her to talk to him to see if we can avoid a war."

Hope's eyes filled. "Drake wantsta go home, Daddy. You hafta let him."

Zane nodded. "I'm happy to take him home. Let's contact his dad."

Promise held out her hand to Drake. "It's nice to meet you."

Drake shook, ducking his head. Was the kid shy? "You too. Now will you call my father?"

"Yes. You two stay here and play. Max will keep an eye on you." Zane smiled. "Drake? I'm sure your dad will want to see that you're okay. I'll talk to him first, and then we'll come get you. Don't worry. You'll be home soon."

Ivar took Promise's hand again, his nerves firing. He'd brought her into a possible target zone, and he didn't have the ability to teleport her the hell out if things went bad. Worse yet, he wasn't familiar with the demon land holding or the escape routes. "Where's Logan?"

"Probably went to see our mom," Zane said, heading downstairs. He reached in his pocket and pulled out an earbud to toss back at Ivar. "If escape becomes necessary, all doors and locks have been calibrated to obey your voice commands. Just in case."

Ivar caught it and shoved it in his left ear. At least now he'd know what was happening up to the minute.

Promise gave him a *wow* expression. This had to seem like a crazy sci-fi show to her. She was holding up remarkably well under the pressure. In fact, even though she looked a mite shell-shocked, there was fascination in her attitude too.

They reached a sprawling computer center and walked right past it to a small room with a camera, huge wall monitor, and green screen background. "Stand there," Zane said, moving to the camera. "They obviously know the location of our headquarters, which we've assumed for a while. But Dayne may try to learn other information from you, and I'd appreciate it if you kept the discussion to the return of his child."

Ivar let her go but remained by the door, prepared to grab Promise and run if necessary.

She stood in front of the green screen and folded her hands together. "I find it peculiar that I'm doing this."

Zane shrugged. "You're female and human and have no reason to lie to him. Most of us have killed people he's known, and he's done the same. Think of yourself as an intermediary." He flicked a switch, and the Kurjan leader came up on the screen.

"Dr. Promise Williams," Dayne said quietly. He was dressed in a Kurjan fighting uniform—all black with medals on the left breast. "This is unexpected."

Promise gazed directly at the camera. "Hi, Dayne. I'm at demon headquarters, and I just spoke with your son. He's healthy, unharmed, and ready to go home."

Dayne's eyes had turned a deep purple. "You don't seem like a liar."

"I'm not," she said. "We can bring him in here for you to see. I assume Zane wanted to make sure you were calm first in order to avoid scaring the child."

Man, she was smart.

Dayne smiled. "I have bombers ready to go, and the missiles are armed. Show me my son, and you bring him to me. Perhaps then we can prevent war."

"No," Zane said, angling Promise out of the shot. "I'll show you your kid. In exchange for the three Enhanced women you kidnapped earlier this year. Call me back when they're free." He pressed a remote in his hand, and the camera went dark.

Promise whirled, and Ivar stepped in, drawing her away. "What have you done?" she snapped.

Chapter Twenty-Seven

Promise could barely breathe she was so angry. "You're supposed to be the good guys." She forgot to shield her brain, and pain instantly slashed into the base of her skull.

Seeing her reaction, Zane stepped back. "I didn't attack."

"Shield," Ivar barked.

She imagined the metal barrier in her head again, and the pain dissipated. "That was unacceptable."

The demon leader looked at her with dispassionate eyes. "I understand you're new to our world, but we've just entered a negotiation, and I used you to do it. I'm sorry if that makes you unhappy."

"That is not an apology," she snapped, wanting to hit him in the nose.

His grin was quick and unexpected. "You're not the first to accuse me of that. I am sorry."

"But you'll use a child to get what you want," she said, her hands shaking even more.

He nodded. "I would never hurt a child, and I suspect Dayne knows that, since he hasn't bombed us yet. But the Kurjans have been kidnapping Enhanced women across the world in preparation for a ritual we don't know enough about, and if I have a chance to secure their release, I'm going to do so."

She whirled on Ivar, waiting for him to chime in. "Well?"

The Viking looked at her. "Well, what?"

There were no words. Her throat ached with the need to yell at him. "Do something." Then it dawned on her. Way too slowly. "You suspected Zane's course of action."

Ivar didn't deny the accusation.

Zane cleared his throat. "Your quarters are down the south hall, third door on the right. It's a nice suite, and the lock is prepared for your voice, Ivar. There are two bedrooms." The demon leader moved to the doorway, all grace and strength. "I do hope the Seven's penchant for getting their headquarters blown to bits is not contagious." With that, he disappeared down the hallway, already issuing orders on his comm line.

Promise rubbed her chest. Her heart hurt. How odd. "I'm surprised you'd be a part of something like this."

His slight nod acknowledged her surprise. "You live in a world of theories where you have the luxury of idealism." He spread his arms out, taking in the whole room. "We don't. Violence and subterfuge are part of every day for us."

"You've had centuries to evolve," she burst out.

He nodded. "Who says we haven't?"

She disliked that he had a point.

He gestured her toward the door. "The only reason I'm not grabbing you and getting the hell out of this place is that the demons have a better missile defense system than any other species or any country on earth."

She stumbled and righted herself, sweeping by him. So many thoughts went through her head, she had to pause to organize them into levels of importance. He took the lead again, obviously knowing where south lay, and soon opened a door to a spacious suite facing the lake. The living area was decorated in comfortable tones with high-end furniture. "Why did Zane assume we'd be staying together?" she asked, turning to face him.

"If you don't know the answer to that, then you're not as smart as I thought," he said, shutting the door and leaning back against it.

Fair enough. "I'm really angry with you right now," she said.

"I'm aware." He smiled. "Want to throw something at me? One of those fancy plates on the bookshelf probably cost a fortune."

She looked past the fireplace to the inlaid bookcases. "I'd rather debate you until you agree with me." It was how civilized people resolved differences of opinion. But nobody said the immortals were civilized. Least of all the immortals themselves. They seemed just fine with their rather primal status. "We need to discuss the mating."

Both of his eyebrows rose. She took a very unscientific delight in having surprised him.

His eyelids lowered. "You still want to mate me? After the other day?"

"Yes." She'd given it a lot of thought, even while working through other problems, and she desired immortality. "I've never been a believer in the afterlife, so staying alive holds a certain appeal. Just think of the scientific breakthroughs I could make." She tried to keep her voice level, but a hint of heat lowered it. "Today notwithstanding, I like you, and you like me. We're sexually compatible, and my odd gifts might be of benefit to you if you try to enter those hell worlds again." There. It was a win-win.

"And if I make it back?" he asked. "If the bubble breaks, and nobody has to align the magnets or whatever the hell Quade has been doing, I'll return and we'll be mated for eternity."

An intriguing shiver tickled through her lower half. "I understand."

"Do you want kids?" he asked.

She blinked. Children? "Yes and no." It made sense to have this discussion now, of course. Her heart fluttered in a peculiar way. "I'm interested in children, and it'd be satisfying to mold a young mind." A vision caught her of a little boy with Ivar's stunning blue eyes and her darker complexion and hair. She shook her head at the sweet thought. "But I'm not what one would call maternal. I don't know how to nurture a child."

"I think it comes naturally at the right time," Ivar said, his tone gentle. "Just look how protective you were of Drake."

Her heart jumped. He thought she could make a good mother? "In high school, my goldfish died," she admitted. "Quickly. Not nearly close to an expected life span." She'd done everything according to the books too.

"I'm sure that wasn't your fault." He looked big and broad covering the door. "I get the feeling that your parents were great at the science stuff and not so much with the nurturing."

"They did their best," she protested, almost too quickly. Though had they?

He watched her. "All right. This is all rational and good. But I've explained to you a mating is primitive, and the male is primal. You have to understand that."

Oh, she'd learned that lesson the other day when he'd kissed her. Yet she'd liked it. "I do understand."

"So you want to mate me." He cocked his head. "Or any immortal?"

"Just you," she rushed to say, meaning every word. "I trust you." She'd proven that.

His eyes flashed green through the blue. "All right. Tonight?"

She nodded, unable to speak. What an phenomenal decision, and she'd just made it.

"It's a date." He tapped his earbud. "I have to go for an hour or so. Why don't you get settled in." He hauled her close and placed a surprisingly gentle kiss on her nose. Then he opened the door and disappeared.

She swallowed. Good grief Newton on a double cracker with cheese. She had just agreed to mate a demon-vampire—and he'd agreed right back.

* * * *

It took Promise about five minutes to get settled in. She missed her whiteboards already. The lake sparkled in the fall sun, and beautiful colors cloaked the coniferous trees near the water. She allowed herself a couple of breaths to admire the beauty. Leaves fell, and she calculated their rate of fall.

She gasped. It was so simple. That was it. She needed results, and she needed them now. If her math was right, the rate of fall, or rather, the rate of the portals closing, could be happening too quickly. There wasn't time to wait. It might be too late already.

She ran out the door, determined to find Mercy. So many theories attacked her that she had to act. Now. Time was running out.

She backtracked to the kids' room, but it was vacant. So she looked around, and nobody stopped her, which worked just fine. Finally, she reached a massive kitchen. Mercy was inside, sitting on an island, eating what looked like microwaved noodles. "Hey."

Excellent. Promise mentally pictured giant shields covering her brain and then proceeded cautiously. "Hi."

Mercy kicked out her feet. "You're doing well."

A slight sting connected beneath Promise's left ear, and she quickly slid the shield in that direction. "Thank you."

Mercy held out the cup. "You hungry?"

Definitely, but there wasn't time for dinner. Promise looked around the sparkling clean space and then pounced on a glass cookie jar. She took out two chocolate chip cookies and devoured them. "Mmm, so much better." How could the studies on sugar be correct? It made her feel calmer. "That works for dinner." She eyed the Fae, trying to find the right words to use. "What are you up to?"

Mercy finished her noodles. "I moved money around for a while and then invested in some new startups focusing on green agriculture. That's about it. Why?"

Promise gnawed on her lip, mathematical equations flashing across her mind. She needed results from an experiment to continue with her math. There was no other way. "Can you get your hands on a compass and a barometer?" Rudimentary but necessary for commencing her practical research.

Mercy set the cup aside. "Sure." She disappeared with a swish of air spinning around.

The cup fell over. Wow. Promise took a couple of steps back. That was amazing. Truly so. Then she waited alone in the now quiet kitchen.

About two minutes later, Mercy reappeared with a compass and a barometer in her hands. "Had to work for these." She grinned. "I take it we're going to do some traveling?"

"Yes." Promise almost jumped when an invisible blade ripped behind her left eye, and she smashed her palm against it. "Shield, shield, shield," she muttered, imagining the protection was made of diamonds this time.

The pain disappeared.

Hey. Diamonds. She smiled. "They are a girl's best friend."

Mercy jumped off the island. "Huh?"

Promise waved her off, excitement and a sense of urgency taking her. There was too much she didn't understand about teleporting, and that had to stop now. "Nothing. So. Are you willing to jump with me and do some work?"

Mercy nodded. "Always. But don't you think you should check with Ivar first? He seems rather insistent that you jump only when he's available."

Promise pinned her with a look. "Are you going to ask permission from your mate?"

Instead of being insulted, Mercy's eyes widened. "Is Ivar going to be your mate? For sure?"

Oh, for goodness' sake. "We've entered into an agreement," Promise said.

Mercy snorted. "Seriously? You've entered into an agreement?" She shook her head, and her dark red hair flew all around. "You have no clue what you're entering into. An agreement." She snorted again. "Girlfriend, you have to stop thinking so logically."

"Ivar has said something similar to me," Promise said slowly. But logically was the only way to think. She was missing something. Subtext? No. "One can be illogical, but one can't think illogically."

Mercy pressed her lips together. "All righty then. Let's just do this and face the consequences later."

"Consequences?" Promise smirked. "What in the world are you talking about?"

Mercy just smiled. "Where do you want to go?"

Promise rolled the question over in her mind. They should start with the familiar, at least to her, and then circle out. "Do you know of any islands in the Pacific? Deserted ones?"

"Sure." Mercy moved forward, watching Promise intently. "Is your head okay?"

Promise nodded and held out her hand. "Yes. I think I have it under control." She kept the diamond shield in place. "Is there any way you can go slowly? As slow as possible?"

"No. I just draw on energy around me, suck it all in, and direct the universe to send me where I want to go." Mercy frowned. "But I'll try to go slow. I've just never done that." She took Promise's hand.

A jolt shot up Promise's arm, and she blocked her brain.

Then the room disappeared. More darkness, more weightlessness, more pressure. Light came first and then sound. They stood on snow-white sand, surrounded by aqua-colored water and healthy reefs. The sun beat down, heating Promise's head instantly. The island was only about twenty yards across with no vegetation. The ocean spread out in every direction as far as the eye could see. "This is thrilling," Promise said, her voice hushed.

Mercy looked around. "Yeah. We should've brought a picnic."

Promise turned toward her new friend. "Thank you."

"Sure." Mercy smiled. "Where to next?"

Exhilaration filled Promise just like when she solved an equation. A hard one. She took the devices from Mercy and read them, not finding any surprises. She handed them back. "Off of this world. Or rather, out of this world. Will you take me someplace else?" It was nearly unimaginable. The idea that she could be on a world, or in a world, other than this one. "Please?"

Mercy faltered. "Um, I don't know. That's the kinda thing you might want to talk about with your contracted-to-be mate. You know?"

Promise swallowed. "Do you talk about all jumps with your mate?"

Mercy shrugged. "Usually. He doesn't like me to jump dimensions without him." She held up a hand as Promise began to protest. "Fine. Jump worlds. Not dimensions." She shook her head. "We should've never given that word to humans. They misused it, and now I can't even use it with you."

The word was in the dictionary, so the immortals should just start employing it correctly. "Well, you did donate the word, so let's go jump into a new world." Promise held her breath, wanting this almost more than anything else in her life.

Mercy sighed. "All right. But I did warn you." She held out her hand.

Promise's hand trembled, and she slid it against the Fae's cooler one. "How do you choose where to go?"

"Some worlds are easier to reach. The same ones are often good jumping-off points for other places," Mercy said. She paused. "I should tell you that a couple of Fae don't like me, and one of them, the ex-king, has been known to bring Cyst soldiers through dimensions to attack me."

Promise blinked. "You're saying that this might be dangerous?"

"Probably not. I mean, the king stepped down, and who knows where he is right now. Niall was a butthead, but he's a better jumper than I am, to be honest. I don't think we'll find trouble, but if we do, I thought I should warn you."

The temptation to move through dimensions was too much to resist. Promise held on tighter. "Let's do this."

Chapter Twenty-Eight

Ivar stalked out of an uncomfortable meeting with Zane Kyllwood, his ears ringing and his gut aching. Kyllwood was less than pleased that the Seven had recruited his brother, and he'd wanted to make sure Ivar knew he'd be eviscerated if anything happened to Logan. The good thing was that Ivar felt as strongly as Zane did about Logan's safety. About all his brothers, actually.

In Ivar's current mood, mating Promise that night didn't seem like a good idea. He'd have to distract her with the plans he'd just arranged with the Queen of the Realm for everyone to undergo MRIs that would test the teleporting zones in their brains. The queen had been beyond delighted at the idea, and he could see why Emma and Faith had built such a fast and quick friendship. He'd like to get Promise inserted in their group, just in case he died when he took over for Quade. It'd be nice to leave her with friends.

He reached their suite and called out her name, surprised at the empty feel of the place. A quick search confirmed she was nowhere to be found.

Perhaps she'd gone looking for food. He retraced his steps and found a kitchen, where Logan was munching on chocolate chip cookies and looking around. "Hey."

Logan glanced up. "Hey. Where have you been?"

"Your brother has been yelling at me," Ivar said. "Well, not yelling, but threatening some pretty impressive and anatomically impossible revenge if anything happens to you."

Logan kept chewing. "Must be Zane. Sam doesn't threaten. He just kills somebody and says they should've seen it coming."

Ivar liked both of Logan's biological brothers. "Fair enough."

Logan threw him a cookie. "I'm sorry about Zane. Sometimes he thinks we're still teenagers running from our asshole of an uncle."

"No problem," Ivar said, scratching his neck. It was tingling again, damn it. "Have you seen Promise?"

"Nope, and I just looked through the entire headquarters for Mercy. Didn't see either one of them." Logan straightened. "Oh, man. That is not a good sign."

Ivar finished his cookie. "They must be here somewhere." Promise wouldn't have left the area without speaking to him.

Logan exhaled slowly. "If those two found each other, they're halfway around the world right now." His lips compressed in a thin line. "At least, they'd better be on this world." He dusted off his hands. "In fact, I believe I asked my mate to stay close since we're in lockdown right now. The world is unsafe. And there's a pissed-off Fae jackass out there who can teleport and likes to take Cyst soldiers with him."

Ivar shook his head, even as his blood thinned. "They wouldn't have teleported out of here. Not without saying a word."

Logan just cocked his head.

Ivar closed his eyes and counted backward from ten. Nope. Didn't help. He reopened them. Fire crackled through him, engulfing the control he'd tried so fucking hard to learn these last three months. Like a whisper, it disappeared. He slammed his fist on the counter, and the marble cracked down the middle. "Tell me you've developed the skill most mates have to talk telepathically to each other."

"Sure," Logan said. "Just tried. Nothing. You know what that means?"

"She's pissed and is ignoring you for some reason?" Ivar asked, his hand hurting as if he'd taken a blade to it.

"Nope. She's off-world. Not here. Anywhere on earth, I can reach her." Logan moved toward Ivar, cutting through the kitchen with long strides. "And I can't reach her right now."

A cold sweat broke out on Ivar's forehead. His last time off-world had lasted an eternity and scarred impenetrable skin. The savage beast at his core, hard to restrain under the best of circumstances, stretched wide awake with almost a gleeful swelling of anticipation. He shook out his hand, even as the flames licked up his arm. Slowly, his chin lowering, he flipped his wrist over.

Logan whistled. "Huh. Well. There you go."

Ivar stared down at the raw branding mark on his right palm. His left one was already a scarred mess from the Seven rituals he'd endured; surprisingly, the brand on the right palm hurt more than those ever had. Maybe because it was unused and wanted to change that status immediately. It pulsed, heated and alive.

Logan moved closer. "The Kjeidsen marking. I've never seen one. That's seriously badass."

Ivar's eyes saw but his brain didn't compute. Not yet. "Kallgren," he corrected. "My mother's side was the demon part of my family—they were Kallgrens." Demons, not vampires, branded their mates.

"Of course," Logan said. "I forgot. Same with us. It's odd that both of my parents had *K* for their surname. You too."

Ivar could only stare at his palm. The dark *K* was surrounded by sinuous knots that crested out like waves from the ocean—the lines darker and thicker than the Kayrs marking. His ears heated, and the blood rushed through them louder than his heartbeat. "Well."

Logan clapped him on the back. "Your mate is in danger. Strong emotions bring the brand out. It's nice to know, isn't it?" His voice remained calm as if he was trying to help Ivar find his balance. Just as he'd done months ago.

Ivar looked up. "Know what?"

"That Promise is your mate. You didn't have to force the marking or anything." Logan's expression sobered. "That's a good thing, Viking."

Just how much danger was Promise in? She was too delicate—too human—to survive a hell world. Ivar grabbed Logan's arm. "Tell me you can track Mercy through other worlds." Most demons couldn't, but hadn't Logan gained the ability after mating Mercy? Ivar couldn't think straight right now as memories of hell smashed into him.

"Of course I can track her. She's my mate." Logan took a deep breath, exhaled, and the world spun away.

* * * *

Light and the smell of freshly baked snickerdoodle cookies impacted Promise first. Soft grass covered her tennis shoes, while three suns shone down, almost gently. She stepped back, her eyes wide, her heart bursting. "Where are we?" Bubbling brooks surrounded them as they stood in the midst of a wide meadow.

Mercy smiled, delight in her eyes. "One of my favorite places. I call it Brookville and have spent days here lounging around. There are no animals, and for some reason, the grass doesn't get any higher."

Incredible. Promise's legs gave out, and she sank to the gentle ground. "Have you been here at night?"

"Sure." Mercy sat and crossed her legs. "The constellations didn't look familiar."

Promise looked up. She really needed to come back at night. "What does the sky look like at night?"

Mercy closed her eyes as if trying to remember. "Maybe some distant planets but no moons or anything. Not like our moon."

This was magnificent. Promise forced herself to breathe normally. "What is that smell?"

"It's from the grass," Mercy said. "The air is a little lighter too."

"So is the gravity," Promise said, lifting her hand. "It's not as strong as at home." Home. The word meant something different to her now. She reached for the devices, and they confirmed her visual solutions. They were not on her planet. How wondrous. Truly so.

Mercy stood. "Want to go somewhere else?"

"Yes." Promise followed suit. "That felt different from when we teleported on earth. It was darker somehow. And the pressure more intense." Before, she'd felt weightlessness. This time, she felt as if she had been moving. If they went to another world, would she sense a different direction? Every point on a graph had a location. "Show me."

"Okay." Mercy grabbed her hand again, and the smell of cookies evaporated. The darkness was the same, but she could swear she twisted three times and then moved in a leftish direction. They landed on a green pod in the center of a purple body of water.

Promise clutched Mercy's hand. "What is in the water?"

"Dunno," Mercy said. "I've been here a dozen times and have never seen anything. Doesn't mean something isn't lurking, though." She grinned.

Promise chuckled and surveyed the readings on her devices before looking around. This place had one sun that was a bright orange color. It was far enough away to give warmth but not burn. "Are there places without stars?"

"Yep, but most are too cold to be habitable. Though there are a few that remain warm," Mercy said, taking the barometer and compass again.

Promise held her tighter. "Where to next?"

The air shimmered.

What in the world?

Two hard male bodies split the day, landing on the pod. It bounced a few times and then settled, sending waves of purple across the water, submerging several other pods.

Mercy sighed. "Ah, crap."

Logan's smile wasn't anything close to sweet. His eyes blazed a deep green. "I believe I asked you not to go off-world for the time being, mate."

Ivar didn't say a word. His eyes glittered, and his jaw looked as if it had been chiseled from the diamond shield she used to protect her brain.

For once, Promise didn't know what to say. Caution overruled logic. How riveting.

"Logan?" Ivar asked quietly, hauling Promise into his side so quickly she didn't have time to protest.

"Yep. Don't move, Mercy. I'll be right back." Logan tackled Ivar, and darkness surrounded them. Promise was jostled more, and she made a mental note that Mercy's teleporting was much smoother than anybody else's for some reason, right before landing on an outcropping of rocks with the sun going down. She shivered.

Logan released them. "See ya tomorrow morning."

"Wait," Ivar said. His gaze was hot enough to melt chocolate. "Promise? Do you still want me to mate you?" The low rasp of his voice echoed through the quiet forest at their backs.

Why did those words sound like a threat? She tried to swallow over a lump in her throat. *When all else fails, use honesty.* No matter how irritated or frightening he was being at the moment, she'd already reached her decision, and the path was one she had freely chosen. "Yes. I do."

Ivar nodded at Logan, who grinned. Then he was gone.

Promise backed away and inhaled the strong scent of pine. The trees towered high around them, and the rising moon showed they were back on earth. "Where are we?"

"My cabin." Ivar pointed behind her.

She turned to see a quaint cabin built into the rocks. In the distance she could see mountains. A bird squawked nearby, and somewhere far off, a coyote howled. She shivered. "I see."

"Do you?" he asked mildly, taking her hand and starting up the rock steps.

She had no choice but to follow, unless she wanted to fall. So she scrambled to keep up with him. His hand nearly burned her, the skin rough. It was his good hand. "Did you hurt yourself?"

"No," he said shortly, turning and releasing her before holding his palm up toward her.

She gulped. Graceful and deadly black lines formed a shield around a *K* on his palm. His marking. The brand was stunningly beautiful. Stark and exquisite. "When did that appear?"

He took her hand again to start walking again, and the marking warmed her palm. "When I'd discovered you'd gone off world."

She endeavored to calm her pulse and reason with him at the same time. A discussion would be beneficial. "It's my understanding that to mate, we need to engage in sex, you must bite me, and then press your palm to my skin."

He paused at the heavy-looking door, which appeared to be metal painted in a manner to appear like wood. "That's what the experience might read like in a dictionary."

His words were calm, but the voice issuing them was raspy with the threat of danger.

She swallowed. Her legs trembled as if they knew something her brain did not. "Yes, I, ah, have decided that the marking should be placed on my center back." She did not have tattoos, and in that location the marking would be easy to cover, even in a swimsuit, should she so desire.

He flipped her around so quickly she yelped. "I'll put the marking where I goddamn want. You're lucky I don't plaster it to your forehead." His eyes had turned that luminous green, which probably blended with the forest—just like a true predator.

She tried to quell her anxious stomach. Even with the panic, heat glided over her skin, beneath her muscles, to tempt her nerves. Why she found his fury at her arousing, she'd have to analyze later. "You're angry."

He exhaled through his nose, his chest moving sharply. "Angry doesn't come close to what I'm feeling."

Her own anger finally decided to appear. "Well, then. Maybe we shall wait until you're more amenable to mate."

He stepped into her, putting her back flush with the impenetrable door. His chin lowered, and then his head did the same, until his mouth hovered right above hers, his gaze burning into her eyes. "Oh, baby. It's way too late for that." Then he took her mouth.

Hard.

Chapter Twenty-Nine

Ivar kissed her, pouring all his pent-up emotions into the act. She'd scared the shit out of him by traveling off-world with a crazy fairy, and then she wanted to be all logical about mating? There wasn't any logic in mating, damn it. If she wanted him, she was going to get all of him. His mouth was fierce, and he took what he wanted, conveying to her exactly how much control he'd shown with her. Until now.

He sensed her move, felt her hands come up with her nails already raking his chest and angling toward his face. Without breaking his hold on her mouth, he manacled her wrists, forcing her harder against the door. Sweeping his tongue inside her mouth, nearly groaning at her sweet taste, he pulled her hands above her head and pinned them in place.

Her tongue met his, and she kissed him back.

Even so, she struggled against his hold, twisting her hips. No doubt so her knee could take out his balls.

A rational voice in the back of his head, one he'd cultivated the last three months as he clawed his way from the depth of darkness to an almost life, told him to release her. Yelled at him that the soft professor shouldn't be mauled by an animal like him. Just as he almost let that voice take hold, Promise groaned. Softly and sweetly.

That sound slid from her chest, through her throat, and into his mouth.

Every still living nerve he had flamed into a hunger so raw it burned. In that second, more so than any other, the voice of reason was flattened and shut off. All that remained was the creature inside him that he truly was. That he'd always be.

He lifted his head, gratified to see her eyes unfocused and filled with need. "You like routine, and you fucking love rules. So let's get a few straight right now."

She blinked, confusion wrinkling her eyes.

"Yes. Rules for you. As my mate." He didn't give one whit that she'd been on her own most of her life. That had just changed. "There will be no teleporting without me. There will be absolutely zero teleporting off of this world until we make sure it's safe to do so, and even then, you will not go without me in front of you." He slid his hand into her hair, jerked, and held her head in place.

She sucked in air while her sexy neck elongated, a vein pulsing rapidly in it. "Ivar—"

"In the likely event that I end up taking Quade's place, I will return. Don't know how or when, but I'll be back. While I'm gone"—he tightened his hold, and her eyes widened—"you will obey the rules the entire time. You can continue being theoretical until I return. That's the path you chose, and you'll stay on it." If nothing else, he had to keep her safe. If they mated, it was his duty and his right.

He expected an argument. A logical, probably irritated, explanation of why he was wrong.

Instead, her gaze darkened. "Or what?" she whispered.

It was a challenge of the most primitive of sort, and he felt it to his battered soul. He knew this woman. She followed logic over safety and experimentation over health. But, without a doubt, she knew no other way than to be loyal and honest. And he knew exactly how to secure her agreement. "There is no 'or what.'" He leaned in, and her breath caught. "You will obey me because that's what you'll agree to do."

Her nails bit through the skin of his shoulders, right above his torso shield as if she knew exactly where to strike. "Humans have evolved past that," she murmured, her gaze dropping to his lips.

"You might have. We haven't," he said, pressing his raging cock against her softness.

A tremble that he could feel wound through her legs. Color slid up beneath her dusky skin. "Are we going inside?"

"Yes." He pushed open the door, keeping his hold firm and her attention on him. He'd wanted to follow her path of logic, and he'd wanted to allow her naïveté about him and his people to remain. But it wasn't possible. Not if he wanted to keep her safe. He moved then, backing her into the main room of the cabin, automatically lifting his nose and searching for threats.

She grabbed his flanks to keep from falling. When they'd finally stopped in the middle of the room, she slid her hands over his abs. "So. Any threats here?"

He liked that she was so attuned to him. That she knew what he was doing. Unfortunately, she was about to know him a hell of a lot better. "Just me, Professor."

* * * *

The chilly night air wandered into the darkened room, and in that second, Promise knew she was safe. She'd gain the precious moments she needed to calm down her body and approach the mating with the logic it required. She tried to keep the triumph out of her expression—she really did.

By the flaring of his nostrils and the straightening of his shoulders, she realized she'd failed.

Even so, he released her, gracefully walking backward and kicking the door shut with one boot. It slammed hard, and she jumped. When he reached behind himself, that impossible gaze still trained on her, and engaged the lock, a shiver took her.

She tore her gaze free and studied the one-room cabin. While the outside had appeared rustic, the inside was all luxury. High-end fireplace with patterned stone, nice sitting area in front of it, kitchen to the left, enormous bed to the right, and a door that no doubt led to a bathroom. Movement caught her peripheral vision, and she turned to see him stride for the fireplace, which was already stacked with kindling and wood. The strike of a match on stone held an erotic tone she couldn't explain, but her legs threatened to fail her.

He straightened and slowly drew his shirt over his head, tossing it on one of two chairs facing the fire. The firelight caressed the hard planes of his chest, gleaming off his smooth skin and emphasizing the dark hollows beneath cut muscles.

She tried to breathe, but her lungs were as much under his spell as her attention.

"Tell me you understand what I've said." His strong hands moved to unbuckle his belt.

A thrill shot through her, pulsing erotically between her legs. She had to try twice to force words out. "Comprehension and acquiescence are two different animals."

"Aren't they, though?" he murmured, drawing the belt free and tossing it to the other chair.

Why the other chair? She tilted her head like a doe she'd once seen spotting an oncoming car. Her legs bunched, prepared to run, but there was nowhere to go. And she wasn't entirely certain she wouldn't run right for him, even though she couldn't grasp exactly what was happening at the moment.

With the firelight so bright, the dark streaks in his hair became more prominent, badges of his time as a warrior. A time she couldn't imagine.

At that thought, self-preservation finally took over. Drawing herself up, she ignored her aching body and turned to the door. "I think we had better reschedule this." Her voice came out almost as hoarse as his. Walking like a newborn colt, unsure of her steps, she turned and strode for the exit.

No wisp of sound came from him. She felt a slight disappointment that caught her off guard, and then she was pinned from behind, pushed against the metal door and trapped in place by a rock-hard body that was all male. His chin brushed the top of her head.

"I wanted to let you be logical," he growled, wrapping his hand around the front of her neck and grinding his hips against her butt. "Wanted to ease you into this life. But it's too late for that. You said yes." His other hand plunged down the front of her pants, finding her clit instantly. He stroked, and her legs gave out, but his body kept her upright. He pressed one finger inside her. "Come now."

Time somehow slowed. The feel of the hard metal against her nipples, his even harder body behind her, and those relentless fingers all took over. An orgasm hammered through her with a brutal blast of heat and electricity. She threw her head back into his chest, crying out, closing her eyes as she bucked against him. She came down with a whimpered sigh, her body still shaking.

He applied pressure beneath her chin, lifting her head more and exposing her neck. "You ready to obey?" His rough tongue skimmed up her neck, and his fang caught her earlobe.

She opened her eyes to see the metal door. "No." Then she held her breath.

He paused, one finger still inside her. "You want to leave?" His breath was hot against her ear.

"No." The word burst out of her before she could think logically. This was about need. Forget the rest.

"Good." He twisted their bodies, putting her against the tall back of the chair, facing the crackling fire. His cock, even in his jeans, ground against her backside with a demand she felt all the way to her toes. His big hand palmed her, stretching against her thighs. "Spread your legs more." He nipped at her ear again.

She jolted, her fingers curling over the chair back. "I—"

He ripped her shirt over her head, and she ducked, the words stolen from her. A soft scrape of his fang against first one shoulder and then the other, and soon her shredded bra joined her shirt near the fire. "I told you to spread your legs." He grasped one nipple and twisted just enough to demonstrate her precarious position.

Her legs quaked, and an orgasm loomed.

He withdrew his fingers a little. "Not yet. You come when I tell you to."

The sound she made was all frustration. But the feeling of his hardness against her was too delightful to ignore. So she closed her eyes and rubbed against him.

The pinch to her thigh had her jerking upright and her eyelids flying open.

His mouth licked along her ear. "If I have to tell you again, I'm pinching somewhere else." His pinkie tapped her clit.

She spread her legs so quickly she fell forward onto the chairback.

His chuckle was dark and raspy. Dominant. "Better." He released her, and before she could protest, he'd dragged her jeans and panties off, along with her shoes. Man, he moved fast when he wanted. He pulled her up, palming both of her breasts. "Hold on to the chair, baby."

She did so out of pure instinct.

He pushed her partially over, sending her up on her toes. Her body quivered while she tried to find her balance. Need shot through her so quickly she could only hold her breath. What was next?

His tongue rasped down her spine, over her ribs, and to the small of her back. Fangs slid along her buttock, and then he bit. Pain clashed into her, and she cried out, turning to push him away when he palmed her core again, his thumb rubbing against her clit. Oh, God. It was so much. Everything. Fire and ice and hunger and craving. She stilled, her body following his lead.

He lifted her a bit more, and she grabbed onto the back of the chair with everything she had. Then his mouth took over for his fingers. They dug into her ass and kept her immobile as his fangs slid along her labia.

She gasped, panicked but unable to move. Then he licked her, swirling his tongue around her clit. Never in her entire life had she been more exposed. His devastating tongue gave her no quarter, and she lost track of his mouth, his tongue, even his fingers.

Her legs shook so badly they hurt, but she didn't care. She strained, so close to an orgasm that a soft sob escaped her. More. She needed more. A tremble uncoiled inside her, and she reached for it—

And he slowed down.

"Nooooo," she gasped, shaking her head wildly.

He chuckled against her, hurling vibrations through her that were a devastating tease. A tempting example of what he could do. "You want to come?"

Her eyelids fluttered several times, and she couldn't stop them. "Yes."

"Then beg me."

His mouth returned to torturing her.

Beg? She didn't know how to beg. "Please?"

He paused, and she wanted to scream in protest. "Better. But not quite."

On all that was holy. "Please, Ivar, master of the entire universe?" she groaned.

His chuckle this time almost sent her over. "I like that. A lot. And I have every intention of mastering you." He gave her one long, slow lick. "Who are you going to obey, sweetheart?"

Even in the throes of a possible stroke brought on by absence of orgasm, she knew not to agree. But her body was quickly overcoming her mind. "I'll try." It was the best she could do.

The hard smack to her clit sent her right up onto her toes, and she almost fell over the chair.

"Do better," he suggested, his tone dark.

"Okay. You've got it. You win. I'll obey." She said the words in such a rush they didn't even compute.

He stroked her, and then his mouth descended. "Come now."

She exploded instantly, her mind shutting down, stars from every constellation bursting behind her closed lids. Right after she'd fallen over the crest, her body beginning to calm, he stood and slammed into her in one hard thrust. She gasped, her body taken over. When had he removed his jeans?

Then he was pounding. Hard and fast, deeper than any human could ever go.

Against everything she thought possible, she climbed up again, her body taking over since her mind was done.

"God, I want you," he rasped against her neck.

She shivered, taking all of him. He thrust into her and tugged her head back. Her heart stopped and then rushed to pump blood as fast as possible. "Come again."

Her body obeyed him, detonating into a million pieces. Pain slashed into her neck from his fangs, followed by an echoing burn above her right buttock, singeing deep enough to capture her soul. He shook against her with his own release and then retracted his fangs, licking the wound closed.

She blinked, her body shutting down with exhaustion. Holy Newton. She was mated.

Chapter Thirty

Ivar finished stoking the fire and then returned to bed, pulling his woman close to keep her warm. Birds chirped outside with the oncoming morning. He brushed his hand down her arm and then tucked her more securely beneath the quilt.

She stirred, her butt to his groin. "Where are we, anyway?"

"Colorado," he said. "Middle of nowhere. It's a place I come to when I need to get away." Which had happened quite often during the last three months. Though he'd never brought another person here. "Are you all right?" He'd been rough with her.

"Yes." She stretched against him. "I don't feel immortal."

"It takes some time, and I'm not sure you will feel different. Well, until you hurt yourself and learn to heal."

She put her cold feet on his thigh, wiggling her ass as she did so. "It felt like you put your mark on my right butt cheek."

He nodded and kissed the back of her neck. "Part on your cheek and part on your lower back." He had a large hand.

"I wanted it in my center back. Why did you put it there?"

"It's where I wanted it." He licked down her neck to her shoulder, and when he found his bite, she shivered. "Which, I believe, is how we firmly established our relationship would go." At least until he could save Quade and then make the world much safer for her.

She shook her head, and her thick hair caught on the pillow. "An agreement made during duress doesn't count."

"You came five times. That can hardly be qualified as duress."
Yeah, he knew what she meant. That didn't change their reality.
"Our lives are dangerous. The second they aren't, you can go
back to being as independent as you want." So long as she stayed
safe. It really wasn't much to ask. Or rather, demand. "There are
consequences to mating, and I spelled them out clearly to you."

He couldn't see her, but he'd bet his left nut she rolled her eyes.

"I can see this is a discussion for another day," she said. "For
now, tell me about Ulric. What did he do that was so bad?"

It was before Ivar's time, when his older brother had helped to
create the Seven. But he knew the stories. "Ulric is a Cyst who
killed a hundred Enhanced women and took their blood. There
was a ceremony, one probably really screwing with the physical
laws of the world, and he fused his entire body. Can't be killed
from outside."

"Like you?" she asked.

"No. I can be beheaded," he reminded her. "Our torsos are
fused like his whole body. So the only way to kill him is to do it
from within. With the blood of his victims."

She shook her head. "That's crazy."

"Reality often is," he murmured. "One of the victims was a
powerful witch who managed to first infuse her triplets with a
drug that'd kill him if their blood was combined. They were the
first Keys. Whenever one dies, another one takes her place." He
kissed her neck again, enjoying her soft gasp. "Grace is one of
the Keys, as is Mercy. We haven't found the third."

She swallowed audibly. "Isn't it possible that Ulric has reformed?
A million lifetimes in hell will do that to a monster."

"Actually, hell creates more monsters." Ivar tried to find the
right words. "The Cyst have been preparing for Ulric's return for
years. Fusing his body was only the first half of his ritual; the
second part remains unfinished. If he completes the other half,
he'll have the ability to kill all Enhanced women. Every single
one of them."

She was quiet for several moments. "Like me?"

"Yes. Like you. Even mated ones." He held her tighter, needing her to understand the danger she was in. "The Seven have diaries and notes on the rituals as well as the science involved. You're welcome to all of it." He knew she'd be eager to study the problem and figure it all out. That was good. Somebody needed to and rather soon.

She nodded. "Another scientific investigation to pursue. I can't believe how many there are."

He flattened his palm across her upper chest, feeling her heart beat. Strong and steady. Beneath his touch, it revved up. "You now have eternity to pursue each and every one. At least you will, shortly." He didn't know how long it would take for her chromosomal pairs to increase. The current theory was that everyone was different, which made sense.

"How much time are we talking?" she asked.

"Anywhere between a couple of days and a week, last I heard," he said. "You can talk to the queen. She's a geneticist and has been studying the issue for quite a while."

"All right." Promise turned in the bed to face him. "Last night was indescribable."

"Agreed." He took in her sleepy eyes and mussy hair. She was perfect in the morning.

She blinked. "I need to get back to my math, Ivar. The boards are calling me."

He grinned. Man, she was cute. From the very beginning, he'd thought so. "All right." He rolled her over, planting himself on top of her. "In a few minutes." Then he kissed her.

* * * *

Even after a lovely shower and serviceable breakfast at the cabin, Promise was more unsettled than she'd been defending her first dissertation when Logan arrived to teleport them back to demon headquarters. The mating had gone way beyond mere bodily functions and sex. "You're kind of kinky, Ivar," she said, following him outside to the rocks.

He snorted. "I'm just me."

Yes. That was correct. And he was far from the growly and easygoing guy who'd cooked stew in her unstocked kitchen. There were depths to him, and they were not at all human. Her visceral reaction to him, to the dominance in him, both thrilled and concerned her.

Never in her life had she found it difficult to handle an issue with her brain instead of emotions. Until now.

Logan waited at the far edge of the rock, dressed in a torn T-shirt and dark jeans, a bandage wrapped around his right forearm.

Promise drew near. "What is this?"

He removed the cotton and showed a three-inch gash already turning red and swollen. "Garrett and I were sparring, and he got me with a good fake. Thought since I was coming to pick you up, you'd like to see healing cells at work."

She gasped, rushing toward him, her mind going on full alert. "That is so kind."

He shrugged a shoulder. "Sure." Then he looked at the wound, breathed in and exhaled evenly.

The wound stitched itself together and then healed, the muscle and sinew beneath the skin smoothing out within a few seconds.

She straightened. "That happened so quickly." Waiting for his nod, she prodded the healed skin, running her fingers along the tendon and finding no ridges or abnormalities. "Truly excellent."

Ivar slipped his arm around her waist and drew her back into his hard body. Her abdomen did a slow roll, and desire flushed along her skin, warming her even more than the hybrid's proximity. "Don't think of attempting that on yourself for a while, little professor."

Heat climbed into her face. She had been considering a couple of experiments. But it did most likely take time for the ability to develop. "We'll see." It wouldn't do to allow Ivar to become too bossy with her.

His hold tightened. "Logan?"

Logan's eyes twinkled. "The queen is ready to perform MRIs on everybody, if you'd like to start with an experiment today."

Promise hopped, exhilaration finally taking over the warning ticking through her. "Wonderful. I want to get started." Her mind flicked through facts she knew about royalty. "With this queen, what's the protocol?" The last thing she wanted was to start off on the wrong foot with the Queen of the Realm.

"Huh?" Logan asked.

Oh, men were clueless. "Is there a curtsy involved? Do I say, 'Long live the queen,' or is there some other form of address?"

Logan scratched his skin where the wound had healed. "We just usually hold out an arm."

Promise ducked her chin. What kind of royal protocol was that? "I'm not comprehending. Is the queen a hugger?" Maybe it was a two-kiss-on-the-cheeks type of situation.

Logan snorted. "No, but chances are, she'll have a syringe with her. If she wants your blood, let her have it."

"No kidding," Ivar muttered. "Benny stayed at headquarters for a week last month, and he was determined not to donate blood for her research. The woman waited until he was asleep and pretty much attacked him."

Logan nodded. "Yeah. Not much Ben could do in that situation. It wasn't like he could throw her across the room or anything."

Promise faltered. She was uncertain how to respond. Then an idea hit her. She'd shielded her mind automatically when Logan had appeared. Hadn't even had to think about it. Was it possible to just remove the shield? She concentrated on sliding it sideways. Ice picks attacked her temple, and she sucked in air, falling back against Ivar.

"What are you doing?" Ivar's mouth touched her temple.

"Just experimenting," she said, drawing the shield back into place and sighing as the diamonds sparkled and stopped the pain.

"A warning next time would be nice," Ivar said, then turned to Logan. "Before we hit Realm headquarters, what's the status with the Kurjan kid?"

"Safe," Logan said. "With us. Haven't sent him home yet."

Promise shook her head. The demons had to be above holding a child hostage. "You should be better than that."

"We're not." Ivar said shortly. "Logan?"

Logan nodded, bunched his legs, and leaped at them. The ride was smoother than the previous night, for some reason. Pure darkness, and even though Promise kept her eyes wide open, all she saw was the void.

They landed in the front yard of a solid wooden lodge. Soldiers patrolled the lawn, somehow stepping around mature rosebushes and colorful annuals just giving up the fight as winter approached.

The door opened, and out rushed a woman wearing a white lab coat opened over jeans and a yellow sweater. Her black hair was tied back in a ponytail, and her blue eyes sparkled with intelligence. Her pink tennis shoes made no sound on the crackled stone walk. She reached them and grasped Promise's hand. "It's so nice to meet you. This ability you have to sense people who can teleport—have you always had it?" She began to draw Promise toward the lodge.

Ivar paused them by grasping Promise's arm. "Missy? This is Emma Kayrs, Queen of the Realm."

This was the queen? Promise stumbled as she turned. Nobody had told her whether to curtsy or not. Did she know how to curtsy?

Emma pumped her hand vigorously.

"Emma, this is Promise Williams, my mate," Ivar said.

Emma's eyes widened. "Mate?" She swiveled to pierce Ivar with a look. "When?"

"Last night?" Promise wasn't sure what to make of the queen.

Emma smiled, color rushing into her face. "Lovely. Just excellent. Great timing." She all but dragged Promise toward the door. "This is our medical facility—halfway between Realm and demon headquarters." Apparently finding too much resistance, she pulled Promise close and tucked her arm around Promise's shoulders, and Ivar had to release her. "We'll do a little blood work before we get started on the MRIs. Since the mating is just taking effect."

Twin groans echoed behind them as Promise let the queen lead her into her lab.

Chapter Thirty-One

As Ivar had suspected, Promise and Emma became fast friends. When Faith joined them, there was so much glee discussing the test results that he wanted to tear his own head off.

Finally, it was his turn. The MRI machine gleamed white with a tiny narrow tube to shove him in. His hands started sweating first. His gut rolled over, and he moved toward the tube, wearing plain cotton pants and a white T-shirt with no metal anywhere.

Promise patted the bed. "Just lie here, and we'll shoot you in. There's a microphone, and we'll get some pictures before asking you to try to teleport somewhere and then return in a minute. If you aren't able to teleport, no worries. We want to watch your brain try."

He swallowed, but his throat had gone dry.

She looked up at him, her honey-chocolate eyes focusing. "Are you all right?"

"I'm fine." He'd faced a dragon-wolf beast in a hell dimension once, and he'd felt better at that moment than this one. After being dragged through so many portals to places with unreal gravity that crushed him, feeling nervous about being shoved headfirst into a tube that would take him seconds to break apart if necessary was fucking crazy.

She ran her hand up his bare arm. "You don't have to do this."

He buried his panic deep inside, where it belonged, so he could force a smile for her. No way in hell was he showing weakness to his new mate. "I'm good." Then he lay down. His heart shook against his fused ribs. Was it possible for a hybrid to have a heart attack? He'd never heard of one, but he could be the first. If his heart blew apart, it'd take ages to mend.

Promise moved into the control room, and the lights dimmed.

The machine whirred and began to slide him into the tube. His fingers dug into the sheet on either side of his body, and sweat broke out down his entire torso.

He came to an abrupt halt, and he shut his eyes, not wanting to see that he was trapped.

Memories assailed him—took him under. Blood and death and paralyzing fear. His fangs dropped, and he pricked his bottom lip, tasting blood. Metallic and familiar.

"Ivar?" Emma's voice came from a speaker right above his head. "Your vitals are off the chart. Do you want to get out?"

"No," he grunted. Of course he wanted out.

"Hey, Viking." Promise's voice came next, and the sound smoothed over him like the soft fur he'd taken off a beast one time. "Take several deep breaths."

He followed her calm instructions, and his heart rate slowed slightly.

"That's good. You're safe." She clicked off for a second. "Okay. We've got a baseline for your brain activity. Go ahead and attempt to teleport anywhere you want. If you don't want to return to the MRI machine, just pop up wherever you decide. It's okay, Ivar. If it doesn't work, we'll just slide you out right away."

Her easy acceptance helped him as nothing else could have. He drew on the forces around him, fighting his own weakness. Power snapped through him and wisped away. Nothing happened. Apprehension tore into him. He reared up and hit his head on the top of the tube.

His shoulders were constrained, and his legs kicked out. His eyes opened upon darkness, and instinct took over. Invisible claws raking him, he roared and punched up as hard as he could.

Then he went nuts.

Metal flew, plastic cracked, and even the sheet tore down the middle as he fought the confinement.

Female voices called out to him through the speaker, but he couldn't make out their words through the raging fire in his head. He punched his arm through the side, and the bed started to move, but he tore pieces with him as he went.

Strong arms grabbed him off the bed and wrenched him to the floor. "You're okay, Viking." Adare shook him, banding an arm around his shoulders, keeping him from flailing anymore. "Breathe, brother."

Ivar punched out and then shuddered. His blood was on fire.

"You're good." Adare hugged him tight and then released him, his eyes the deepest of blacks. "I've got you."

Ivar panted out heated air, the raging in his head dissipating.

"Ivar?" Promise's voice came from the doorway.

Adare held up a hand to ward her off. "Stay there for a second, Professor." He angled his head, watching Ivar. "Right, buddy?"

Ivar took in several more shuddering breaths and then sat back on the cold floor. His body stopped shaking, and he turned to look at the demolished equipment. He blanched.

Adare slapped him on the back, grabbed his arm, and hauled him to his feet. "Yeah. The queen is gonna be pissed. You're on your own for that one." Then he held tight until Ivar's legs were able to hold him up without help, silently giving the support of a brother.

Promise ran inside and collided with his chest. "I'm so sorry. I had no idea your claustrophobia was that bad." She hugged him, her hands flattening above his waist. "Or that you had claustrophobia."

He lifted her chin, shocked to see tears sliding down her smooth face. Tears? For him?

It was like a kick to the heart and a kiss at the same time. "I'm fine, sweetheart." He leaned in and soothed himself with her scent.

She held him, rubbing his back, making soft noises.

He looked over her head at the queen, who stood in the doorway, her patrician features set in concerned lines. "I'm sorry, Emma."

Emma's face, already kind, softened even more. "I didn't know, Ivar. I'm the one who's sorry."

He looked toward the mangled machinery. "Ah, shit." It was worse than he'd thought. "I have funds to replace that," he said. "Mercy can transfer the money today."

Emma shrugged. "We have three more rooms like this one, so no worries. However, I think we'll stick to blood and physical intensity tests for you." She turned and slipped out of sight.

Ivar gently wiped the tears off Promise's cheeks. "You always cry for your subjects?" he asked.

She sniffed. "This is the first time."

Yeah, that's what he figured. There were emotions between them, which made sense after the mating. How was he going to leave her sweetness and return to hell?

It didn't matter how. He had no choice. The day he'd agreed to undergo the ritual to become one of the Seven, and the moment he'd survived that agonizing ordeal, his path had been forged.

Life sometimes sucked.

* * * *

"Your playroom does not suck," Drake said, sitting cross-legged in front of the video console. "These games don't even come out for another six months. How did you get them?"

Hope shrugged, sitting next to him with her purple game controller in her hands. "My uncle Kane makes a bunch of these games with different companies. He said that's how he gets money to buy me presents." She grinned.

Drake grinned back, his eyes a lighter green today. "I've heard of Kane. He's supposed to be brilliant."

"Yeah. He's super smart," Hope said, her heart all warm. Kane made the best ice cream too.

"Isn't he working with the Seven?" Drake asked, his fingers fast on the controller so that his bear leaped over a bunch of snapping turtles on the screen.

"Uh-huh," Hope said. "The Seven are good guys. You don't hafta worry about them." She had her bear do a summersault over a wild river with hungry crocodiles.

"Nice," Drake said.

Hope sat up straighter, her shoulders back. He thought she was good at the game. That was awesome. "Thanks. You're super at this too."

Drake shook his head. "Not as good as you. And you're wrong about the Seven. They did some bad stuff years ago and put away the guy who's kinda like a priest to us. To do that, they broke a lot of laws."

"Nuh-uh," Hope said, her face getting hot. "My uncle Garrett would never break a law." He'd joined the Seven this year. "My uncle Logan might, but he wasn't there years ago, so he couldn't have broken laws." Somebody was lying to Drake, and it was just too bad. She had to get him to see the truth.

The door opened, and Paxton walked in. He had a purple bruise on his right cheekbone.

Hope stood and rushed to him. "Pax? What happened?"

Paxton turned red. "I was training this morning with a couple of demons, and one got a good shot in." Even his ears were bright.

Drake stood and walked more slowly, his gaze on the bruise. "Looks like you caught a couple of big knuckles." He shook his head. "Those hurt. It's happened to me."

Paxton lifted his chin. "Why are you still here?"

Drake shrugged. "I don't know. I got to talk to my dad yesterday, and he wants me to come home, but the demons are keeping me here. Didn't know you guys kidnapped kids."

Hope shook her head, panic hurting her throat. "They're gonna let you go home soon." She needed to talk to her daddy. He'd come in late last night after she'd already gone to bed. Drake had stayed in their guest room.

Her mama poked her head in. "Hey, kids. You guys hungry?"

Both Paxton and Drake shuffled their feet but looked at her mama funny. Kind of like with curiosity and wishes. They nodded.

She smiled, her blue eyes sparkling. "Well, come on. I have mac and cheese, sandwiches, chips, and noodles. And for dessert I have ice cream or cookies."

Hope bit her lip. Neither boy had a mama anymore. She could share hers with them, and she usually did with Pax, but Drake was gonna have to leave soon. She wished he could get a mama, but immortals usually couldn't re-mate. Maybe she should tell him about that virus in case the Kurjans didn't know.

"Hope?" her mama asked.

Hope jumped. "Oh. Yeah. We're all hungry. Pax got hurt training today."

Janie moved to Pax and gently lifted his chin. "Ah, sweetheart. I didn't know there was training earlier today."

He leaned more toward her. "A bunch of shifters were working out, and I joined them."

Hope frowned. "You said demons."

He jerked. "It was both. The shifters were, ah, training, and a couple of demon kids joined in. It was a demon that caught me with my guard down."

Hope's mom tilted her head. "Are you hurt anywhere else?"

"No," Pax said, backing away from her. "I'm fine, Mrs. Kyllwood. Honest."

"I've told you to call me Janie," she said, sliding an arm around his shoulders. She turned and motioned for Drake, who walked forward slowly and took her hand. "You too, sweetheart."

Drake blushed and leaned into her side. "Okay. Janie."

Paxton looked him over with no expression.

Hope watched. Maybe they could eat lunch, and Pax and Drake would finally become friends. She wanted to find a way to bring

Pax into the dreamworld with them, but so far, she hadn't figured out how.

"Come on, Hope," her mama said. "Let's eat and then we'll figure out how to get Drake home to his daddy. We've waited long enough for *your* daddy to figure it out."

Ah, good. When Hope's mama took over, things got done. Her daddy was good at leading the nation. But her mama would help Drake see his daddy soon. "Okay, Mama." She followed behind her mom and two of her best friends in the whole world.

Things were getting better.

Her daddy appeared from a doorway down the hallway. "Janie Belle?" He walked toward them, his big boots clonking on the tiles.

Her mama stopped. "Did you make the arrangements?" Her voice had that tone that said things had to get done.

Her daddy's green eyes sparkled, and he'd taken off all his weapons. "Yes." He looked down at Paxton. "What happened to your eye?"

"Training," Paxton said, pressing closer to Janie. "I'll do better next time, Zane."

Daddy ruffled Pax's hair. "You're doing fine. We'll talk later." He looked at Drake. "Hey, Drake. Have you ever teleported?"

Drake shook his head.

Daddy smiled. "It's no big deal. I'll just hold your arm, we'll fly through a little tunnel, and then I'll take you to see your dad. How does that sound?"

Her mama reared back. "*You're* taking him?"

Daddy nodded. "Yes. Our requests have been satisfied." He reached for Drake, who held out his arm. "I'll be right back." Then they zipped out of sight.

A moment later Daddy was back. He leaned over to kiss Mama on the nose. "It's fine. We made arrangements earlier, and Dayne was waiting in a public place. Drake and I popped in behind a few trees, he ran to his dad, and I left before anybody could shoot me." He looked toward Hope. "So. I guess we should talk about being grounded now for going into town without permission."

Ah, man. That stank. She'd hoped her daddy would forget and would need to go back to work. There was lots going on with the Seven.

She knew because she'd had dreams that night about the Seven and her uncle Ivar. He was gonna get hurt again, and she hadn't figured out a way to save him.

But she would.

Chapter Thirty-Two

The week flew by for Promise at demon headquarters. She spent her days conducting experiments with Faith and Emma while Grace recorded everything with her camera, wanting to participate but falling asleep with irritated groans whenever Promise tried to explain string theory to her. They'd quickly discovered the areas of the immortal brain that lit up when teleporting happened, and it was true—different areas were triggered for demons and fairies.

The search for the female demon-Fae hybrid had intensified, with both Realm and demon computer experts working around the clock to find her—if she had survived her childhood.

Promise's nights were spent with Ivar Kjeidsen, learning that her body was made to enjoy as much as her brain was. The sense of urgency surrounding their scientific investigations only amplified her feelings overall.

It was also fascinating to see him try to heal himself. Since she'd been able to identify the area of the brain that controlled teleporting, she was able to use a scan to show Ivar exactly where to send the healing cells. He said he could feel a change in that area within a day of concentrating on it.

One night she was typing furiously in her laptop from the university, sitting on their bed, waiting for Ivar to return from training. Apparently the demon soldiers had new moves to share with him. She muttered to herself, really not liking where the math was heading. Ivar was going to like her results even less. Her stomach cramped, but she forced herself to keep diagramming and working the numbers.

Her laptop dinged, and she pressed a button, bringing Mark Brookes on-screen. "Mark. Hello," she said, smiling, grateful for a break. "How are you?"

His thinning hair was swept back, and his eyes glowed with excitement. "Excellent. I've been working on my grant and have managed to incorporate your last two research papers with my current theories. I think my math could help you with your theoretical application for interdimensional travel. Maybe. Or it would be just fun to work together again."

She kept her smile in place. Honestly, she'd give anything to be able to tell him about her actual travels, but that amounted to treason in the immortal world. Ivar had been exceptionally and irritatingly clear about that fact. More than once, actually. "That's wonderful." She ran back through her mind to remember the two papers. Right. String theory and dark matter had been the main subjects. "Most mathematicians don't believe we could use gravity to bend time."

"Meh." He lifted a shoulder and angled closer to the camera. "So, what do you say? Want to come into the school and collaborate? Nobody said you had to work from home."

"I'm not at home," she said, pushing a wayward curl away from her face. "I've decided to travel some while I work."

He frowned. "I know you. When you're on a problem, you're obsessed. You're telling me you're taking in sights while doing a little math on the side?"

She grinned. "Of course not. I just decided to rent a place in the mountains and work in quiet and solitude. But I'd love to collaborate if possible." Mark was a brilliant mathematician and he might be of great help. Unfortunately, she couldn't share any of her results as of yet. "I'm just getting started and don't have anything to share."

"What mountains?" he asked.

"Washington," she said, lying almost easily. She'd been spending too much time with immortals who thought everything should be secret. At least the queen was on her side and wanted to share results with humans if necessary. How odd. A realization smacked Promise in the head. She was no longer human.

Then what was she? She was immortal but not an immortal being. Huh. Fascinating.

"Promise?" Mark asked. "Are you listening?"

"Of course." For goodness' sake. She'd lied again. The outer door opened. "I have to go. I'll be in touch." She clicked off as Ivar walked in, dropping weapons on the duvet near the window.

"Who was that?" Ivar toed off his combat boots. His eyes were a dusky green, and his shoulders tense. Lines fanned out from the sides of his generous mouth, making him look exhausted.

"Mark Brookes," she said, tilting her head to study him. "What's wrong?"

"Nothing is wrong." Ivar reached her and took the laptop, gently placing it on the bedside table. "I'm just tired. The healing cells are working constantly on my brain, and they take a great deal of energy. Add in training with knives and dealing with crazy Benny, and I could use some sleep." He sat on the bed and dragged her onto his lap, kissing her deeply. "What did Brookes want?"

"He wants to collaborate on the grant proposals," Promise said, her voice husky. Ivar could kiss. Her entire body went from tired to full burn.

"Oh." Ivar kissed her nose. "I guess we should announce the winners of those grants so people stop working on them. Hey. By the way, congrats. You won a grant."

She grinned. "No kidding." Her funds were apparently unlimited now, anyway. "Does the money go to the university?"

"It does, and it's unfortunate you don't," he said, rubbing his chin on the top of her head. "Unless you really want to go teach for a couple of decades. Then you'll have to disappear for a while, though."

She shook her head. "No, I'm on this teleporting problem and can't think of teaching until I solve it. But it's nice the university will get the funds." She'd done a good thing for her alma mater, and that satisfied her. A moment or two to bask in that victory was all the time she had, though. Her closed laptop mocked her. "I checked the news, and there haven't been any more reports of kidnapped physicists."

"We have guards stationed around the world protecting whomever we think needs it," Ivar said, raking his hand through his long hair. "There have been a couple of attempts, but we have good resources in place."

That was sweet. She swallowed. "I have to talk to you."

"Ditto." He smiled. "I teleported today."

Her breath caught. "No way."

"Way."

He was quick and funny. She hugged him as much as she could from his lap. "That's so wonderful. Let's go somewhere." Before she had to give him the bad news.

"Not yet." He yawned. "My control wasn't great. I'll need a couple more days to get it down, but I'm close. Then we can go anywhere you want." His chin lowered, and his gaze ran over her face. "You're tense. What's going on?"

She gulped. Giving bad news was often a normal day for a theoretical physicist. "The math doesn't work, Ivar." She used his name and not the Viking nickname to make sure he understood the seriousness of her statement. "I've worked the equations back and forth, studying all that we've learned." And using theories she'd created along with Kane Kayrs in the application of traveling through dimensions via wormholes. "You can't take Quade's place, and you can't set him free. The results of either eventuality could be catastrophic. I'm sorry."

* * * *

Ivar set Promise on the bed and backed away, his gaze on her. No way had she said what he'd thought. "There has to be some mistake."

She shook her head. "No. I tried to avoid Newton's first law, and so did Kane. But it's true. There's a status quo in the configuration of the, let's call them bubbles, right now. After Ronan's broke, the other two probably, as much as we can theorize, used gravitational pulls to find a new normal. Every world is connected, or you wouldn't have been able to go there. If one world were to be shattered, it'd change all the rest." She straightened, her voice strengthening as she tried to explain. "Don't you see? When Ronan's bubble burst, it created those hell worlds. Or it revealed them or brought them in from elsewhere. We're not sure exactly what happened."

"But Quade is in a hell dimension," Ivar countered.

"Now, he is. But he probably wasn't until Ronan's dimension burst." She tapped her laptop on the table. "We think. And since time is different in different dimensions, three months here could be eternity there."

"No." He shook his head and moved toward his weapons. "You need to find a way." His breath was heated in his chest, and it burned up his damaged throat. "I don't care if we cause chain reactions in other worlds so long as we get him here. How can it matter?"

Her eyebrows lifted. "How can it matter? For one thing, it could destroy this world. For another, just because you haven't come across other humans or intelligent beings in those other worlds, it doesn't mean they're not out there. If the bubbles are infinite, then you've visited less than one-zillionth of a percent of one-zillionth to the nth degree."

He didn't care. Not one part of him cared. "Thank you for figuring it out. I appreciate it." He strapped his knife back in place. Surely Adare would be up for a few hours of sparring.

"Of course." She frowned.

"But you need to go the next step and discover how I get back to Quade." He tried to make the statement sound like a request, but it definitely sounded like an order. So be it. "Whether you like the results or not, that's your job. That's why you have the grant."

"Are you doubting me? Do you think I'm lying?" she asked.

The woman thought she was all brain, but in truth, she had an enormous heart. "I think you're giving up. Part of you doesn't want me to go, and I think you're limiting your math."

Her head jerked. "You're an arrogant jackass. My math is spot on, and I've been working nonstop every second since we met."

How could he get her to see beyond the numbers? "Your job is to do the math. So do it."

"Is that why you mated me?" she asked, her voice soft. "You mated me for my mathematical abilities, and you're not getting the answers you wanted. You made a mistake."

He paused. "That's why you mated me. For access to this world and its physics." She didn't get to rewrite history now. "I agreed because that's what you wanted." Words were bottled up in his chest, and he swallowed through the sandpaper of his throat several times. "I know there's more between us than science and exploration, and so do you." But at the moment, he wanted to yell at her, so he needed to get the hell out of there. They'd been playing house with the kissy face and sex, and he'd enjoyed it. But he had a mission to do and a vow to keep. "Don't think for a second you're getting out of this mating."

"My job is bigger than your wishes," she said, her eyes dark.

He tried to grab his temper. He really did. "That's all well and good, but you'll do as you're told. The repercussions are mine to worry about."

Her chin lifted and firmed. "That's where you are incorrect. I have a duty to science and the preservation of life that transcends your wants. You don't want to work against me on this."

Was that a threat? A fucking threat? A part of him—a far distant part from the one blowing up in fury—admired her for it. The other part. Well now. That one was going to take control of the situation in a way she surely would not like. "Stick with the theoretical, Professor. I'll worry about the practical applications." He strode toward the door, forgetting his exhaustion.

"I'll stop you, Ivar," she said, her voice a mere whisper.

He paused in front of the door and closed his eyes. Oh, she had not. He turned to look at her over his shoulder, trying to ignore how sweet and vulnerable she looked on his bed, even though her eyes were now shooting sparks. "Oh, baby. You just try it." Then he turned and walked out the door, shutting it so quietly it was only a whisper.

His blood heated, he strode to the end of the hall and turned down a stairwell. Demon headquarters had an excellent training area in the basement, and hopefully Adare was down there. Instead, he found Garrett finishing up with a weight set in the far corner.

"Hey," Garrett said, straightening to study him. The kid's metallic gray eyes caught everything. "What's up?"

"Looking for Adare to spar," Ivar said.

Garrett looked around the vacant area covered by mats. "He's not here, but I'm available."

"I'm pissed," Ivar warned.

Garrett shrugged. "Dude, I spar with my dad. He's often pissed." Talen Kayrs was the strategic leader of the entire Realm and was known to level buildings with his temper. "And stop calling me *kid*." He shook out his hands and moved toward Ivar.

"You are a kid." Yeah, he might be twenty-five or so, and he might've fought in a war and then survived the Seven ritual— "Yeah, okay. That's fair." There was nothing kid-like about Garrett Kayrs. Ivar swung out, testing, and Garrett ducked easily.

"So. What did she do?" Garrett asked, his feet light on the mats.

Ivar kicked and hit him beneath the chin. "How did you know my mood has something to do with my mate?"

"Please." Garrett swung and connected with a solid punch to the neck.

Fair enough. "She told me the math says we can't get Quade out."

Garrett's head went back, and he flipped backward, landing on his feet and sweeping Ivar's feet out from under him. "So you feel betrayed."

Ivar hit hard, rolled, and kicked Garrett in the gut before striking behind his knee. "Well, yeah."

The fight intensified, and they stopped talking, just hitting and kicking. An hour passed and then two. Finally, they both lay on their backs, breathing heavily and bleeding, maybe coughing up shit that shouldn't be coughed up.

"Feel better?" Garrett groaned.

"Yes. Thanks. Owe you one," Ivar panted.

Garrett snorted, blood dribbling down his face. "Just don't let me get mated. Ever."

Ivar grinned, his tongue touching the spot where he'd lost a tooth. "Oh, man. I can't wait to meet your mate." Now that was going to be an interesting day.

For now, Ivar had his own mate to deal with. Somehow.

Chapter Thirty-Three

Promise awoke from dreams about the universe exploding and rushing back to the moment of the big bang, when time stopped, never to move forward again. She blinked. The bed shifted, and heat instantly enveloped her. Then Ivar hauled her up against him, her back to his front, his mouth at her ear. He was nude and rock hard behind her. "Did you have time to think about your position?"

Her position was rather vulnerable in her T-shirt and panties. Desire clawed through her, and she tried hard not to shiver. She failed.

His chuckle sent ripples beneath her skin, even as one big hand moved up and caressed her nipple through the shirt. "While I'm not having an effect on your brain, your body knows who it belongs to."

Her nipples, both of them, turned tight and achy. She dug her hands into the sheets to keep from reaching for him. "I thought you were pouting elsewhere," she breathed.

He pinched.

She moaned, delicious flames streaking from her breasts to her clit. "That's not fair."

"I've never planned to play fair." His fang caught her earlobe with a hint of threat.

Her womb convulsed. How did he do this?

He licked along the shell of her ear and tugged the shirt over her head to toss it across the room. Then his warm palm moved to her other needy breast. "I kicked Garrett for a while, he punched me, and once we were done, I realized a couple of things."

"That you need to be hit in the head a lot?" she asked, her voice breathy.

He pinched again, and she arched against him, pressing her thighs together against the painful ache there. "No. That you belong to me. Every stubborn inch of you."

She opened her eyes, having not realized they were still closed. "Says the man determined to disappear into hell without me."

"It's a mission." His fangs scraped along her neck, providing an erotic reminder of the danger in him. He tugged on her panties, and she scooted her butt up to let him remove them. "Like any soldier, I'll have missions. And I'll return. Didn't know that until I met you. But I will be back."

She settled back down, need rioting inside every cell. Not one molecule of her wanted him to stop, so she'd argue with him while heading toward orgasms. Who knew? Maybe they could reach an agreement somehow during sex. It was certainly worth the experiment.

His free hand flattened over her abdomen, sliding down.

She caught her breath, sucking in her stomach, willing him to go faster. To get there sooner. "Please."

"Ah, so sweet." He lifted her thigh and pulled it over his before shoving the bedclothes down.

Cool air hit her private parts, and she gasped. She was open, exposed, her body nude. They'd been in a fight, and they needed to talk. But no words would come. Her body took over, wanting him. Needing him. Was this what craving felt like? If so, it hurt. She tried to move, to protect herself, but he held her in place. She shuddered, need licking inside her. "Ivar," she murmured.

"Yeah." He touched her, so lightly, and her body jumped. "Is it possible, Professor, that you don't want me to return to hell?"

She rolled her hips, trying to get closer to the hand held tantalizingly out of reach. "At the moment, I want you right where you are. Except closer." She rested her head back on his chest, pushing, needing more of him. Wanting all of him.

"Could it affect the math?" His fingers grazed over her clit, one at a time, forcing shock waves through her extremities.

Math? What the hell was math? She breathed out, her brain catching up. "No."

"Sure it could." He lifted her thigh and slowly penetrated her from behind, his fingers working her clit so she'd take him all the way in.

Pain and pleasure mingled until she couldn't tell one from the other and didn't care. So long as he didn't stop. "Math is math," she gasped.

"Ah, my theoretical bunny." He wrenched her head to the side and nipped her neck with enough pressure to send her heartbeat skyrocketing. "You sometimes start with a conclusion. A hypothesis, if you will. Then you take the math there to see if it works."

She swallowed, overtaken. "Did you just call me 'bunny'?"

His chuckle moved his chest behind her, vibrating along her spine to her butt. "Started to say 'brat,' but figured you wouldn't like that since I was about to do this." With one final push, he shoved all the way up and inside her with a force that pushed her toward the headboard. Only his strong hold kept her from hitting her head.

She cried out as an orgasm washed over her before she could identify what was happening. He held on to her as she shook. She moaned, her shoulders relaxing, letting his warmth comfort her. He waited, silent and unmoving, until she realized they weren't done.

She stiffened. "Ivar."

Soundless, he used his body to roll them over, her on her stomach, allowing himself one second to flatten her to the bed, her face in the pillow.

His heaviness pushed her into the mattress, and she jerked, unable to breathe. Then he was off her, pulling her hips up and using his knees to force hers up, while remaining fully embedded inside her. His cock stretched her, filling her beyond mathematical possibilities. Maybe her math was off.

She scrambled up to her elbows to keep from suffocating in the pillow. Behind her, he clamped both hands on her hips and drove into her without pause, without a hint of mercy. He pounded into her, hard, hot, huge, his grip bruising and absolute.

He leaned over her, dragging his fangs up her shoulder blade.

She shut her eyes, unable to move. The feelings took her over, more than she could've ever imagined. This wasn't sex. It wasn't making love. It was a claiming on a level she had never anticipated. No human could. But it was there, the immortal power, the animalistic reality of a connection beyond all comprehension. Or maybe just beyond hers. Even though she couldn't define it, she felt it.

She couldn't have stopped him if she wanted to. That idea, simple and primal, cascaded a fiery brand through her, quaking her into a second orgasm. This one rolled over her, took her, and left her panting for more. She'd die before she tried to stop him. She'd kill him if he stopped.

He struck, his fangs going deep, slashing through muscle to bone. Maybe deeper.

She cried out again, arching her spine, her head thrown back. His hand snaked along her rib cage, over her breasts, to her opposite shoulder, tugging her face up, holding her immobile. Her body was his to command as he hammered into her. Heat uncoiled inside her again, this time with a raw edge that embraced pain.

His fangs retracted, their imprint forever embedded in her. He licked her neck, sliding his mouth to her ear. "Tell me you're mine," he rasped in that damaged voice.

It wasn't a request. There was no plea, no cajoling. It was an order, clear and dark, conveying more than words ever truly could.

She was his. Everything in her knew it. A part of her rebelled against it. The terminology and the reality of it. She was a human born in this time, a successful woman in her own right. But here and now, with him inside her, with his power, his strength, everything he'd become demanding what he wanted, denying the truth was wrong. "I'm yours," she whispered, understanding it to the soul.

His thrusts turned wild, searing her with galvanizing heat, illustrating his might and his control. His next violent thrust propelled her into an orgasm so strong she could only shut her eyes and jerk violently through it.

His fangs slashed home again, increasing her tremors until she wound down just as he ground against her and came, his breath harsh and his groan dark.

She gasped several times, aftershocks taking her. Vulnerability was next. The world had changed once again on her.

* * * *

It was intriguing that his heart still beat so wildly in a chest fused by fire, blood, and bone. Oh, it couldn't be split in two, but even so, what power. Ivar pulled out of his woman and turned her on her side, wrapping an arm around her waist and drawing her against his body. Fine tremors still shook her, so he reached down and hauled the bedcovers up and over them both.

She yawned, stretching and then settling into place with the sigh of a satisfied kitten. "Bunny." She snorted.

He smiled against her hair, his tension ratcheting down a couple of notches. He'd been rough with her—even more so than when they'd mated. But his point had been made, and while it probably proved him to be a bastard, he was content with that fact.

She didn't seem to be complaining either.

He played with the soft skin over her wrist. Delicate bones— still so breakable. How could he keep her safe while he was out of this universe? Hopefully the math problems would keep her entertained at demon headquarters until he could return. She was

Enhanced and mated to a member of the Seven. That put her in danger on a level he wasn't sure she truly understood.

"What you said about the math—I'm not sure," she said quietly into the darkness.

He tilted his head on the pillow. "Explain."

She was quiet for a moment, and he could almost hear her mind working. "My initial goal is always to protect this earth and its people. You know that."

"Yes." It was one of the things he truly liked about her—when it wasn't a pain in his ass. "Go on."

She kind of ducked her head. "I may have begun in a conservative place with my theory, which is a good place to begin." The last was said rather defensively. "And we're talking theoretical physics."

Exactly. "Find a different hypothesis," he said.

She exhaled, her shoulder blades rubbing against his chest. "You don't understand. The only way to move from hypothesis to conclusion is with experiments, and in this case, one experiment could destroy the world as we know it. Many worlds. How can we take such a risk with other people? It's irresponsible."

"Have you no faith?" he asked softly, truly curious.

She stiffened. "Faith?"

"Yeah." He caressed her arm up to her shoulder and back down. The tension in her waned slightly. "Faith. A sense that there's something bigger. That we're part of a whole and that there are reasons for everything. Reasons beyond the math and your theory and the reality of right now."

She swallowed audibly. "Faith is for children."

Something in her tone caught him. "I bet it wasn't for you. Not as a child."

"No," she said softly. "I brought up the subject of God once, and my dad made me study Darwin for an entire week before I could do anything else."

Ivar wished he could go back and punch Promise's dad in the head. "Aren't theoreticists, scientists, supposed to be open to all eventualities? All possibilities?"

"Well, yes."

"Before last week, did you think vampires existed? Or were they like God or Santa Claus?" he asked.

"Oh, Santa Claus exists." She waited and then gave a slight chuckle. "Fair enough. But I have to ask, as somebody who has lived centuries, do you really believe in God?" She seemed to hold her breath.

He lifted a shoulder. "Yeah. I mean, I know Fate exists, so why not God? Maybe we don't truly understand the concept of God, but we also don't understand much beyond three dimensions, and even you cynical physicists believe there must be more than three. Otherwise, nothing else makes sense. I don't believe you can create this world or any other out of nothing. Something had to be there first, and that something has to be omnipotent."

"I don't know," she said. "My sense of reality, of what I know to be true, has been shaken. I might be open to other possibilities."

It was all he could ask of her at the moment. "It's like sex and your vibrator," he murmured.

"What?"

He grinned. "You didn't know the kind of pleasure that existed, and now you do. You've admitted it." He kept his voice gentle as he tried to explain. "The same might be said for how you're working the math for me. Maybe you're including assumptions and limitations you don't even realize you have."

She was quiet for a moment. "That might be brilliant. I've never seen the connection between the physical or emotional status and the cerebral one."

In other words, she was realizing that emotions held power and could help with math. All right. He'd let her mull that over. "Go to sleep, chipmunk."

She laughed, and the husky sound soothed his soul. "I think you should stick with 'Missy' as your term of endearment."

"I think you might be right." He smiled and kissed the top of her head. "I'm glad we've reached an understanding."

"I'm not agreeing with you about experimentation," she said. "I'm willing to examine my hypotheses and investigate alternatives, but that's all." Her voice lowered. "My parents did their best, but I'm learning that emotion can have a place with intelligence, and it's okay to be angry with them and still love them."

Did that mean she could love him and still be aware of the beast deep inside him? Maybe. Hope burned deep inside him. "Sleep now," he murmured.

She scooted closer and was asleep within seconds. Was her tiredness caused by the change in her chromosomes? Or just exhaustion?

Lightning flashed through the window, and the skies opened up with a fall storm that held a new chill. Soon it would snow. He held her close, his eyelids shut, trying to remember how he'd gotten from this world to the hell loop. And it was a loop. The more he'd studied her math, the more he'd recognized a pattern. He could trace that pattern again if he had the right skills, skills beyond the power of a normal demon.

He'd get them somehow. His last brain scan had shown engagement in areas of his brain more connected to fairies than demons. Was he changing, evolving, from mating Promise? Her ability to instinctively identify those who could teleport might translate into a whole new skill for him.

He was hoping. In fact, he was starting to get interested in fractal math, and he'd spent a half an hour actually enjoying playing Sudoku the other day. How weird was that?

He drifted in between dreams and reality, memories and hopes for hours.

A knock on the door had him stiffening. "What?" he called out, knowing his voice would carry through the suite.

"We think we've found the Fae-demon hybrid," Logan yelled back. "Be in the conference room in ten minutes."

Ivar awoke fully immediately. He kissed the back of Promise's neck. "Get up, Missy. It's time to work."

Chapter Thirty-Four

Promise sucked down the cup of coffee Ivar had handed her as if it was an elixir of life itself. Even though she'd slept well, her body ached in all sorts of delicious places, and she could use a long bath. But it was not to be. Ivar led her into the conference room at demon headquarters, where Logan and Garrett awaited.

A screen took up the entire west wall, and a small picture in the bottom left showed Faith, Emma, Mercy, and Grace in a room at the medical facility.

Mercy grinned. "We've been working for a couple of hours. Where have you been, Promise?"

Heat slid into Promise's face. "I was sleeping. Sorry about that." The rain slashed hard against the windows, and she wrapped her cardigan tighter around her body. "What did you find?" She'd been surprised to discover that Garrett and Logan both were excellent with computers as well as being superb fighters. They'd been on the search to find the Fae-demon hybrid for the entire week.

Garrett kicked back in his leather chair. He had a couple of bruises down his cheekbone that he hadn't bothered to heal yet. Were those from Ivar? They must've really gone at it. "Have a seat."

Ivar pulled out a chair at the conference table for her, and she sat, careful not to spill her coffee. He sat next to her, while Logan was situated closer to the screen, his green eyes serious and his long form in a torn T-shirt and gray jeans. The mood in the room felt heavy, as if gravity was pulling everyone down. How did the immortals affect the atmosphere in such a manner?

Garrett reached for a remote control on the mahogany table and clicked it toward the screen. "Meet Haven Daly, formerly known as Mary Agnes Lockship."

A California driver's license came up on the screen showing a twenty-something woman with white-blond hair, one black eye, and one green eye. Her skin was smooth and pale, and her expression somber.

"Whoa," Ivar said, leaning forward. "White hair of a demon, multicolored eyes of a Fae. That had to cause some questions through the years." He whistled. "Just five feet tall and what my mama would've called 'willowy.' The females of both species are petite, and she definitely fits that bill."

Garrett nodded, his head cocked. "She hasn't had an easy time of it." He clicked the button again. "As a newborn, she was found outside of a church in Minnesota, taken into child protection services, and adopted at the age of three months by a minister and his wife." Records flashed one after another on the screen. "An investigation conducted years later showed a multitude of attempted exorcisms by the good pastor and his flock."

Bile rose in Promise's throat. "I take it those weren't pleasant."

"No," Garrett said, his jaw firming and his eyes blazing. "Not even close. She then spent time in different psychiatric hospitals, some good, and some terrible. Three of them have been shut down for abuse." He growled low and then coughed to cover it.

Logan stared at the screen. "We managed to secure some of the records from those places. She thought demons were real. Thought her dreams were real, as well as the creatures that peopled them. They used drugs and therapy to convince her otherwise." His voice was pained. "No offense, Mercy, but the Fae leaders are going to be held accountable."

The screen image of Mercy was pale. "That's fine, but most of the leaders who experimented are dead, mate. Do what you need to do."

Promise reached under the table for Ivar's hand. He'd gone stone cold and silent. Hadn't he mentioned feeling protective of abused women because of his sister? He was probably planning murder right then of any Fae responsible. She wasn't entirely sure she wanted to stop him.

He held her hand, his grip firm.

Garrett clicked again, and a picture of a skinny twelve-year-old Haven came up. "She was still Mary Agnes at this time—when she left the last psychiatric hospital and returned home." His voice darkened and turned almost as hoarse as Ivar's. "Two years passed, and child services were called in by a concerned neighbor after another exorcism. She was taken from the home and put into foster care for another two years."

Promise held her stomach. It was terrible. "Tell me that time was all right for her."

"I don't know, but I doubt it," Logan said. "She ran away at sixteen and didn't show up again for five years. There are no records of her, and she might've lived on the streets, but she sends money every month to a commune called Mark's Mountain off the grid in Northern California. She may have found a safe place there."

Garrett clicked again to show a small house on a street with other small houses, all neat and tidy. "She reappeared at twenty-one and changed her name to Haven Daly. Attended community college for a semester and a half and then dropped out."

If anything, the tension in the room had increased. Promise sipped her coffee, trying to shield herself from the stress the same way she protected her brain. Nope. Her skin still pricked, and her focus narrowed. "What is she doing now?"

"Working as a waitress," Logan said. "And painting."

"Where?" Ivar asked, leaning forward.

"She's been selling online and has a showing set up for next week in Oregon. Her first showing." Garrett pushed a button, and painting after painting flashed across the screen. Disturbing, angry, wild oils of hellish landscapes and dark places.

Ivar gasped. "Stop. Go back two."

Garrett reversed the paintings to show a purple world with black mountains and a gray sky. The power of the painting made Promise catch her breath. It was starkly beautiful and yet terrifying.

"I've been there," Ivar said, the muscles in his arm clenching. "That place is real."

Garrett nodded. "We figured." He looked down and punched in something on a keyboard. "Because we came across this one too."

A painting came into focus with a man standing in front of jagged rocks, fury on his face, his body scarred. His eyes were a deep aqua, just like Ronan's. And his jawline was exactly the same.

Ivar released her hand. "Holy fuck. It's Quade."

* * * *

Ivar shoved away from the table. "We have to get to her. Secure her. She's definitely Enhanced."

"Wait." Promise swiveled her chair toward him. "That woman is Enhanced and possibly has no idea what that means. She's been through hell in her life already. Do we have a right to drag her into more?"

Ivar tried to think through the logic. It looked like Haven had found a way to live despite the pain she'd known. How could they cause her new trouble?

Ronan burst into the door, his phone in his hand. "We have to get her. Now."

"Agreed." Ivar clapped his back. They'd protect the woman, but she needed to help them get to Quade. He'd find a secure place for her. "Let's get a helicopter."

"Wait a minute." Promise jumped to her feet. "Stop it. Both of you. Take a step *back*."

Ronan exploded before Ivar could. "Back? Not a chance. She's seen my brother. Maybe she's even visited him. At the very least, she knows something, and she's going to tell me everything."

"Exactly," Ivar said grimly.

Promise pressed both hands to her eyes in an obvious attempt to rein in her temper. "Listen. We have no idea how she'll react to either of you. She's dreamed of or met Quade, and she might've dreamed of one or both of you. This is a woman who has spent a significant amount of time in psych wards being drugged and possibly enduring electric shock therapy."

"Not to mention a series of forced exorcisms, and we have no clue what that entailed," Faith added through the speaker. "If you two show up, it might just shut down her entire brain. She could be half-crazy already."

"Look at her paintings," Garrett said, his voice thoughtful. "She's definitely tortured."

Ivar swung on his youngest brother. "You're on their side?"

"No." Garrett sat back in his chair, not fazed in the slightest by the fury. "We need to contact her, but it shouldn't be any member of the Seven who does it. Nobody she might've dreamed about." He scratched a barely healed cut along his forearm from the day before. "In fact, power recognizes power. We shouldn't have an immortal approach her first." His gaze went to Promise.

She nodded vigorously. "Yes. Exactly. I'll go. Just to meet with her."

"Me too," Faith piped up. "I'm a neurologist. That could come in handy."

"I'm coming too," Grace said, her voice slightly higher than her sister's through the speaker. "I'm the only artist among you, and she'll relate to me better."

"What is this? You ladies need a blasted field trip?" Ronan growled, his fingers already balled into fists.

Promise reached for Ivar's hand. "Yes. Obviously nobody has found this woman yet. We can't bring attention to her either. This is the correct path, Ivar. Take a deep breath and start planning the approach."

Ivar looked down at her intelligent eyes. Then he took a deep breath. "Ronan?"

The vampire's nostrils flared, but his shoulders lowered. "Fine. But we secure the entire area before anybody goes in."

Ivar nodded. "We'll fly three helicopters under the radar." This was what he'd been good at before going to hell. Strategizing and organizing. "Satellites are watching us, but the cloud cover is good right now. We can take three copters, head toward the Pacific; it will look like we're going on maneuvers if spotted." His hands itched with the need to steer one of the copters.

Ronan opened the door. "Two pilots in each craft. The lead craft with six additional soldiers and same at the rear. The center craft will take us."

Ivar turned. "We'll secure both ends of that street." He looked toward Garrett. "Bring up the entire neighborhood." He waited until the map showed on the screen. It was a nice street in a small community near the ocean. No way would demon and vampire soldiers blend in. "We'll have to go after dark and hope the cloud cover still provides some secrecy."

"We could just kidnap her," Logan said, eyeing the map.

"No," Promise said, shaking her head again. "If she doesn't know anything, we'd be harming her. She'd never be able to return to her life. If nothing else, the Kurjans would learn of her."

Ivar's neck felt like a broad hand was squeezing his flesh, making breathing difficult. "She knows something."

"Maybe not," Promise said gently. "Her paintings may be from dreams. Or rather, she may think they're dreams. We don't want to cause her pain, Ivar. She's had enough."

That was a fair point. Even so, if the woman could provide any information about a way to save Quade, Ivar was going to take it. "All right, ladies. You need to figure out how to get her to meet with you."

Promise tapped her unpainted nail against her lips. "I'm thinking I need to buy a painting or three."

Chapter Thirty-Five

Promise smoothed back her hair and then straightened her flowered blouse, making sure the miniscule camera was pointed at the light green door.

"Stop messing with the button," Ivar growled through the earbud in her left ear.

She stilled. What a bossypants. Faith stood on her right and Grace on her left, both sporting hidden cameras too. She felt like an undercover cop from a television show, and even though this was deadly serious, she couldn't help the flush of excitement rippling through her. A quick glance at her friends revealed pink cheeks and sparkling eyes.

Ivar had secured the entire neighborhood, taking point in a vacant house on the other side of the block, along with Ronan and Adare. Soldiers were stationed out of sight throughout, and the three helicopters had headed out to sea to pretend some maneuvers, just in case the Kurjans had caught wind of their leaving Realm headquarters. But the rain slashed down, and the clouds remained dark over the night sky, so hopefully it was just a precaution.

Promise knocked on the door, her adrenaline flowing freely.

She could hear somebody press against the door to look through the peephole. The porch light came on. Then a series of locks, at least five, were disengaged.

The door opened. "Dr. Promise Williams?"

"Yes. Hi." Pain hacked into Promise's temples from within, and she gasped, pulling shields into place.

"Promise?" Ivar asked, sounding as if he was already moving.

Promise coughed. "Excuse me. Sorry about that. Allergies." Her eyes watered from the pain, and she doubled the diamond in her shield, pushing most of the pain out. There, that was better. "I'm okay," she said. Partially. Obviously Haven had a lot of power, because the pain echoed still, not horribly but still present.

Promise held out a hand to the very petite blonde. Small to the point of appearing fragile. Both of her eyes were a dark green, so she obviously wore a colored contact in at least one eye. Did she ever allow the black iris to show? "It's nice to meet you. I take it you checked out my credentials?"

"I wouldn't have opened the door otherwise," the blonde said quietly. "I'm Haven." Her voice was throaty but not as much so as any of the male demons. "Who are your friends?"

Maybe two doctors would reassure the woman or at least impress her a little.

Faith stepped up. "Faith Cooper. I'm a neurologist, and I'm interested in the thoughts behind your paintings." They shook hands.

"Don't like doctors. I just paint." Haven released Faith and looked toward Grace. "You?"

"Oh." Grace switched her dark camera to the other side so she could shake. "Grace Cooper. Big fan."

Haven's chin lowered. "Grace Cooper the photographer?"

Grace straightened. "Well, yes." A smile bloomed across her face. "You've heard of me?"

"Now I'm the big fan," Haven said, animated for the first time. "What happened to you? There were tons of photographs and then you just disappeared."

"Oh, head injury, coma, and now recovery," Grace said with a wave of her hand.

"I see." Haven stood back to look them over. "Promise, Grace, and Faith. Huh. Who would've thought? All we need is a Hope to make it complete."

Promise coughed. The woman had no idea. "It is funny."

"Isn't it, though?" Haven opened the door wider and gestured them inside. "Come on in. My studio is actually upstairs in the attic. Well, what used to be an attic."

They stepped inside a small living area decorated with bright splashes of jewel colors. A tuxedo-type cat with luminous green eyes looked up from his perch on the back of the sofa, blinked, and then returned to sleep.

Haven waited until they'd moved farther inside before reengaging all the locks, one at a time, and then double-checking them afterward. She peered through the peephole for several seconds and then turned off the porch light.

"Is there a lot of crime here?" Faith asked, sounding merely curious.

"No." Haven turned, patted the cat, and walked into the kitchen. "Follow me." The woman moved gracefully past a fifties-diner-style table, older but well-kept appliances, and comfortable, light yellow Formica countertops to a steep staircase hidden by a narrow door. She walked up easily, flipping on lights as she went.

The smell of paint and turpentine filled the air.

Promise followed her, grabbing the noncompliant handrail, and made sure her button camera faced the front to capture everything. They emerged into a sprawling attic space with paint splotches covering the floor and every visible part of the walls. One whole wall was made of glass, no doubt remodeled to let in more light. "Wow."

Haven pulled tarps off a couple of paintings. "Most of my work is in Northtown for a show I'm having in two weeks. But as I told you on the phone, I do have a few pieces still here, if you're interested."

"Exquisite." Grace moved to the first painting, her attention clearly caught. "The movement in this is almost painful."

The colors were deep purple and red with a hint of orange. Jagged rocks rose out of a bubbling amethyst ocean that spewed angry spray into black clouds tumbling across a furious sky. The harsh paint strokes almost conveyed sound, they were so wildly vibrant.

"Holy shit, I've been there," Ivar muttered through the comms.

Haven pulled cloths off several more paintings. Each conveyed raw, brutal beauty.

Promise walked closer to a large painting of a swirling vortex that almost drew her in. "This is amazing. Where do you get your ideas?" She made sure to stand for a moment at each painting so the camera could record.

"Dreams, mainly," Haven said, picking at dried paint on her left thumbnail. "I'm driven to be precise to a point of almost creating a photograph."

"This place looks real," Faith said, bending down to view a series of mountains in front of three suns, which turned the peaks a blood red. "The contrast between the wild, imaginative subjects and the style here creates a sense of astonishing power."

Haven leaned against the one empty spot on the wall. "That's the goal."

The woman didn't speak much. Promise took a deep breath and turned to face her. This was unbelievable. The ultra-preciseness of the brushstrokes were mathematical in nature, as was the way the rippled skies suggested the presence of dark matter. Or nearby dark holes. She had to force herself to finish her job here and not run off and immediately start working the math. "On the website, I saw a painting of a man with aqua-colored eyes. He was so compelling I couldn't look away. Do you have that one here?"

"Nope." Haven smoothed down black yoga pants beneath a pink T-shirt covered in paint stripes. "I don't like to paint portraits, although the few times I have, they sold quickly."

"Oh, shoot." Promise forced a smile. "I really want that one. Any chance you remember who bought it?"

"No," Haven said, straightening, her gaze direct and open.

If she was lying, she was exceptional at it. Of course, somebody raised the way she'd been would certainly learn to mask emotions and tell falsehoods, just to survive. "Do you remember the painting?" Promise pressed, infusing curiosity into her tone.

"I remember all of my paintings," Haven said. "The guy you're talking about is made up. I think I saw a movie, a horror story really, and he kind of looked like the guy in it. A combination of the guys in it." She shrugged. "Sorry."

That had to be a lie, since the painting was so obviously Quade. So yes, the woman could lie convincingly. Promise nodded. "I see."

"I want this one." Grace picked up a 2 x 3 abstract oil painting with greens, yellows, and oranges that moved as if it was running away. To something with light. "How much?"

They haggled over the price, and Grace pulled out the cash that Adare had given her.

Haven's eyebrows lifted as she accepted the money. "You walk around with that kind of cash?"

"I knew I'd buy something," Grace said, her eyes alight with intrigue.

Faith moved around. "Do you have anything more upbeat? I love these, I really do, but I often work with coma patients, and something soothing would probably be better for the family members who regularly visit and read to them."

Haven studied her for a minute. "I do have something new. Just finished it last week." She walked over the paint-riddled floor and moved several of the darker works out of the way. "It's a little silly and so different from the others that I decided to keep it out of the exhibit."

Promise's gasp made all three women look at her. "Oh, I just love it," she covered, her legs trembling. Haven had captured Mercy's Brookville world perfectly, right down to its bubbling brooks and sweet grass meadows. The three suns shone down, glimmering off the gently waving grass. "You say you've dreamed of this place?"

"No. Not that one." Haven pulled the canvas out. "I was just playing around and decided to paint something lighter. Even smelled sugar cookies when I did it." She smiled for the first time, looking years younger and not so closed off.

What Promise wouldn't give to get the woman in an MRI machine. Had she traveled to these places? It seemed unlikely she would've survived the hell worlds she'd painted.

So what did that mean?

What about the Seven ritual? It was Promise's understanding that the males' bodies had stayed on earth while their consciousness had traveled. What if that wasn't the case? Mathematical equations filtered through her brain faster than fireworks on the Fourth. What if—

"Promise?" Faith asked. "You okay?"

Grace sighed. "She just started working on a math problem. See how her eyes gleam?" Her voice lowered. "Haven, our friend is one of those genius types who forgets other people are in the room. Your painting must've inspired her somehow."

Promise shook herself out of it. Briefly. "Sorry. It's the precise lines and the depth of the strokes. I got lost in math land." She smiled and tried to look rueful. "Surely, you leave this world too when you paint, Haven."

The woman nodded, understanding lighting her expression. "I do. Can paint for hours and forget to eat."

Oh, Promise wished the woman trusted them. She had so many questions. But pushing Haven would be a mistake; she knew that to her bones. They had to proceed cautiously while keeping Haven's existence a secret from not only the Kurjans but other immortal species as well. "I definitely want to purchase this painting." She'd give it to Mercy. "Faith, would you please negotiate for me?" She turned her most guileless smile on Haven. "Would you mind terribly if I used your powder room?"

Haven looked at her for a moment and then shrugged. "Sure. First door on the left after the kitchen."

Promise nodded and walked to the stairwell as Faith began to negotiate for the painting, hopefully keeping Haven occupied. She reached the kitchen and edged her way through, ducking her head into a small bathroom decorated in rich colors. Trying to keep quiet, she moved to the only other door and swung it open, holding her breath.

Haven's small bedroom held a bed covered in a purple comforter, a nightstand, and a dresser, all decorated with knickknacks. No pictures. Her closet door was already open to reveal clothing and an impressive number of tennis shoes.

Disappointment filtered through Promise, but time was running out, so she turned back to the kitchen again. An enclosed mudroom was beyond the stairs going up, and she peered inside to darkness. Biting her lip, she swung the door open to find a washer and dryer across from a bench with shoes lined up beneath it. Another closet was adjacent to the door. She quickly flipped on the light and stepped inside the room to open the closet door, expecting to see more coats and boots.

Paintings filled the space. One fell out, and she grabbed the canvas before it could hit the floor. She pulled several out, looking at them, making sure the camera caught them all.

Every single painting was of Quade Kayrs, surrounded by hell.

Chapter Thirty-Six

Ivar didn't let his body relax until the helicopter rose above the town, turned sharply, and headed back toward safety. They remained beneath the cloud cover, enduring the rainstorm, the Realm-upgraded fighting helicopter making no noise.

Promise waited until they'd leveled off and then looked around. "Why didn't you all tell me how those worlds looked? Even though I saw the paintings on the computer, seeing the actual brush strokes, the mathematical precision of them, is different. I told you I need to go to those hell worlds to get data. There are equations within equations in those scenes. Something completely new, damn it."

Ivar's eyebrows rose. What was she talking about?

She looked at him. "Paper. I need paper." Urgency colored her words, and her tension clawed his spine.

He shook his head. "No paper, honey."

She growled—it really sounded like a growl—and looked frantically around. "Pen or pencil. Anybody?" Her voice rose shrilly.

Ronan looked around from the pilot seat, reached in his rear pocket, and threw back a partially chewed black marker.

Faith looked around again and zeroed in on Grace. "I need your shirt."

Grace glanced down at her white T-shirt, her eyes wide. "Huh?"

Promise grabbed the bottom of Ivar's shirt and yanked hard enough that he ducked to give it up. She tossed it at Grace. "Put this on."

Adare was sitting next to Grace, his eyebrows raised. Without a word, he partially turned to block his mate. Her shirt soon sailed over his head, and Promise grabbed it, her body vibrating. She dropped to the floor, flattened the shirt, and started diagramming equations. "Yes, that's it," she said, her shoulders still shaking.

Faith leaned over to watch her. "Fascinating. I wish I could stick her in an MRI machine right now."

Promise drew out complicated equations, but Ivar thought he recognized a couple pertaining to string theory. But then she went far afield, writing quickly, mumbling to herself as she worked.

Man, she was impressive. Cute and fascinating. Now that they were safe, somewhat, he sat back and enjoyed just watching her mind at work.

"No—no." She scratched out part of the equation, digging deep with the marker. "Damn it." She moved to the side of the shirt, her pen working so fast it caught on the cotton several times. "That's it," she muttered, making what looked like a checkmark. Then numbers started appearing along with parentheses and more.

Faith scratched her head and looked toward Ivar, who shrugged. It was new math to him.

A gust of wind battered the helicopter, and Promise fell over. He slid down the bench, grasped her shoulders, and put her between his knees. Then he spread out the shirt in front of her and placed his boots at the very edges of the cotton to hold it in place.

"Thanks." She leaned forward, her shoulders protected by his calves, and kept diagraming.

They landed with a soft bump, and he scooped her up, T-shirt and all. She protested, but he ignored her. Ducking his head over hers, he protected her from the rain and ran inside the demon headquarters, straight for the room where he'd had her whiteboards moved from the cabin. A row of computers on a wide desk took up one wall of the room.

Her sigh was one of relief as she jumped down and leaped for the nearest marker.

Faith stood to Ivar's side and shook out her long auburn hair. "Man, I want a look inside her head."

"Doesn't look very comfortable," Ronan said, putting his arm around his mate's shoulders. "Faith? You wanna get that button camera from her?"

"Nope," Faith said.

"I've got it." Ivar angled around a desk and reached his mate, flipping the camera free while she continued to write furiously on the whiteboard. He tossed it to Ronan, who caught it easily. "Get those downloaded, please. I'd like a printed picture of the woman."

"Why?" Ronan asked.

Ivar turned and studied the equations. "Something tells me we're going to be able to visit your brother soon." It had to be Quade she'd painted.

Promise paused, and they all turned to look at her. She partially pivoted. "Faith? I need the results of the MRIs. All of them."

Faith nodded and hustled for one of the computers, typing quickly. A printer soon shot out reams of paper.

Promise leaped for them, throwing several on the floor. "There it is," she muttered, taking one sheet back to the board to start formulating equations again.

Ronan shook his head slowly. "I've never seen anything like that."

Faith pursed her lips. "Agreed. She might be here for a while. You guys want to grab something to eat? I'm starving."

Promise made a frustrated sound that had them all pausing again. She fumbled behind herself for a yellow marker, rushed to a far board, and diagrammed something with Hope Kayrs-Kyllwood's name on top. "Later. Get to this later," Promise muttered, throwing the yellow marker over her shoulder and returning to the main board and her black marker.

Ivar leaned back against the wall, bemused.

"Food?" Ronan asked, his gaze remaining on Promise.

"You guys go ahead," Ivar returned. "I want to watch this." He couldn't look away. The idea that he'd have to leave her soon hurt somewhere he hadn't realized existed. Even if she didn't realize he was there, he wasn't leaving her. Not yet, anyway.

* * * *

Being grounded stank. Hope snuggled with her stuffed dragon in bed, her lip out. She hadn't gotten to play with her friends or watch television for a whole day so far. It wasn't fair. The sky cried big tears for her. Yeah. That'd teach them. The sky was on her side and would rain until she wasn't sad anymore.

A tapping at her window made her sit up. It was dark outside.

She looked at her door, but it stayed closed. Holding her dragon close, she slipped out of bed and padded to the window.

Pax was on the other side, his nose flattened against the glass. She gasped and struggled with the heavy pane, shoving it up. "Paxton Phoenix," she whispered. "What are you doing?"

"Move back." Water dripped off his too-long hair and onto his shoulders.

She kept her stuffed animal away from the rain and stumbled back.

Paxton's chubby hands grabbed the sill, and he jumped inside, landing really quiet. When had he learned to be so quiet? Without saying anything, he pulled the window shut with one hand. "I wanted to check on you." Her butterfly nightlight was on and made the bruise on his face stand out.

She rushed forward and hugged him. "I missed you."

He patted her back and leaned away to look at her face. "You're okay, right? They were mad. Your dad was super mad."

"No." Her lip trembled. "I'm not okay."

Pax straightened. "What did he do?"

She paused. "Huh?"

"What did your dad do?" Paxton's silvery blue eyes glowed in the darkness.

She sniffed. "He grounded me. No television or toys." It was terrible.

Pax's shoulders went back down. "That's all?"

That's all? It was awful. "Yes." She sniffed again and handed over the dragon. The green guy was Pax's favorite, and since his daddy didn't let him play with stuffed animals, he played with them at Hope's. "Are you in trouble?"

"Um, yeah. Grounded. But I snuck out." He looked down at his wet shoes on the rug. "My dad is on patrol and won't be back until tomorrow afternoon."

She blinked. "Who's staying with you?"

"Nobody. I'm eight," he said, his shoulders kinda hunched.

Her mama didn't know he stayed alone. Hope shivered. "Wanna stay here until morning?"

He nodded, not looking at her eyes.

She went to her closet and pulled her daddy's shirt off the floor. She'd worn it to sleep in a few nights ago. "Here. Put your clothes on the chair to dry," she whispered, turning back around and looking at her bed.

When he'd changed, they jumped in the bed, giggling. Pax still held the dragon, so Hope picked up the teddy bear Uncle Logan had given her last week. Pax held her hand and snuggled into his pillow. "Hope? If you go and see Drake, try to take me with you, okay?"

"Okay," she whispered, her eyelids closing. She had known they'd like each other if they ever met. Things were working out just how she wanted. "Night, Pax."

"Night, Hope." He went to sleep right away.

She listened to his even breathing and wondered if he should stay with her all the time. He didn't seem to like his daddy and tried to come to her house a lot. Pax could be her brother. That'd be fun. She snuggled with her bear, keeping Pax's hand in hers. It was time to see if she could bring him into the dreamworld.

She had to kinda fall asleep first, so she let herself drift.

Then she walked on a light pink sand that was warm on her feet. A deep blue ocean rolled in pretty waves, and on the other side was a forest with green trees. A bird flew above her, its bright purple wings gliding on the barely there wind.

She kept walking, enjoying the warmth. She heard Drake before she saw him.

He walked out of the trees, this time wearing black jeans and a red T-shirt.

Good. He was there. She closed her eyes and drew on the idea of Paxton as hard as she could. Then she opened her eyes. Nope. He wasn't in the dreamworld. Darn it.

Drake moved nearer, kicking off his tennis shoes and socks to walk on the sand. "How much trouble are you in?" he asked, reaching her.

She winced. "Grounded. You?"

He nodded. "Really grounded. I got lectured for hours too. You?"

"Yes." Danger, Kurjans, enemies, and a bunch of other stuff. "I told them you wouldn't hurt me."

"They kidnapped me," he said, his eyes widening.

She bit her lip. "Yeah. Sorry about that."

He shuffled his feet, kicking up sand. "I had to tell my dad everything. I didn't see a lot of headquarters, but what I saw, I told him about."

Hope wiped sand off her leg. "Yeah. I would've told my daddy too. Don't feel bad." If they were gonna stay friends, they had to tell each other the truth. "Did you try and tell your daddy that the Seven are good?"

He looked at the huge ocean. "They can't be good because they want to hurt Ulric. He's our religious guy. Like your prophets." Glancing down, he studied the blue markings on her neck. "You're a prophet. Can you reach others like you? Maybe you can reach Ulric."

She shrugged. "I don't see the other two prophets much." Lily and Caleb were super nice, but her daddy didn't let her spend time with them since she was just a kid. Something about choosing her own path or whatever. "I don't think I can reach him. This is the only dreamworld I can get to." *Right now, anyway. It got easier every year, so maybe someday she could visit other dreamworlds and even talk to Ulric. But then she'd really get grounded.*

Drake scrunched his toes in the sand. "You and Paxton are good friends. No?"

"Yes," *she said.* "Him and Libby are my best friends. And you, Drake."

"Hmm." *He watched the bird fly by again.* "Do you see the future?"

"Sometimes." *The bird came back, and she waved at it.* "But I don't get to choose the stuff I see. What 'bout you?"

He nodded. "Same. I can see some stuff but not others. Me and Pax? We're not gonna be friends. I've seen us fighting each other as grown-ups." *He sighed.* "But I can't see who dies. Somebody does for sure."

Her stomach did something funny. "Nobody dies." *Drake just couldn't see the whole picture.* "We're gonna fix it all."

He turned his head suddenly. "I have to go. Meet you back here soon." *He smiled, but his green eyes didn't twinkle.*

She wanted to tell him it'd be okay and to trust her. Instead, she woke up back in her room with the rain splashing against the window, her hand in Paxton's. She turned to watch him sleep.

How was she gonna save them both?

Chapter Thirty-Seven

Promise awoke and stretched against a hard male body, wincing as her butt hit his hip. The night before came crashing back. She'd been working on her boards when they'd blurred and become fuzzy, forcing her to sit suddenly. Ivar had insisted she get some sleep, and she'd protested, saying she just required more coffee. When he'd grasped her arm in that no-nonsense hold, she lost it and punched him in the thigh.

The world had instantly spun, and she'd faced the computer to receive a hard smack against her ass.

She blinked into awareness. "I cannot believe you slapped my butt," she muttered.

"You punched first," he retorted, his voice grumbly in the morning. "You're lucky you were exhausted. Ever punch me like that again, and you'll be facing the floor over my knee for a good long while."

Oh, he did not. Yes, she'd punched first. But there was no need to get all alpha on her in the morning light. "I was not in my right mind at the moment."

"I was, which is why you're still able to walk today."

Well. Whatever. She slipped from the bed and headed toward the bathroom for a quick shower and blush of makeup. Returning, she grabbed her laptop from the table and gave him her haughtiest look.

He sat up in the bed, the blankets to his waist, his magnificent chest revealed. His eyes were a lighter blue today, and he watched her like a hawk spotting a rabbit. "You need to eat something."

She rolled her eyes. "I'll grab a bagel on the way to the board room." She paused, her mind racing. "I'm ready to talk to everyone." Numbers and solutions clicked through her brain, and she nodded, adding them to what was already there. "In fact, I don't have a choice. The earth is at the right position for the journey to be made."

He stretched from the bed, a hulking warrior taking up more than his fair share of space. "You can get me back to Quade?"

She swallowed. "I think so. But I need more information." There was still no way to know what he had to do when he got there.

"You can't break the bubble?"

"Not yet." Even if she could, she wasn't certain she would. For now, she required more information. "You need to take me with you to at least one of the jump-off points." No way could he take her into the hell worlds because the wormhole was closing too fast.

He paused in the midst of pulling up his jeans. "Oh, hell no."

"Yes." She tried to sound conciliatory instead of commanding, but it was difficult. "I have to see what's happening." She needed to feel what was happening. This ability of hers, the one dealing with teleporters, enhanced her theories so well. "You don't have a choice."

His smile provided more warning than an outlandish neon sign. "You don't want to use phrases like that with me, Professor."

She shivered and failed to conceal it. "Is it just me, or are your possessiveness and authoritarian tendencies progressing to the point of being tyrannical?"

His eyebrows lifted. "Perhaps you're just starting to notice."

How irksome. She met his gaze directly. "You are aware, are you not, that I'm about to give you the possibility of entering Quade's hell world?"

"I am," he said, reaching for his shirt.

"Then you might wish to remember that you'll need me to help you return." She flounced toward the door. "Make sure I don't decide to just leave you there."

He flattened her against the door with a whisper of sound, his body bracketing her. "I guess we should get some things straight, then," he murmured, his hands at her waist. Her shirt soon flew over her head.

* * * *

Ivar stirred more sugar into his coffee at the conference table, his body satiated after the discussion with Promise. Oh, there hadn't been a lot of talking, but in between a couple of orgasms, he was pretty sure he'd gotten her to agree to stop bugging him about teleporting. Hadn't he? He frowned. Maybe not.

All the members of the Seven, save for Quade, sat around the table along with Zane Kyllwood, Kane Kayrs, Emma Kayrs, and King Dage Kayrs, who led the Realm. Faith, Grace, and Mercy ate donuts or bagels with their coffee. It was a full group.

Promise stood up front by a large screen covered with equations from her laptop. She waited for everyone to see it, intelligence in her eyes.

"Oh, man," Kane Kayrs said, leaning forward and staring at the notations. "That's fucking beautiful."

"Isn't it?" Promise eyed the equations like most women would diamonds.

All right. It looked like a bunch of numbers to Ivar. "How about you explain, sweetheart?"

She clasped her hands together. "I know how we can reach Quade's world."

Ivar stilled, head to toe. This was happening. Right now.

She nodded. "All right. Here it is." Her laser pointer glided to a bunch of the equations, and turning, she read the room. The laser zipped out of sight. "Um. Okay. Without math." She breathed out.

"The key, I think, is the ritual of the Seven and what you went through."

Ivar frowned. What did that have to do with Quade?

She swallowed. "Demons teleport on earth; the Fae go elsewhere. But during that ritual to become one of the Seven, it's different. As far as I can see, you actually existed in two different places. Both your physical being and your consciousness. It wasn't split."

Ivar took another drink of the too-strong coffee. "How?"

She swept her hand toward the screen. "You entered another dimension. I think." Her grin was impish. "Yes, I know. I just said you managed to be in the middle of crossing dimensions." She pointed at the solution on the board. "It's only a hypothesis. But that's the only way I can think of right now for you to exist in two different planes. They had to have combined somehow." She waited for questions, but the room remained quiet. "And"—she was so animated, she looked delicious—"I think that teleporting paths are like brain waves."

Faith sat back and whistled. "Of course. That definitely makes sense."

Ivar scratched his back. There was some logic there, and now Promise had math that proved it? "Go on."

Promise smiled. "The first point is that demons can only go where they've been before…or to places described to them. There has to be some sort of connection." She nodded at Mercy. "The Fae can travel more broadly, but they usually take the same paths. One jumping point to another, and they've never hit that hell loop."

"But I did," Ivar said.

"Yes." She nodded. "You were forced into a hell dimension by that Niall. Maybe it was the only one he knew of, and once you were there, you crossed over somehow."

"Into another dimension?" Ronan asked.

"More like a crossing of two dimensions," Kane murmured. "Right?"

"Yes." Promise slapped Kane on the shoulder. "Exactly. I think you combined two, which created a time flux, the only way you

could be in two places at once. You guys interfered with time."
She shook her head. "You messed with a whole lot more than that
when you created those three worlds." She frowned. "Strike that.
You didn't create three worlds. You found your way to three and
bound them together—by using gravity and time. The magnets you
told me about, Ronan. The ones you had to arrange religiously so
your world stayed stable. Those affect the gravity. Don't you see?"

"No," Ivar said.

"All right." Promise set down the laser pointer. "We know from
studying the brain that paths are created. Maybe by good habits,
maybe bad, and so on. Anxiety makes a doozy of a path as well."

The woman was comparing brain paths to teleporting paths?
All right. "I'm with you," Ivar said.

She sobered. "You've been down the path. Now that you can
teleport again, you should be able to go where you've been by
creating those paths in your mind. You teleported instinctively
before, and that's how you'd need to do it again, now that you've
healed your brain." Her lips drew tight, and she took a deep breath,
obviously not wanting to give him the information. "However you
teleport, whatever you draw on, I think you, and probably only
you, can return to that world."

Only because she'd identified the injury in his brain that he'd
been working on healing. "So I can take Quade's place?" Ivar asked.

She sobered even more. "Not in the time frame we have right
now. But if there's a way to do it, we'll find it, and we can fight
about it then. For now, you need to seek information before we
can determine if the worlds are failing—and you're the only one
who can make a definite return trip."

Garrett breathed out. "You have elite status to travel to hell
and back."

Ivar snorted and quickly lost his amusement as Promise gave
him a glare.

She cleared her throat. "Quade is important, I know. But entire
worlds are at risk." She looked at Ronan. "When your world failed,

I think the catastrophic disaster created these hell worlds. And I believe the reaction nearly destroyed Quade's."

Ronan blinked. "So if Quade's world breaks…"

She nodded. "More worlds could be destroyed. Every action has a reaction. Using unnatural forces to combine those three bubble worlds left voids in the universe, and some of those were filled. You altered more than we can probably comprehend." She made a sound of frustration. "Okay. Imagine that the earth disappeared. What would happen to the moon?"

Since the earth's gravitational pull kept the moon in orbit, it would…what?

Promise tapped the screen. "The moon would either continue circling the sun, fall into the sun, or zip off in a straight line and get caught in another planet's or star's gravitational pull. We don't know exactly what."

Kane nodded. "Yep. That's right."

"So we need more information before we do *anything* with Quade's world. Or Ulric's. A lot more, and you're the only person who can get it for us." She focused on Ivar. "If you want this mission, which means you'll have to go twice and somehow return twice. The first time will be doable, based on the math. I'm not sure about the second time. Are you sure you want to do this?"

"I do," he said soberly.

She studied him and then nodded, her eyes darkening. "I've had Emma's scientists working on instruments with the 3D printer that aren't made of metal. If you return to Quade's world, you have to look for differences since you were last there, and you need to take measurements and leave several instruments if possible. We need that data to determine how much danger that world is in. All the worlds, actually."

Ivar finished his coffee, his gut roiling. "Is there a chance I could take the path and not find Quade's world?"

"Absolutely," Promise whispered. "You had three worlds balancing each other with inertia, gravity, time, and who knows what else. One blew up. The other two have certainly shifted as well as changed, and unless one is much more powerful than the other, they're heading for a collision." She sighed. "Such an event could take a millennia…or two days. We have no way of knowing absent a practical experiment."

Ivar stood. "Then it's time we conducted an experiment. The faster the better, right?" he asked.

Promise nodded. "It's even bigger than that. We went through all the data the Fae supplied as well as your memories, and for every journey, there's a starting point."

Of course. Ivar cocked his head. "Earth, right?"

She swallowed. "More importantly, earth at certain times of the year, which means certain positions in space. This week is one of the optimal times."

That figured. "Okay." Ivar's brain had been healing for long enough. He drew on the power of the universe, letting it sing through his blood. Then he jumped through the void and landed at his cabin again. Yeah, he was stronger, back to normal. Grabbing a pinecone, he jumped back to the conference room.

"Show off," Mercy said, licking maple syrup off her fingers. "So, Professor. Just how dangerous is this? I mean, should you two go spend a few nights together?"

Regret filled Promise's eyes. "No. Faster is better. We're definitely in a time crunch."

"Now," Ivar agreed. "Let's do this right now."

Mercy nodded. "Promise, I'm thinking your man will need assistance reaching the first jump-off point. Correct?"

Promise nodded. "Definitely. He could do it alone, but he's not accustomed to otherworld jumping, so he should conserve his energy for the jump to Quade." Worry glimmered in her eyes for the briefest of moments. "I would very much like to visit at least to that point."

"I'll take Ivar," Logan Kyllwood said, looking at his mate. "I'm well familiar with Brookville."

Ivar lobbed the pinecone at Promise. "Nice job, Professor. I knew you could do it." But she was staying safely at demon headquarters whether she liked it or not.

She looked at him across the conference room, past the others present, her gaze serious now. "This is a quick hop type of mission. You had better come back."

Ah, shit. She did know him. He had no intention of leaving Quade there, and if somebody had to stay, it was gonna be him. "We'd better suit up," he said. It was time to go. If he waffled, she'd talk him into staying.

There was a flurry of discussion, issuing orders, and expressing good wishes, and then he stood outside the headquarters with Promise and Logan.

He drew Promise aside.

"I want to go to the first point," she said, urgency in her tone. "In case there's something to observe."

"No." He didn't have time to treat her with kid gloves. "Stay here and stay safe so I can do my job." He leaned down to press a kiss to her mouth. They'd been leading up to this moment since their first second together.

"You don't have much time." She picked a backpack off the ground. "We don't know if you'll make it through carrying anything, but it's worth the risk of losing these. Here are the instruments I've had Emma create with notations on each for how to use it. Bring the atmosphere readings back. Also, you understand the Doppler effect, right?"

He nodded and slung the pack over his shoulder.

She clutched her hand against his forged ribs. "Promise you'll return."

"I will." He didn't know when or how, but he'd be back. "I promise." She meant more than he could say. The woman was both cerebral and physical, and they were perfect together.

She handed him a picture of Haven. "Find out if they've met."

He nodded. "I will." Logan took his arm. It went against his nature to let Logan take the leap, but he did it to conserve his energy.

The jump to Mercy's Brookville was smooth, and Ivar landed on the soft grass, releasing Logan instantly. He looked around the peaceful meadow and turned to face the farthest right sun. "We went this way." Sucking in air, he tried to remember the paths he'd taken to get to Quade's world, and then finally zeroed in just on that world. He was a demon, and he flew by straight paths. So that's how he'd go. "Take care of Promise for me. Just in case."

"You know I will, brother." Logan grabbed him in a bear hug that would've broken his ribs had it been possible to break them. "Your woman is right in that you have to come back with information before we do anything else. There are worlds at issue."

Ivar nodded. "I understand." And he did. But if there was a way to bring Quade back, he was going to do it. "Bye, brother." He shut his eyes and imagined the paths he'd taken so long ago to get to Quade's hell world. Was instinct and subconscious memory going to be enough? He drew on the energy of the brooks, on the sweetness of the grass, on the power of the brother next to him.

And he jumped.

Chapter Thirty-Eight

The ride was impossibly long and complex until Ivar barely twisted a hard left and then squeezed through the final vortex that tossed him around so violently his teeth cut into his mouth. It hadn't been that tight before. He landed on ice and skidded several yards. He covered his head to protect it, but shards of ice slashed up and tore his thighs to shit. He finally came to a stop, his body freezing. He shoved himself to his feet, perched precariously between two blade-sharp pieces of ice. Something howled in the distance. He blinked, shivering. This was the wrong world.

Quade's world had held jagged rocks surrounded by lava and the stench of burning sulfur. Ivar looked up. The sky was a swelling purple and the atmosphere painfully heavy. Wait a minute. That was familiar. As were the brutal burnt-gold color of the trees, but now thick icicles bent their massive branches.

Where was the lava?

He slid over the ice toward the forest, avoiding the sharp blades the best he could. Either this was a twin world with opposite weather, or things had changed. Just how much time had passed in this world during the last three months of earth time? He clambered through the trees, avoiding the sharp branches.

A crack popped from high up, and the sky seemed to open, showing red on the other side. Wait a minute. This had happened before, but there had been silver. The crack was wider and stayed for longer this time. Then it closed.

A body dropped from high up, landing in front of him. The figure was covered from head to toe in fur, including a mask.

"Quade?" Ivar asked, settling into a fighting stance, even though he was bleeding from both legs.

Quade ripped off the mask, his eyes a burning aqua. He looked Ivar up and down. "Vike?"

"Yes." Ivar moved to him. "You're still alive." He looked around. "Where's all the lava?"

"World changed." Quade shook his head, and his long black hair swung in clumps. "Why are you here? I saved you. Sent you home."

A creature howled in the distance, sounding closer than before.

Ivar tensed. "I made it home, and now I'm back. Need to take you home."

"Can't go." Quade motioned for Ivar to follow him. "The fire is coming. Hurry."

Fire? It was all ice. But he'd been through this before, so he ducked his head and followed Quade through the ice field to another forest made of burnt trees holding branches with razor-sharp bark. Now all of it glimmered with ice everywhere, which only served to sharpen the bark. Quade took several different trails, winding around and finally reaching a series of tall rocks.

They climbed, hand over hand, to reach the same cave as before.

Ivar panted, trying to heal all his cuts. He dumped out the backpack and set the odd boxes along the far wall to record whatever it was Promise wanted.

Quade sat and leaned against the smooth rock of the cave. "What the fuck are you doing back here?"

A complete sentence. So the Kayrs brother did know how to speak.

Ivar sucked in air. He'd forgotten about the difference in gravity or altitude or pretty damn much everything. He retrieved the devices to put back inside the pack. "I've been gone three months. How long has it been for you?"

Quade shook his head. "Centuries? Long enough for the lava to dry up and then turn to ice. The creatures still live, though." He reached for what looked like dried jerky. "Hungry?"

"No." Ivar looked toward the entrance. "When Ronan's bubble burst, it changed yours and Ulric's."

"Yeah." Quade chewed thoughtfully, looking more barbarian than vampire. "The cracks in the sky are longer, and I've seen Ulric. We're getting closer to each other. Soon we'll collide." He scratched his neck. "Will we get the chance to fight or just die?" He didn't sound concerned about either possibility.

"Which do you want?" Ivar asked, curious.

"Doesn't matter so long as Ulric dies," Quade said, ripping off another piece and dropping parts in his overly long beard. "I stopped feeling a long time ago. Millenia or two. Maybe more." He focused, his eyes so much like Ronan's it hurt to look at them. "Ronan is well."

"Mated and happy. Wants you home."

"This is home," Quade said. Fire flashed across the rock entrance, throwing intense heat inside that boiled their skin.

Ivar bit his lip to keep from screaming. Then it was over. He sent emergency healing cells to his bubbling skin. "That happen a lot?" he gasped.

"Three times in a cycle day," Quade confirmed, the bubbles on his face remaining. "Takes me that long to heal now." He scratched a second mark in the dirt. "As soon as the third one comes, I have to run and move the magnets again." He sighed, the sound soul weary. "They're weak. Not sure what happened when the worlds changed, but they've lost their charge. Any idea how to recharge them?"

"No," Ivar said. "But I'll find out."

"It'll be too late. The less they charge, the faster we fall. Maybe that's good. A hard collision will serve better to kill Ulric."

"You need to leave. Tell me what to do to protect the world, and I'll tell you how to go back home," Ivar urged. It was his turn to serve. To protect Quade.

"Can't." Quade shrugged. "Every day I draw closer to Ulric and his world. I can stem the tide briefly by the routine with the magnets, but it'd take too long to teach you. If I knew we'd just collide and die, I'd stop. But his world is bigger. More powerful. I might die and he might be set free. Can't allow that."

"Teach me. I'll learn fast," Ivar urged, ready to throw Quade through a portal. But how could he set Quade on the path through the portal? Only the Fae had that skill, and he hadn't had time to learn it.

"Nay. You have to leave. The balance is absolute." Quade tugged at the fur of his boots. "Whenever there's a change, the lava gets worse. If one animal is born, another must die. But not two. See?" He leaned forward, a look of madness crossing his hollowed cheekbones. His arms were thinner than last time—too thin. "Can only kill rarely to eat."

"I don't need food," Ivar countered. "Just tell me what to do."

"No time. You have to leave after the second fire, or we descend. Can't descend any faster." For a second lucidity glimmered in his eyes. "Find out what happens if we collide. If I should let it happen or not."

The fire hit again, this time with a bright blue color, burning even the walls.

Ivar ducked his head and let the pain wash over him. God, it was excruciating. "Please let me help."

Quade jumped up and grabbed Ivar's arm in an iron grip. "No time. Trust me. It wants my blood, anyway. You have to go or we'll go faster. Get answers if you can. A direction."

Ivar had known, deep down, that Quade couldn't leave yet. "Do you remember how to read?" Ivar handed over the other pack.

"Yes." Quade took it, frowning.

"Follow the instructions. I think those need to go by the magnets and at any other far points you find. Once they finish working or wear out, just bring them back here." That would definitely happen before Ivar could return. "That'll get you the answers we need."

"All right. You need to go. Now," Quade said.

Ivar tore the picture out of his back pocket and unfolded the paper. "Do you know her?"

Quade took the photograph and remained perfectly still. "Where did you get this?"

"We met her. Sought her out. She has skills—"

Quade pivoted and rammed Ivar into the wall. He leaned in close, his breath foul. "Leave her out of this. She does not exist. Got it, brother?"

Ivar didn't try to break the hold. "She's part demon and part Fae. If anybody can help you out of here, it's her." Especially if the path was closing, as Ivar suspected. He probably had only one more chance to make it here, now that he knew the path. "We need her."

"Promise me," Quade growled. "I've asked for nothing. For centuries, for an eternity, I've asked for nothing. Except for this. Leave this woman be."

Ivar could give nothing but the vow. "I promise."

Quade released him, taking the picture. "If you can get answers, then do so. If not, I'll fight the collision until my last breath, and then if there's a chance, I'll fight and kill him."

"I'll get you answers and be back to help. To take your place if nothing else, so be prepared to tell me how." Ivar clutched his brother's arm. "Until then, stay alive. We'll get you freedom."

Quade's mangled lip half lifted. "Don't want freedom. Just want to end this with Ulric dead. That's all."

A swirling mass of wind billowed up.

Ivar's fangs dropped, and he ripped open his wrist, grabbing Quade and shoving it in his mouth. "Drink. I don't need it."

Quade fought him for two seconds and then groaned, clamping on with his mouth and drinking deeply. He took enough to suffuse his face with color and then jerked his head free, panting.

Ivar gave him a second to compose himself and then yanked Quade back for a hug. He couldn't just throw Quade into the void, because he had no idea what to do to keep this world safe for the time being. "I'll be back, brother."

"Don't forget your promise about the woman. Keep her away from all of this." With that, Quade stood back.

Ivar drew on the power of the wind, turned, and jumped, hoping he reached Brookville.

Darkness swallowed him with a heavy anticipation.

* * * *

Promise paced the physics room, muttering at her equations. How the heck had she allowed Ivar to go alone?

Mercy popped her head into the doorway, sucking on a popsicle. "You still busy?"

"It's all math all the time," Promise murmured. "I take it Logan returned safely?"

"Yep. We're going for a boat ride and wanted to see if you'd like to join us. It could get your mind off Ivar." Mercy finished the orange treat.

Promise couldn't leave her boards. "No, but thank you." She paused and stretched her neck. "I can feel Ivar. Somehow, I feel him close." It didn't make sense.

"It's the mating," Mercy said. "So long as there's a way to connect, you'll feel it. The connection should help you to relax."

Promise tried to calculate her new reality and hit pause on it. "I'll figure that out later. Tonight, I'm going to keep working."

"Suit yourself." Mercy stepped inside to read the boards. "Logan is getting the boat. Wow. You've done a bunch more work already."

Promise turned back to her boards just as her laptop dinged. She moved to it and found Mark on the screen. "Hi. Any progress?" she asked.

He angled closer to the camera. "What's up with all the boards?"

"Working hard," she said, drawing out a chair to sit.

"Where are you, anyway?" He pushed his glasses up his nose.

She grinned. "A very nice research room."

"At demon headquarters?" he asked, his gaze serious.

Mercy gasped and moved closer to the computer. "You told somebody? A human?" she whispered tersely.

"No." Promise sat back. Her head spun. "How in the world do you know about—"

He shook his head. "You get too caught up in the equations and ignore the reality. I've enjoyed your innocence and dedication to saving the planet, but come on. This research, this discovery, is too much to sit on. The equations you've computed will win a Nobel Prize."

Her math? She gasped. The laptop from the university that she'd brought with her. She hadn't thought for one second that he'd try to gain access to her files. He'd always been trustworthy. Even so, she had nothing about other species in there. "Mark? Who are you working for?"

"That would be us," responded a male voice from behind her—*in her room*. In demon headquarters. Her mind went through a million thoughts before her body caught up. She jumped up to see a blond-haired male and two huge Cyst soldiers right inside the research room. How in the world had they teleported? All her research indicated that the Cyst didn't have the ability.

"Niall," Mercy snapped, pressing her hands to her hips and staring at the blond-haired guy. He was much smaller than the two Cyst soldiers. "You total dick." She jumped for Promise.

Niall drew a gun from his hip and fired it, hitting Mercy midair. She cried out and crashed into Promise, smashing them both into the desk.

Pain rocketed up Promise's arm to her neck. "Teleport," she hissed.

"Can't." Mercy rolled to her feet, her body vibrating. "Dickwad hit me with a blaster gun. Shit. This is bad. Scream."

The Cyst solder in the lead lifted a green gun. "One sound, and I'll end you."

Mercy angled herself in front of Promise. "Niall. You want me. Not the human."

"Oh, bitch." Niall's teeth gleamed in the computer lights. "You're right I want you, but the Kurjans want the physicist. Badly. Your buddy Mark has shared your research with us, and we need your help. We're going to demand it, actually."

Mercy's body still shook from the laser stream that had hit her. "I should've let Logan kill you."

"Oh, we'll get to him again soon," Niall said. He motioned them forward. "Bring them over here."

How could there not be some sort of alarm to warn that the enemy had just teleported in? Wait a minute. They had to know the space, the point on a graph to land. How had they known where to find her? Promise slapped at the Cyst soldier who reached for her first. "Drake, the kid. He managed to explore this area a little bit." Add in Mark's view from the laptop, and the Cyst had been led right to them.

An alarm blared through the rainy day.

"Finally," Mercy breathed, kicking up at the other Cyst solder with both feet. He grabbed her, lifting high and turning. The second Cyst solder manacled Promise, lifting her against his chest. With a furious bellow, Niall charged them all, hitting midcenter, and then the earth dropped away.

Chapter Thirty-Nine

Ivar landed in Brookville, barely. The vortex or wormhole or whatever it was tried to rip off his legs and keep him. He lay face-down on the sweet grass, panting heavily, his blood running red to the brooks. What was left of it, anyway. He'd given Quade as much as he could. The pain engulfed his entire body so completely that he couldn't concentrate on one area.

Did he have to sit up to teleport? Probably not.

Turning his face to the side, blowing grass out of his nose, he closed his eyes and tried to pull on the energy from the brooks around him. He imagined demon headquarters, and the air fizzled around him. Then he pictured Promise's face, alight with intelligence and excited to talk about equations. That did it.

He shot through time and space, almost in slow motion, and landed flat on his stomach and squarely on Adare.

Adare coughed and fell on his butt, wrapping his arms around Ivar's waist. "Holy fuck. You're bleeding out." His eyes a glittering black, he shoved Ivar to sit up and then ripped open his own wrist, holding it to Ivar's mouth.

There wasn't time to argue or talk tough. Ivar took enough blood to launch his healing cells into motion and then shoved Adare's arm back. "Thanks, brother." Man, he hurt. Everywhere. Then he caught the commotion around him. Soldiers dressed in black, fully armed and loaded. In the research room, shoving the whiteboards out of the way. "What happened?" His heart kicked hard, and he stood, looking for Promise. If there had been a breach, she'd be locked down safely. "Where's Promise?"

Adare stood and planted a hand on his shoulder. "She and Mercy were taken about an hour ago. Video shows two Cyst soldiers and that Fae ex-king Mercy got fired. Teleported right in here and took them. We need defenses against that—better than we have."

Rage catapulted through Ivar so quickly, his wounds started bleeding faster. "Where are they?" He threw the two devices he'd brought back for Promise on a table. Then he pulled open the door and ripped the damn thing off the hinges.

Ronan and Logan came running from the far hallway, already dressed in combat gear. Fury darkened Logan's face until his eyes glowed. "It's my fault. I thought the Fae king was a harmless douchebag, and I let him live. Never thought the coward would work with the Kurjans." The dark growl in the demon's voice was as hoarse as Ivar's. "I'll rip off his head this time."

"Oh, that bastard is mine," Ivar said, his nerves firing with the need to kill. Niall had been the one to throw him into the hell loop, and Ivar had planned to hunt him down after getting Quade home safely. If the bastard hurt Promise in any way, he'd suffer before dying. Horribly.

Ivar could barely think. Oh, God. They had Promise. Helplessness mixed with rage inside him, and he had to banish all emotion to think. "What do we know?" His gut hurt worse than his wounds.

Logan pulled out an odd black scanner. "They jumped to a place outside of Seattle." A little green blip showed on a map.

Ivar passed. "What the hell is that?"

Logan looked up, his eyebrows rising. "A plastic scanner. My mate is a smart-ass fairy who can teleport anywhere on this planet or world she wants. You're crazy if you think I didn't tag her first chance I got." He frowned. "You haven't tagged yours yet? Highly recommend it, brother." Even though the words were light, the fear in Logan's eyes promised death.

Ivar started for the outside doors, going into battle mode even while bleeding. He sent as many healing cells to his legs as he could. "You're the only one who can teleport with metal because you mated Mercy. You and I will go in first via teleportation, and backup will have to arrive in helicopters."

Logan looked him over. "You're burned and bleeding."

Ivar grabbed his arm. "I don't give a shit. Let's go."

"Wait a minute." Ronan pushed him toward the conference room. "We have a satellite feed bringing up the entire area. At the very least, let's see what we can see before you just jump in. You can also take three minutes and heal your fucking legs. And face. You're a mess."

He didn't like it, not a bit. But Ronan was right. "Okay. Three minutes, and we go."

Logan nodded sharply. "Agreed." He followed Ivar toward the room.

Zane Kyllwood burst through the front door, followed by Benny. "We're teleporting in with you," he said.

Ivar looked at the demon leader. Just as he was about to answer, King Dage Kayrs jogged in the back door, his black hair tied at the neck and his silver eyes pissed. Seriously so. "I'm coming. Helicopters will be backup, but those of us who can jump are jumping."

Logan nodded. "Everyone should know that I haven't learned the ability to transport weapons yet. No metal, gentlemen."

Benny smiled, his expression fierce. "Good. That should at least even the odds in a fight. Fuckers."

Ivar's chest swelled. He had family, and he had friends. Even though he'd been lost and nearly destroyed, these men were his family. They'd help him protect Promise. His throat closed. "Let's do this." She had to be okay. She had to be safe. They wouldn't tear her apart like they did the other physicists until they understood everything she knew about teleporting.

He had to believe that. He just had to.

* * * *

Darkness surrounded her, and it was as if time slowed down and pressed in, trying to break Promise's ribs. Then, blissful light. The five of them landed, and Niall the Fae rolled toward the far wall, groaning. Apparently transporting four other people, especially the two massive Cyst soldiers, had been too much for the jackass who was the very embodiment of coccydynia.

The Cyst soldier holding her set her down in what looked like an abandoned elementary school classroom and backed away.

She panted wildly, staring at him. The guy was at least seven feet tall and almost as wide, with reddish purple eyes and that strange white strip of hair down his head and back. His skin was thick and white, while his lips were a shocking red. He stayed away from the light coming in the window and moved for the door. She couldn't get the leverage to tackle him toward the window and would just break her neck trying.

Mercy had no such hesitation. The second she landed, she turned and kicked her Cyst soldier beneath the chin with a solid thump. The guy took a step back and swung out with a beefy fist.

Promise rushed to her friend's aid, but Mercy had already ducked and then kicked the solider in the groin.

He bent over with a harsh growl.

Impressively fast, Mercy slid on her knees toward Niall and grabbed the silver gun from his back pocket. She was already firing at him when she stood, shooting him in the back of the neck with what looked like a laser. He jerked once. "Ha." She threw the gun toward an old teacher's desk crammed into the corner. "Now neither of us can teleport, asshole."

Niall coughed several times but didn't turn around.

"Enough," said a male voice by the door. "General? Please continue making preparations for our exit once darkness falls."

Promise knew that voice. She turned, her seizing lungs constricting the flow of oxygen to her extremities. "Dayne."

The Kurjan leader half bowed. "It is an honor to see you again, Dr. Williams." He strode into the room, looking tall and dangerous in his Kurjan soldier uniform with all the shiny medals on his breast. "And you, Mercy O'Malley. You're my first fairy."

"Fae," Mercy said, her teeth gritted together. "And you're my first asshole."

Promise sent her a look. It made zero sense to antagonize the guy holding them captive. She glanced toward the window. The one advantage they had at the moment was the sunlight. If she could get Mercy out there—

"I wouldn't," Dayne said easily, leaning his long body against the nearest chalkboard. "I truly don't wish to harm you, but my men have standing orders to shoot you if you leave the building before dark. They're positioned all over the property, several in sniper posts well guarded from the sun. The area outside that window has five guns pointed right at it ready to shoot." He glanced toward Niall, who still lay on the floor in the corner. "Hey, Fae King? You dead?"

It appeared that all immortals gained a somewhat macabre sense of humor through the centuries.

Niall groaned and rolled to sit up, his face pale and his body shaking. "I told you the Cyst soldiers were too heavy to transport at once."

Mercy stepped toward him, menace in every line of her small body. "I am so going to kick your balls through your ears."

"Mercy," Promise admonished. They had to keep clear heads to gain their freedom, and first she needed to discover exactly what was happening and why they'd been taken. Her legs trembled, and she locked her knees. She focused on Dayne. "You said you wished us no harm, but didn't you kill Dr. Rashad and Dr. Fissure?"

"Well." He spread his large hands. "I didn't kill them. My general did, and that's because they didn't give me what I wanted. You're going to give it to me, aren't you, Promise?"

The way he said it was mildly creepy and monumentally terrifying. Those people had been torn apart, piece by piece.

What kind of a monster would do such a thing? As if reading her mind, the nearest Cyst soldier licked his lips.

Her stomach revolted. "What do you want?" she asked.

Dayne ticked his head toward the boards. "Your brilliant mind. Help my physicists discover how to reach Ulric and bring him home. I know you're close to understanding the way teleportation works."

Her breath heated, and she threw out her hands. This was crazy. They truly didn't comprehend the mysteries of the universe. "I'm nowhere near close." She shook her head. "The math you're talking about, the advances in theoretical physics will take centuries. Maybe longer."

He lifted his head and...sniffed? His eyes swirled purple through the red. "You've mated a demon." His lips curved. "Make that a hybrid." Then he laughed, long and hard.

"H-how did you know?" she asked.

"I can sense it," he said. "So can any immortal. Your mate's scent is all over you. What is it with you Enhanced females getting yourselves bitten and tied down for an eternity? It just makes this so easy."

"How so?" Promise asked.

He sobered, his gaze piercing. "Their weakness is you. Always has been and always will be. What do you think is happening at demon headquarters right this second?"

Hopefully they were trying to bring Ivar back from the hell world. Had he returned? Was he safe? Promise cleared her throat. "I don't know."

"I do," Dayne said. "They're gearing up to find you, which will take some time since we teleported you out of there. No satellite, no cameras, no witnesses to see you go. They don't know where you are." He smiled, flashing sharp canines. "And on the off chance they find this place, we'll be long gone. Never to be found again."

"Why?" Promise asked, her voice shaking.

Dayne studied her as if truly surprised. "We're at war. It never really ended, you see."

"We took good care of your son," she protested as Mercy edged even closer to Niall.

"That was kind of you," Dayne said.

She looked him over and found several weapons—guns and knives. "How did you let him get so far away from you, anyway?" The child was only eight. It couldn't have been by design, could it? Who would use their own child in such a manner?

Dayne didn't answer. Instead, he glanced over his shoulder and then moved to the side.

Mark Brookes walked into the classroom, his gaze earnest. "I'm so sorry about this, but we needed you here. I'm struggling with some of your equations."

Her hand shot out and slapped him right across the face. The sound echoed loudly in the room, bouncing off the chalkboards. She gasped, her shock mirrored in his expression. "You have no idea what you've done."

Mark stepped away from her, a red handprint on his right cheek. "You have turned into such a bitch. Now help me get the math right, we'll give the information to these nice people, and then return to the university to enjoy the grant and work our way to a Nobel."

Dayne straightened. "As far as I can see, she doesn't need you, Brookes."

Promise's skin pricked. "That is incorrect. I do require his assistance."

"That's too bad." Faster than a blur, Dayne broke Mark's neck. The snap was deafening, and Mark fell to the ground with his eyes still open. "You have three hours to give me results that make me happy, or the redheaded Fae is next." With another bow, he turned to leave the room. "Niall? Bring the body with you. I don't want any distractions for our ladies."

Chapter Forty

With the satellite images clear in his mind, Ivar landed on the roof of the abandoned school and punched out, taking the Kurjan soldier by surprise. The guy was hidden beneath a tarp, and Ivar dragged him into the sun, covering his mouth with a forearm to muffle the screams. The bastard jerked against him while his body went up in flames. His weapons dropped to the ground along with his charred bones. But the fire spread. Ivar patted out the fire on his arms, wincing at the pain. Grabbing the weapons, keeping low, he ran around the other side of the roof toward where the door should be. A Cyst soldier guarded it from beneath an awning.

Ivar was on him before he could move, shoving the knife up beneath the soldier's chin all the way to the hilt. He followed the body down and wrenched, cutting several times until the head rolled into the sun and ignited into flames.

The smell of burnt flesh and death choked him for a moment. His knees weakened from blood loss. There hadn't been time to heal from his visit to hell.

He wiped off the knife and opened the door, heading inside, his only thought to find Promise. The demons had always enjoyed the sole power to teleport, and having their enemy employ the gift by working with the Fae had been unexpected. Even so, he was pissed at himself for not considering the possibility.

He limped down the stairs, coming across Adare and a red-haired Kurjan soldier trading furious punches. The Kurjan yanked a knife from a sheath at his belt, and Ivar threw his blade to Adare, who caught it without missing a move. The knives flashed, hard and fast, and blood sprayed.

Some arced across Ivar's arm, and he winced. He'd forgotten how badly Kurjan blood could burn.

Seeing that Adare was gaining ground, Ivar stumbled down more steps, turning at a landing and barreling into a Cyst soldier at least five inches taller than Ivar's own six-foot-six. They paused simultaneously. Then Ivar ducked his head and charged, sending them both tumbling end-over-end down the hard concrete stairs.

The agony in his legs and head nearly dropped him, but he fought hard. He rolled at the bottom and brought up the gun he'd taken, shooting several times into the Cyst soldier's eye, straight to the brain. The soldier flopped back down, blood leaking from his ears and spurting from his eye, out cold. The injury wouldn't kill him, but he'd be out of commission for a while.

There wasn't time to decapitate him.

Ivar's body tried to shut down, and he sucked deep, sending healing cells everywhere. Then he stumbled down the rest of the stairs and burst into a hallway, right into Logan, who'd come in the front door.

Benny fought with two Cyst soldiers at the far end, his punches almost gleeful. Dage Kayrs flew out of a classroom to join him, and the two were brutal grace in motion.

Logan looked down at his black box. "This way." He pointed down a far hallway and started into a jog, following that green blip on the screen.

Ivar tried to stay calm, memories assailing him. Of him leaving Quade in hell, not once but twice. Of rolling with Promise on the bed, of making her laugh. He hadn't told her. Not once had he told her how he felt. Knowing he was going off mission and probably not returning for eons was no excuse. He should've saved Quade, and he should've let Promise know she was loved.

His boots echoed dully on the dusty old wooden floors, his chest heating until he swore fire filled his breast. Panic clutched his hands into fists. Where was his mate?

They reached the end of a hallway and turned down another one, this one with damaged blue lockers lining the way, some having fallen into the middle. He jumped over two, following Logan, a growl rising up from his soul. Where were they?

Logan paused in front of a series of classrooms, swinging the black box around.

The sound of a helicopter lifting pierced the sunny day outside.

Ivar's head jerked. What if Promise was in the helicopter? His legs shook with the need to run and find out, but what if she was here? He opened his mouth to say something to Logan, and the nearest door exploded open. The force lifted him off the floor and threw him high against the far wall. His head impacted on the cement wall, and he dropped fast, landing on his knees.

Logan landed next to him, shoving backward and drawing his gun.

Smoke filled the hallway. A burning torch burst out of the smoke followed by a second one, swinging for his face.

He ducked and rolled, coming up and grabbing the wooden handle. Promise came with it, kicking and punching, holding fast. "What are you doing?" he snapped.

She blinked up at him. "Ivar?" Her hold on the torch loosened. He claimed it, noting the damn thing was actually a broom with the bristles on fire.

He pulled her close, breathing in her scent.

Logan stood with Mercy, who had a similar broom. He looked toward the smoking classroom.

Promise leaned over and coughed, her body shaking.

Ivar pushed her behind him. "What's in there?"

"Nothing," she wheezed. "We found cleaning supplies and made a bomb."

Admiration and pride swelled through his fear for her. "You made a bomb?" The back of his head was still bleeding from smashing into the wall. It was a hell of a bomb.

"Yes." She straightened up and grabbed his arm. "Mercy was shot with a blaster. She's unable to teleport."

That explained that. Ivar looked over at Logan, who had his arm wrapped around his mate. "Let's get the hell out of here," Logan growled, throwing the still burning broom back into the classroom.

"I don't think so." A Kurjan soldier, gun held on them, dashed out of the farthest classroom with Niall on his heels.

Everything in Ivar went silent. He positioned Promise more squarely behind him. He could teleport, but the bullet might hit them first. If it impacted anywhere except his torso, could it go through him and into Promise?

Two Cyst soldiers dropped from the ceiling, breaking tiles that rained down. Promise yelped and ducked against Ivar's back to avoid the sharp pieces.

Logan cut him a look.

With a short nod, Ivar focused, trying to banish the weakness in his limbs.

Then he charged.

* * * *

Ivar went for one Cyst while Logan focused on the other, trying to end this quickly. Niall moved out of the way, to the side, where Promise started smacking him with the burning broom. Mercy ducked for hers, grabbed the handle, and followed suit. The Fae king was unsuccessfully trying to shield his face from the fire.

Ivar kicked the Cyst soldier beneath the jaw and threw him back several feet. The soldier grabbed a knife from the back of his waist and advanced. Shit. It was a blade made specifically to kill one of the Seven by striking right above their fused shield. Ivar circled, waiting for the attack, wanting to get Promise to safety.

The fight behind him raged on, hard and fast, with Logan beating the other Cyst around the head and neck.

Another Kurjan soldier ran from the far hallway, firing green lasers as he moved. Several hit Logan in the legs, and he dropped with a shout of pain.

Mercy leaped for him, trying to cover the wounds with her hands.

"Teleport, damn it, Logan," Ivar yelled, driving his knife up into the head of the Cyst nearest him. The guy fell back, hit the wall, and went down for now. Promise was too far away for the demon to grab her. "Get your mate out of here since she can't teleport. Find a doctor. I've got this."

The Kurjan soldier aimed and hit Logan right in the throat with a bullet. The demon's eyes widened, and he grabbed his larynx. Mercy screamed and pressed her hand over his, but blood welled through her fingers. He closed his eyes, and tingles popped in the air around him. Then they both disappeared.

God, hopefully Logan had enough strength to get them to the Realm medical building.

Ivar stole the gun from the guy he'd just dropped and turned, already firing at the Kurjan who'd shot Logan. The Kurjan stopped cold, bullet holes in his forehead and cheeks. He dropped forward, hit the wooden floor, and stopped moving. His legs flopped twice.

Pain blasted into Ivar's head from a full-on punch aimed by the remaining Cyst soldier. The power flung him into the row of lockers, which immediately crashed to the ground at the impact.

Promise screamed.

Her voice centered him. He backflipped off the damaged metal and landed on the Cyst soldier's back, where he dug his fingers in as hard as he could, seeking the larynx. Blood coated his hand, burning him to the bone.

Niall yanked the broom from Promise and threw it over his head, lunging for her. He grabbed her by the neck and took her down. She slapped and fought him, but he started to strangle her.

Ivar roared, and his fangs dropped. Holding his prey tight, he struck, ripping half of the Cyst's neck out with one strong pull

The Cyst soldier dropped to his knees and then fell forward, out cold. Ivar landed on his feet and jumped for Niall, tackling him off Promise and rolling him down the hall.

They both rose to their feet, panting and bleeding.

Promise coughed and struggled to stand, coming up on Ivar's side. "Let's get out of here."

Niall smiled, his teeth bloody. "How was your trip to hell?"

"A little warm," Ivar said, taking a step toward the Fae king who'd nearly caused his destruction. "But I did see my brother, so there was that."

Niall held up both hands. "I'm not armed, and I can't teleport." He motioned his head toward Promise. "You should take her out of here before more Kurjans come. They really want her brain."

Ivar's rage settled hard and cold in his gut. The Fae king didn't have a weapon, and this wasn't a fair fight. But if Ivar let him live, he'd gain his ability to teleport again, and then what? "Are you the only Fae working with the Kurjans?" he asked, advancing another step.

Niall sighed. "Yes." He wiped blood off his chin. "Most of my people aren't interested in politics." He motioned them away. "You really should go."

Ivar smiled and enjoyed the way the color drained out of Niall's face. "I don't think so."

Niall hesitated, his blue and brown eyes moving to Promise and back. "You wouldn't hurt an unarmed man in front of your mate, would you? It's not like I'm a threat."

"But you could be." In one smooth motion, Ivar punched through the ex-king's chest and pulled out his heart. He squeezed the muscle into nothingness as the body dropped to the ground. Then he threw the heart toward the lockers and smoothly walked to the downed Cyst and removed the knife from his neck. The only way to kill Niall was decapitation. "Promise? You're gonna want to look the other way, baby."

Chapter Forty-One

Promise starting throwing up the minute Ivar grabbed her to teleport. Blood covered his face and neck, and she tried to turn away, but then they were traveling through space and time. Everything stopped, including her. Light came first, and then he released her. She bent over and vomited all over the grass near the lake.

Rain splashed down, cooling her heated cheeks. Her body lurched, and she emptied the rest of her stomach.

Ivar moved down the beach and bent to wash off his bloody hands. Then he turned toward her, his chest still bloody. The fierce blueness of his eyes cut through the gray storm, making him look like that ancient Viking she knew him to be. Deadly and primal. "You okay now?"

She heaved a couple of times, clutching her stomach. "Yes." Walking around the mess on the sand, she crouched and washed her hands in the chilly water before splashing her mouth and face with lake water. The rain pinged off the lake, bouncing up at her. "Was that necessary?"

"Yes." He grasped her arm and gently helped her to stand. "I'm sorry you had to see it."

She hadn't watched. The second he'd moved toward Niall with the knife, she'd heeded his words and turned away. But the bleak sound of cartilage and bone separating would always be with her, no matter how long she lived. While she understood Ivar's reasoning, she just couldn't look at him right now. "I need to brush my teeth." She turned to the back entrance of the demon headquarters building.

Zane Kyllwood opened the doors and strode outside, rubbing a cut along his neck. Had he been at the fight? She hadn't seen him. He nodded at Ivar. "Logan is in the medical building healing his neck. I already radioed that you're safe." A bruise above his left eye made him look even more dangerous than usual. "Dayne?"

Ivar shook his head. "Didn't see him."

Zane's lips tightened. "A helicopter made it out. The bastard was probably on it. What about Niall?"

"Dead," Ivar confirmed. "Head and all."

Zane's gaze flicked to Promise and then back to Ivar. "Thank you. He would've been a threat to the demon nation forever, especially since he's been here at headquarters."

"I'm aware." Ivar took Promise's hand and began walking toward the door. "Promise needs a quick shower and then has math to do so I can get back to Quade as soon as possible. Hopefully tomorrow since the earth is still in the correct position. His world has deteriorated horribly, and I don't think he has much time left. This is my last chance to bring him home." He helped her inside, and she blinked rain out of her eyes.

Promise stayed silent, her mind oddly quiet. Then she asked, "Do you have the results from the instruments I had Ivar bring back this time?"

"The results are still downloading, but I can tell you already that Quade's world is heading toward Ulric's. We can't stop it," Zane said.

Oh, equations were running in the background of her mind, and maybe even a way to get around the magnet problem, but right now, all she wanted was a hot shower and a toothbrush. She stumbled along with Ivar until he finally just picked her up without so much as a hitch in his stride.

They reached their suite, and he carried her into the bathroom, setting her down gently. She moved to the sink and brushed her teeth, feeling better already. Then she looked down at the blood now covering her shirt and swayed.

"Whoa." Settling her against him with one arm, Ivar reached into the vast natural-rock shower and flipped on the water. "Let's get you warm, sweetheart. I think you might be going into shock." He gently removed her clothing and then his own, carrying her inside and shutting the glass door to let the steam surround them.

She let the warm water wash over her hair and stepped back from him.

His eyes darkened. "I'm sorry if I scared you."

Everything inside her, from her head to her heart, knew he'd never hurt her. "I'm not scared of you," she whispered. "I know why you ended the threat of Niall. Intellectually, I understand. But it was just overwhelming." She shivered at the natural violence that Ivar so easily employed.

Ivar engaged another set of showerheads closer to him and washed all the blood off. The red pooled around the drain and then disappeared. "I know." His impressive back and rock-hard butt made her mouth water. He planted one hand on the wall and lowered his head, letting the water slide over the impressive shield that covered his entire back.

Maybe it was the shock or the multiple jumps, but she could feel his pain. His guilt. What drove him. She walked across the smooth stones and placed her hand on his lower waist. "You need to let go of the guilt," she said quietly.

He turned, his eyes nearly black in the steam. His naked body was a study in male perfection. "I don't feel guilty about killing Niall."

"I know." She stepped into him, going on her instincts for the first time in her life. He accepted all of her—even the parts she'd never liked. Her imagination versus her rational brain—he wanted them both. Her belly cushioned his already hardening penis. She smoothed the wet hair away from his face, noting the darker strands through the blond. "You're so driven to save Quade. It wasn't your fault that you escaped and he stayed. You have to stop carrying that with you." At some point, it'd destroy him. She wanted to prevent that with a determination that heated every cell in her body.

He looked at the shower door and then back at her.

She reached up and palmed his whiskered jaw. "It wasn't your fault. Forgive yourself before you risk your life again."

He stared at her, his lids half-lowered. "Promise, I do, don't wanna, ah…" He shook his head, and her hand slipped down. He looked at her shoulder. "Don't, can't talk about that."

Her heart hurt for him. Completely. "I know. But when you can, I'm here to help." They were mated. He needed to know that. Why the urgency caught her now, she'd figure out later.

He gave a slight nod.

She stepped closer and leaned up to kiss him. His eyebrows rose, and he watched her. "Promise?"

"You saved me." A part of her she hadn't explored before sang at the thought. That he'd risked his life, forcing his way through the enemy to fight for her. To bring her home safely. He definitely planned to return to Quade, to fiery danger, but right now, they had this. Sometimes a moment was all there was. "You came for me."

"I'll always come for you." He gripped her jaw and swooped in to kiss her, taking over as she'd known he would. "When I found out you were taken, I nearly lost my mind. I love you, Promise. It's real and it's only for you." He kissed her deeper, pressing her against the slick tiles.

"I accept all of you, Ivar." She kissed him back, running her hands down the hard planes of his breathtaking chest. He loved her? She had feelings she couldn't identify. How was it possible they were just chemicals and the biological imperative to find the strongest mate for protection? It had to be more. He'd taught her that emotion and intelligence could make her smarter. Stronger. "Ivar," she murmured.

He clamped his hands on her butt and lifted her. Then his mouth took hers, and she kissed him back, giving him everything she couldn't figure out how to put into words.

* * * *

Ivar held Promise aloft, pressed against the shower wall, needing her more than he'd needed anything in his long life. After having almost lost her, he was on fire. His blood, his soul, both pumping to the wild beat of near madness. There was only right here and now, only sensation, only this voracious hunger, one only she could satisfy.

She moaned his name, digging her nails into his shoulders, her thighs like a steel trap on either side of her hips. The one trap he never wanted to escape from. He slowly pressed inside her. Her eyes widened, and he tilted her to take more of him. "Ivar."

He licked her lips, kissing, going deep. "You need to know. My loyalty is absolute." He pumped harder, watching her full breasts jiggle in response. Her dusky nipples were a treat he could feast on for his entire life. "When I give my heart, it's once only, and it's for you." He had to make sure she understood.

"Ivar, I love you," she breathed, looking more than a little surprised as the words came out of her mouth.

He wanted to shout and laugh and kiss her some more. But he had to be sure she truly understood. "You're everything to me, sweetheart." The feel of her around him, of her taking all of him, was pure fucking bliss that nearly took his head off. His fingers dug into her rear, and he tried to slow down, but her internal muscles clamped down hard on him.

Desperation ripped through him, throwing him into a frenzied lust.

She cried out and held him harder, her thighs trembling on his hips.

He powered into her, plunging again and again, going deeper than even he would've thought possible. Closer. He wanted to be closer, to be a part of her, to never leave. No matter what it took, he'd come back to her. His fangs dropped.

Her eyes widened, and she slowly turned her head, revealing her delicate neck. It was a moment of absolute trust. She'd seen him rip out the neck of the enemy, and yet, she exposed herself to him. Willingly.

He grazed his sharp fangs beneath her ear and down her neck, enjoying the way her curvy body shuddered against his. She was vulnerable and trusting, and she gave him everything he could've ever wanted. Slowly, he pressed the twin blades into her skin, marking her yet again.

She tensed and cried out, an orgasm taking her with a power beyond them both. He pounded harder, his fangs inside her, finishing in a white-hot explosion that left him gasping and for the first time in his life feeling like he had a place. Just for him.

For once, he felt whole.

He licked her wound closed, and she mumbled something, her head back on the wall, her eyes closed. Satisfaction filled him at the sight of his mark on her delicate flesh.

The rain beat outside, cocooning them together for this brief moment.

Her eyelids fluttered open, and she smiled, her expression full of contentment. "Loving you has made me even smarter. I can imagine even more now."

His cock jumped inside her. He kissed her sweet mouth, drawing in her taste to keep him sane on the journey to come. "I need to leave tomorrow morning first thing."

She started and released his shoulders. "I understand the timing, but I have to go work the equations first."

He let her legs drop and then held her until she'd gained her footing. He studied her precious face. "All right." His hand swept down her back and over the stunning K marking on her butt. She purred. He'd swear to his last days that in the second, she purred. "You're in my heart. In my soul." He had to make her understand. Just in case he didn't return.

Chapter Forty-Two

Promise paced back and forth in the research room, mumbling to herself and shaking her head. This wasn't good. Not only was it terrible, it was unfixable. Was that even a word? When was the last time she'd slept? She took a cookie from the tray at the end of the computer table and ate it. Perhaps the sugar rush would help. Demon headquarters was abuzz with everyone working hard to prepare for morning.

Ivar and Adare walked inside and sat down, both wearing comfortable-looking jeans and shirts.

"We thought we'd ask for an update," Ivar said, fixing her with that intense gaze.

The look shot straight through her body to land in her heart. Hard. She swallowed and pointed to the equations on her newest board. Her stomach cramped, and her throat felt scratchy. "The instruments are interesting but not useful until you get new readings we can compare." But he'd already reported a change in Quade's world, so the world was changing. It was simply disintegrating.

"And?" he asked, his gaze intense.

The male was certainly getting to know her well.

She rubbed her temple. "Based on your last experience jumping from Quade's world, I extrapolated the time left in the wormhole or whatever it is." She shook her head. "You can't rescue him."

The wormhole is closing, and there won't be room for two of you. No way."

He straightened up in the chair, looking like a tiger about to pounce. "No, it isn't. I have to at least try to save him."

"Yes." She swept out her hand, ignoring the blue marker in it. "I think you have time to jump there, but it's closing, and you know it. You can't bring him back through." No matter how she worked the problem, the solution was the same. "And from what Quade said about balance, you both can't be on his world. I don't know why, but you have to believe what he said." Her heart hurt as if she'd taken a punch in the chest. "It's a suicide mission. The path, or wormhole, or whatever it is might not hold even one person for a return trip. It's closing."

Her words hung in the air.

Ivar sighed. "I don't want to leave you, but I have to save him. I can't let him die."

Grace stepped into the room, a bandage on her arm. She took a seat next to Adare.

He looked down at her. "You did not give blood."

She met his gaze evenly. "Sure, I did. Why not?"

The Highlander's eyes flashed a hot black. "You've only been out of a coma for a short time. For the love of all that is holy, do I need to lock you up?"

Grace rolled her eyes. "No. In fact, once we're finished with this mission, I'm out of here. Ronan said he can get me a new identity, and I can start living my life. There's no reason for me to stay here." She looked pale but determined.

Adare's jaw firmed, making him look like one of those ancient warriors.

Ivar kept his focus on Promise. "Forgetting the wormhole for the moment, tell me about the magnets."

She needed more time for the math. Like a century or two. "From what I understand, the magnets polarize the worlds somehow, keeping Ulric's in place. Or at least they did." She needed a better description. "Like poles repel each other, and unlike poles attract. Imagine using magnets with gravity and possibly time." There wasn't time to diagram it. "When Ronan's bubble burst, the destruction may have created a demagnetizing field."

"Shit," Adare said. "This is all theory, right?"

She nodded. "Based on what Ivar reported from his last visit, but yes." She looked at the diagrams. "My theory is that the magnets on Quade's world were permanent, or what we call rare earth magnets."

"Can we remagnetize them?" Grace asked, looking at the formulas on the boards.

"Of course," Promise said. That was the easy part. "You'd want to use lodestone, which isn't made of metal and can be teleported." She swallowed and set the marker down. "But this is irrelevant. You're not going, Ivar. This is most likely a one way trip. Nobody will come home."

Adare looked at Ivar and then pushed his chair back, taking Grace with him. "I'll go see how fast we can hunt up lodestone." With a nod at Promise, he took Grace's hand and disappeared out the door.

Ivar stood and moved toward her, all grace and sleek muscle. "Trust me."

She lifted her chin, facing him calmly. "I do trust you."

"Then tell me how to get to Quade. The wormhole moved as I was going through it, and I can see by your equations that you know exactly how much." He cupped her chin. "I'm asking you for this. I have to try and save him. I made a vow."

Her entire body hurt all of a sudden, the pain spiraling out from her chest. "You can't bring him through this wormhole."

"I'm asking you to trust me, and somehow, at some point, I'll bring those instruments back with readings. Just think of the decades of research they'll have in them since time moves so quickly there." The intensity in his blue eyes was almost blinding. "Trust me. I will come back to you."

She swept her hand to the board. "The math says otherwise."
All her life, she'd depended on math. It was real and could be
proven. In fact, she had proofs right there on the boards.

He leaned in, his masculine scent washing over her. "I know
what the math says. Trust me, not the math."

She looked up at him. Did he have any idea what he was asking?
By the expression on his face, he did. Her heart thumped. He'd
said he was all in. Did she have that strength? "I love you, Ivar."

"I know," he whispered, kissing her again.

She leaned back, her heart cracking. She did trust him. Even
more than the math. "All right. This is how you get there after
these new changes." Then she took the marker and diagrammed
the solution for him.

* * * *

Dawn was finally arriving in hues of gold and pink across a still
dark sky. Ivar finished dressing in the protective outfit and took
a moment with his brothers, looking at each in turn. Logan and
Ronan were happily mated, while Garrett and Benny were very
happily not mated. Adare, on the other hand, had shit to work on.
But for now, as the six of them stood outside in the rain, he tried
to find the right words. "I—" His chest flushed.

"Ditto," Benny boomed, slapping him on the back.

The rest nodded.

Ronan stepped up. "If I could go instead of you, I would." His
aqua eyes were so much like Quade's, it hurt to look at them.

"I know, brother," Ivar said. "I made Quade a promise, and I
have to keep it." They were bonded in blood and bone. To the soul.
He trusted his woman, so he needed to draw on her mathematical
skills for a solution. For now, they just had to make sure Quade
had time to survive. If there was a way for Ivar to take his place
in the meantime, he'd do it. But he needed Quade's cooperation.

Logan and Garrett hugged him, and he was careful of Logan's
still healing neck as he hugged them back. They all moved away,

and Adare stood before him. "You dragged me out of every funk I've gotten into the last few centuries. Thank you," Adare said, his jaw grim.

Ivar nodded. "You're my best friend. Always have been." He searched for the right words. "I'm coming back. Take care of Promise until I do."

"You know it," Adare said, emotion in his dark eyes.

"And give your mating a chance. Stop being a bossy asshole and get to know the woman. Grace is special." Which was probably why Adare was running like hell in the opposite direction.

"Come back, and you can Oprah me all you want. Here. The packs are all full of what you wanted." Adare hugged him hard and then stepped back, handing over several backpacks. The final pack, a light blue one, would remain in this world.

Promise came out the back door and ran to him, hitting him hard. Her eyes were cloudy. "Please be safe. Remember the path."

He had memorized her equation already. A twist to the left, more than last time, and hopefully he'd end up where he wanted to be. Hopefully the path wasn't closing even now. "I love you." It humbled him that she'd believed him over the math telling her the opposite. That she hadn't fought him when he'd said he had to keep his promise to Quade. His heart was full of her.

"I love you too." She swallowed and handed him a notebook. "If there's a way somehow, bring back any of the instruments that have survived. Remember that you have me." She stepped back, tears in her eyes.

His heart swelled. Even though she had a gigantic brain, her heart was even bigger.

He cleared his throat and handed over the one blue backpack, which was moving.

She blinked and took it. An adorable furry puppy popped out, big brown eyes wide, and licked her face. She gasped and helped the dog out of the pack. "Ivar."

He nodded. It was the mutt he'd seen on the internet and had Adare get for him. For her. "He's half golden retriever and half a bunch of other stuff. I thought he could keep you warm until I return."

Her eyes welled, and she hugged the squirming puppy close. "You gave me a dog."

He nodded. Yeah. She should've been given one years ago.

Logan and Garrett ran up with more backpacks for him that nearly knocked him to his knees. But he stayed upright. He pulled the protective face guard over his head. Looking at his family one last time, he drew on the power within himself and from them and jumped.

Pain cut into him immediately, and he tried to aim his trajectory the way Promise had said. The wormhole closed in on him, pinching his legs, slicing into his thighs. He screamed into the vortex, but no sound emerged. Then he fell, landing hard on sharp ice and skidding toward the forest.

Holy fuck.

It was nighttime, and stars sparkled down, bright in the black sky. The orange forest glowed somehow, inviting him. He lay on his back, looking up at different configurations, more than he'd ever seen. Than most people would ever see.

He glanced down to double-check that his legs were still attached. Thank God. He'd lost one once, and it had taken forever to rebuild. Scrambling up, he skidded over to the backpacks and gathered them before gingerly moving past spikes of ice for that forest.

It was colder than before, and the forest too sparse. At least half of the trees were gone and buried beneath more ice. The silence was devastating. How much time had passed in this place?

The sky crackled open, revealing a purplish red ocean, pulsing against a whole other mountain. It stayed open, and his world tilted, knocking him on his face. He landed, and ice sliced right through his protective face covering to rip his lip. Blood sprayed.

Seconds later, a creature screamed. Did something smell his blood? Heat squeezed his heart. The crack in the sky closed. Another scream, this one closer. He put his head down and ran, hoping the trail had stayed somewhat the same. This time he wore protective gear on his body and face, so it took longer for the blade-sharp bark to cut him. All too soon his clothing was in tatters, but he was climbing hand over hand, so he took a deep breath.

Something rustled through the trees below.

He climbed higher, finally hauling himself into the cave. "Quade?" He lit a match to see better.

Quade was on his side, facing the wall.

He couldn't be dead. Ivar rushed inside just as Quade rolled over, his face a blistered mess. "Quade." Ivar ripped off his coat and slashed his wrist, shoving it against Quade's mouth.

Quade sucked deep, and color returned to his face. His blisters began to heal. "Shit, Viking." He sat up, his back to the wall. "You came back. Dumbass."

Ivar snorted and hitched the backpacks off. "We have blood, food, weapons not made of metal, and lodestones to remagnetize whatever it is that needs magnetizing." He shoved them toward Quade. "Tell me how to place the repaired magnets, and I'll do it. You can go home." He moved a rock out of the way to sit, noticing a worn piece of paper. Looking closer, he could see it was the washed out photograph of Haven Daly he'd brought before. How much time had passed since he'd been there? The paper had yellowed and faded as if it had been hundreds of years.

Quade's beard was even longer but had a streak of gray this time. "It takes me from the last fire to the first to move the rocks. There can't be two of us on this world that long. Balance, remember? I've seen this place without it, and we'd die." He squinted. "Did you find out about the worlds?"

"Not yet. I was only gone a day," Ivar said. "We need more time."

Quade snorted. "Time. I have too much." He reached behind a rock and drew out a ripped backpack. "The devices stopped blinking, so I brought them all back here. Hope they did what you wanted."

"Thanks," Ivar said, taking the pack. "We think we can use these to figure out if the worlds are going to collide. Maybe even when it'll happen."

"Good." Quade reached for the second pack and drew out a granola bar. "What the hell is this?"

"My mate told me two of us couldn't make it back in the wormhole, so I brought provisions for whoever stayed. I trust her," Ivar said. He'd known, deep down, that both Promise and Quade were correct in that he couldn't take Quade's place right now. Not this time.

Quade twisted the bar around. "All right. What is this?" he repeated.

"Food," Ivar said. "I packed as much as I could. The blood is good and labeled. Use the human first." He had to keep Quade alive until they could figure out the bubble worlds. "The plastic weapons should help too." He drew out an album. "Here's a history of the world along with photographs of your family." He handed it over.

Quade's dirty hands shook as he gingerly flipped open the front page.

Ivar ignited a ceramic lantern and handed it over. "Next to Ronan in that picture is his mate."

Quade nodded and looked through the pictures, taking one of Haven Daly out. "I haven't talked to her in a while. Used to, but not for a while. You left her alone."

"Yes."

Blinding light burst into the cavern, and Ivar jumped, spinning around to face the threat.

"It's morning," Quade said wearily, shoving himself to his feet. "I have to run now. So do you. The next fire will come shortly. Get out first." He yanked Ivar close for a hard hug. "Stay safe, Viking."

"We're going to save you," Ivar vowed. Now that he'd left Quade with some provisions, he'd figure out a path where two people could travel home. Or Promise would find it with these new readings. "Are you sure you have to stay?"

"Yes. There's no other way." Quade studied him and then nodded. "Good to know you, brother." Setting the picture down gently, he turned and leaped out of the cave.

Well, shit. Ivar looked around. Okay. He had facts to report to
Promise as well as the silent devices from the 3D printer. Hopefully
they hadn't been broken. The forest had lost half of its trees in
the time he'd been gone. The sky had stayed open longer, and the
ocean had appeared closer. But for now, Quade was safe. And
Ivar had news about Haven. Somehow she'd communicated with
Quade? If so, she was the answer to this problem.

Ivar moved to the edge of the cave and looked down. Two yellow-
fanged animals with bright blue fur crossed each other, jumping up
and falling down the cliff. One spotted him and howled, even its
purple eyes looking hungry. Ravenous. He removed his protective
clothing for Quade to have, even leaving the face gear. His jeans
and thin T-shirt were all he needed. Thinking for a moment, he
toed off his boots and socks.

Then he readjusted his aim, corrected for a new twist if the
thing was still changing, and tried to jump into the wormhole.

He hit a rock-hard wall, his ears ringing as he fell back into the
cave. The wormhole was closed. Gone. Destroyed. He chuckled,
blood bubbling off his lips. Promise's math had been correct.

Well. Good thing they'd mated. This math, he could do now.
He ducked his head, worked out the equations in his brain, and
jumped in a different direction.

Chapter Forty-Three

Promise paced along the lake as rain splattered down, soaking her T-shirt. Ivar was gone. The math had correctly predicted that the wormhole would close. She just knew it. She also knew he'd find a way home, because he'd promised he would. She bit her lip, muttering to herself, fully aware that Faith and Emma watched her from a window. Yes, she looked like a crazy person.

If the wormhole had closed, how the heck would he get home? The spray of water on the lake caught her attention. One drop, many ripples. Mathematical equations ripped through her head. That was it.

Turning, she ran right into Mercy. She hadn't heard the Fae approach and grabbed her arms. "I can't feel him." Panic grabbed her and tried to shoot through the solution in her brain. "Anywhere. I can't sense him, Mercy."

Mercy let the rain fall on her face. She paled until her freckles stood out. "I'm sorry."

"No." Promise shook her head. "That's just it. I keep trying, kind of aiming where he went, and that wormhole closed. The math said it would." She released her friend and wiped rain off her cheeks. "But before. When Ivar went through the hell loop. He didn't come back the same way." She looked back at the ripples in the water. "There's another way."

Mercy nodded. "Yeah, okay. I've never paid a lot of attention, but I've jumped to Brookville from other worlds besides this one. What does that mean?"

Brookville was a jumping-off point for the hell dimensions, because that's how Niall had thrown Ivar into it. Promise whirled around, spraying water. "You have to take me to Brookville." Hope filled her chest.

Mercy's eyes filled. "I can't. I won't be able to jump for a week or so. Niall shot me, remember? My abilities are gone."

"Mine aren't," Logan said from the doorway.

Promise pivoted. "Will you take me?"

Logan studied her with those deep green eyes for a moment.

Promise started toward him with Mercy by her side. "Please. If I can feel him from there, then he should be able to sense me too? Right? Maybe there's a way to catch his attention. I don't know, but we have to try." Yes, she was actually going on faith. For Ivar. There wasn't time to test her hypothesis.

Logan nodded. "All right. He held out his hand. "Let's go."

She grabbed it and shut her eyes, letting Logan take her out of the world. They landed harder in Brookville than she had with Mercy, and it took her a minute to catch her balance. She opened her eyes.

"What now?" Logan asked, stepping away from her.

"I'm uncertain." She walked around the meadow, trying to sense Ivar. Then she focused on a graph point, reaching out mentally, receiving nothing, and then moving a foot in the other direction, like the dial on an old-fashioned clock, moving clockwise.

Logan stepped farther away, keeping an eye on her. She ignored him.

A slight buzzing caught her attention, and she turned quickly to what felt like west. More strength. Her mind opened up, and the marking on her lower back started to heat. "Ivar," she whispered. He was there. She could feel him. Shutting her eyes, she reached out with senses she couldn't explain. She reached out with every feeling she had for him, throwing them all beyond any universe she could imagine.

The sky opened, and he dropped down, landing hard and bouncing, his body engulfed in fire.

"Ivar," she yelled, running to him and sliding on her knees the last several feet. She patted the flames on his chest. Logan rushed over and grabbed Ivar's shoulders, swinging him around and dunking him in the nearest brook. Steam rose up, hissing from the contact.

"Geez." Ivar winced and pushed himself up from the water. Burn marks covered his face and down both arms. "I have totally figured out all this math shit. Nailed it."

Logan's fangs extended, and he cut into his wrist, pushing it against Ivar's mouth.

Ivar drank, and the burn marks slowly disappeared. He lifted his mouth away. "Thanks, buddy."

"No problem." Logan flopped back on his butt, his chest heaving.

Promise gasped. "How are you here?"

"Math and science, baby." Ivar grinned. "I used those equations you were doing in the helicopter, projected a different trajectory, and kept on twisting and turning until I could sense you again. You're right. Math rocks."

She sniffed and smiled. "Math can save us all. How's Quade?"

"Living. Hopefully surviving until we can figure out how to save him and leave Ulric," Ivar said. "I left him enough provisions and I believe he'll live until we get to him again. Soon."

Promise crawled to him, hugging him tight. "I totally can't explain the math. Not completely."

He chuckled and pulled her into his lap, holding her tight. Then he rocked her, kissing her neck. "We have forever to figure it out, sweetheart. And I'm going to make you very happy. I have those 3D devices for you."

She sniffled, holding on with all her strength. He'd promised to come back, and he had. Oh, they had work to do, and they had to get to it, but right now she just wanted to hold him. He was safe, and he was hers. Always.

Logan cleared his throat. "Let's get back home."

Ivar leaned back and kissed Promise on the nose. "Home sounds good."

* * * *

Ivar tipped back his beer bottle and watched the jubilant kids play the games on the other side of the pool table. It was his first time in the adult rec room at demon headquarters, and he liked the place. Pool tables, dartboards, game consoles, and a huge-assed television screen showing the football game. The bar was wide and fully stocked as well.

It was a birthday party for one of Hope's friends, a cute kid named Paxton, and the children played over near the windows, while the adults mingled around the screen. The king's kid, Hunter, seemed to be directing the other kids in some sort of game involving beanbags and dartboards. Two blond twin boys appeared to be winning when they weren't wrestling with each other, and a kid who looked just like Jase Kayrs egged them both on.

Promise approached him, smiling and sliding beneath his arm snuggling into him. She had a margarita in her hand, and her eyes were nicely blurry and her body relaxed. "This is a lovely party. We should do this more often."

He should get her tipsy more often. The woman was a lightweight, and a hilarious one at that. The debate she'd gotten into with Kane over the tenth dimension in string theory had been quite enjoyable to watch.

Adare approached and handed him another beer, taking the empty bottle and tossing it into the trash across the room. "Bad news, brother." He took a deep drink of his brew before continuing. "We sent a squad to bring in Haven Daly after your report, and she's gone. Fled the coop without a hint of a location."

Promise gasped, her pretty auburn eyes focusing. "Do you think she was taken?"

"Nope," Adare said. "Cleared out her bank account, and we have some camera feeds showing her leaving town, but she disappeared somewhere toward San Francisco. Nothing has picked up her trail since. She told the art gallery to go ahead with her show, but she wasn't going to be there. Is playing at being a crazy and mysterious artist, and it looks like it's working."

Promise looked up at Ivar, her hand on his chest, right where it belonged. "Do you think Quade told her to run?"

"Maybe," Ivar said, running through his last conversation with the Kayrs brother. "He seemed a little out of his head, so he might have. *If* they are somehow communicating, which I'm not sure about. He could be insane by now." But it didn't matter. They'd get Quade home and find him the help he needed to heal. It's what brothers did. He knew that firsthand or he wouldn't be standing there now.

"I don't have any new data yet." Promise sipped her drink. "The computers are downloading any and all information from the 3D instruments right now." She took a healthy gulp. "We should have preliminary results tomorrow. I love results. Even preliminary ones."

Yep. Adorable buzzed. Man, he loved her.

Grace bounced up, pool sticks in her hands. Her dark hair was up on top of her head, highlighting her pretty hazel eyes. As usual, her camera hung around her neck in case a good shot appeared. "Adare? Want to get your ass kicked?"

Adare straightened, looking down at his mate, appearing to be almost twice her size. He reached for one of the sticks. "I've wanted to teach you a lesson for a while," he said mildly, turning to follow her.

Promise watched them go, cuddling even closer to Ivar, her thigh to his. "Think they'll figure things out?"

Ivar settled against the wall, enjoying having her in his arms. Her wild purple heather scent washed over him, easing his guilt over Quade. For now, anyway. "I'm not sure. There's something between them, but they seem to fight a lot."

Promise leaned up and kissed his cheek. "Not like us. We have logic and math to guide us."

He captured her lips, kissing her deep. "And love and faith." No matter what she said, the woman had shown faith in him when she'd chosen him over math. For his entire life, he'd never forget that. The next day, they'd have to get back to work. But tonight, he was going to enjoy every second with her, and soon he was going to get her away from the party so he could have her all to himself. All night.

She settled back against him with a soft sigh of contentment. "You came back to me. I knew you would."

He grinned, basking in her trust. "Of course and always. In fact, I always knew, even in the darkest times, that when it really mattered, I would be able to keep my Promise."

Read on for an excerpt from Rebecca Zanetti's next Deep Ops novel, *FALLEN*, coming soon!

CHAPTER 1

The smell of wood polish and lemons mixed with the smooth male scent of the way too respectable man sitting across the round table from Brigid. Everything about Raider Tanaka was clean cut, upstanding, and unyielding. Even his perfectly tailored navy blue suit and striped green power tie made him appear like a guy who daily helped old ladies cross the street. "You look like a Fed," she whispered.

His black eyes glimmered. "I am a Fed," he whispered back, his voice low and cultured.

Yeah, and that was a problem. She looked around the darkened Boston tavern, where the attire of the patrons ranged from guys wearing worn dock clothes at the long bar to handmade silk suits over in the corner. Bodyguards with bulges beneath their jackets stood point near the guys with nice suits.

She shivered. "I don't think we blend in."

"I believe that's the point, Irish," Raider said, using a nickname he'd given her the first day they'd met. He finished off his club sandwich. His angular features showed his part-Japanese heritage, giving him an edgy look that contrasted intriguingly with his stockbroker suit. Just who was this man?

She shook her head. "I don't get it. Angus sent us here just to have lunch, didn't he?" The plane ride alone from DC would've cost a mint, even though they'd sat in coach. Of course.

"The boss always has a plan," Raider said, tipping back his iced tea while eyeing the suits in the corner.

Aye, but it would be nice to know the plan. Brigid enjoyed working for the rag-tag Homeland Defense unit run by Angus Force, but her job was hacking computer systems or writing code. Certainly not having a weird lunch with her handler in Boston. "Should we be doing something?"

Raider shrugged and gestured toward her Cobb salad. "You going to finish that?"

"No." Her stomach was all wobbly.

"Okay." He slid his empty plate to the side and tugged hers toward him, digging in.

Her mouth gaped open. Straight-laced Raider Tanaka did not seem like the kind of guy to share somebody else's food. Not a chance. She'd figured him for some dorky germ-a-phobe, even though he was impossibly good looking.

"What?" His dark eyebrows lifted. When she didn't answer, he glanced down at the lettuce. "When you grow up on the streets or in foster care, you take food where you can get it." Then he munched contentedly on a crouton.

She blinked, her mind spinning. "You grew up in foster care?" She'd have bet her last dollar, if she had one, that he'd grown up in Beverly Hills somewhere with a maid or two cleaning up his room and making his bed. His suits had to cost a fortune, and he had that prep-school look.

"Yes." Raider leaned back in his chair. "You're not the only one who's tough to figure out."

She tried to maintain eye contact but found it difficult. Her abdomen warmed, and an interesting tingling licked along her skin. She had to do something about this impossible attraction she had for him.

His gaze narrowed, while his back somehow straightened even more. That quickly, he went from lazily amused to alert and tense.

Her breathing quickened in response.

A man appeared by their table. One of the guys with the bulging jackets. "Can I help you?" he asked.

Raider looked up, a polite smile curving his lips. "Not unless you're serving dessert."

Brigid breathed in through her nose and exhaled slowly. Adrenaline flooded her system. "We're fine," she said.

The guy didn't look at her. His brown hair was slicked back, revealing beady brown eyes and a nose that had been flattened permanently to the left. A scar cut through the side of his bottom lip. "You look like a Fed."

Raider smiled, flashing even white teeth. "So I've heard."

"It's time for you to leave," the guy said, resting his hand on his belt.

"No," Raider said, his voice almost cheerful.

Brigid began to rise. "Raider, I think—"

"Sit down." Raider kept his gaze on the man with the gun, but the barked command in his voice had her butt hitting her seat in instant response.

She blinked. What the heck had just happened? "Um."

The armed man leaned in toward Raider. "I tear apart Feds for fun. Now get the pretty lady out of here before I decide to rip off your head and show her what a real man can do with an hour or two."

Brigid's hands curled over the table, and she looked frantically around. The door was so close. She focused on Raider again.

If anything, he looked a little bored. "My money would be on the lady," he said, losing his smile. "Now, friend. You can either go get us a dessert menu, or you can fuck off and slink back to your bodyguard duties."

Brigid swallowed a gasp. Had Raider just said the F-word? She glanced toward the corner, where one of the other bodyguards had started walking their way. This was about to get ugly. She wasn't armed. Was Raider? He couldn't be. They'd flown commercially, and he hadn't declared a gun.

They had to get out of there. Right now.

The guy grabbed Raider by the tie, and then everything happened so quickly that Brigid didn't see all of it.

Raider stood in one easy motion, manacled the back of the guy's neck, and smashed his head so hard into the table that it cracked in two. Dishes and utensils flew in every direction while the guy and the wood crashed to the floor.

Brigid's chair rocked back, and she yelped, scrambling to her feet to keep from falling. The guy on the floor didn't move.

Raider's easy and brutal violence shocked her more than the fight itself.

"Hey!" The other bodyguard, a red-headed man with a barrel of a chest, ran forward while yanking out his gun.

Raider pivoted and kicked the guy beneath the chin, sending him down and following like a blur of motion. Three punches and a quick twist, and Raider stood with the gun pointed at the back table. When he lifted his chin, the two men there lifted their hands.

The remaining patrons looked on without moving.

Raider straightened his tie.

Brigid could only gape, her mind fuzzing. What had just happened?

Raider backed toward her. "Door. Now."

She turned and stumbled toward it just as sirens echoed down the street. Running outside into a light rain, she rushed to the passenger side of the compact they'd rented at the airport. Raider calmly entered the driver's seat, ignited the engine, and drove away from the restaurant.

Brigid gulped down panic, struggling to secure her seat belt. "I don't understand. Why in the hell were we sent to that restaurant?"

Raider set the gun between them and maneuvered around traffic. "I have a feeling our mission went according to plan." His hands were light on the steering wheel but his voice held a tone she couldn't identify. She studied him. He looked like he'd been out for a relaxing lunch with a friend, not like a man who'd probably just put two guys—two tough guys—in the hospital for a week.

Just who was Raider Tanaka?

After a silent plane ride back to DC, where Brigid ran over every moment of the day in her head and Raider read a series of HDD reports, they finally ended up at their headquarters just as night began to fall. As usual, the dilapidated elevator shuddered to the bottom floor and then remained quiet.

"I hate this thing." Raider smacked his palm against the door. "Open, darn it."

The door opened with a hitch.

Amusement bubbled through Brigid's unease. "You're magic."

He looked over his shoulder. "You have no idea, Irish." Then he crossed into the small and dimly lit vestibule of the basement offices.

Had he just flirted with her? For Pete's sake. She moved out of the too small space on wobbly legs, feeling overwhelmed on several levels. Enough of that silliness. Reaching the wide-open room, she sighed. Fresh paint had brightened the office a bit, but the myriad of desks were still old and scarred, and the overhead lights old, yellow, and buzzing.

Raider looked down at the cracked concrete floor and shook his head.

"We're supposed to paint that next," Brigid said. Wasn't that the plan? "And I think there's art coming, or screens that show outside scenery." The basement headquarters were a step down from depressing, even with the new paint. The big room was eerily silent, as well.

Three doors led to an office and two conference rooms, while one more door, a closet for the unit's shrink, was over to the west.

A German shepherd padded out of the far office, munching contentedly on something bright red. It coated his mouth and stained the lighter fur around his chin.

"Roscoe," Brigid breathed, her entire body finally relaxing. Animals and computer code, she knew. It was people who threw her.

The dog seemed to grin and bounded toward her, his tail wagging wildly. She ducked to pet him. "What in the world do you have?" This close she could see that the stuff was thick and matted in his fur. She frowned and tried to force open his mouth. "Roscoe?"

As if on cue, Angus Force stepped out of the second conference room, also known as Case Room Two. "Hey, you two. How was Boston?"

Brigid looked up. "Roscoe has something."

"Damn it." Angus made it through the desks in record time. "Is it Jack Daniels?"

Brigid craned her neck to see. "No. It's red." The dog had a drinking problem?

Angus glared at his dog. "Drop it. Now." The command in his voice would've made Brigid drop anything she was carrying.

The dog sighed and spit out a gold-plated lipstick.

Brigid winced. "That looks expensive."

The dog licked his lips.

Angus sighed. "I told everyone not to leave makeup around. He likes the taste."

"No, you didn't," Brigid countered.

Angus pierced her with a look. "Well, I meant to. Roscoe, get back to the office. Now."

The dog gave her a "what a butthead" type of look and turned to slink back to Angus's office.

"You two, come with me." Angus turned and headed back to the case room, no doubt expecting them to follow.

Raider motioned her ahead of him. Yeah. Like she'd return to that death trap of an elevator. Though it was preferable to dealing with Angus Force. The former FBI profiler now headed up this division of the HDD, and he seemed almost able to read people's minds. Was he reading hers? Did he have one clue that she wasn't who she was supposed to be? How much had he guessed? More importantly, why had he sent her to Boston?

She crossed into the case room to face a whiteboard across from a conference table. Several pictures of men, some in their early seventies and some only in their twenties, were taped evenly across the expanse. "New case?" she asked.

"Yes." Angus gestured for them to sit. "Did anybody recognize you in Boston?"

It took her a second to realize he was talking to her and not to Raider. "Me?"

"Yes," Angus said.

What the heck? "Why would anybody have recognized me?" she asked, her senses thrumming.

Raider eyed her and then Angus. "Nobody recognized her. My best suit, which you asked me to wear, did get some attention, however."

Angus nodded. "I've already read the report."

Curiosity took Brigid as she sat down with Raider beside her.

Angus moved around to the board. "New case kicked to us by the HDD. They think it's crap, and I think it has merit. Either that, or somebody is messing with us."

Raider stiffened just enough that Brigid could feel his tension. "How so?"

"While the Irish mob is no longer a serious threat in Boston, there are criminals, past associates of the mob, that have risen in the ranks and become dangerous recently," Angus said, standing big and broad on the other side of the table.

Brigid perched in her seat, still not seeing what this had to do with her. She had no problem hacking into criminal networks, so perhaps that was why she'd been included on this Op?

"How so?" Raider asked, all business.

"Instead of working within the usual, or rather former, hierarchy of the mob, these guys are outsourcing work to incredibly skilled computer criminals," Angus said.

"Like me," Brigid said quietly.

Angus nodded. "Exactly. We have a line on a group using a site on the dark web. We think they're running drugs, but we don't know what else."

The dark web was nearly impossible to hack. "I can't just find a site without knowing where it is," Brigid said. "The key to bringing down somebody on the dark web is—"

"Getting them to meet you in person," Raider said. "Guess that's my part of this op."

"Partially," Angus said, eying them both. "There's more."

Warning ticked through Brigid. Why, she didn't know. But her instincts rose instantly, and she stiffened. "What?"

"We think this man might be one of the key players." Angus turned and taped one more picture to the board.

Brigid stopped breathing. She stared at the picture. He had aged. His skin was leathery, his nose broken more than once, and his hair now all gray.

Raider glanced at her. "Who is that?"

"My father," she whispered. The man she hadn't seen or talked to in years. She coughed. "You're crazy. He's a farmer. Always has been."

Angus winced. "No. He was involved with the Irish mob way back when. Then he supposedly got out, but now we think he's back in."

That couldn't be true. No way. "That's why you sent us to Boston. Those guys in the corner were mobsters?" Brigid gasped.

"Yep. Just wanted to see if you'd be recognized," Angus said.

"Damn it," Raider muttered. "You could've given me a heads up."

Brigid tried to rein in her temper. "Of course nobody recognized me. You're wrong about my father."

"Prove it," Angus said mildly. "You and Raider go talk to him and prove I'm wrong. But be prepared to discover I'm right."

Brigid shook her head. "You want me to take an obvious government agent to my father's farm and what? Just ask him if he's involved in cybercrime?" No way. "Believe me. My dad wouldn't talk to a Fed if he was dying."

Angus's smile didn't provide reassurance. "No. You're going home to reconcile with your father because you've finally found your way in life with the man next to you—one with possible criminal ties that we're still working out. Who you want to introduce to your father before you marry."

"Marry?" Brigid blurted, her mind spinning wildly. "Are you nuts?" She turned to Raider. "Tell him this won't work."

Raider hadn't moved. "This is important, Force?"

"Crucial," Angus affirmed. "There's more going on here than drugs. I just know it."

Raider turned and studied her with those deep, dark eyes. "Well Irish. Looks like we're engaged." His smile sent butterflies winging through her abdomen. "This is going to be interesting. Now that you're mine, I will finally figure you out."

About the Author

New York Times and *USA Today* bestselling author **Rebecca Zanetti** has worked as an art curator, Senate aide, lawyer, college professor, and a hearing examiner—only to culminate it all in stories about alpha males and the women who claim them. She writes dark paranormal romances and romantic suspense novels.

Growing up amid the glorious backdrops and winter wonderlands of the Pacific Northwest has given Rebecca fantastic scenery and adventures to weave into her stories. She resides in the wild north with her husband, children, and extended family who inspire her every day—or at the very least, give her plenty of characters to write about.

Please visit Rebecca at: www.rebeccazanetti.com
Facebook: www.facebook.com/RebeccaZanetti.Books
Twitter: www.twitter.com/RebeccaZanetti

Printed in the United States
by Baker & Taylor Publisher Services